HIGH PRAISE FOR EDWARD LEE!

"The living legend of literary mayhem. Read him if you dare!"

—Richard Laymon, author of *Into the Fire*

"Edward Lee's writing is fast and mean as a chain saw revved to full-tilt boogie."

—Jack Ketchum, author of *The Girl Next Door*

"Lee pulls no punches."

—*Fangoria*

"The hardest of the hardcore horror writers."

—*Cemetery Dance*

"Lee excels with his creativity and almost trademark depictions of violence and gruesomeness."

—*Horror World*

IT CAN'T BE REAL

The coroner nodded curtly. "It's just kind of odd, and it's difficult to explain in any way that makes sense. But every now and then any medical examiner's office will get a cause of death that simply can never be determined."

Patricia frowned at the sheet. This was much less than she'd hoped for. "How was his head cut off, is what I want to be able to tell the family. Was it cut off, shot off? Was it knocked off in some sort of freak accident?"

Another curt look from the pretty coroner. "It was...none of those things, and that's about the only thing we *do* know. No blade striations, no evidence of severe impact to the body, no evidence of firearm discharge."

"But the head was never recovered—that's what I heard from the locals, anyway. Is that true?"

"Quite true, ma'am."

This was frustrating. "I'm sorry, but I just don't get it."

"Look on the next page, Mrs. White."

Patricia followed the instruction and immediately fell silent.

What she looked at now was the most macabre photograph she had ever seen in her life....

Other *Leisure* books by Edward Lee:

FLESH GOTHIC
MESSENGER
INFERNAL ANGEL

THE BACKWOODS

EDWARD LEE

LEISURE BOOKS

NEW YORK CITY

This book is for Pam Herbster.

A LEISURE BOOK®

October 2005

Published by

Dorchester Publishing Co., Inc.
200 Madison Avenue
New York, NY 10016

ISBN 0-8439-5413-2

Printed in the United States of America.

ACKNOWLEDGMENTS

I'm grateful to have so many people to thank for their friendship, inspiration, and support: Tim McGinnis, Dave Barnett, Rich Chizmar, Doug and Matt, Don D'Auria, Jack Ketchum, Tom Pic, Michael Slade. Cooper, Keene, Mike R., and all the Horror-finders. The proofing committee: Pam (whose blood on the print-out exponentially increased its value!), Bob Strauss, and Ben Ricciardi. Special thanks to David Graham and Lord Gore, and, next, to out-standing friends: Christy and Bill, Darren, R.J. Myers, Kathy, Sarah S., Karyn Valentine & Patti Beller, and Jeff Walton, and of course Charlie Meitz and Tim Shannon—for international crustaceans, particularly *Portunus halsatus.*

THE BACKWOODS

Prologue

The moon smeared in his eyes. He'd been staring as he waited, staring across the gulf of night to the other side of the river. He smiled. *Soon . . .*

The moonlight revealed sleeping bulldozers, stacks of foundation molds, and telltale trailers erected as construction offices. *It's progress,* his benefactor had said not too long ago. *Progress equates to more jobs, more satisfaction, and more money. In your pocket and mine. It's exponential.*

Dwayne's command of the English language excluded that particular adjective—but he got the idea. He was going to help speed progress along, and that was a good thing, wasn't it?

The voice grated out of the dark: "Do a good job."

"I always do, don't I?" Dwayne Parker said. Huffy redneck that he was, he felt mildly insulted by the other man's comment.

"You do, yes. I'm not denying that."

"Ain't none been found, right?" Dwayne challenged.

"Right."

Workboots came forward, crunching softly. In the moonlight Dwayne could see leaves and moss stuck to the tops of the boots, but no mud like Dwayne's. Here was what Dwayne guessed was the real difference between white collar and blue collar, the brains and the brawn. *Big fuckin' deal,* he thought. *Bet I get laid twice as much as he does. . . .* It seemed a fair recompense for brawn.

"Sounds like you don't trust me to get the job done," Dwayne finally got out. "The tone of your voice 'n' all. Like maybe just 'cos I ain't no big college graduate like your cronies."

"Don't be insecure." Now there was something else to the tone. Dwayne didn't like it, yet he didn't push it. The boots crunched forward another few steps, twigs crackling. Moonlight flowed through the trees, bars of shadows from branches splayed across the other man's face. "I have the utmost confidence in you," he told Dwayne, and passed him an envelope.

That's better. . . .

The envelope contained five crisp hundred-dollar bills.

The other man's voice seemed to resonate, a dark flutter from the face barely visible. "You won't have to do this too many more times before they all leave."

"What happens then?" Dwayne asked.

"Your wife sells the land to me. She'll be rich and so will you."

Dwayne pocketed the money. *Yeah, that's right. And until then, I'm gonna have a lot of fun.*

The cicadas were thrumming, a nearly electric drone that issued out from the woods in all directions. If a sound could be cloying, this was it. It pressed down on him like the sickly sweet humidity of the marsh.

"Here's fine," Dwayne said.

The girl seemed surprised. "Here?" she questioned. "Don't'cha wanna go back to my shack?"

Dwayne frowned. He'd seen where the Squatters lived: mostly sheet-metal huts on the bayside of the Point. He hesitated, "Well, uh—"

"Oh, it's nice," the girl promised. "Not like lots of 'em. My brothers built it for me, and I got it all to myself now that I'm eighteen."

Dwayne repressed a grin. *Eighteen? Shit, this girl looks fourteen, if that.* She was a twig of a thing, ninety pounds maybe, but then all the Squatters seemed small—Stanherd's clan. The tallest males stood five-seven if they were lucky, and the girls? They were all like this one: four-eleven, five feet tops. Must be something hereditary, in the ancestral blood. Stanherd's Squatters were *small* people.

But what had she been saying? *Don't want to turn her trick in the woods,* he remembered. *Wants me to go back to her shack—well, fuck that.* Someone might see him.

"Naw, here's fine," he repeated. "All I got time for is a quick one."

The girl was the sleekest shadow in the dark. "Oh, right," she said. "It's gettin' late, and I guess yer wife'd wanna know where you been."

"Just you let me worry about my wife," Dwayne said, annoyed. "I don't answer to her."

"Don't she ever get suspicious of ya?" The girl had asked the question calmly and, unabashed, kicked off her flip-flops and took off her shorts. "We all love her so much, generous as she is to us."

Minimum wage to pick fuckin' crabs, Dwayne thought

with another hidden smile. *And these pinheads think that's a lot of money. Shit.* Of course, Dwayne had done the same thing quite a bit in his life, or any other menial job where employers weren't discriminating. Dumpster cleaning, refuse removal, oil-change jockey, and the like—any job his parole officer could land him. Dwayne was almost forty now, and he'd done three jolts with the Russell County Department of Corrections, totaling seven years in stir. After the last one (two years, assault with a baseball bat), he'd landed here for a job picking crabmeat at the Agan's Point Shellfish Company. Not the best job he'd ever had. After a while he'd begun to smell like crab guts; no matter how many showers he took, the dank fishy stink emanated from him. But then he'd met Judy and his life had truly changed. She owned the company, which her sister up in D.C. had helped her revamp, a small-time operation that turned secretly lucrative. When Dwayne had pulled enough wool over Judy's eyes, she'd practically been begging him to marry her. And now?

Made in the shade, he thought.

Dwayne wasn't picking the crabs anymore; he was the supervisor of the Squatters and other lowlifes who did.

But there was never enough, was there?

The five hundred dollars in his pocket reminded him of that.

When the girl turned in the wedge of moonlight, Dwayne saw that she was fully naked now. *Bitch don't waste time,* he mused. He also saw something else: evidence that she was indeed at least eighteen. Full, fresh breasts, dark nippled; very feminine lines from shoulders to waist to hips; a plush outgrowth of untrimmed pubic hair. Not that Dwayne would've been worried about statutory rape . . . *No. Not with this one,* he thought. Or those six others.

"Still can't believe you wanna just do it here instead'a my shack," she was saying. In the dark she was bending over, a gesture like someone putting on stockings. But why would she do that? In the woods?

"And like I was saying," she went on, "what with your wife bein' so kind to us, givin' us good work." She looked up, looked right at him with dark sparkles for eyes. "I don't feel too good 'bout doing this, you bein' Miss Judy's husband and all."

Dwayne cut a frown. "Hey, a buck's a buck, right? You don't want to do me because of my *wife?* Then one of your other little friends will. In a heartbeat."

"I know. . . ."

"Besides, the twenty bucks I'm payin' you for five minutes of your time, you'd have to work three hours pickin' crabs."

"I know," she repeated.

That said it all. The Squatters were poor, and they weren't even on the books as citizens. Invisible, like illegal aliens. They worked hard for their low wages, and the better-looking gals—like this one—utilized other resources for increased income. The way of the world since humans came out of the caves.

Dwayne squinted in the dark. *What's she doing?* She bent over again, which replayed his notion that she was putting on stockings or garters or something. Yes. She'd slipped something up high on her bare thighs.

"What's that you're puttin' on yourself?" he finally asked her.

"Wheat bands," she said. "Has to be a special kinda wheat, though, and they're hard to make. Hard to get the kernels to stay together when you sew 'em on the band."

The hell? he thought. But suddenly he felt distracted by a number of things. For one, the endless chorus of cicadas, these being the three-year variety. This part of Virginia, Agan's Point got them all—the three-year, the seven-year, the thirteen-year, and the seventeen-year. As a kid, Dwayne had always found these waves and waves of insect sounds to be mysterious and captivating. But now—as an ex-con pushing forty—he found them annoying. The girl's voice distracted him too, the accent. All the Squatters had it, at least those from Everd Stanherd's clan. No one could ever quite place it. Part backwoods hillbilly drawl mixed with something that didn't even sound American. There was something rich and swoony about the way they talked. When they spoke, their lips didn't seem to move enough.

And then this new distraction. *What the fuck?* Dwayne thought. *Wheat bands, she said?*

Now she stood more directly in the moonlight, her fresh young body nearly luminous, breasts jutting, her belly button a perfect black shadow. She'd pulled a band up on each thigh, like corroded garters.

"Those bands are made of *wheat?*"

"Um-hmm. It's middling wheat, and it ain't from around here. The clan mother makes 'em, and every girl gets a pair soon as she gits her period. The magic goes back a long way."

"Magic," Dwayne said.

"Yeah. It's for when you're gettin' with a fella. If ya wanna baby boy, ya put it on the left thigh, and if ya wanna girl, ya put it on the right." She adjusted the strange bands daintily with her finger. "And if ya don't want nothin', ya put 'em on both."

Dwayne shook his head. *Squatters. Jesus.* He knew there was a lot of weird superstition with them, but this was one he'd never heard before. Deep down he laughed to himself. *Stupid cracker. The last thing she needs to be worryin' about is gettin' knocked up.*

It was getting late. "Time to get down to business," he said next, and walked right over to her. He dropped a twenty-dollar bill down on her clothes, then turned her brusquely around, her bare back to him, and reached around to slide his calloused hands over the soft skin of her breasts and abdomen. He rubbed his groin against her buttocks, feeling that forbidden charge. Her skin seemed to rise in temperature as he maintained his rough caresses, and she began to breathe harder. Dwayne thought with an inner chuckle, *Look at that, I'm turnin' the bitch on, gettin' a whore all hot 'n' bothered. Guess them dirty little clan boys don't do the job for her. Dwayne to the rescue . . .*

He figured it was the least he could do, considering. . . .

He sucked her neck, playing intently with her breasts. The nipples felt pebble-firm now, and when he gave them a hard squeeze with his fingers, she squealed delightedly, rising on her tiptoes.

"I always had a big thing fer you," came her strange accented whisper. "Just somethin' about *you* . . ."

The evidence of that was plain when he delved his fingers through her thatch into her sex. Dwayne felt electrified below the belt. "I've had my eye on you, too, for a while."

"Ya have not!" she playfully challenged.

"Sure, I have. You're about the prettiest of all the clan girls—"

"I am?"

"—and I've seen you on the line a lot. One of the hardest workers at the picking den. That's what I told my wife."

"Bet'cher just sayin' that," she toyed. "Why, I bet ya don't even know my name, even though you do the pay envelopes every week."

"Of course I remember your name," Dwayne insisted, still cossetting her breasts, but then he thought, *Fuck? What's this hosebag's name?* "Uh . . ." He paused. "Sunny, right?"

"Close," she told him, seeming at least pleased by that. "It's Cindy. Least, that's what I'm called mostly."

Dwayne didn't really give a flying shit what her name was . . . yet the comment nagged him. "What'cha mean, mostly? It's either your name or it ain't."

"It ain't my clan name. It's awful."

He worked her breasts harder, with more focus. "What's your clan name, then?"

"I ain't tellin'!" She seemed ashamed. "You'd laugh!"

"No, I wouldn't."

"Everd says when we're 'round local folks, we use our other names; we only use our clan names around ourselves. Everd says it's easier for us to fit in. We all know we don't fit in with ya all."

Dwayne was only worried about one thing fitting in, and it had nothing to do with names. But the man she referred to—Everd Stanherd—was a strange coot indeed. He was the clan's elder, the wise man, so to speak, for all the Squatters. The fucker claimed to be sixty but he looked eighty . . . except for his hair. Not a gray hair on his head anywhere, just jet-black. All the clan had weird shiny jet-black hair, even the older women. Dwayne couldn't see folks like this using hair dye.

"You feel really good . . . Cindy," he guttered. As his own arousal steepened, the dense chorus of cicadas seemed nearly deafening. Now his hands roamed all over—she felt tiny in them, the lithe frame, the reed-thin physique almost disproportionate to breasts firm and full as the popovers Judy made on holidays—and just as warm.

Playtime was over; Dwayne was more than ready behind the zipper. He urged her through trees hanging with mops of Spanish moss, sort of pushing her along with his groin, and his fingers slid back up to her nipples. She was panting when he got her to the clearing.

"Yeah, right here," he said. He turned her around, placing her hands on his belt, telegraphing that it was time for her to take off his pants.

Now her words sounded parched from desire. "You sure you don't wanna go back to my shack?" she almost pleaded.

His jeans fell down. "Naw."

"It'd be lots more comfortable. What's so special about this place?"

Dwayne dragged her down into the dirt, and as he pushed her knees to her ears, his thoughts answered her question: *This place? It's only about ten feet from where I dug the hole last night. . . .*

One

(I)

I wonder how he died, came the spontaneous thought. Even as a lawyer, Patricia White never imagined herself to be capable of such mental ill will, but here it was, secretly staring her in the face. Her promotion couldn't have been farther from her mind, nor the idea of so much extra income via the profit sharing. No, there were only these fleeting thoughts of darkness and morbidity. *Judy said he'd been murdered but she didn't say how.* The next question bloomed as she gazed numbly at a series of Ming Dynasty–styled statues:

I wonder . . . how. . . .

Yes. Exactly *how* had her sister's husband been murdered? What circumstances? And what modus? Gun? Knife? Bludgeoning?

Then: *I'd better get my head back on straight, before my own husband thinks I've completely flaked out.*

Byron sat across the table from her, trying not to look like he noticed her distraction. His first tack—when he knew something was bothering her—was to get her talking from any tangent available. "I'm not yet sure if this is the best Chinese restaurant in town," he said, "but I'm prepared to proclaim even at this early interval that it's the best-*smelling* Chinese restaurant in town."

So deep was Patricia White's distraction that she hadn't noticed until he'd mentioned it, but when she did, her eyes widened. Slim Asian waitresses scurried back and forth, bearing huge trays of food that seemed to draw aromatic banners throughout the restaurant. "Oh, Byron, wow. You're right. The aromas here are almost . . ."

His broad face widened as he grinned. "Erotic."

"You would say that, Mr. Perverted Food Critic."

He splayed his hands over the soup bowl that had until a moment ago been filled with shark-fin soup. "Good food is supposed to involve a sensual reaction; it has since early man began cooking. I see nothing *perverted* about it."

She couldn't help it, leaning over to whisper, "Except for maybe the time when we were in L.A., and you insisted on bringing the slice of Chocolate Martini Cheesecake home from Spago's and eating it off my stomach when we got back to the Beverly Hills Hotel."

"Um-hmm. And I think I can honestly describe your reaction to that as particularly sensual. And don't forget, Mrs. Perverted Power Attorney, what *you* did with the whipped cream first."

Patricia blushed immediately. How had she forgotten that part? More wonderful aromas rose to her face when their own entrées arrived: tangy sauces and elaborate spices and herbs carried upward in steam.

"So before we dig into our northern-China feast," Byron said, "why don't you tell me what's bothering you?"

Why not just say it? "I feel bad," Patricia admitted, "for not feeling . . . bad." Her eyes glanced up from the exorbitant plate of seared langoustines in shallot sprouts. Her normally stable gaze was confused now. "Does that make any sense?" she asked.

Byron's chopsticks stalled as he would have plucked up a strip of flash-fired abalone, his broad face contemplative in candlelight. "Honey, in this case it makes perfect sense. It's hard to put into words because we're not supposed to speak badly of the dead. That's what you're talking about, right?"

"Yes . . ." She set down her own chopsticks on the porcelain prop. The circumstances were obviously killing both their appetites, which was a shame in such an upscale restaurant known for such exotic cuisine. "Part of me feels so bad for Judy, but most of me feels . . . Oh, damn it. I feel like such a shit heel for even thinking it."

"Let me finish for you; tell me if I'm on track. Most of you feels good for Judy, because she's too good a person to be married to a guy like Dwayne. Dwayne was a pretty crappy person. He was a liar and a criminal and a con man, and now he's dead. And some part of you is *glad* he's dead. And you feel guilty about that. I do too a little, but I'm also glad he's dead. Nobody ever liked that guy. I only met him that one time, and I could tell at a glance that he was a shifty redneck who only married your sister to make his own life better. He was causing her great grief that she didn't deserve. He used to slap her around, for God's sake. Well, now he can't do that anymore. All in all, Dwayne's getting killed was a good thing. The world's a better place without him, and Judy is better off."

"I know," Patricia confessed, "but—"

"But she's your sister," Byron continued, "and you love her and you know that you're not supposed to feel happy that her husband is dead. A situation like this can never be simple."

"She was always convinced that he'd change eventually, that it was just his background that kept him down—"

"Of course, because that was the only thing she *could* think to ever have hope. The truth is, guys like Dwayne don't change. They're predators till the day they die. You can blame environment or upbringing or bad education or whatever, and sometimes those really are factors that need to be considered. And sometimes they're not. Dwayne was simply a bad person, and always would have been."

Patricia shook her head. "But she loved him so much."

"Sometimes love is blind and very illogical," Byron added. "Your sister's always been a bit insecure. She bought into Dwayne's phony charm and that rugged, tough-guy look, and she wound up getting screwed. She should've sent him packing a year after they got married, but that's when the insecurity kicks in. Happens a lot with women her age; after forty, they look at whoever they're with like it's a last stand."

"A woman her age?" Patricia questioned, but it was more as a joke. "She's forty-two; I'm forty-three."

"Yes, but the difference is, she was married to a brawny redneck; you're married to a bald gourmand. *I'm* the insecure one in *this* marriage. Most men my age have beer bellies." Byron patted the girth in his lap. "I have a foie-gras-and-chateaubriand belly."

They both shared a laugh, which was more than welcome in the midst of the bad scene. Byron was a food critic for the *Washington Post*. He made a good living eating at the best restaurants in the D.C. metropolitan area, yet he was constantly poking fun at himself. Patricia's salary was five times what he earned, and now that she'd made partner, it would be even more. And she wore her middle age quite deceptively, looking more along the lines of a woman in her early thirties. In spite of her workload, she still managed to make it to the gym three times a week, and nature or God had been kind enough to keep the wrinkles at bay. The wall by their table, just beyond an elegant, white-brick-bordered fish pond, was a mirror that doubled the restaurant's proportions, and when Patricia stole a glance at herself, she remained quite satisfied with the image that reflected back. Her silken, straight red hair shone about her face, long bangs pushed back. She'd just had it cut a few days ago, collarbone length, straight as a bezel. The sleek black jersey skirt only highlighted her slim physique, made even sexier by a bosom ample enough to leave most of Byron's friends convinced that she had implants when in fact she didn't. She looked exactly like the in-shape, attractive D.C. businesswoman that she was. Byron, on the other hand, incarnated the word *jolly*, and he knew it, which was just another reason why she loved him. He was overweight but he was genuine, and in the Washington power circles such men were rare indeed. She truly had married her best friend, and she knew she'd be at a loss without him. *I lucked out*, Patricia thought in a grateful calm. *I wish Judy had. . . .*

The restaurant busied itself around them, soft chat haunted by barely audible Oriental harps, and soft accents explaining tonight's specials: Thai-style cuttlefish in three spices, Peking duck, and Szechuan beef proper.

More seriously now, Byron said, "I'm sorry this other matter's darkened your celebration dinner. I wanted this to be special."

She squeezed his hand under the table. "It's very special. It could be McDonald's and it would be special, as long as you were here."

Byron smiled meekly. "Anyway, a toast. To your promotion."

They tinked tiny glasses of rich plum wine. Patricia was a real estate lawyer whose firm had just officially elevated from number two to the number one spot in the field. For the last ten years the realty market in the entire Washington and northern Virginia area had been going nuts, and it had never been nuttier than now, which meant prime business for attorneys such as she. Making partner gave her a share of company net earnings, and their Georgetown brownstone was already paid off and worth five times what they paid. She and Byron had always had a good life together, but now it was going to be a great life.

"I don't like it, though. It seems sexist." Byron returned to some levity, expertly chopsticking a piece of rumaki. "Your firm, McGinnis, Myers, and Morakis. You're a partner now. Shouldn't it be McGinnis, Myers, Morakis, and *White?*"

"Bad aesthetics, Byron," she answered. "That would screw up the marketable ring—the three Ms. Besides, I don't need my name on the door. First thing I do with my signing bonus is take my wonderful husband to Hong Kong so you can finish your fine-dining book."

"It may sound like a foolish indulgence for me to have this gluttonous dream, but what you must understand is that a preeminent critic such as myself *needs* to experience tao fu fa smoked bean curd and fish-head soup at the best Cantonese restaurant in the world—"

She smiled, looking at him. "Whatever turns you on, honey. I admire your passion. Me, I love good food too, but I don't have the same appreciation." She gestured at her plate. "This, for instance. It's great; it's even probably the best shrimp I've ever had—"

Byron winced automatically. "Honey, they're not shrimp; they're langoustines from Morton Bay in Australia. Not shrimp at all, but actually a genus of crevice lobster—"

Patricia nodded it off. "Fine. But to an unsophisticated taste like mine it's shrimp, and it's great, but I just don't have your knack for communicating that to other people. I don't have your *love* for that. You'd probably describe this as—"

Before she could finish, Byron plucked a langoustine off her plate, savored it in his mouth, and said, "A mysterious conspiracy of authenticated spice work, punctuating the sweetness of this distant and very exotic crustacean. The wild bite of tender shallot sprouts has been sufficiently tamed by just the right heat, all to impart a magnificent delectability rarely available to American palates. In all, the dish equates to culinary poetics."

"Exactly," she said, and laughed. "Hong Kong will definitely be your element, and I can't wait to see you in it." And it was true. They'd been together for twenty years, and it was Byron who'd worked so many extra hours while Patricia had been in law school and doing associate work. "You helped make my dream come true," she said more quietly, "and I know a lot of the time it seems like I've forgotten about that."

"Nonsense, it's *our* dream, and we get to live it together," Byron said.

She wondered, feeling even more guilty now. Most of the time she was too busy writing interrogatories for pretrial hearings to remind herself that she was a part of his life. *I'll make it all up to him, starting now,* she promised, hoping it wasn't just another excuse. He'd always wanted to go to Hong Kong—for the restaurants—and in twenty years, she'd never had time. She'd always been too busy. *Well, not anymore,* she thought. *I'm one of the bosses now.* "So like I said, the first thing I do as partner is take you to Hong Kong." But then a troubling thought intervened. "Well, I mean . . . the second thing."

"Of course,the funeral," Byron said more soberly. "Why don't you let me go with you? It's a long drive by yourself."

"It's only three hours or so."

"Well, that's not what I mean. You won't want to be alone in that crowd and that situation."

She knew what he meant. She'd never felt in place down there in Agan's Point, because she simply *wasn't* in place. *They all think I'm a conceited cosmopolite . . . which I guess I am.* "Judy's fine with me," she assured him, "and as far as the others go, to hell with them." It was a strange sentiment. Only ingrates left their birthplace for the city, people who thought they were better than everyone else. "I won't lie to you: I don't want to go, and if you want to know the truth, they can drop Dwayne's body in a trench and cover it over with dirt and not even *have* a funeral service . . . but—"

Byron nodded. "But you need to be there for Judy. Of course you do. That's how any real person would feel."

But her own thoughts, and what Byron had finished for her, made her feel awkward. *I was never there for her when she* really *needed me, was I?* Family loyalty and careers often warred with each other—a trademark of modern nuclear families—and in Patricia's case, the family loyalty had lost out. *Deep down Judy never forgave me for not staying in town to go to a closer college not too many years after Mom and Dad died. . . .*

More war, between her life as it was now, and however familial responsibility might be interpreted. Instead, she changed the subject. "I also want to look at the company records, see what kind of damage Dwayne may have done behind her back. The deal was, she did the accounting and Dwayne supervised the personnel, but I have my doubts. I wouldn't be the least bit surprised if he was skimming some kickbacks off the crabbers."

"Don't change the subject. I still think I should go with you," Byron prodded.

She sighed. It was out of the question. His family crises had never interfered with her; hence, she was determined not to allow the opposite. "You can't take off work just for that," she deflected.

"My monthly column's already finished—the piece on local caviar lounges—and I could zip out this week's feature review tonight. Going back to Agan's Point under these circumstances will be pretty damn uncomfortable for you. Let me go—even if it's only for the first few days. It might keep some of the stress at bay."

Patricia dearly wished she could say yes—she wanted to so much. *But it's not fair to him. That backwoods place is just as weird and awkward for him as it is for me.* "No," she declared. "You stay here and do your job.

You're the best culinary critic on that whole paper. I can't have you slipping because of me."

"But—"

"No," she repeated. Then she leaned over and whispered, "Just give me some great sex before I leave."

Byron's rotund face seemed to brace for a moment. Then he shrugged and said, "No problem."

The dim morning light seemed to make the street feel more desolate. Just this moment, it looked like anything but summer in the city. Only the faintest tinges of sunlight began to filter through the smog, which would only get worse when rush hour commenced. At least she wouldn't have to drive through any of that this morning.

Patricia felt disconnected as Byron placed her suitcases in the trunk of the sporty Cadillac SRX. In the meager light, the car's sumptuous burgundy paint job looked black.

Byron glanced up a moment, puzzled. "If you drive with the ragtop down, you'll cause multiple wrecks, you know."

She returned his expression, just as puzzled. "What?"

"But I have to admit, I like the idea of all those Virginia rednecks envying me."

"Byron, what are you talking about?"

"Your bra, or I should say lack thereof."

She briefly touched her bosom and then stifled her shock. She almost always wore a bra, yet at that moment she didn't consciously recall deciding not to this morning when she'd dressed. Her sizable bosom in addition to the plain white blouse would likely incite any gawkers on the highway. "I'd keep the top up to avoid sunburn anyway, Byron, so the jealous male sexual animal in you can relax. The only person I'll probably come in contact with today will be my sister."

"I'm relieved," he joked. "Believe me, this convertible plus that blouse plus *your* set of boobs would definitely cause a ten-mile pileup."

"See? I'm thinking solely of public safety."

The condo building loomed behind them. Byron smiled, the little bit of hair he had left disarrayed in spikes, stubble dark on his face. "Last chance. I could change real quick and go with you."

She hugged him a bit too desperately. "No, honey. I'll do this by myself while you hold down the fort. With any luck, I'll be back in a week."

"Give your sister my condolences. I'll order flowers today and have them delivered. Oh, and not to sound too insensitive but . . . could you bring back a few of her crab cakes?"

Patricia chuckled. Crabmeat packaging seemed about as obscure a business as anyone could imagine, but Judy had done very well vamping up the old family business since Patricia's investment of some venture capital. She'd paid back all the cash with interest, and the company was still growing. Judy had found her green thumb. Something rare and ideal about the waters of Agan's Point produced unusually large blue crabs in abundance, and the meat was so uniquely sweet that the restaurants in the county outbid other crabmeat suppliers simply due to the quality. Hence, the long-shot business had succeeded tremendously. Even Byron, with his persnickety attitudes toward food, admitted that the best crab cakes he'd ever eaten were those made by Patricia's sister. "I'll bring you a box of them," she promised.

The empty street sucked up the muffled echo when Byron closed the car trunk. But Patricia caught herself: "I'm such an airhead. I forgot my laptop—"

"You hope to do legal work in Agan's Point?" her husband asked in amusement.

"Just to keep in touch with my associates on e-mail; plus I need my records with me in case there's an emergency at the office," she said, and scurried back into the condo.

It was an old, homey stone building, six large units total, and the equity had skyrocketed in the ten years they'd lived there. Patricia took the elevator up, listening to the drone that cleared her head and helped her feel solid about going "home" today. As for the condo's interior decor, she'd deferred to Byron's more modern, urbanized tastes—something that might be called post–art deco. It didn't bother her, considering how little time she actually spent here; too often, for most city lawyers, the office felt more like the homestead. She brushed through the stark, light-toned living room, into the bedroom—the only room in the unit that she'd decorated to her own taste. Heavy paneling, dark hardwood furniture, and a plush four-poster bed. Colonial styles, though essentially passé in the modern city, had always appealed to her. She supposed it did remind her of her childhood on Agan's Point, which seemed odd, since she never thought fondly of either her childhood or the town, a repressed, poor community in which she and her sister had been raised by dour, insensitive parents. *God rest their souls,* she paused enough to think. Their creaky old house on the hill, though, had been decorated similarly in the Colonial style. When she passed the dresser to grab her laptop and case, something made her pause, flicking her eyes to the framed picture of her and her sister smiling on the wide, heavily railed front porch of the house she was about to return to today. She'd been fifteen at the time the picture had been taken, Judy fourteen, both dressed in the modest sundresses they wore so frequently during the hot, southern Virginia summers. They were both freckleless in spite of inherent fair skin and bright red hair, and something about the photo made them appear even younger than they were. A glance back into youth gone by. Behind them both stood the oversized front door whose threshold Patricia would be crossing again in three or four hours. She wondered what memories would be waiting.

The next picture on the dresser showed her mother and father standing in the backyard. They'd begun parenthood in their late thirties—a late start that made Patricia wonder if she and Judy hadn't really been accidents. Hard work in the crabbing business added still more years to her parents. Her father's eyes looked back hard from the old photo, while her mother's seemed bored. Both had grayed early, and just as neither of them smiled in the photograph, they'd seldom smiled in life. A mundane traffic accident had taken their lives the year Patricia would graduate from college. One thing she regretted was that they hadn't lived long enough to see their daughters succeed, but not living long enough to see Judy marry Dwayne was something Patricia clearly *didn't* regret.

Without thinking she turned the photo to face the wall. Her honesty about the matter had always bothered her, plaguing her with guilt. Patricia may have loved her parents, but she'd never really liked them very much. Her upbringing was an endless, unpleasant memory.

But there was one memory that hooked her right there when she was about to turn and go back out. *You bad, greedy girl,* she thought. The high, veiled bed she shared with Byron remained in disorder from last night's gluttonous frolic. *Maybe it was that plum wine from the restaurant?* she wondered. It was definitely something, though, something that lit all her fuses at once. Byron wasn't the greatest-looking man in the world, but Patricia knew that at their age, being sexually comfortable with a person was much more of a turn-on than muscles, a chiseled jaw, and other images of virility. She blushed at more recollections: He'd sensed her need all night, hauling her dress up to her waistline, dragging her panties off, and bullying her to the bed. He knew what she liked best, and he'd wasted no time in providing it, not even bothering to take his own clothes off before beginning an oral excursion of her body that lasted for over an hour, so delicately and featherlight at first, but graduating to animalistic fervor. Patricia came in multiples, biting her own knees like apples. Several times her shrieks of pleasure reverberated throughout the condo. *We're lucky the neighbors didn't call the police,* she thought now. A cruder thought occurred to her, maximizing her guilt: *Last night I practically used my husband's face for a bicycle seat, and I didn't even do anything for him afterward.* Her orgasms had so worn her out that she fell sound asleep immediately afterward. . . .

I keep telling him that I'm going to make things up to him now that I'm a partner. She frowned to herself. *Great start, Patricia. You're a selfish bitch.*

She gave herself a final checkover in the mirror, happy that faded jeans, sneakers, and an old blouse wouldn't be overdoing it for returning home. True, her bralessness left little to the imagination, but she hardly cared. *Maybe I skipped the bra on purpose and just didn't realize it?* she wondered. Her breasts stretching the blouse and her nipples ghosting through it would leave her husband with a final sexy image of her when she left.

Ready. she thought. She took a breath and turned out the light. Then she went back outside, kissed her loving husband good-bye, and embarked on the three-hour drive that would take her back into the heart of her childhood memories—

—and the unbidden recollection of the awful thing that had happened to her so long ago.

(II)

Sometimes you just can't win. The thought occurred to him when he opened his wallet and saw but four single dollar bills in there just after he'd walked in to the Donut King at the edge of town. A dozen doughnuts, by the way, cost $4.69, and he didn't dare ask Trey for the extra.

That would be humiliating. After all, Sutter was the chief.

So he bought one doughnut and a cup of coffee and walked out.

"Cuttin' back?" Trey asked. "Usually ya git yourself a dozen."

"Yeah," he lied. "Doc said to lose weight if I wanna live to collect my Social fuckin' Security. I've been payin' into the bitch for damn near fifty years, so I ain't gonna let myself get ripped off."

It would be just his luck, wouldn't it?

Chief Sutter wasn't generally prone to cynicism, an attitude he was inclined to regard as unhealthy. He was a levelheaded man, a fair one and probably more goodhearted than most police chiefs nearing retirement. Father Darren at church reminded them every Sunday that taking for granted what one had was a sin, sort of a slap to the face of God, Who'd made this world and everything in it as a gift to mankind. Every day above ground was a good day, a blessing and another opportunity to celebrate the joy of life, and most would probably agree.

Fuck me and the horse I rode in on, came the sour thought.

Even good men had bad days, and that was what Chief Sutter woke up to this morning, his three hundred-pound frame smothered in a swelter, and his wife, who weighed not much less, snoring like a mountain gorilla. The air conditioner had crapped out overnight—what a splendid thing to happen in the South, during summer's tightest squeeze.

It would probably cost him two grand to replace, and with the two mortgages, property taxes going up, and a wife who'd maxed out the credit cards, Chief Sutter didn't know *what* he was going to do.

Just ain't right, he thought later, on his way to the station. *I've worked my ass off my whole damn life helping other people, and what have I got to show for it?*

Not much, right now. Just a lot of debt, and damn little satisfaction.

"Still bothered about your money problems?" Trey asked from the passenger seat. Sgt. William Trey was Sutter's second in charge and officially the department's deputy chief. Second in charge didn't mean a whole lot on a two-man police department, but Sutter figured he deserved the acknowledgment. Trey was fifty now but tended to still act like the brazen, feisty cockhound he'd been when Sutter'd hired him almost three decades ago. A local boy with good intentions, and who respected his home. He sort of looked like Tom Cruise, if Tom Cruise had never made it. But he was still agile and fairly fit, which—considering his weight—Sutter sadly was not. When he needed someone to jump over a fence to run down some punks, Sutter was glad for such a deputy. And he had a way of painting a bad situation with a happier color. "Look at it this way, Chief. All married men got money problems. Take us, for example. We both got wives the size of a coupla full-grown Berkshire hogs, and the only difference is they eat *more* than a coupla full-grown Berkshire hogs. That costs *money,* Chief, and it's the husband's job to provide it. A fat wife is a sign that a man is providin' for her, which is what God wants."

Chief Sutter appreciated the spin but wasn't sure if it was working.

"We'se both married in the eyes of the Lord; that's how it's supposed to be," Trey went on. "You're not seein' my point now, are ya?"

"Well . . ."

"Here's what Father Darren would say. Why is it you think you ain't got enough money?"

"Well, 'cos—"

" 'Cos yer wife spends half the money you work your ass off for on food, and you spend the other half on keepin' a roof over her head and her big ass in a car, right?"

Sutter gave him an alarmed glance. "Yeah, and it's a right pain in the ass and it's pissin' me off."

Trey nodded knowingly. "And here's what Father Darren would say. He'd say that a wife who's fat 'n' happy is the wife of a God-lovin' man, a man who's doin' his best to live by His laws."

Sutter blinked. "That what he'd say?"

"You can roger that, Chief, and here's why. 'Cos if yer fine wife, June, was bone-skinny and didn't have no cable TV, or no car a' her own, and had ta live in a shit little house, then that'd mean that you *weren't* livin' by His laws."

Sutter sighed. "I hope you're right, Trey, but what ya don't understand is I'm *chokin'* on a right *shitload* of debt, and now I somehow gotta find me *two grand* for a new air conditioner. I'm real happy that I'm livin' by God's laws, but I sure don't see God buyin' me a new air conditioner."

Trey pointed. "But don't ya see? He will. All you gotta do is ask Him. God provides to those who rightly deserve His provisions. Do it right now, in yer head. Ask God ta forgive ya for not managin' your finances proper, and ask Him to help ya out. Go on. Do it. Remember what Father Darren says: A man should never be embarrassed to talk to God."

Sutter slumped behind the wheel of the cruiser. *Can't hurt, I guess.* He closed his eyes and prayed: *God, what I'm askin' ya to do is to forgive me for bein' selfish 'n' ungrateful 'n' for takin' your gifts for granted. Forgive me for not lookin' hard enough to see how you want things to be, and forgive me for not managin' my finances proper and for lettin' things get outta hand. I need your help, God, and I mean I really, really need the scratch for a new air conditioner, 'cos if I can't dig it up, June'll be whinin' worse than a truckload of weasels. . . .*

When Chief Sutter opened his eyes again, he felt

better. He didn't feel any richer, but he definitely felt better.

"Good man, Chief. When you talk, God listens." Trey sipped his coffee in some seeming assurance. "He listens to me, I can tell ya that. I ain't braggin', but let me show ya something." He slipped out his wallet and withdrew two slips of paper. "Now, I make less than you, and if anything my wife, Marcy, eats even more than your wife, but look at this."

He passed the slips of paper to Sutter.

Holy . . . shit! They were bank balance receipts. "Trey, I say you sure *do* manage your money proper. Jiminy Christmas." Trey had five grand in his checking and eight in his savings.

Trey took back the papers, nodding. "It's 'cos God listens when I talk to him. God looks at me and ya know what He sees? He sees a man who's had plenty of chances to go astray but chose not to. He sees a cop, same as He sees you. He sees a man bustin' his ass to uphold the law and maintain peace and decency. So God don't leave a man like that out to dry. Instead, He helps him out every so often. Just like He's gonna help you."

Sutter reflected on the words. He remembered Trey back in his younger days, before marriage, before typical social and domestic responsibilities had come into his life. The man had been an absolute nutcase, a hard-drinkin', hard-partyin' character. *Gals would follow that boy down the street,* Sutter thought. *Spent mos a' his money on bar-hoppin', hot rods, and women. . . .* But life had changed Sgt. William Trey—a change for the good. He'd used the force of his will to change himself into a *good* man, and now *good* things were befalling him.

Would the same good things befall Sutter?

He needed some good things now.

It was almost as if Trey were reading his mind when he said, "Good things, Chief."

"What's that?"

"Good things happen to men who put their trust in God."

Sutter stared out the window. What Trey was telling him just made him feel better and better. He shook his head. "Trey, I known you for goin' on thirty years, and in all that time I had no idea you had so much religion in ya."

"Ain't no secret; ain't no big deal." Trey calmly sipped more coffee. "Live by God's laws, and He will grant blessings upon you." But in that same moment, Trey's eyes shot wide out the window at a figure at the side of the road. It was a woman, a woman flagging them down, and that was when the very God-fearing Sergeant Trey exclaimed, "Holy sufferin' *shit,* Chief! Would you get a load of the tits on *that* piece of ass?"

Two

(I)

Patricia, of course, had forgotten. It had been five years, hadn't it?

Five years since her return to Agan's Point.

The Cadillac cruised silently, comfortingly, but as the city had faded behind her, and the interstate highways had eventually given over to long, winding, and very rural county roads, the words began to haunt her:

Oh, my God, girl. How could you let something like that happen?

They were her father's words, less than a week after her sixteenth birthday. . . .

The look in his eye, and the words he'd chosen. *Like I* let *it happen,* she thought now in an overwhelming mental darkness. *Like I* wanted *it to happen . . .*

She'd never been more hurt in her life.

She'd felt good, hadn't she? Her wonderful, if selfish, love session with Byron last night might have had something to do with it, but when she pulled away from the condo, knowing full well where she was going, she felt good, and that was something she didn't expect. Watching the sun bloom as she drove, opening the Cadillac up on Interstate 95, and moving forward . . . It seemed to clear her head of all the city's stresses and the endless intricacies of work. Indeed, Patricia felt clean, new; she felt purged. Until . . .

Her mood began to wilt in increments. She knew what she was doing. *Putting it off. But I* can't *put it off. All I can do is dawdle, procrastinate.* She wound up driving through the historic district in Richmond, and blowing an hour looking for a place to have breakfast. Same thing through Norfolk, for lunch. She was turning the three-hour drive into an all-day journey, as if getting to Agan's Point later would ease some of her distress. But she knew it wouldn't. *I'm torturing myself,* she thought.

Hours later familiar road signs began to pop up, signals that she wasn't so much driving away from her exhausting lifestyle in Washington, but instead driving *to* something much more stressful. The far less traveled Route 10 seemed to throw the signs in her face as she raced past, towns with names like Benn's Church, Rescue, and Chuckatuck. More and more of her frame of mind began to melt. Then a sign flashed by:

DISMAL SWAMP—10 MILES.

And more signs, with stranger names:

LUNTVILLE—6 MILES.

CRICK CITY—11 MILES.

MOYOCK—30 MILES.

Oh, God, Patricia thought.

She was beginning to feel sick, and with the sickness came a resurfacing. She hadn't thought of the psychologist in a long time, a keen, incisive bald man named

Dr. Sallee. And she'd seen him only once, just after her return from her last trip to Agan's Point five years ago, when her despair seemed insurmountable.

"We bury traumas," he'd told her. "In a variety of different ways, but the effect remains the same. Some people deal with their traumas by confronting them immediately, and then forgetting about them, while others deal best by forgetting about them first and then *never* confronting them because there's no apparent need. That's what you're doing, Patricia, and there's nothing wrong with that. There's no apparent need because you relocated yourself from the premises of the trauma."

The premises of the trauma. She thought over the odd choice of words. But he'd been right. *I moved away as fast as I could. . . .*

"What happened to you will always be there," he continued, fingering a paperweight shaped like a blue pill that read STELAZINE. "I'm a behavioralist psychologist; I'm not so liberal in my manner of interpreting human psychology. Other professionals would tell you that it's unhealthy to *leave* your traumas because they remain in your psyche whether you know it or not. That's not true with regard to how we must function in our lives, in our society, and in the world. If not living in Agan's Point restores you to that kind of functionality, then you've done the right thing. Your trauma becomes neutered, ineffectual—it becomes a thing that can't affect you anymore. It no longer has any bearing on your life, and never will . . . unless you let it. You don't need a regimen of antidepressant drugs and costly psychotherapy to deal with your trauma; all you need is to be *away* from the area of the occurrence. Your life right now is validation. You're a fabulously successful attorney enjoying a fulfilling career and a wonderful marriage. Am I right?"

Patricia splayed her hands on the couch. "Yes."

"You aren't *traumatized* by what happened to you when you were sixteen, are you? You aren't a psychological *basket case*; this event in your past hasn't *ruined* you. You can't tell me that this twenty-five-year-old tragedy still rears its head and exerts a negative force in your existence, can you? Can you tell me that?"

Patricia almost laughed. What he was forcing her to admit to herself was now replacing a creeping despair with a frivolous joy. "No, Doctor, I can't tell you that at all."

He looked at her with a blank expression. "So your problem is . . . ?"

She conceded to him. "You're right. I don't have a problem anymore."

He raised a finger. "Proximity to the scene of the trauma is your only problem. Whenever you return to Agan's Point, your despair recommences. When you're away from Agan's Point, your mind functions as though the trauma never occurred. We know I'm correct about this because every aspect of your life verifies it. Let me put it in the most sophisticated, clinical terminology I can, Patricia. *Fuck* Agan's Point. *Shit* on Agan's Point. To *hell* with Agan's Point. How's that?"

Now Patricia was laughing outright.

And he finished, "Your despair is activated only when you return to Agan's Point, so my professional advice is never to go back there. You don't have to. You don't have to do anything you don't want. If you want to see your relatives, then they can come to you. You don't have to go to them. Agan's Point is a bowel movement that you flushed down the toilet years ago. Solution? Don't go back to the sewer."

And that was that. Not only had Patricia gotten a great laugh from Dr. Sallee's acumen, she'd needed to see him only that one time for all to be set back to rights. When she'd gone home from her sister's wedding, it all returned to her—indeed, like a toilet backing up. *Now that I'm away from that hellhole . . . I feel great. . . .*

And she continued to feel great . . . until she'd received the call from Judy reporting her husband's murder.

I'm going back to the sewer, she recalled the doctor's metaphor as the Caddy brought her closer and closer. *I don't know what else to do. She's my* sister. . . .

This was all she *could* do, and she knew it. "And I'll just have to make the best of it," she said to herself. "It was so long ago anyway. I'm acting like a baby." Admitting that to herself was easier than admitting her optimism was forced.

She let more of the road take her, the Cadillac almost too quiet and smooth as more roads turned rural, and more turnoffs took her farther away from her metropolitan world. The wilds of southern Virginia were an *opposite* world—farms instead of skyscrapers, old pickup trucks and tractors lumbering along quiet, tree-lined roads, quite unlike the manic traffic streams of the city. She knew that home grew ever closer by still more telltale signs: AGAN'S POINT CRAB CAKES, boasted a roadside restaurant. Then a market: WE SELL AGAN'S POINT CRABMEAT. Her sister's crabmeat was locally renowned. Eventually the scenery began to calm Patricia's nerves, and she actually smiled. Would she really be able to forget about her trauma of decades ago? *Maybe it's all just worn off,* she hoped.

Then another sign swept by:

AGAN'S POINT—3 MILES.

She steeled herself behind the wheel. *It's no big deal, no big deal. I'm* over *it!*

And then the awful words came back to haunt her just as effectively as she was being haunted by her past:

Yes, her own father's words . . .

How could you let something like that happen?

Patricia's eyes suddenly flooded with tears. She couldn't control herself; she couldn't even remember what she was doing, her sensibilities jerking away from her like something being stolen. Without even realizing it, she pulled the Cadillac to the shoulder and got out, her heart hammering, sweat pasting her red bangs to her forehead. A passerby would've dismissed her as a crazy woman about to run amok into the woods. Tears blurred her vision. Her feet took her in a blind run away from the car. When she fell to her knees several minutes later, she looked up, choking through sobs, and then saw a smaller sign just before the turn onto a narrow country road. She had to squint through her tears to focus until she could finally read the sign, a right-turn arrow and the words:

BOWEN'S FIELD.

Patricia shrieked, vomited into the grass, and passed out.

(II)

"It just seemed weird to me, Mr. Chief," the slim, curvy girl with tousled black hair was relating into the driver's-side window of the Agan's Point police patrol car.

The strange accent was more of a giveaway than the pale skin and black hair, not to mention the "Mr. Chief." *One of Stanherd's Squatters,* Chief Sutter realized. They always called him Mr. Chief. He didn't recall seeing this one around, but then he didn't typically pay much attention to the Squatters—he didn't have to. They kept to themselves, stayed out of trouble, and worked hard, most of them taking minimum-wage jobs at the crab company. Chief Sutter was a reasonable man. *Work your job, pay your taxes, and obey the law, and you'll have no problem with me.* Right now, however, Chief Sutter was having a problem of his own, with this girl who'd flagged them down on Point Road. As she leaned over the window, to convey some mishap at the Qwik-Mart, her breasts stared him bold in the face. The homemade tomato-red jumper top restrained a pair of breasts that might be getting close to D-cup territory. The hand-set stitches of the top, in fact, were stretching enough to show lines of flesh in their seams. She also wore an equally tight threadbare skirt hemmed uncomfortably high on the thigh. The Squatters made their own clothes from fabric scraps they bought at Goodwill, and this little thing was obviously still growing into her getup. A heat wave flashed in Sutter's groin when, as he listened, his eyes shot a quick glance down the front of her abdomen and hips. *Oh, lord,* he commiserated. Her right foot crossed over the back ankle of her left, a dollar-store flip-flop hanging off the sleek, voluptuous foot. *Jiminy Christmas, even her fucking* feet *are hot . . .* Hence Chief Sutter's "problem." The images distracted him, such that he found himself nodding as if in attention but hearing almost nothing of what she said.

"—and they was kinda grinnin' and lookin' me over," she went on, "the way fellas'll do, makin' me really uncomfortable, and when I told 'em I didn't wanna buy none, they said somethin' like, 'Well, that's all right, we'll give ya some fer free if ya come and party with us.' "

The Squatter girls weren't much above the neck, sort of wide faces and flat noses, not the best teeth, and that ratty black hair. But below the neck?

Jiminy Christmas, Sutter repeated the thought. They all had bodies that would make a calendar girl feel insecure.

"What's that you were sayin' there, hon?" Trey asked. Sutter could tell by Trey's squint and the tone of his query that he too was experiencing a problem with distraction. Any officer's job was to get all the facts, and that wasn't working well here, not with this Squatter bombshell's pair of absolutely state-of-the-art breasts practically falling out of that top in front of them.

"What was it you say these fellas were tryin' ta sell you?" Trey blinked hard enough to get out.

Her hip cocked, which caused her bosom to sway delectably in the hand-stitched top, and she explained in that weird accent that all the Squatters seemed to have, "Ice! Can ya believe that? They asked me if I wanted to buy some *ice!* Sure, it's hot 'n' all, but we got a bunch a' ice trays in our freezer just like dang near everyone, and even if we didn't, I could walk right in the Qwik-Mart and buy me a bag. Dumbest thing I ever heard anyone tryin' ta sell right out front of a convenience store. Who sells ice out of a truck, Mr. Chief? So's that's why I flagged ya down, just 'cos that whole thing seemed really weird and so did them fellas. Thought the police'd wanna know."

Sutter and Trey exchanged glances. At least now they had some police business, which was good, because if Sutter had to spend another minute looking at this girl's outrageous body he might have a heart attack right there in the cruiser.

"That was right of you to flag us down, missy," Sutter said, "because fellas like that are definitely not the type we want in Agan's Point. You see which way they went?"

Now she stood on both feet, legs parted, and leaned back with hands on hips. More distraction: she was so *short*—all the Squatters were—and as she leaned back like that, she nearly appeared unreal, like something manufactured at a scaled-down size. When she pointed across the windshield, Sutter's eyes bugged as one immaculate breast rose in the top, and in that little gap underneath he could see the bare bottom of it in all of its orbicular glory. "They ain't went nowhere yet, Mr. Chief, 'cos see? They're still there. That's them in that orange boxy-looking truck parked right out front of the Qwik-Mart, and that's one of 'em standin' right there talkin' on the pay phone."

Trey's expression revved up. "Well, ain't that grand, yes, sir!"

"You got that right," Sutter agreed, then back to the girl: "You've done a fine civic duty today, missy, and we appreciate it."

She seemed delighted by Sutter's response, and then her not-so-comely face lit up with a big smile—not that Sutter nor Trey, was focused on her face. "You have a fine day, Mr. Chief, and . . . and . . . and Mr. Chief's partner."

Sutter paused to himself. *Shit. I gotta know.* "By the way, missy, if you don't mind my asking . . . how old are you?"

Her eyes beamed. "Why, it's funny you should ask, but I just turnt fifteen yesterday!"

Trey spit out a mouthful of coffee while Sutter thought in a long, low groan: *Oh, my great God in heaven. . . .*

The girl waved giddily as the cruiser backed up and began to turn. "Jiminy Christmas," Sutter muttered like a man with a bad bellyache. "That dizzy brick shithouse was almost the death of me just lookin' at her."

"Damn near busted my pants, Chief. And did'ja see how *little* she was? Bet she wasn't five feet. And who cares about the butt-ugly face? Them Squatter chicks got bods on 'em that make me wanna howl at the fuckin' moon." Trey may have momentarily rubbed his crotch when Sutter wasn't looking. "I got myself a leapin' lizard down here."

"Tell me about it."

His slapped his thigh. "And she's only *fifteen!*"

"Tell me about it," Sutter repeated, pulling around.

Trey was shaking his head. "But just as they got bodies from hell they ain't got but shit fer brains." He let out a hick laugh. "She thinks those guys are selling ice cubes! How's that for a dumb shit?"

"Aw, give her a break. She's had a shit life, no proper schooling, and works her ass off at the crab plant."

Trey belted out another laugh. "Shit, Chief, with that bod, she can work *my* ass off anytime she likes!"

Sutter shot him a reproving glare.

"Er, I mean, once she turns eighteen," Trey added in haste.

"That's what I thought you meant. Christ, ten minutes ago you were runnin' your mouth all about how God helps us out if we obey His laws." Sutter chuckled.

"You sure lost your religion quick enough, lustin' after that Squatter."

Trey roused to object. "I was just speakin' figurative, Chief," he said, pronouncing the word as *figgur-tive,* "as men will do when they're amongst themselves, but in my heart—and I say this 'cos I know it's in your heart too—men married in the eyes of the Lord wouldn't even *think* of havin' any carnal knowledge with no gal other than his lawful wife, no matter what age she is. I asked Father Darren 'bout it once."

"About what?"

"About lust in the heart, and he said that since all men was born in original sin, we're all guilty of lust—can't help but be—'cos it's all in our genes. So it's okay to eyeball a hot gal now and again, 'cos it's a manner of appreciatin' the beauty God gave to women."

Sutter's eyes narrowed. "Father Darren said it's *okay* to eyeball other women?"

Trey raised a finger to finish his point. "As long as you know in your heart that ya wouldn't really have sex with her once it got down to brass tacks. I know you'd never cheat on yer fine wife, June, and I sure as shit'd never cheat on Marcy. Don't matter that they both gone to fat and got tits hangin' down to their thighs. That's 'cos God blesses us in our love."

Sutter sighed.

"Anyway, Chief, that's what Father Darren means in a nutshell. It's okay by Him that you look at other chicks every once in a while as long as ya'd never really hobnob with 'em."

Well, that's sure good to hear, 'cos I still got half a hard-on in my pants from lookin' at that little thing, Sutter thought sourly.

Trey grinned. "And look at it this way, Chief. That little piece a' eye candy got your mind off your money problems, huh?"

The recollection of those breasts, those curves, and those legs waylaid him. "It got my mind off 'em, but I still *got* 'em, Trey."

"Patience is a virtue, Chief. Says so in the Bible. God smiles upon a patient man. . . ."

Sutter shook off the after-imagery as he pulled into the convenience store, where a gleaming, brand-new Humvee occupied one of the parking spots, tangerine orange and ten coats of lacquer. A shifty-looking black guy in his mid-twenties, in baggy pants and gold chains, had just hung up the pay phone and was coming back to the car, giving them the eye.

"Fucker's got more gold chains than Mr. T.," Trey observed with a smirk. "And look at the watch on the son of a bitch. Looks like a Rolex."

"We know where he gets that kind of money," Sutter remarked. His own watch cost $7.95 at the drugstore. "And look at those rings on him, too. Fucker's all decked out like a Harlem pimp."

In the Hummer's driver's seat sat a long-haired white kid with scruff on his chin, and similar gold chains and watch.

"We know what these scumbags are all about, so keep on your toes," Sutter said. "I'll take the rapper and you take the white guy."

"Gotcha, Chief. Thumb snap's off." He grinned at his boss and released the snap on his holster. "We ain't had a tussle in a spell. I'm ready."

"You keep your dander down unless ya need it." Sutter hit his own thumb snap; then he added, "And it can't hurt for us to mitt up."

"Roger that," Trey assented. They each slipped on

their pair of Bianchi elastic-stretch sand mitts with nude trigger fingers and heavy-duty leather sand pouches reinforcing the knuckles and palms. Ideal for punching through doors or busting a scumbag's face without consequently busting one's own knuckles.

Sutter moved his own considerable bulk out of the car. He blocked off the black guy before he could get back to the Hummer, while Trey leaned against the driver's door, arms crossed.

"Is there a problem, Officer?" the black guy asked a bit haughtily. His T-shirt read, RAPPIN' AND CAPPIN', and he had a tattoo of an AK-47 inked over one apple-sized bicep.

"Oh, there's a problem," Sutter confirmed. "Turn around, hands flat out on the roof, and spread 'em. No sudden movements. Don't fuck with me."

"The fuck?" the white guy complained.

"Pipe down, Kid Rock," Trey said, "or *I'll* pipe ya down."

The black guy glared. "I haven't done anything wrong! You're just shaking me down 'cos I'm black!"

"Don't give me that racist jive," Sutter said back. "I don't give a shit what color a man's face is. The only kind of black man I call a nigger is a black man trying to sell crystal meth to kids."

That was all the black guy needed to hear—"crystal meth"—before he realized he could either run his ass off or do three-to-five for possession and distro of Class II narcotics with another five tacked on for attempted distro to a minor. He chose to run his ass off.

Shit!

He bolted off the car. Sutter, since he was not exactly dextrous nor physically fit, being obese and close to sixty, managed to get a handful of T-shirt, which sufficed only to slow the guy down around the corner of the car, whereupon the T-shirt tore away.

As for Trey, he didn't appear to even break a single bead of sweat when in some impressive synchrony he—

Whap!

—landed a solid fist right smack-dab into Kid Rock's forehead, then—

"Holy Jesus, man, that hurts like a motherfucking motherfucker!"

—emptied half a can of GOEC-brand chemical spray into his eyes and bleeding, split-open face.

"Got ya covered, Chief," Trey said next, sidestepping forward. He moved fast enough to cut off the black guy before he could get clear. Then—

Thud.

—palm-heeled him once in the solar plexus.

Which sufficed to circumvent the attempt to flee.

"Getcha a case of beer for that one, Trey," Sutter said approvingly, then lumbered over. "You simmer down the long-hair while I read this suspect his rights." The black guy was sprawled out belly-down on the pavement, bug-eyed, barely able to move. He was sucking wind. Sutter promptly stepped on the back of his head, treating his face to a little dermabrasion the hard way. The guy flip-flopped on the pavement, shrieking like a little girl who'd just been scared out of a carny house of horrors.

Kid Rock had managed to stop screaming long enough to make the very unwise decision to attempt to drive off. Hair hanging in blood-drenched strings, he jerked his hand forward, touched the keys in the ignition, was about to start the car, when—

"Holy Jesus, mother of God, you gotta be fuckin' shitting me!"

—Trey emptied the rest of the GOEC into his eyes.

Sutter dragged a dozenish bags of crystal methamphetamine, aka "ice," out of the black guy's pockets, not to mention a pipe, and—of all things—a 1964 Topps Mickey Mantle baseball card. Sutter pocketed the card, then allowed the point of his steel-toed black oxford to come into direct proximity with the area of space that was occupied by the black guy's scrotum. That took the rest of the zing out of him.

Finally got me another Mantle card for my collection . . .

The cowbell on the door clanged. Pappy Halm, a well-known Agan's Point local and the store's proprietor, hobbled out front, aghast. He clacked toward the scene on his cane and objected in his typical loud rail, "What the hell ya doin' Chief? I seen ya in the winder! All that fella done is make a blamed phone call! What right ya got to beat him down like that?"

Sutter showed him a handful of ice. "This walkin' piece a' shit here and his hippie buddy are selling these hard drugs to kids. Just tried to sell some to a fifteen-year-old not five minutes ago."

"Oh, yeah?" Halm replied, then cracked the end of his cane hard up into the black guy's crotch. Now the guy was gasping, screaming, and blubbering all at the same time.

"Want me to cuff Kid Rock, Chief?" Trey asked.

"Naw." Sutter dragged the black guy up. "If we write this one up and take 'em to county detent, I'll miss dinner. And you know how fierce the wife bitches at me when I miss dinner. Fuckers'd be out on bail in the time it takes me to fart."

"Roger that."

"But we better look the vehicle over. Check that guy's

pockets and under the seat." Sutter opened the Humvee's back door for a quick search. *Jesus* . . . He found a tackle box full of more ice. "Bet there's a thousand bucks' worth of dope in here," he said.

Trey peeked between the front seats. "More'n that, by the looks of it. Just think of all the kids they'd be selling it to. And look at what the hippie was carryin'." He held up a small pistol.

"Jesus. These guys."

Sutter shoved the dizzy black guy back into the front seat, but before he closed the door—

Crack!

—he raised his fiberglass nightstick high over his head and whacked it down across the guy's thigh. The thighbone snapped like a stout bough.

Trey whipped out his own billy. "A limp to remember us by. The same for this one?"

"Naw. He's gotta drive. But I think a Southern-style haircut might do him justice. Fucker must think he's in Lynyrd Skynyrd."

Trey twirled a finger around a lock of Kid Rock's hair, pressed his other hand against his head, and yanked as though starting a lawn mower. The kid barked a righteous yelp when a clump of hair popped out of his head along with a square inch of scalp.

Sutter's temples pounded in sudden disgust as he looked at the shining vehicle and the gold chains on the wheezing black man. "It ain't fuckin' fair, ya know? I ain't an ungrateful man, and I ain't greedy either. But I got my problems just like any hardworkin' man. Them two mortgages I was telling you about are bleedin' me dry, car insurance just gone up again and so did county property taxes, not to mention the damned Ay-rabs keep jacking the price a' gas. Got a wife that eats more than the Redskins defensive line, God love her, and who runs my credit cards up like she's Bill fuckin' Gates's wife insteada the wife of a small-town police chief, and now the blasted AC up 'n' broke, so *that's* gonna cost me out the ass . . . so I am pinched to the max. I'm so broke I can barely pay fuckin' attention, and then look what we got here." He glared intensely at the shuddering black guy and his accomplice. "We got two piles of walkin,' talkin' garbage wearing gold jewelry and drivin' a brand-new Hummer, and how'd they get the kind of bread for all that?" He looked at the bags of crystal meth. "By sellin' this shit. Yes, sir, these pieces a' shit live large and got enough cash to choke a fuckin' horse, and what do I got? Enough *debt* to choke a fuckin' horse." He slammed the Humvee door, made a fist of his right sand mitt, and said directly to the black guy, "We don't take kindly to people sellin' drugs in our town, so listen up."

He pinched the guy's cheeks together. "You 'n' your buddy are gonna turn this jalopy around and drive outta here, and you ain't gonna stop till you're plumb out of this county, and you're never, and I mean *never*, gonna come back here again, and if we ever, and I mean *ever*, see you anywhere near Agan's Point in the future—"

Whap!

He rammed his sand mitt right into the guy's mouth.

"—we might have to rough ya up a little."

The black guy was spitting out teeth. Kid Rock convulsed behind the wheel, backing the Hummer up and spinning wheels out of the lot.

Trey rubbed his hands together. "All in a day's work, huh, Chief?"

"Damn straight. And I snagged myself one hell of a Mantle card. Pisses me off, though."

"What's that, Chief?"

Sutter dropped the tackle box and rest of the drugs into the garbage. "A small fortune worth of dope, and those punks probably sell that much shit to kids every damn day."

"Sure they do."

"Driving around in a brand-new fifty-grand Hummer—"

"That tricked-up model? Sixty, sixty-five at least."

"Yeah, and we drive clunkers. Gold chains, too. Shit. Only thing I can afford to wear around my neck is a line of sweat. Ain't right."

"No, it ain't, Chief." Trey crossed his arms with a look of concern. "But I'd say we done a lotta good today. Ain't no drugs gonna be sold by them fellas fer a while. And . . ." Trey paused to reflect on something. "Let me ask you somethin', Chief."

Sutter scratched his belly, trying to shake off the irritation. "Go ahead."

"Is stealin' from a thief really stealin'?"

"Huh?"

"If a fella breaks the letter of the law but the only person he victimizes is a lawbreaker himself, is that really a crime?"

Sutter didn't get where this was coming from. "Well, you told me Father Darren said lusting after another woman ain't really lust so long as you wouldn't really get it on with her. So I guess . . . no, it ain't."

"I didn't think so neither, 'cos, see . . ." Trey reached

in his pockets. "While you were checkin' the backseat, I took the liberty of lightening up those boys' wrists—"

"The Rolexes?" Sutter queried with some excitement.

"Yeah, Chief, the Rolexes." Off of two fingers, Trey dangled two genuine Rolex Submariners. He passed one to Sutter. "No doubt it was drug money those guys used to buy these."

Sutter inspected the watch with a gleam in his eye. "No doubt."

"So we could sell these fine watches and give the money to the charity of our choice, or we could even—"

"We could even wear the fuckin' things ourselves," Sutter finished, and put the watch on. *Perfect fit.* "It's legitimate for officers of the law to own accurate timepieces."

"Roger that." Trey put his on too, admiring it. "And one more thing. Since we agree that lustin' after a chick you wouldn't bone ain't lust, and stealin' from a criminal ain't stealin' . . ."

Sutter's eyes widened.

"Look what my fingers found in Kid Rock's pocket." Now Trey held a wad of bills. Mostly hundreds showed when he fanned the stack. "A little more than two grand here, Chief, and tell me if I'm wrong, but this here pile of cash is pure drug profits. It ain't money those fellas earned mowin' lawns."

"It's ill-gotten gains procured during a critical police procedure, Trey," Sutter embellished. "We'll split it."

Trey handed over the whole wad. "Nope. You take it, Chief. You buy you 'n' your wife the brand-new air conditioner you need. You asked God fer help, and He just answered your prayer. Me? I'm fine. When I need some help, I'll ask the Lord myself."

This shitty day just turned really fine, really fast. Sutter pocketed the money with some haste. "I'll remember this, Trey. Thanks."

Trey grinned. "Don't thank me. Thank the Lord."

I damn straight will. . . . "We'll drop the gun off next time we go up to county. And right now?" Sutter looked at the Qwik-Mart. "Coffee and doughnuts on me."

"Make way fer the law!" Pappy Halm celebrated behind the counter. "Our fine boys in blue! Agan's Point is damn proud to have such brave officers protectin' us!"

"Proud enough to slide us free coffee and doughnuts?" Trey asked.

"Hell, no! What do I look like? Fuckin' Santa Claus?" Halm winked. "But refills are half-price."

"You're all class, Pappy."

Sutter wended to the doughnut display and began to tong out a box of cream-filled and glazed. "Guess that poor black fella'll have to sell some of his gold to cover his dental bill."

Trey guffawed. "Yeah, and Kid Rock'll have to comb his hair funny to cover up the permanent bald spot."

Pappy Halm slapped his thighs. "They picked the wrong guys to fuck with today!"

"Never seen a worse pair of scumbags in my life," Trey added, eyes cruising over the mag rack full of *Hustler, Penthouse,* and *Playboy.*

"Speaking of scumbags . . ." Sutter noticed a copy of the town's weekly paper, the *Agan's Point Messenger,* and the blaring headlines: LOCAL MAN MURDERED. He picked it up and scanned over the short article about the mysterious death of Dwayne Parker. "Damn near forgot about this. Feel so bad for Judy—the poor dumb girl don't even realize that Dwayne wasn't no good for her."

"Wasn't no good for anyone or anything," Trey pitched in. "There's a bad seed in every crowd."

Sutter read more of the article. "This came out the day after they found the body; it don't say when the funeral is. Hey, Pappy? You know when they're holdin' services for Dwayne Parker?"

The name seemed to slap Halm's age-lined faced. His eyes lit up in a furor. "Dwayne Parker! That no-good, low-down rat bastard! Ya ask me, they can't bury that fucker deep enough. He ain't worth the lumber it takes to build the coffin! Ain't worth the elbow grease it takes to dig the hole, nor the fuckin' air ya gotta breathe whiles yer gettin' the job done."

"They ain't buryin' him," Trey said, skirting the point. "Crematin' him is what I heard."

"Then fuck it! That cracker ain't worth the gas it takes to burn him. Ain't worth the effort it takes me to grunt out a whiskey-piss into his urn. Cryin' shame the way that prick treated Judy, broke her damn heart, slappin' her around like that. You ask me, any man who beats his wife should have his own ass beat twice as hard."

Sutter nodded, chewing a cream-filled. "We're not in disagreement there, Pappy. But I wanna show my face and offer my condolences to Judy. When's the funeral?"

"You ask me, they shouldn't even *have* a funeral for that worthless piece a' shit. He pulled up here one night all pissy drunk, and I could see in the car he had a woman with him, and that woman sure as shit wasn't Judy, and he walks in all stinkin' a' beer and talkin' loud, grabs himself a twelve-pack and just looks at me 'n' says 'Put it on my wife's tab, ya old fuck,' and then walks back out. Hocks a big looger on my front winder ta boot. That son of a fuckin' dirty mutt. I ever tell you about the time he—"

Trey slapped a hand down on the counter. "Pappy! Chief wants to know when the services are!"

Halm blinked. "Oh, yeah. Saturday noon, at the Schoenfeld Funeral Parlor. I'll be there, fer Judy a' course—but not fer that rat bastard."

Sutter rolled his eyes. *Gee, I guess he didn't think much of Dwayne.*

"Hearin' some damn funny stuff, since we're on the topic," Trey said in an aside.

Sutter put the paper down, listening.

"Funny ain't the word," Halm said. "Nonstop fucked-up is more like it, since the day they found that fucker dead."

Shit . . . Sutter asked with some hesitation, "What's fucked-up, Pappy?"

"The talk about Dwayne is what. You fellas are the *cops*, fer Christ's sake. Ya musta seen the body."

"We didn't get the call; Luntville EMTs did," Sutter said quickly.

"Well, ya musta heard that somebody cut his head off."

"Aw, we all heard that, Pappy," Trey stepped in. "That ain't the half of it. I *know* some of Luntville's EMTs—they're buddies of mine—and they said there was something really fucked-up about the *way* he lost his head . . . but they didn't say exactly what. Something really screwy, though."

Sutter frowned through an uncomfortable tremor in his belly. "Don't listen to every rumor you hear, 'specially in a hick burg like this. Stuff gets all blown out of proportion."

"I don't know, Chief. I went down to the county morgue to take a look myself and they wouldn't even let me in. Why's that? I'm a police officer in the jurisdiction of the murder. It was *our* crime scene. Ain't our fault we weren't the first responders."

"Trey, it ain't even positive yet that it *was* a murder. Could've been an accident. See? Folks start talkin' without knowin' all the facts and they jump to conclusions. County didn't let you in 'cos I'd already been there to ID the body."

Trey stalled at the information. "Shit, Chief, you didn't tell me that."

"Right, I didn't tell no one except Judy, because she's the official next of kin. She wasn't up to seein' the body, so I went in there on her behalf."

Halm and Trey both looked at him.

"So?" Halm asked.

"Was his head really gone?" Trey finished.

Sutter sighed. "Yeah, Trey."

"And they never found the head," Halm added. "Somebody cut off his head and run off with it. That ain't murder?"

"We still get gators," Sutter hedged. "It coulda been a gator. He could've fallen down the bluff and lost his head on the rocks. Fuckin' truck could've been barrelin' around the bend and knocked his head off with the rearview. It could've been anything. So relax 'n' stop talkin' shit, 'cos that just makes the rumors worse. We don't want all this weird talk getting back to Judy. She's bent out of shape enough as it is."

Trey and Halm quieted but only for a moment.

Trey began, "Was there anything screwed-up about the neck wound?"

"No, Trey," Sutter replied, aggravated. "His head got cut off. Simple. It happens. It was a decapitation. Said so in the autopsy report."

This was Chief Sutter's first lie.

Pappy popped some chaw in his mouth: Red Man. "They're also sayin' it was Squatters who killed him. Everd Stanherd's people. Makes sense."

Jesus, Sutter griped. *These boys won't get off it.* He couldn't tell the truth about it, could he? He didn't even understand the truth himself. "It makes *no* sense, Pappy. Ain't no reason for Squatters to kill Dwayne Parker. You don't kill the husband of the woman who keeps your ass out of the welfare line. And you seen these people. I'll bet the biggest of the men don't even stand five-six. Dwayne was six-three and was still packin' all them muscles from working out in the joint all those years. Shit, there ain't *ten* Squatters who could take down Dwayne Parker."

"There are if one of 'em had a machete in his paw," Trey pointed out.

I just can't win here, Sutter thought.

Pappy spit brown juice into a Yoo-Hoo bottle. "And ain't it funny 'bout how Dwayne gets his ticket punched right in the middle of all this talk about some Squatters disappearin'. Like maybe he had somethin' to do with it."

"Or done it himself," Trey said.

Now Sutter was grinding his teeth. "Done *what* himself, Trey?"

"Offed some Squatters. Dwayne hated the Squatters; everyone knows that."

"Listen to me, both of you." Sutter's voice hardened. "There ain't no Squatters who *disappeared.* It's *bullshit.*"

"Nearly a dozen's what I heard," Pappy offered.

"Here one day, gone the next," Trey said.

This was getting hairy. "You two boneheads listen up. Ain't nobody's *disappeared* 'round here. It's a free country. Some of these people think they can do better somewheres else than here . . . and that's their right. There ain't nothing wrong with Squatters just 'cos they're a little funny-lookin' in the face. They're just as smart as anyone else and just as able to work. Some of 'em get tired of crabbing, so they move on. Like anywhere."

Sutter's sensible explanation didn't seem to convince the others. It was true that an unusual number of Stanherd's Squatters had left their abode on the Point, some quite suddenly. Stanherd himself had reported it several times, but even he admitted that they probably did just leave town of their own accord. Sutter did know of the anomaly regarding Dwayne Parker's death, but of missing Squatters? He knew nothing, nor did he believe any foul play was involved. *I swear to God. Gossip mouthpieces like Trey and Pappy Halm just make my job harder. . . .*

"So I don't want to hear no more crap about Squatters disappearing into the night and Dwayne's fuckin' head never being found," he finished.

All three heads turned when the cowbell clanged, and in walked a lean, fortyish man with short blond hair, blue eyes, and an expression that could be deemed somber. He wore a beige windbreaker in spite of the heat, work pants and boots without a speck of dirt on them.

"Howdy, Mr. Felps," Pappy said.

"Mr. Halm, Chief Sutter, Sergeant Trey," the man said in return. His voice was light yet somehow edged, sibilant. "Things are going well for you all, I trust?"

"Yes, sir, Mr. Felps," Sutter replied. Felps's presence always affected Sutter and most townspeople as something close to regal, for some disjointed reason. He wasn't necessarily the town's savior, because Agan's

Point had always been self-sufficient—but just barely. Instead, Felps was the bearer of some energetic new blood that was sorely needed. His Riverside Estates luxury condo complexes would siphon upper-income families out of the state's overpopulated big cities. There were already several hundred preconstruction sales, along with pricey television ads throughout Virginia. This transplantation would divest Agan's Point of some of its natural beauty but deliver a much-needed economic shot in the arm. Sutter saw it as the progress he'd waited for all his life, and he saw Felps as its herald. "Things are just dandy 'round here."

"And they'll be getting even better soon," Felps said, picking up a coffee and Danish. "You've probably noticed that the foundations have already been laid. Things will change around here fast. You'll all be very pleased." The man's enthusiasm, however, seemed dulled, lost in his businessman's veneer. Sutter supposed any successful construction magnate carried the same air. And what did it matter, anyway? *All our lives will improve because of this fella,* Sutter realized.

Felps's stay was brief, to the point. He paid up, bade them a good day, and left.

"Not the friendliest fella in the land," Pappy said, "but do you think I give a flying fuck? My business'll triple the first year those condos start opening."

"He's a big-city builder, Pappy," Sutter reminded him. "Guys like that are no-nonsense and all business. That's why they're millionaires."

Trey shrugged, leaning on the counter. "He ain't such a poker face once ya get to know him. Matter of fact, I had a few beers with him at the bar the other night."

Sutter felt secretly jealous. "You're kidding me?"

"Naw. He and a few of his managers walked in. They asked me to join 'em and we all sat there for an hour shootin' the shit and pounding a few. When Felps is off the clock, he's a regular guy just like you and me."

Sutter's jealousy remained. If there was one man he wanted to be pals with, it was Felps. *I'll have to work on that. . . .*

"Later, Pappy," he said. "We're out of here."

"You boys take it easy the rest of the day." Pappy cackled. "Don't wanna wear yourselves out kickin' scumbag ass."

"Just another day in the lives of two hardworkin' cops," Trey said, casting a final glance at the men's mags.

Back outside, Sutter didn't even have time to grab his keys before a shadow moved behind him. He hadn't heard a sound. Had those drug dealers come back for revenge? *Impossible,* he thought. *They're lucky if they made it to the nearest hospital on their own. . . .* Sutter spun, instinct charging his gun hand, but then found himself looking into the face of a gaunt old man.

"Hey, there, Everd," Trey greeted.

Everd Stanherd stood like a meticulously dressed scarecrow, neat as a pin in his typical faded black suit and tie. Short jet-black hair didn't look right atop the old, waxen, and deeply lined face, yet the deep-socketed eyes appeared vibrant, the eyes of a twenty-year-old set in an old man's skull. The only detail that might tell him apart from any elderly man was the pendant around his neck: a black silk cord connected to a small black silk sack.

Everd lived with his wife, Marthe, in the only house at the end of the point, a decrepit slat-wood mansion built a hundred years ago. Judy Parker let him live there, and he shared the house with other elders of his Squatter clan. The rest of the Squatters lived all about the property surrounding the house, in surprisingly well built tin huts erected in the midst of the heavy woods—Squatterville, most people called the area. Judy let them all live there rent-free as a benefit of their employment with the crab company. In all, the Squatters were respectful, law-abiding, and industrious in their own simple way, and this frail yet vibrant man standing before them was their leader.

"It's good to see you, Everd," Sutter said. "Any word on those couple of folks in your clan who can't be accounted for?"

"No, sir," Everd replied. They all spoke so strangely, yet Everd's tone and diction were the strangest of all. His thin lips barely moved around the words, almost as though they were being projected from elsewhere. And that indefinable dialect. "As a matter of fact, two left for Roanoke last week, quite verifiably. I suspect the same can be said of the others, as you suggested. It's just uncharacteristic for members of our clan to leave without notice."

"Everd, when I was a kid, I ran away a bunch of times, and never told my parents where I was headed," Sutter pointed out. "There's over a hundred Squatters you got livin' on the Point. You can't keep tabs on them all."

"You're correct, sir," Everd returned. He stood absolutely motionless as he spoke, save for one crabbed hand fingering the black pouch about his neck. "However, a third member seems to have disappeared—a young girl named Cynabelle—Cindy, to you. But I must confess that she may have fallen with a bad crowd and vacated, too, for more adventurous exploits in the city." Everd paused, as if about to say something difficult. "She lacked the standard of morality that my clan lives by, and I'm afraid several of the girls have fallen by the same wayside in the past. Not many, but a few. I feel it's my failing ultimately."

"Trickin' herself out, you mean." Trey got the gist. "Everd, your Squatters have a lower crime rate than the general population. From a police officer's point a' view, they're about as low-maintenance as you can get."

"Don't kick yourself in the tail," Sutter added some consolation. He was actually relieved by the extent to which Everd was reasonable about things. "You run a tight ship with your people, and we're grateful. But you can't go blamin' yourself because a few girls go bad. They're ain't nothing you can do about it. In any community, there's always gonna be a few girls who decide they can make more money with their bodies than workin' a proper job. Been that way for thousands of years. And there's always gonna be a few fellas who go bad too. Don't worry about it."

"Nevertheless, I apologize for such mishaps," the man intoned. "I will try to keep a closer rein on it. But I've also come to thank you."

"For what?"

"Just earlier," Everd said. He kept touching the pouch. "Some ruffians from the city attempted to corrupt one of our young girls. She came immediately and told me. She said that you and your deputy repelled these two criminals convincingly."

"Oh, yeah," Trey said. "Couple drug dealers tryin' to sell their crap in our town. We sent 'em packin', didn't we, Chief?"

"You won't have to worry about them boys anymore, Everd," Sutter guaranteed. Every so often, he'd cast a glance to the pendant, at first paying it no mind, but gradually growing more curious.

Everd looked him right in the eye, his own eyes green as emeralds, flecked with blue—another trademark of Squatter heredity. "You men have the utmost gratitude of my clan. This I cannot emphasize enough. I'd like to invite you both to my home tonight for a meal prepared in the tradition of our ancestors. Marthe will be serving an andouille-style sausage made with slow-smoked muskrat, crab-and-chickpea bisque, cattail cakes, and the seasonal delicacy this year, something we call custa."

"Custa? What's that?" Trey inquired.

"Cicadas roasted in wild mint and cracked white peppercorns."

Yow! Sutter's doughnut-filled stomach lurched as if kicked. "That's, uh, mighty generous of ya, Everd, and we definitely will take you up on that kind offer down the road. But, see, Trey and I have some important police work to do for the next few weeks."

Everd nodded. "In the future, then, when it's more convenient to your busy schedule. You're always welcome at my home. And remember the clan cookout next week."

"We'll be there for sure," Trey said.

"So until we meet again, gentlemen, I bid you a pleasant day." But before Everd turned to leave, Sutter couldn't resist: "Everd, tell me somethin', will ya? What *is* that thing around your neck?"

The old man seemed unfazed by the question, untying the sack. "It's called a tok." He removed something stiff and twisted.

What in shit's *name!*

It was a chicken head.

"It's the severed head of a black cock—not an ordinary chicken, mind you," Everd explained. "Upside down in the pouch. It preserves wisdom." He started to take it off. "Here, I'd like you to have it, as my gift."

Yow! Sutter held up his hand. "Aw, no, Everd, I couldn't. But thanks just the same."

"Very well. But it's been a pleasure to be in your company these few minutes. I look forward to our next meeting." And then Everd slipped away, silent as a shadow.

"How do you like that funky shit?" Trey chuckled. "With all the shit he said he was servin' for dinner, I'm surprised there ain't no *chicken* on the menu. Ain't that some weird superstitious jive they got goin' on?"

"You got that right," Sutter said. "And I'll definitely pass on the muskrat and cicadas."

"Roger that."

"Hey, Chief, why don't ya hang a chicken head from the cruiser rearview? Maybe it'll give us *wisdom!*"

Sutter looked after the old man, who'd already made it halfway up the road. "The Squatters are tough to figure. They're kind of like Indians, but they don't look it. All those charms they're into."

"Or like Gypsies," Trey compared. "But they don't look like Gypsies, either. They don't even look European."

"The accent's weird too. One time I asked Everd where he and his people were from, and you know what he said? He said 'the Old World.' Then I asked him what the hell that mean, and he told me Agan's Point is where they're from. That his ancestors've always been here." Sutter pinched his chin. "I wonder where they're really from. . . ."

"Yeah, then there's always the one question that's more important than that," Trey posed.

"What's that?"

"Who gives a flying rat's ass?"

Sutter was inclined to agree. He looked down the road again and saw no sign of Everd Stanherd. Trey had his back to him, looking off in the opposite direction. "Ooo-eee, Chief! Would you look at that Caddy!"

"Yeah. Nice set of wheels."

A snappy, late-model Cadillac coup was cruising along past them, a ragtop, with a deep, rich paint job the color of red wine. The driver obviously spotted the two police watching her, and slowed down a bit.

Trey squinted. "Looks like some dandy tail drivin' it, too. Looks hiiiiiigh-class."

"Yeah, too high-class for this town, now that ya mention it," Sutter considered. "Bet that car runs eighty grand outta the showroom, Trey. What the hell's a rich gal like that doin' in Agan's Point?"

"Red-hairt, too," Trey could see. "Ah-oooooo-gah! Bet she's got red carpet to match those red drapes." He elbowed Sutter. "Looks like she's doin' about five over the limit, Chief. What say we pull her over, see what she's got to gander?"

Sutter frowned. "Git your mind outta the sewer, Trey." But it wasn't that bad an idea. Cops worked hard. They needed a perk now and again.

Then, as the car flashed by, the driver waved and honked.

Both men looked behind them. Trey scratched his head. "She wavin' at us?"

That was when the red hair and upscale look clicked. "Ah, I know who that is, and so do you."

"Huh?"

"Patricia, Judy Parker's sister."

Trey stared off after the vanishing car. "Ya don't say? Ain't seen her around here in—"

"About five years. Looks different 'cos she cut her hair. Came back for Judy's marriage to that scumbag Dwayne, and now it looks like she's here again—"

"—for the scumbag's funeral."

A silence passed between them. The Cadillac disappeared around the road's bend.

"Too bad about her, ya know?" Trey said.

Sutter nodded at the words. "I remember Patricia since she was tiny—shit, I wasn't but twelve or thirteen myself when she was born. Fiery, chatty little kid, she was. Full a' life, always happy."

"Yeah. Then she just turned cold. Bet I didn't hear her say two words before she ran off to college and law school."

Sutter jingled his keys. He remembered. "Poor girl never was the same," he said, "after the rape. . . ."

Three

(I)

An instant reminder: the odd knocker on the center stile of the front door. *I've always hated the knocker,* Patricia thought. She had parked the Caddy in the cul-de-sac, and had sat a while looking up at the house she grew up in. The great wooden edifice went back to pre–Civil War days, and had been refurbished incrementally over the decades. It looked the part: a Virginia plantation house with a high, sloping roof and awnings, and a screened porch that defined the entire circumference of the lower level. A grand house. There were plenty of ghost stories dating back to the days of slavery, when previous owners often executed unruly workers and buried them around the foundation to fertilize the hedges and flower beds. It made for excited talk, but in the eighteen years Patricia had lived here, she'd never seen a ghost.

She did now, though.

The door knocker. It was an eyesore and it was just

plain peculiar: an oval of tarnished bronze depicting a morose half-formed face. Just two eyes, no mouth, no other features. In those last two years here before college, the knocker's expression had reflected her own.

In truth, however, she had to admit that Judy had kept the place up beautifully, and were it not for the bad memories, Patricia would see the house as a gorgeous abode.

It was just getting dark. *I forgot,* she thought. *Another cicada season.* They had so many varieties down here; there were more seasons with them than without. The unique sound in the dark, surrounding her on the porch. She'd looked forward to that sound as a child, but now the throbbing drone served only as another jolting memory.

The summer she'd been raped had been a cicada season, too.

Soft lights lit the front bay windows, but there was only Judy's car in the court. *She shouldn't be alone. . . .* It was too soon. Patricia's younger sister was a Rock of Gibraltar when in her element, but she was also terribly codependent. With Dwayne gone—abusive as he'd been—Judy would be unstable, flighty, and off-track. *She knows I'm coming today,* Patricia thought. Knowing her sister as she did, it was surprising that Judy wasn't pacing the foyer with the front door open.

Can't stand on the porch all night . . . Patricia winced, raising her hand to the unsightly knocker, but then saw that the door stood open a crack. *The house is half-mine,* she reminded herself, and stepped in.

The pendulum clock ticked to her left, and to her right stood a long walnut table containing knickknacks and candles, centered by an old framed photo of their parents as newlyweds. For a moment she imagined her father frowning in the frame, as though he disapproved of her arrival. "Judy?" she called out. Only silence returned her call. The interior seemed smaller than she remembered, cramped. Pictures on the walls seemed to hang lower, and had the wallpaper been changed? *Everything looks different, but I know Judy would never change a thing.*

She turned into the sitting room and stopped cold. A breath caught in her chest and wouldn't come out.

Judy lay slumped on the old scroll-footed sofa.

"Judy? It's me."

Her head tilted aside, her mouth agape. She looked pallid and years older. Patricia's heart tightened up when she noticed an open bottle of pills on the old tea table next to the couch. She rushed forward, then sighed in relief.

Just a bottle of vitamins . . .

But there was an irreducible instant when she'd believed that her sister was dead. She certainly looked it, lying there as if dropped amongst the tasseled pillows.

Judy stirred in her sleep, mouthing something unintelligible, but then real words formed:

"His head," she whispered. "My God, his head . . ."

Patricia leaned over and gave several firm nudges. "Judy, wake up, wake up. I'm here."

It was like looking at a countrified clone of herself; Patricia and Judy had near-identical faces, possessed similar figures and the same plenteous bosom. But Judy's hair lacked the bright red fire of Patricia's, and instead of being short and straight, it lay long and thick, with high bangs that their mother always called "kitchen-curtain hair." Five stress-laden years with Dwayne as a husband had streaked her hair with some gray and had blanched the once-vibrant color from her cheeks.

"Judy? Wake up."

The crow's-feet at the corners of Judy's eyes began to twitch. Her breasts rose quickly once; then she gasped herself out of sleep and was finally looking up at Patricia.

"Hi, Judy."

No recognition at first, just a puzzled stare; then Judy's arms shot forward and she hugged her sister for dear life. "Oh, God, thank God. I thought . . . Oh, Jesus, I was dreaming—a terrible dream."

Patricia sat down and put her arm around Judy's shoulder. "It was just a dream, and it's over now. Everything's fine."

Judy actually shuddered in her sister's arms. "Thank you for coming. I've just . . . I feel like I'm falling apart. I sleep all the time; I've just been so tired. The house is a mess; I haven't even had the energy to pick up."

"The house looks fine, Judy," Patricia assured her. "You've been under a lot of stress, but things will get better."

"I hope so. . . ."

Patricia could smell alcohol; whenever Judy got depressed, she drank, which only worsened matters. "Come on; you're exhausted. Let's get you up to bed."

Judy offered no objection. She trudged up the carpeted stairs, clinging to her sister. *She's lost weight, too,* Patricia observed. She felt thin, bony. Patricia helped her down the dark hall, passing more framed pictures that should seem familiar but somehow didn't. The house was too quiet, save for when floorboards creaked, then the keening hinge of the bedroom door.

"I'm sorry I'm so out of it," Judy finally said. "I shouldn't have had that wine. I'm just so lonely now. . . . Doesn't that sound pathetic?"

"Of course it doesn't. You've suffered a loss. It takes time to work through it. But what you need more than anything tonight is a good night's sleep."

An exhausted nod. Patricia got Judy out of her housedress, then saw just how thin her sister had grown in her despair. Her ribs showed beneath the bra. She looked like she'd lost a cup size, too. She also had tears in her eyes. *This is going to take a while,* Patricia realized. *She's falling apart.* She got her into bed and under the covers, then sat down beside her and held her hand. "You want me to get you something, some warm milk, water?"

Judy looked back at her very wanly, but she finally managed a smile. "No, I'm fine now that you're here. I guess I'm not dealing well with being alone."

You never did. "But where's Ernie?" Patricia asked after the family yardman and housekeeper. "Don't tell me he's not working for you anymore. I can't imagine him anywhere else."

"He just keeps the yard in order now. Dwayne never liked him, so since the wedding Ernie's stayed outside, never does anything in the house anymore."

"Well, that can change now, can't it? This is a big place, Judy. You can't keep it up on the inside all by yourself, not with the crab company too."

"I know, and it *will* change." The tired smile even brightened then. "But when I saw Ernie this morning, I told him to make sure the yard was cut, 'cos I didn't want it all shaggy for you comin'. You shoulda *seen* the way his face lit up when I told him you'd be comin' back for a spell."

Patricia nearly blushed. Ernie Gooder had been her "boyfriend," back in seventh grade. They'd stuck together like glue all through childhood, but as middle-school years faded—and her body ripened early—she'd lost interest in Ernie and potential sweetheart romances. Ernie was a tried-and-true local, would never think of leaving Agan's Point, and, like most of the men in these rural areas, he was also a tried-and-true hayseed. He'd dropped out of school early to work his father's farm and stagnate like so many who'd grown up here. *They don't know they can move somewhere else and make their lives better,* she thought, but maybe she was being pretentious. There was nothing wrong with staying close to one's roots and working the land, but it just seemed so shallow to Patricia, that or maybe she was just more adventuresome than everyone else. At any rate, Ernie's crush on Patricia had never died, and he'd been disheartened when she'd left for college.

"He's still got that torch burnin' for you," Judy said. "And he's still as handsome as ever."

"I'm sure he is," Patricia played along, "but my husband's still got all my bases covered."

"Oh, I know, and I'm so glad you're happy with Byron. How is he, by the way?"

"He's fine . . . and you're exhausted, so . . ." Patricia snapped off the bedside lamp. "You go to sleep, and we'll have a big breakfast together in the morning." She kissed her sister's forehead, then stood back up. Judy wouldn't let go of her hand.

"Oh, Patricia," came the whisper. "You don't know how much it means to me that you come all this way to be with me."

"You're my sister and I love you. Now go to sleep!"

But Judy's eyes kept staring up. "I-I never told you . . ."

"Never told me what?"

"How . . . Dwayne died."

"Of course you did." Patricia bent the truth. Actually, her sister had never elaborated. "An accident, you said."

Judy's voice piped up like a child's. "His head was cut off, and nobody knows how it happened."

Patricia stood in a silent shock. *She's serious. . . .* She had no idea what to say in response.

"And the head was never found," Judy groaned out the rest.

Murder, not an accident. What condolence could she add now? But when Patricia looked again, Judy had already fallen asleep.

My God . . .

The windows stood open at the end of the hall, letting in the cicada sounds, and the house's deep, old Colonial decor made her feel a thousand miles away from her condo in D.C. She stepped into her bedroom, felt odd at once, then backed out. Sleeping there would just remind her of more childhood memories, but she couldn't stay in her parents' old room, either—that would just be worse. *One of the guest rooms downstairs,* she decided, then drifted back down the stairs to go out and get her bags from the Caddy. The macabre distraction was sidetracking her: *Dwayne's head. Did she mean that somebody cut off Dwayne's head?*

She stopped midway down the step. *How the heck did—*

Her suitcases sat neatly stacked at the bottom of the steps.

"Didn't know where ya'd wanna be sleepin'. . . ."

Ernie Gooder stepped from behind her baggage, looking up.

"We was expectin' ya much earlier," he said next,

"like about noon." He glanced to the window. "Looks like ya barely beat sundown."

Patricia felt a shock: *Judy wasn't kidding. . . .* Ernie had always been attractive: well contoured, strong arms, broad-backed. Dark eyes glittered in an appearance of youth that should've disappeared a decade ago. If anything he looked late twenties instead of mid-forties. The only difference, now, was his hair. For all the years she'd known him, Ernie had had a nearly military cut, but now he'd grown it out shoulder-length. When she finally found words, she blurted, "Your hair!"

He looked sheepish. "Yeah, I growed it out fer the hell of it; now everybody likes it, so I guess it's here to stay."

She came down the stairs and gave him a hug. "Ernie, did you find the fountain of youth somewhere out in the woods?"

"Huh?"

"You look the same as you did years ago. You look *great.*"

The remark embarrassed him; he almost blushed. "Aw, well, thanks, Patricia. You look really fantastic your own self. I like your hair shorter that way; ain't never seen ya with it like that."

"It makes me look more like a lawyer, I guess." Then she remembered his first comments. "And, yeah, I did plan on getting here this afternoon, but I wound up dillydallying. Had breakfast in Richmond, lunch in Norfolk. I burned the whole day driving around."

He seemed instantly uncomfortable. "Well, yeah, that sure is understandable—that you wouldn't be in any hurry to get here. This old backwards town's gotta remind ya of . . . well . . . you know."

His stilted compassion was sweet, the way he awkwardly talked around her obvious motive. Naturally she hadn't been in any hurry to get back to the place that made for the worst memory of her life. It didn't bother her, though, which seemed strange. Nor was she bothered by the obvious difficulty that Ernie was having in keeping his eyes from roaming her obviously braless bosom. He'd always had a thing for her. Always. The silliest thought occurred to her then: *Maybe I subconsciously didn't wear a bra because I knew it would rile Ernie up. . . .*

But that was ridiculous.

If anything, his darting eyes flattered her, even caused her to want to tease him a little. *No harm in that. The poor lug is probably still nuts about me.*

"So how's yer, uh, yer husband?"

"Oh, he's fine, Ernie. He was going to come down with me but he's busy with his job. What about you? You *must* be married by now."

More embarrassment. "Aw, no, never did tie the knot with no one. One day maybe." But as he spoke he kept looking down. *Still as shy as ever,* Patricia thought. *Like a little boy.*

"Anyway, it's good to see ya, Patricia," he went on, shuffling his feet in place. "Well, not like this, a' course, but . . . you know what I mean."

"Sure I do, Ernie. A funeral is always the worst occasion to see old friends."

"We all know you don't like to come down to Agan's Point much, but what'cha gotta know is that it really means a lot to Judy."

"She looks really shaken up," Patricia said. "It'll take time for her to jump back to normal."

"I hope she *can* jump back to normal." Ernie shook his head. "She sure was crazy in love with Dwayne. No one could ever figure it out. Enough of that, though. You want me to put your bags in your old bedroom, or would ya rather—"

"The guest room down here would be better, if that's okay."

He seemed visibly enthused. "It's bigger and catches the sunlight in the morning. Plus it's right down the hall from my room, in case ya need anything."

No wonder . . . "It'll be fine."

He picked up her bags and led her through the back of the house. *I feel good all of a sudden—hell, I feel great,* she admitted to herself. All day long during the drive, and even the first few minutes back in the house, a heavy oppression seemed to be hunting her. Now it was all gone. *Maybe this trip won't be as bad as I thought. . . .*

"Really bad about Dwayne," Ernie made conversation.

Patricia couldn't take her eyes off the strong, tapered back as they moved on. "Oh, yes."

"He wasn't a good man by any stretch, but *no man* deserves to die like that. I believe that ya get what's comin' to ya in this life. What goes around, comes around. But *that?* Jesus."

Patricia touched his arm, urging him to stop and turn. The contours of his silhouette opposed her, the strong legs in tight jeans, the bulging biceps. She frowned at herself. "I didn't know the details until just now—she told me when I put her to bed. He was decapitated?"

"Somebody cut his head clean off, I guess."

Strange way to say it. "You guess?"

"That's what Chief Sutter told Judy. Judy wasn't up to seein' the body, so he did it for her, for proper ID 'n' all. But there's all this talk now."

"What kind of talk?"

"Rumors about somethin' really *wrong* about Dwayne's body, and I mean . . . somethin' *more* than just losin' his head."

Patricia couldn't imagine. *What could be more wrong than losing your head?* It was something she could look into, though. As a lawyer, she was an expert at expediting Freedom of Information Act requests. *There must be a death certificate and an autopsy report. . . .*

"But that's probably all it is when ya get right down to it—just talk. You know what this place is like. People got nothin' better to do than run their mouths 'bout every little thing that ain't their business."

One rumor generates more rumors, she knew too well, *and at the end of the line there's no truth left at all, just distortions.* "It's really odd, though, and Judy does have a right to know all the details concerning her husband's death."

"I went down to the county morgue myself and tried to see the body, but it had already been cremated. Then I asked to see the autopsy report and they told me it was confidential," Ernie said, pronouncing the last word *confer-din-shul.*

We'll see about that confidential part, Patricia vowed.

The guest room was cozily decorated and large, with fat, tapestried throw rugs and tasseled drapes. It felt unlived-in, which was what she wanted. French doors, closed now, showed a charming little porch over looking backyard flower beds. In the moonlight she could see the flowers swaying in a night breeze: pansies, baby breath, daisies.

"Will this do ya?" Ernie asked. "There's a smaller room on the east wing."

"No, this is perfect, Ernie."

"And you can open the windows if ya want, catch

the breeze off the bay most of the night. It comes right through the pine trees, brings that scent right into the room."

"I just might do that." She sat down on the high bed, testing the mattress. Suddenly the day's long drive caught up to her, and she couldn't wait to fall asleep on the comfy bed with the moon on her face. "What time are the services tomorrow?"

"Noon. I'll be fixin' breakfast at eight."

"That sounds great. See you in the morning."

"Night."

She leaned over to untie her sneakers, and in the fringes of her vision noticed his shadow still there. Before she even looked back up, she could guess the reason. *I'm leaning over . . . and I've got no bra on.* Ernie was getting an eyeful.

Then she looked back up at him with the thinnest smile. "Was there something else you wanted to tell me, Ernie?"

His eyes darted out of her cleavage. He quickly cleared his throat and said, "Oh, yeah, just that it's great to have you back in town for a while." And then he rushed out of the room and closed the door.

Men. But some would say she was asking for it, wasn't she? Wearing no bra, with *her* bosom? But then part of the tease in her returned. *I guess it's not that big a deal. At least I gave the poor guy something to think about.*

Alone now, she switched off the bedside lamp, undressed, and shouldered into her typical nightwear, a soft spearmint-colored lounger, which she quickly zipped up the front. Without thinking, next she took Ernie's advice: she opened the window. Warm air and cicada sounds instantly flooded the room; she felt tranquilized. And Ernie was right—soon the moonlit room began to flux between sultry summer heat and a fresh, pine-scented coolness from the bay breeze filtering in through the woods.

As if they were a lover's hands, the dark air and pulsing sounds pushed her down to the mattress. Her fatigue left her dopily giddy as she stretched out, flexing her toes, arching her back. An impulse from out of the dark brought her hands to her thighs, slipped them up under the lounger. When she closed her eyes, she imagined that it was the darkness feeling her up, exciting her nerves. Her hips squirmed around in unbidden horniness, and when her fingers walked up her belly and threatened to slip beneath her panties, her conscience dragged them away. *What are you doing?* she scolded herself. *You're exhausted. Go to sleep. What am I all hot and bothered about? I'm going to a* funeral *tomorrow. . . .*

The dark thickened around her, broken only by the wedge of moonlight that lay right beside her, a pearlescent bedmate. The cicadas thrummed and thrummed, rocking her in a strange and primitive lullaby. Then she faded off, but—

Oh, my God . . .

—at once, her sleep dropped her into a dream gushing with sex. She lay cringing, raw, and naked on her living room floor, her ankles locked desperately around the back of a faceless man. Patricia knew it was her living room back in D.C. because she saw her business dress, high heels, and blouse flung over her litigation bag, which she always set down right next to their coffee table. The Rothko print that she'd bought for Byron for a past birthday hung just above the faux fireplace, and on the mantel sat the crystal carriage clock he'd bought her years ago for an early anniversary. These were familiar things, things that rooted her to her life with Byron, and she *loved* these things. But through her cringing sexual angst—as she was being fastidiously penetrated on the floor—she noticed the clock's glass dome bore a crack, and the Rothko hung upside down.

A climax clenched her up—she couldn't breathe for a moment—and then she looked up at her aggressive lover's face. She fully expected it to be Byron's, but she could see no face, and it wasn't his rotund body atop her but a lean, muscle-rippled physique. *Oh, my God, do it harder, harder,* she thought, teething her lower lip, and then the desires of her mind were answered. The rigid penis boring in and out of her stepped up its delicious tempo, pile driving her loins into the bed. Another orgasm rippled through her as her lover withdrew and released himself across her belly and breasts. He knelt between her legs now, looking down at her; then he grabbed her hand and glided it over the lines of warm sperm—an earthy love lotion.

Patricia lay quivering, heaving in breath. *Who is he? Who is he?* The question reeled around and around in her head. She could see every detail of his chiseled body shellacked in sweat, but his face still remained shrouded, as if by smoke.

The smoke moved downward; he was lying beside her, his mouth sucking pink marks on her neck, and his fingers playing lower. Just the touch of his hand riled her up; she was just about to come again, but then her eyes darted off a moment and she saw Byron sitting fat and naked on the couch, his face forlorn as he watched this other man electrify her.

Patricia didn't even care.

She lay back, tensing more, begging for this strange mystery lover to take her again right there in front of her husband, the rough hand expertly gentle with her most private parts, and then her legs shot upward, toes straining toward her living room ceiling when she recognized Ernie Gooder's face on the man who was burying her in the most wanton ecstasy—

Patricia shrieked in the throes of another climax . . . and—

—then awoke naked and clenching in her sister's guest room.

Oh, jeez . . .

There was no one beside her, of course, no Ernie finishing up, and the only hand between her legs was her own.

What's gotten into me? she thought. Her confusion melted into a drowsy disorientation. It frustrated her, even half-asleep as she was, because it made her feel unaware of herself. The cicada sounds seemed twice as loud now, the moonlight dimmer yet somehow edgier. During the fitful dream she'd kicked the covers off the bed and cast her cotton lounger to the floor, and now she didn't even bother putting it back on. The moonlight made the sweat on her breasts, belly, and thighs appear frostlike.

She let her confusion fade away behind her fatigue, then curled up into a nude ball. Her sex still tingled as she drifted back to sleep, completely incognizant of the face peering in at her naked body through the window.

(II)

Wilfrud and Ethel Hild were the clan's dowsers. But it wasn't water they sought; nor did they hold any forked branches for divining rods.

They'd shed their handmade clothes—for nakedness better solicited the spirits of the Earth—and stood now as pale stick figures painted ghostly white by the moon. Wilfrud's gut looked sucked-in beneath the ribs, Ethel's breasts losing some plumpness. Divining required a three-day fast, and they'd been divining a lot lately—hence the emaciation. Their eyes looked huge in thin faces—huge in the trance they put upon themselves.

"A minute or two more," Everd Stanherd intoned from the side. "It takes time for the ashes to reach their blood."

Wilfrud and Ethel had been dowsers since early childhood, and now, fifty years later, they'd honed their skills—which some would call sorceries—to expertise.

No, no forked branches. Instead they'd slit the belly of a newborn snake, eviscerated it, and then burned its threadlike innards in a brass censer, along with dried coneflower petals, sweetbriar oil, and some fabric from one of the girls' tops—something well-worn and close to the heart.

The others watched from moonlit trees as Wilfrud and Ethel then ate the ashes out of the censer to begin the trance. Some wore stone pendants about their necks, while others wore *lao* pouches, and still more wore crude crosses fashioned from animal bones or dried vine cuttings. They all looked on silently in their inexplicable faith.

They walked nude through the woods. The others followed. No one spoke.

A while later, they stopped in a small clearing near the river and pointed down.

Everd was the *sawon,* the keeper of the clan's heritage—and its magic. His voice croaked in the dark, his wife, Marthe, beside him. "Dig here, men. You can see the upturned earth."

It was obviously a makeshift grave they all surrounded now. The younger men quickly wielded their shovels, routed and emptied the sad mound. Their women watched from the trees, some sobbing. It didn't take long before the pallid body was hauled out.

Marthe clutched her husband's arm and burst into tears. *The monster didn't even kill her first,* Everd thought, shielding his wife's eyes. The young girl's fingers were locked in an upward clench. She'd been trying to unearth herself when she'd finally smothered. *A monster, yes, a monster.* The wheat bands around both death-white thighs confirmed what she'd been doing. Another one had gone astray, prostituting herself for extra money instead of living by the clean, honest way of the clan. *And Cynabelle's dead. Another one dead. Murdered by that monster.*

"At least it'll stop now." Wilfrud's sorrowful words crept through the dark. "Now that you've taken care of the soulless bastard."

"I pray so, my friend."

They hadn't found all of the others who'd gone missing over the past few months, and perhaps Chief Sutter was right in his suggestion that they'd simply left town for a chance at a better life. *But not all of them.* The dowsers had found four others buried like this. The men murdered, and women *raped* and murdered. Everd would not leave them to graves like this. They'd rebury them on clan land, in earth consecrated by Everd himself.

"I pray so," he repeated, "but I fear not."

"I won't hear it, Everd!" Ethel nearly cried out at the remark. She was coming out of the trance. "Dwayne's dead now. He hated us, but now he's dead! There's no reason for more of us to wind up"—she shivered when she looked at poor Cindy's body—"like this."

"We fear there is, dear." Marthe spoke up in her smoke-light voice. "It's that Felps man. Everd has foreseen this."

The *sawon* nodded. They all paused in a moment of silence as the others lifted Cindy's body and began to take it back to the property. "He wants this land, so he's having us killed. People are *doing* this for him, for money."

"For what purpose? Miss Judy would never sell the land out from under us."

"She would if we weren't here. She would if we all left. If more of us continue to disappear, if more of us are found murdered, then our people *will* get scared. And they *will* leave."

No one argued with that.

"We must tell the constable."

"That violates our own laws, and he wouldn't do much to help us anyway. I haven't even let on to Chief Sutter what I know. I let him believe that I think the missing ones left on their own accord. We take care of our own, Wilfrud; it's our law, and it has been since longer than we can conceive. We will never go to outsiders. We will always take care of our own."

At least Wilfrud seemed satisfied with what he said next. "And we can thank heaven and earth that you took care of Dwayne. . . ."

(III)

It appeared to be the makings of a great dream—no, a *fantastic* dream. Chief Sutter, behind the wheel of the town cruiser, was on routine patrol, ever diligent in his oath to protect and serve. The cruiser prowled through dark, Agan's Point backstreets as the moon followed over treetops and the cicadas thrummed. Ever vigilant, he kept his eyes peeled for suspicious persons and signs of foul play. Police work was a thankless job, but Sutter was proud to have it. Who knew, for instance, that he was out here on the job right now? As Agan's Point residents slept soundly in their beds, they could sleep ever more soundly with Chief Sutter maintaining watch over their safety in these wee hours of the night.

Even at this early juncture, the dream was proving to be damn good. Why? Because as he drove, his right hand regularly reached over to the passenger seat to withdraw a piece of his wife's homemade fried chicken, which, as he recalled, was the best he'd ever eaten. She hadn't actually prepared this favorite of his for many years, electing instead to tell him, "I feel like fried chicken tonight, honey, so why don't you bring home a twenty-piece bucket from KFC on your way home from work?" But that was irrelevant here. This was a dream. This was not reality.

He ate the drumsticks first, peeling away the crunchy, delectable skin, then sucking the meat off the bone.

That was when he saw the girl.

Looks like a woman in distress, he noted, and properly switched on his flashing Visibar. She emerged from the darkness at the bend in the road ahead, a short woman with a curvaceous figure, raven-haired. *Looks like she's wearin' a white bikini,* Chief Sutter reasoned. *And . . .*

His eyes widened.

And she looks to be quite possibly the best-lookin' gal I have set my eyes on in quite *a spell!*

Deeply tanned legs, belly, and arms. And a bosom . . .

Jiminy fuckin' Christmas . . .

The bosom satcheled high in the big white bra looked about big enough to lay Thanksgiving dinner out on.

At the end of the headlights, she began to wave.

That was when Chief Sutter became aware of a serious discrepancy in his previous assumption as to her apparel. Was that really a white bikini she was wearing, or . . .

He squinted harder.

An exciting darkness seemed to lay triangularly at the crotch of the white bottoms, and as for the top: large, dark circles were centered . . .

And the final realization:

That ain't no fuckin' bikini! Those are tan lines!

The approaching woman wore no bikini at all. In fact, she wore *nothing* whatsoever.

What to do now? the chief asked himself. An errant rub to his crotch alerted him to a rising turgidity. The woman was obviously a Squatter; he could tell by the short stature and mussy black hair, and, of course, that—

Jiminy Christmas, Sutter thought again.

—and that jaw-dropping, one hundred percent *perfect* body.

Sutter was thrown for a disturbing loop. *Looks like I'll have to arrest this gal for public nek-it-ness, I suppose. What the hell's she doin' walkin' 'round here at this time of night bare-assed?*

His libido and human sexual responses in general didn't ponder an answer to his question. She traipsed around the car, the headlights glaring over every perfect detail, breasts gently jogging, and then she—

Oh, Mother of God!

—she leaned over the passenger-side window and shot Chief Sutter a giant, sultry smile.

"Evenin', there, Mr. Chief!"

"Huh-huh-howdy," he stammered.

"What'cha *doin'?*"

"Ruh-ruh-ruh-routine patrol, miss."

The Southern twang blended with that indefinable Squatter accent enriched her voice to something dark and syrupy and most definitely sexual. "Well, me, I'se just out fer a walk."

Without being asked, then, she opened the passenger door and plopped her exquisite rump right on the seat. Chief Sutter did not raise an objection.

She grinned shyly at him in the dash lights. "Can I tell ya something, Mr. Chief?"

Sutter's mouth opened but no response seemed possible. The mere sight of her body choked him up, circumventing any possibility of reply.

Her eyes looked dreamy, green gems filled with bright-blue chips that seemed to glow. "Just somethin' about officers a' the law, and the uniform 'n' all . . ." She sighed. "Just gets me all flustered. Cain't really even say why."

More proof that this was a dream. In Sutter's forty years of police work—and forty years of obesity—no woman had ever voiced this cliché to him. And no woman *this* attractive had ever given him any kind of notice as overt as this. Still speechless, he felt his eyes struggle to stay in one place: her crotch, her tight belly, her bodacious breasts. Eventually the breasts won out as those dark pink jutting nipples bigger than silver dollars began to hypnotize him as surely as a mesmerist's pendulum.

The voice oozed further. "Yeah, Mr. Chief. You fellas in uniform . . . 'specially big, strong ones like you . . . git me so hot I cain't rightly sit still. . . ."

Current as fierce as electricity speared through him when her hand—soft as a little bird but unduly *hot*—found his knee, then began to inch up higher on his leg. The humid night air hanging in the car drew the sweat out of her skin; soon her nakedness was shining, her breasts and belly aglaze. This pinpoint image of glimmering flesh, compounded by the sensation of her hand creeping toward his groin, made Chief Sutter feel as though his small and almost always flaccid penis had magically transformed into something the size and stiffness of a summer squash. It strained against his police trousers in an absolutely thrilling agony.

Now her voice seemed desperate with need. "Mr. Chief, ya turn me on so much I'se just goin' *crazy!* Let's git'cher pants hitched down—" She was almost in tears now. "If I don't have ya right now, I swear I'll just die!" And then her hands slipped up to his belt, her slick breasts bobbing, sweat visibly dripping off the points of the nipples.

Sexual malfeasance be damned! Chief Sutter made no effort to stop her.

"You can do me right in this here car." She was panting. "I'se about to git off just thinkin' about it!"

Oh, my, Chief Sutter thought as he ground his teeth.

His pants were down, his knees quivering. The girl

came very close to gasping when she looked down, and when Chief Sutter looked down himself, he, too, came very close to gasping.

Where did that fuckin' log come from? he asked either the universe, God, or fate. The knobbed baton of flesh that throbbed up in his lap was at least three times larger than the actual member nature had tacked onto him. And then he remembered, with a cunning smile: *That's right. This is a dream.*

And what a *grand* dream it was, when the girl crawled forward in the seat.

She spoke quickly now, in words that were scalded by desire. "Guess ya don't remember me, huh, Mr. Chief? Just a bit ago?"

"Huh?"

"Them bad men in the funny truck who wanted ta do bad things ta me? You mussed 'em up right fierce."

Then somehow, through her words, an awareness snapped. *The Squatter gal in the road today. The chick that black guy and the hippie were tryin' to sell crystal meth to . . .*

"I'se so grateful to you fer protectin' me, Mr. Chief, and I'se gonna show you just *how* grateful right now," she promised, and began to lift her leg over, to bring herself crotch-to-crotch with him in the front seat—

Oh, yeah, he thought, *what a great fuckin' dream!*

Then she froze. Her excited expression wilted. A second later she withdrew and sat back on the passenger side.

"What's wrong?" Sutter nearly bellowed.

Her breasts and shoulders slumped when she let out a long, frustrated breath. "Dang it, Mr. Chief! I'se forgot. . . ."

"Forgot *what?*" Chief Sutter shouted.

"We cain't do this."

"Why?"

"'Cos I'se only fifteen years old, like I told ya today. You're a police officer 'n' I'm a minor." She shook her head, smiling innocently. "It was silly a' me ta even think this." And then she opened the door and began to get out of the car.

Sutter's lips twisted up into queer shape as he tried to form words for his objection. Finally, he managed to bark out, "Wait a minute, honey! We *can!* It don't matter that you're a minor because this is just a dream!"

She looked back into the car, magnificent breasts swaying. "Aw, no, Mr. Chief. It'd still be immoral 'cos you'd feel really bad about it once ya woke up."

"No, I wouldn't!" he assured her.

"Oh, yeah, I'm sure ya would, 'n' I cain't have that. It'd make me feel guilty."

Sutter shouted again, "You can't feel guilty! You're just an image in a dream! *My* dream!"

"Naw, naw, still wouldn't be right," she said. Her face perked up. "But I'll tell ya what! You just wait three years when I'm eighteen and then have this dream again! We'll have a *fine* time! I promise!"

And then she closed the door.

Sutter lay back in the seat, on the verge of tears. *What a fuckin' ripoff. . . .*

She came around the other side for one last tease. Perfect legs parted, her perfect elbows planted on the edge of his open window, perfect breasts still swaying, still shining from all that desiring sweat. "But lemme give ya a peck on the cheek, okay?" she said. "I'se pretty dang sure *that* ain't against the law."

Well, it was better than nothing, wasn't it?

She leaned over further, bringing her head into the car, and just as she would kiss him on the cheek—

Whup . . .

—her head fell off her shoulders and landed in Chief Sutter's lap.

A sound screamed through his head like a jet turbine, and suddenly he was falling through darkness, and after what seemed hours of falling, falling, falling—

—he awoke in a tumult on his bed.

Oh, God . . .

His heart *thunked* in his chest; he thought of an old engine trying to restart. His eyes hurt as he stared after the nightmare, and the inside of his mouth tasted rancid. *What a ripoff,* he thought again. Why should his subconscious produce such a dream, such intense erotic images, only to leave him unfulfilled?

He winced.

Unfulfilled and with a severed head in his lap.

The entirety of his bulk flinched at a hideous noise. He rolled over in bed and noticed the even larger bulk lying beside him. June always slept naked. Her blubbery belly and breasts vibrated through each cycle of that awful noise—her snoring. Sutter looked at her aghast in the moonlight. *Is that my wife or did someone dump three hundred pounds of vanilla pudding in my bed and put a wig on it?* This new image only doubled the cruelty of the dream: first the Squatter girl and her perfect image of sexual beauty, then this pale pile of human lard that he would spend the rest of his life with.

Suddenly all the unfulfillment of his life landed on him at once. *Over-the-hill, up to my neck in debt, and married to* that, he realized.

This was it. This was his life, staring him in the face in all its irrevocable truth.

He actually could've cried. The bed jostled like a small earthquake when he slid off and stood up, pasty, belly sticking out under hairy man-tits, forty-eight-waist boxer shorts bunched up his ass. Comfort food was the only ticket to cure this grim hour of the wolf, so he trudged out of the noisy bedroom to the kitchen.

He clumped through the darkness, and finally a smile found his mouth. *Nice and cool,* he reminded himself. *At least I have air-conditioning, and yesterday I didn't.* The brand-new unit was doing its job on the summer heat, purring away. He'd thought about it and thought about it, and he'd finally come to the honest decision that taking that dope money off those scumbags represented no infringement on his sense of professional ethics. *It was just drug money. If I'd turned it into the county sheriff's, they would've confiscated it.* One thing to feel good about was better than nothing. He'd done his job beyond the call of duty, and . . .

And I got a little perk, he rationalized. *Ain't no harm in that.*

The refrigerator light flooded the kitchen when he opened the door. A little less dejected than before, he pulled out a fat Boston cream pie that June had picked up at the grocery store and cut himself a sizable slice, but before he could take his first sloppy bite . . .

He smirked in the dark.

Snippets of the dream swept around his mind's eyes like a flock of birds. The girl's stunning, earthy, sweat-glistening beauty unfolding before him and then—

Whup . . .

Her head falling off right into his lap.

I must be really fucked-up in the head to have a dream like that, he considered. *Why in God's name would I dream something like that?*

Her head falling off.

Her head . . .

Heads, he thought.

It couldn't help but remind him: Dwayne Parker's funeral was tomorrow. The most bizarre death his little town had ever seen.

He knew about the rumors. The EMTs had run their mouths, and probably so had some folks down at the county morgue. *Can't say that I blame them. Who could see something like* that *and not mention it to anyone?*

At least they were just rumors at this point, and he hoped they'd fade away after Dwayne's ashes were cast to the four winds. Even minus the head—which still had not been found—there'd been no doubt as to positive identity. The tattoos were right, the clothes were right, and the ID in the wallet was right. Two days later the fingerprints came back from NCIC, and they were Dwayne Parker's. The death certificate had read: *Anomalous death—COD: Decapitation via smooth transection of levator scapulae muscular process and #5 & 6 cervical vertebrae. Mode of transection as yet undetermined and curious.*

That was the tech talk. Sutter himself had been one of the few to see the body. The coroner's remarks—*undetermined and curious*—were understatement. Sutter had never seen anything so strange, nor inexplicable.

He'd never forget the sight of the body when the attendant had opened the body bag.

Jesus . . .

It seemed less like his head had been cut off and more like it had vanished off his body. There was no telltale "stump." No cut marks or blade striations. Dwayne Parker's skin, in fact, seemed to cover the area of space between his collarbones as though the skin had impossibly *grown over* the decapitation wound.

Sutter sighed, his appetite lost. He put the pie back in the refrigerator.

Goddamn Dwayne, he thought, wincing the vision out of his mind as he headed back to the bedroom. *Almost like he'd never had a head in the first place.*

Four

(I)

When Patricia opened her eyes, the bedroom was shimmering in sunlight. She felt warm and rested, ready for the day in spite of its circumstances. *The funeral,* she thought. She'd dreaded it, hadn't she? Because she'd dreaded coming back here, but so far her return had provided the opposite of what she'd expected. *I feel great,* she realized, and then she hopped up from the big bed and looked at herself in the dresser mirror. *And I look great, too.* Her skin shimmered like the light in the room. Her eyes looked back at her, vibrant, bright. Her naked body had never appeared healthier, her breasts heavy yet high, her waist tight, bereft of even a trace of middle-age flab. *And I'm starving,* she reminded herself. The aromas of coffee and bacon drifted into the room, seducing her. She quickly pulled her robe over her shoulders and rushed into the hall toward the shower. She grabbed a towel from the linen closet, then opened the bathroom door—

A blue-jeaned and shirtless Ernie looked at her, a toothbrush sticking out of his mouth. His eyes widened, and he flinched at the sight of her. "Jesus, Patricia," he mumbled through lips foamy with toothpaste.

Patricia stalled, blinked; then a shock bolted through her brain. *My God, I'm practically naked!* It had taken her a second to realize that her robe hung wide open, affording Ernie a complete full-frontal glimpse. Then her face must've turned nearly as red as her hair. She pulled the robe closed and sprinted back to her room, squealing in embarrassment.

She slammed the door shut and leaned against it, bug-eyed. *What in God's name is wrong with me? What kind of a complete airhead am I?* Was she that distracted by coming here? She didn't feel distracted at all; in fact, until she'd opened the bathroom door, she'd been marveling at how good she felt, and how together. *Ernie's going to think I'm an exhibitionist!*

Then she reflected further: *Maybe I did it on purpose. . . .*

Something in her subconscious. She even admitted to herself that she'd been sort of teasing him last night, when she'd bent over braless to untie her shoes. She knew he'd been looking down her blouse . . . and she didn't mind.

And now this.

He just saw everything. . . .

More reflections spun around her head. *Something weird's happening to me. Since the minute I got back to town, I've been horny as hell. Then last night I dream about having sex with another man right in front of my husband—the lewdest dream of my life. I took my nightgown off in my sleep, and I even had orgasms* during *the dream, and then . . . then I wake up masturbating. And to top it all off, the first thing I do after I wake up is expose myself to Ernie! What is going on in my head?*

Patricia was a very logical woman, but she could find no logic in this. *Agan's Point is the town where I was raped. I should feel very* unsexual.

So why the opposite?

The good feelings she had wakened with were ruined. She waited till Ernie was finished in the bathroom, then showered quickly. She made a point to wear a bra this time, an old baggy crewneck T-shirt and a cotton ankle skirt. The frumpy clothes made her feel very *un*sexy.

Now for the hard part . . . She couldn't sit here all day. *What am I going to say to Ernie?* A worse consideration: *Did he tell Judy what I did?*

And what might he say to any male friends? She knew how guys talked amongst themselves, and in her mind she could hear it now: *Yeah, guys, I swear to God, she just walked right in with her robe hangin' wide open showin' the whole package! Tits stickin' out—damn near poked me in the eye! And that red-hairt beaver? Yeah, man!*

"Oh, please," she muttered.

She summoned her courage and walked straight to the kitchen.

"Good mornin', my sweet big sister!" Judy greeted her. She smiled brightly as she was pouring the orange juice at the table.

"Hi, Judy," Patricia said dolefully.

"Sleep well, I hope?"

"Yes, fine . . ."

Ernie stood at the stove, flipping eggs. He glanced over with half a smile. "Mornin', Patricia."

She let out a frustrated breath. "Ernie, I don't know what to say."

"Aw, don't worry 'bout it," he dismissed. "Probably

groggy when ya got up and forgot you weren't in yer own house. No biggie."

"What are you two talkin' about?" Judy asked.

"Ain't nothin', Judy," he said fast, then severed the subject. "How ya want your eggs, Patricia? Judy likes hers sunny-side down, 'n' I take mine up."

Thank God he didn't tell her what a ditz I am. "I'll take mine up, too."

"Ernie makes the best eggs," Judy bragged. "He kind of floats 'em in butter and bacon grease."

"See, Patricia, out here in the country we don't worry 'bout none of that citified hogwash like cloresterhall're whatever the hail it's called."

"Fine with me. Mine's always been low." Patricia sat next to her sister. "How are you holding up?"

Judy crunched into a piece of buttered toast. "Honestly, I feel much better than I thought I would, and I *know* it's because you're here. I can't thank you enough for makin' the trip—"

"I won't hear talk like that."

"And I'm so, so sorry for bein' so out of it last night—"

"It's all right, Judy—"

"All drunk and weepy and sleepin' most of the day. I'm just ashamed to be like that for your arrival."

"Quiet, I said," Patricia ordered. But Judy's mood was actually encouraging. *Today she's going to scatter her husband's ashes. I'd expect her to be a wreck right now, but . . . so far, so good.*

The three of them chatted casually during breakfast, mostly Judy talking about her business, which locals had died, gotten married, or left town, etc. Eventually Ernie excused himself for some outside chores he needed to get done before the funeral services.

Patricia found it almost impossible to keep her eyes off him as he walked out the door.

"Oh, yes, I'm afraid Ernie never quite got over you," Judy was saying over her coffee.

Patricia smirked, more at herself than at the comment.

"But I'm glad you found the life you truly wanted with Byron." Judy chuckled. "Ernie's quite a good-looking man, but not your type at all."

"He'll find his Miss Right one of these days," Patricia said for lack of anything else. "I'm totally in love with Byron, and I'm sure I always will be." But she continued in thought. *If I'm so in love with Byron, why am I having sex dreams about Ernie?* She wondered what her old psychologist, Dr. Sallee, would say. *Midlife crisis, I guess . . .*

Later, they walked out back in the garden, which glowed resplendently in sun and flower blooms. Every so often a cicada would fly cumbersomely across their path, in search of a tree to hide in. Judy seemed more circumspect now, her mind mulling things as she ambled along over the fieldstone trail that snaked through the back property.

"I know what everyone thinks," she said, plucking yellow petals off a small touch-me-not.

"What do you mean?"

"Everybody's glad Dwayne is dead."

Patricia's train of thought stalled. *You've got that right,* she thought, but said, "Don't be ridiculous." She struggled to say something positive without sounding fake. "Dwayne was a difficult person to read. He was misunderstood and . . ." *Careful!* she thought. "He had a pretty bad upbringing. When you grow up around a lot of negativity . . . it has a negative effect on a person."

"Oh, no. Everybody thinks Dwayne was a bad person and full well wanted to be." Judy grabbed her sister's arm. "But he *wasn't.* He was a *good* man. He helped me so much. He *loved* me."

He loved the free roof you put over his head, Patricia thought. *He loved eating your food and spending your money.* "I know, Judy. I'm sure he was a good man."

"And those two or three times he cheated on me?" Judy's eyes were wide. "That was all my fault."

Patricia ground her teeth. "Judy, how can that be your—"

"I gave him no choice. A wife has more responsibilities to her husband than just to run a business. I never made time for him. I was so busy with the company, I'd neglect my duties to him as a lover."

Patricia wanted to wail. Dwayne had likely engaged in sexual infidelities more than two or three times. "Don't stress yourself over it now," was all she said.

"And those times he hit me?" Judy vigorously shook her head. "I had it coming."

At that Patricia had to object. "Judy, no woman ever has *it* coming. No woman should ever be hit by a husband."

"You don't know, Patricia. I'm sure I frustrated him, and then when I get to drinkin' . . . I can understand why he done what he done."

This was going nowhere. *Be a lawyer,* Patricia ordered herself. *Judy is the claimant and she's just lost her case in litigation. Offer your summation, Counselor. . . .* "It may be true that a lot of people here didn't like Dwayne, but that's only because nobody really knew him. Only you knew the real Dwayne, Judy. *You* know he was a good man. *You* know he was a good husband. He's gone now, in a terrible accident, so the best thing you can do is honor his memory by *not caring* about what other people might think. Remember Dwayne to yourself as the positive force he was in your life and all the happiness he gave you."

Patricia nearly gagged on her words, yet they seemed to do the trick. Judy's angst was quelled now, and she quieted into contentedness, a sedate smile on her face.

Patricia held her hand as they continued their walk through high ranks of flowers and hedges. She felt awful at her next thought. *My God, I'm so glad that ex-con prick is dead. Maybe now my sister will find a man who'll be good for her for a change. . . .*

They sat down on a stone bench at the end of the path. Sparrows frolicked in a birdbath. The air around them hung still in the sun, and through the trees Patricia could see the glint of the river that emptied into the bay around the other side of the Point. *It really is beautiful here,* she realized. The thrum of the cicadas pulsed.

"It's going to be hard to keep on . . . without Dwayne," Judy said. "The business 'n' all, I mean."

Patricia smirked. "Any loss takes a while to get over, but you'll be fine." Her words hardened with insistence. "Your company is turning ten times the profit that Mom and Dad got out of it. You're a very successful, self-made businesswoman."

"Oh, that's silly. The only reason the business thrives now is because of the new boats and equipment that *you* loaned me the money for."

She's just feeling sorry for herself, Patricia knew. She supposed that was to be expected. *The future of the company might seem overwhelming right now.* "Judy, you paid that money back twice as fast as you ever needed to, with interest. The company's success comes from *your* brains and *your* hard work. You'll do just fine."

Judy seemed reluctant. "Without Dwayne it'll be so much harder. Sometimes I get to thinkin' . . ."

"What?"

"Oh, I guess I never told ya. You saw the construction on the other side a' the river, right?"

Patricia remembered from her drive in. "Yeah, waterfront condos, it looks like. Judy, that's just the way things are. Everything gets bigger. It's social growth. All those condos'll do is bring in more people—rich people, by the way—who'll spend more money here. More growth for you, too, and your business."

"Oh, I know, but I never told ya about the offer, 'cos it's so recent."

"Offer? Someone offered to buy the crab company?"

"No, the land, the entire Point. The construction man. His name is Gordon Felps. He wants to turn the entire Point into a waterfront residential community. He offered a million dollars for everything, and remember, half of that land is yours, from Daddy's will. You'd get half the money. That's a *lot* of money."

Patricia rolled her eyes. *My poor sister is such a hayseed.* "Judy, a million dollars for your company and all this land isn't nearly enough. Try three or four million, and you'd still be foolish to sell. Where would you go; what would you do? I know you enjoy running the business; you've told me that too many times."

Judy seemed doubtful. "I know, but I'm getting old for this."

"You're only forty-two!" Patricia exclaimed. "What, you want to sell everything now and *retire?* That's ridiculous. Wait till you're *sixty*-two, when you can sell everything for *twenty* million. *That's* when you retire, little sister." Patricia wanted to object further, but then she took a moment to consider the reality. *She's still in mourning. She'll be a little kooky for a few weeks, but then she'll come to her senses.* "And besides," Patricia went on, "What about the Squatters? You've had offers before and didn't sell. Remember the last time when you called me about it? You'd said you'd never sell the land because the Squatters would be kicked out and have no place to go. Those people adore you; they're like your children. Don't tell me you've changed your mind about them."

"I don't know. Things are changing. I keep hearin' things, and it makes me think."

Patricia just kept frowning. "You keep hearing *what* things?"

"Well, that the Squatters are startin' to turn bad. Some of 'em are startin' to get into the drugs, and some a' the gals are sellin' themselves 'n' all."

Patricia could've laughed. "Judy, the only difference between the Squatters and the Pennsylvania Dutch is that the Squatters are even *more* puritanical. They make the Amish look like party animals."

"I don't know," her sister repeated. "I get to thinkin' that maybe they're startin' to turn bad 'cos of me."

Patricia was getting close to wringing her sister's neck. "Okay, let me see. You give them work. You give them a free place to live, free electricity, and free water. So how are they turning bad because of you? You're the best thing they've got going for themselves."

Judy dismissed the notion with a wave of her hand. "I feel like a welfare lord. I give 'em work, sure, but it ain't nothin' but minimum-wage work. The men go out 'n' catch the crabs and the women pick the meat. It's sweatshop work, and most of 'em got nothin' but tin shacks to live in. Don't matter that I don't charge 'em rent for the land. It ain't much more than ghetto life, and I'm the one danglin' the bait. Lot of 'em think there ain't nothin' else, nothin' that might be better for them out in the world."

Patricia shrugged. "For people like that there probably isn't. The Squatters exist in their own little society. They're self-sufficient, living off the land. They're pretty much uneducated and unskilled. The world can't save everyone. All that matters is they're making the best of what they've got and they're very happy. They practically worship you—you're like their queen. I'm not saying that you have an obligation not to sell the land if you really want to. It's just that there's no reason to do that. And for God's sake, Judy, you're not keeping them from greener pastures by giving them full-time employment. If they weren't here, they'd be standing in breadlines, living in homeless shelters. If they think they can better themselves somewhere else, then they're free to leave. But they don't, because they know they probably can't. They're simple people who live a simple, hardworking life. Same as the Amish, same as the Quakers, same as a lot of the Appalachians. You're not keeping them down by keeping them employed."

Patricia felt winded after the philosophical exchange, and she felt frustrated as well. *Where is she getting these nonsensical ideas?*

Judy mulled it over in the silence, then said, "You're probably right. Guess I'm just in a mood."

"You've got a lot on your mind. Just focus on today."

It was about the only advice Patricia could think of. *This guy Felps,* she thought next. *Maybe he's the one filling her head up with this crap.* "So tell me about this construction man who made the offer."

"Oh, yes, Gordon Felps. He's very successful, been buildin' luxury homes all up 'n' down the East Coast for a long time. And he's very nice." Judy blushed, looking down at her knees. "He even asked me out when he first come to town. Didn't know I was married, a' course, till I told him. But he really is a nice man."

By now, Patricia thought she'd develop permanent wrinkles from frowning so much. *She is so friggin' naive I can't* believe *it!* "Judy, you own a lot of valuable property. You have to be very careful with people who seem 'nice' if they have an ulterior motive. You know, like wanting to buy your land for several times *less* than what's it worth!"

Judy didn't even hear her. "And I'm sure you'll meet him today at the funeral. I think he 'n' Dwayne were even friends. I saw 'em talkin' several times, gettin' on real fine."

Naive, naive, naive! "I will definitely look forward to meeting Mr. Felps," she said. *Oh, you can bet on that.*

She was relieved at the break now in the conversation, Judy keeping any further thoughts to herself. Patricia just relaxed in the sun, peering around at the spacious yard's beauty. The cicada sounds seemed more distant, lulling her. *A wine cooler would be nice right about now,* she considered, but then looked at the time. In another hour they'd have to start getting ready for the services.

In the distance, she could hear . . . something.

What is that?

A sharp *thwack, thwack, thwack!*

The noise persisted, drawing closer.

"Here comes Ernie," Judy said.

Patricia glanced around, then at the edge of the yard noticed a shirtless Ernie going at the blocks of hackberry bushes with a pair of hedge clippers.

Thwack, thwack, thwack!

"He does such a wonderful job with the yard," Judy commented through a drowsy smile.

The image caught Patricia off guard. "Oh . . . yes. Yes, he does." But her focus was elsewhere—not on Ernie's hedge work; it was on Ernie himself.

On Ernie's body.

His toned back muscles flexed with each *thwack* of the clippers. Then his angle changed; she could see his chest, the well-defined pectorals tensing, his six-pack abdomen running with lines of sweat. He paused for a moment, wiped sweat off his brow with a toned bicep. Then he got back to work.

Oh, for pity's sake, Patricia thought.

She couldn't take her eyes off him, off the magnificent physique, and her mind dragged her back to last night's dream.

The terrific sex.

Patricia could only shake her head at herself. Her eyes stayed fixed on Ernie's sweat-drenched chest. *I'm turning into a sex-obsessed floozy!*

She knew it was going to be a long day.

•

(II)

"Hey, Pappy Halm!" Trey called out just as he stepped out of his cruiser in front of the Qwik-Mart. "What'choo think you're doin'?"

The old proprietor stopped, cane in one hand, dragging the large front garbage can with the other. "I'm takin' out the fuckin' garbage, ya moe-ron. What's it look like?"

"Looks like an old codger tryin' ta pull twice what he weighs. Let me take care a' that for ya."

"Aw, fuck you, ya young fuck!" the old man railed. "I was bustin' beaver when you was a tadpole in yer daddy's sack. Back in my day I could haul ten of these, with you on my back."

"I'm sure ya could, Pappy. But that was back when Roosevelt was in office. *Teddy* Roosevelt. So why don't ya let me take that?"

Old man Halm jerked on the big can a few more times, grunted, then gave up. "Fuck it! My taxes pay your salary, so *you* empty the sucker!"

"My pleasure, Pappy. You can gimme a free coffee once I'm done."

Halm waved his cane in the air. "Yeah! I got'cher free coffee for ya right here, so you come 'n' get it!" And then he grabbed his crotch and hobbled back into the store.

Sergeant Trey laughed at the old man's spunk. A tightwad pain in the ass, but Trey liked him. Pappy Halm was a black-and-white, commonsense kind of fella, and Trey felt that he himself was too.

What he was doing right now, for instance . . . it made sense, and no, it had nothing to do with giving the old man a hand taking out the store garbage.

The point was the contents of the garbage can.

If I don't do it, someone else will.

Trey knew he was a lousy cop deep down, but he felt confident that that didn't mean he was a lousy person. *It's all give and take. Dog eat dog. Shit, I'm a decent guy mostly. I pay my bills, provide for my wife, even go to church at least twice a year. . . .* Perception was interpretive and abstract. Trey arrested bad people, so that was good, right? He helped make the world a little bit safer by submitting to an ungratifying and often sordid job. He and Marcy never had kids—because, after knocking up a good dozen gals before tying the knot and paying mightily for abortions, he got a vasectomy. See, one thing was for sure: he sure as *shit* didn't want kids. Marcy wanted kids bad, but he never told her about his trip to the doctor, because if he had she never would've married him, and back in her day she was one hot number. Trey wouldn't stand for her marrying anyone else, especially as good in bed as she was. So that was the short version. He lied. He let her marry him believing he would give her children when in fact he was shooting big-time blanks.

Which was beside the point.

The point, relative to the true nature of Trey, was that if he did have kids, he'd be a decent father. He knew that. He wouldn't neglect his kids, wouldn't beat 'em, and would make sure they always had food in their bellies. Period. And as far as husbanding went? The same. *I'm a good husband, damn it,* he felt sure. He kept a roof over Marcy's head, kept food in the fridge, and never slapped her around, even when she mouthed off. Five years after they got married, her looks went to shit in a handbasket, legs turned to cellulite tubes, tits dropped down to her belly like a couple of limp sacks full of flour, but even with all that, Trey never cheated on her. Oral sex on the side wasn't cheating (it was a Southern law: "Eatin' ain't cheatin'," and by God, Trey was a Southern man) because it lacked the intimacy of intercourse, that parameter of closeness that coupled the body and soul, so a few blow jobs per week from hookers and bar tramps hardly constituted a breach of the covenant of matrimony. So, yeah, Trey was a faithful husband to boot.

And as for certain private activities that he might engage in on occasion . . . did that make him a bad person?

No, he felt determined. *No way.*

He had some connections—all cops did. *Ain't no force on earth can stop the drug trade. Better me makin' some cash than a dealer.* After all, he'd spend the money more responsibly, wouldn't he? Once he dragged that big garbage can around to the back of the store, it didn't take too much plowing around before he came up with the tackle box full of crystal meth that Chief Sutter had dropped in there yesterday.

Yes, sir, Trey thought.

He tossed the box in the patrol car, emptied the garbage, and brought the can back around. *Fifteen more minutes,* he thought, looking at his watch, *and I gotta go pick up the chief.* He was about to go in the store for a quick coffee, just when his cell phone rang.

"Sergeant Trey here."

"You recognize my voice? Just say yes or no."

"Sure do."

"Good. Don't say my name." A pause. "You recall our previous conversation? About the backup plan?"

"Sure do," Trey said.

"Things aren't working as well as I'd like. So I'm going to implement that plan. Are you up for it?"

Trey smiled. "Sure am." Then he remembered what he'd tossed into the patrol car a moment ago. "And you ain't gonna believe what I just pulled out of the trash. . . ."

Five

(I)

". . . and so whoever believeth in me shall never die.'" The loud voice reached across the field. Father Darren stood tall, broad-shouldered, with brown hair sweeping past his shoulders—an imposing figure. His gentle expression and blazing eyes seemed to maximize the effect of the words he was saying.

Patricia struggled not to shield her eyes. All dressed in black like that, the congregation appeared as stark shadows in blazing sun. The moment felt odd, the thrumming of the cicadas adulterating the silences between the service intercessions.

And it was stiflingly hot.

Judy stood next to her, holding her hand and sobbing very quietly. Patricia's eyes darted around as the minister read on. There were a number of townspeople gathered around, but she didn't remember their names. Chief Sutter and his deputy—Trey, she thought his name was—stood off to the side, and then she spotted old Mr. Halm, who ran the local convenience store. Angling off in another direction stood a dozen or so Squatters, all dressed in austere black clothes. The oldest face there she recognized at once—Everd Stanherd. This elder of the clan looked deceptive, black, black hair belying the lined face. The short hair was so dark it could've been a badly chosen wig. Next to him stood his wife, Marthe, graceful, swanlike in some aura of backwoods stature; Patricia remembered her too, still slim and attractive in her sixties, black hair lustrous around the set face. Both of them wore odd pendants about their necks, pouchlike things, which Patricia couldn't identify until she thought back. *The Squatters are so superstitious,* she remembered. *All those trinkets and charms they wear.* A number of the other Squatters in attendance wore similar items, either pendants or bracelets, and to confuse her more, several others wore crosses.

But something was bothering her—not her sudden recollection of the Squatters' superstitious totems but . . . something else. Something seemed to nag at her. . . .

A moment later she sensed more than saw a presence behind her.

More of Father Darren's words resounded around them: " 'So we fix our eyes not on what is seen but what is unseen. For what is seen is temporary, but what is unseen is eternal.' "

Patricia had a hard time paying attention. She'd never been particularly religious; to her funerals as well as weddings were just fancy words in a ceremonial show. It was the figure behind her that distracted her.

She finally stole a glance to her rear, then, and saw Ernie standing solemn-faced, hands clasped in front.

Seeing him in a suit seemed jarring, but with him dressed as he was, and with his long hair pulled back, Patricia had to admit that he looked . . .

Really good . . .

She smiled briefly, then turned back around. *Yeah, he looks really good, all right. . . .* The delayed reaction smacked her consciousness like a slap, an edgy sense of shame. *There I go again—my God. I'm standing here at the funeral of my sister's husband and I'm checking out the handyman's bod.* That bizarre sexual flux she'd noticed since she arrived had never felt more apparent. Then she yelled at herself. *Jesus, Patricia! What is wrong with you? You're lusting after other men at a friggin'* funeral *while your loving and very faithful husband is sitting back at your home paying the bills!*

She chewed her lower lip, hoping the tingling in her nipples would pass. . . .

"'We brought nothing into this world, and it is certain that we can carry nothing out,'" Father Darren continued, this time quoting the Book of Job. "'The Lord giveth, and the Lord taketh away. Blessed be the name of the Lord.'"

The minister's hands were outspread before them all, his sedate smile exuberant. He held up the urn. "Blessed Lord, we sing praise and thanks to your name! And we beg you to commend the eternal soul of our brother Dwayne unto the kingdom of Heaven—all unworthy servants that we are." Then Father Darren broke from his portable podium and approached Judy. He handed her the urn full of her husband's ashes.

Ricky and Junior Caudill were twin brothers, Junior being so named due to the fact that he emerged from his mother's womb six minutes after Ricky. The Caudill name carried some infamy throughout southern Virginia, which perhaps lent credence to some recent scientific research that suggested antisocial, psychosexual, and overall criminal activity were indeed genetically inherent. Both were stocky, fat-faced, sizably bellied, and both had short, dung-colored hair always sticking up as though they'd just climbed out of bed. Ordinarily their everyday apparel consisted of jeans, boots, and dingy T-shirts, but today they'd dressed up in dark suits each a bit too small, yet suits just the same. Even disrespectful fellows such as these needed at least to *look* respectful on select occasions.

Ricky spit a loogie between his shoes, but he did so very quietly. See? Even a shiftless sociopath knew some facsimile of ceremony. "Gettin' boring," he muttered.

Junior watched as a tearful Judy Parker took the urn from Father Darren. He elbowed his brother with a chuckle. "Bet'cha that urn weighs less than most, huh?"

Ricky didn't get the joke for a moment, but then he pondered the remark further. "Yeah. Shit, I wonder . . . I wonder how much the *ashes* of a head weigh?"

Deep thinking for this pair. Ricky scratched his ass as Judy Parker began to toss plumes of ash into the open air.

"You think he wants us to do like he was talkin' the other day?" Junior asked.

"Hope so. Been a pretty borin' summer. Somethin' to jazz it up'd be just fine."

Junior picked his ear. "Oh, yeah, that'd jazz it up, all right."

Ricky's eyes scanned the crowd. "Lotta Squatters here. Shit, ain't that a laugh. Dwayne hated the Squatters."

"Yeah, but they practically worship Judy. Only reason they got work is 'cos of her."

"You really think it was Squatters who kilt Dwayne? That's the story."

Junior's chubby face pulled into a smirk of doubt. "Naw. One a' the construction crew's what I heard. Dwayne was fuckin' the dude's girlfriend, so the dude showed him what trouble really was."

Now Ricky was squinting. "Check out the trim standin' in front of Ernie. I swear I seen her before."

Junior squinted too. "Never seen her before, and I'd remember a rack like that. Fuck. She got a pair a' milk wagons or what?"

"Oh, now I remember!" Ricky cited with some whispered enthusiasm. "That's Judy's sister. She moved to the city a *long* time ago, married some rich, fat fella. Don't'cha remember? Patricia's her name. She was the biggest talk a' Agan's Point 'bout twenty-five years ago."

Junior crudely calculated in his head. "Twenty-five years ago? Shit, I'se pretty sure I was doin' my last stint in juvie hall."

"Yeah, yeah, I remember *tellin'* ya 'bout it when I come to visit ya." Ricky's face turned up in a big pumpkin grin. "She's the chick who got raped out at Bowen's Field. Weren't but fifteen or sixteen. She was skinny-dippin' by herself one night at the pond and someone hauled her out and put the blocks to her right there in the dirt. Staked her to the fuckin' ground, too, while he was doin' her."

Junior popped a brow. "Shit, brother, don't'cha be talkin' like that. You're gettin' my willy jumpin'." Then he shot his brother a suspicious glance. "Bet it was you who raped her and you just ain't tellin'."

"Naw, boy, if I'd ever carved me a piece of box *that*

fine, you'd be the first I'd tell." Ricky rubbed his hands together, still staring at the attractive redhead. "I'd be *proud* to have a cutie like that screamin' under me. . . ."

The highly intellectualized discussion faded now, as Judy was finished dispersing her husband's ashes.

Father Darren, ever smiling, spread his hands to them all and said, " 'I know that my Redeemer liveth, and that he shalt stand at the latter day upon the earth.' Go in peace, to love and serve the Lord!"

The congregation's reply strayed across the field: "Amen."

"It's about time," Junior said. "I'm tired a' standin' around."

Ricky's eyes roamed the crowd as a line formed, townsfolk waiting to convey their condolences to Judy. "Where is he?"

"Here they come. Shit. Sutter's coming too."

Sutter and Trey approached the two brothers, neither looking happy. "What'choo boys doin' here?" Chief Sutter demanded.

The brothers shrugged. "Just payin' our last respects to Dwayne," Junior told him.

"You boys didn't give a shit about Dwayne," Trey said, standing right up to them.

Ricky frowned. "We knew Dwayne, all right. Didn't always get along, but now that he's dead . . . like my brother said, it's only right fer us to pay some respect."

"Bullshit," the chief said. "You're about the two biggest lowlifes in all of Agan's Point—"

"You ain't got no right to say that!" Junior said back.

"—and neither of ya got any respect for no one. I told you two last time after Harriet Farmer got all that jewelry stole out of her house—I don't wanna even *see* either of you nowheres around me. You see me walkin' down the street, you turn around and walk the other way."

Ricky glared back. "We didn't have *nothin'* to with that break-in, Chief," he lied, "and it ain't proper for you to hassle us just 'cos you don't like us."

"You guys busted into that old lady's house and ya know it," Trey told them, jabbing a finger hard against Ricky's chest. "Oh, you don't like me pokin' ya? Do something about it."

Ricky's eyes lowered, and under his breath he said, "This is bullshit."

Next, Chief Sutter bellied right up into his face. "And I know it was you two peepin' on the Chester girls and their babysitter. Truck just like yours was seen leavin' the street. What a pair a' scumbags."

Now Junior tried to get right back in Sutter's face. "We didn't peep on nobody," he lied just as well as his brother. In fact, they'd been doing the same since adolescence. Junior's voice increased in volume. "And that's downright shitty a' you to say we'd do somethin' like that. The Chester girls ain't even in high school yet."

"That's what I mean," the chief countered, and then he jabbed a hard finger. "And you better keep your lyin' voice down, 'cos if you disturb this service with your bullshit, I'm kickin' both your asses."

Junior's face began to twitch, as it often did when he was riled. But was he stupid enough to assault the chief of police?

Junior opened his hand, prepared to give Sutter a good, hard shove.

Trey jumped in front of him, pushing him back. Even Ricky, the slightly wiser one, grabbed his brother by the arm to stave off the blow.

"Forget it, Junior," he ordered. "Don't give 'em an excuse to bust us."

Trey kept pushing Junior away from the chief. "Grow a brain for a change and listen to your brother, you asswipe." He leveled his gaze on both of them. "Get your deadbeat asses out of here while you still can. We will *not* allow a scene here. You fuck this up for Judy, me 'n' the chief are gonna fuck *you* boys up but good."

Junior's eyes were red with rage. He shook off his brother's hand, then turned and stalked off. Ricky followed him.

When they were back at the road where everyone had parked, Ricky slapped Junior's shoulder. "Shit, man! I thought you were really gonna shove Sutter!"

"Damn well had a mind to. I'd love to roust that fat fuck."

"So'd Trey slip ya the contact?"

Junior reached into the back pocket of his slacks. "Fucker should be a pickpocket. Slippery, ya know? I didn't even feel it." He slipped out a small piece of paper.

The paper read: *The Hilds. Tonight. Glove compartment.*

"Hmm," Junior said.

They both lumbered to their pickup truck, a dented hulk. Ricky excitedly flung open the door, then popped down the door to the glove box.

"The man came through!"

Junior eyed the contents of the envelope. "Yeah, and he ain't foolin' around."

A thousand dollars in cash filled the envelope.

(II)

Later, the house sprawled with friends, neighbors, and other well-wishers. *This is definitely a Southern-style funeral reception,* Patricia observed. The gathering began quietly but soon unwound into something close to a party. Local women had all brought food—cakes, salads, cold cuts—but it didn't take long before the banquet table took a backseat to alcohol. *This is how they do it. . . .* Younger Squatter women silently aided Ernie in dispensing the drinks, yet Patricia didn't see any of the Squatters actually drinking themselves. *Oh, that's right,* she remembered. *They're teetotalers.* Just about everyone else, though, was proving the opposite.

But Patricia was surprised by how well composed her sister remained during the service. There were tears, of course, but nothing close to the breakdown Patricia foresaw. Again, it seemed that Patricia's mere presence was her sister's main source of comfort.

As late afternoon became evening, Patricia began to feel more at ease herself. At first she'd felt a bit like an outcast in this crowd of seeming strangers, but eventually many of the faces sparked her memories of when she'd last lived here; she was greeted cordially time and time again, even by some whom she didn't remember until names were mentioned. The entirety of the affair was rich with sentimental talk, like, "Dwayne surely will be missed," "What a tragic passing," "We'll really miss him," and on and on—things Patricia knew were being said only for Judy to overhear. In the parlor, some older local men spoke more along the lines of the truth: "Judy's so much better off without that lyin', cheatin' prick," and "Good riddance to the bastard." Patricia's city-born cynicism forced a smile.

She kept her own drinking on the light side—she wasn't in the mood, and she didn't want to make a bad impression by getting too tipsy in front of the others. *I'm here for my sister, so I don't need to be getting pie-eyed.*

But every so often—she couldn't help it—she cast a glance toward Ernie.

Not this again . . .

He had his suit jacket and tie off now, the sleeves of his white dress shirt rolled up over toned, tanned forearms. He'd unbuttoned the shirt a few notches, and she could see his pectorals flexing when he lifted a tray of sandwiches.

Her eyes raked down his body, and suddenly she was imagining him naked, on top of her. . . .

I have to stop this! This is crazy!

"You must be Patricia, Judy's sister from Washington."

The sudden voice hawked down on her; she flinched as a child might when caught doing something naughty. A very well dressed blond man stood beside her, hard blue eyes, a flirting smile. She'd been so caught off guard musing about Ernie, she was nearly annoyed.

"Yes, I'm Patricia," she said when she recovered. "And you are?"

"Gordon Felps," the man replied. His hand felt cool, strong. His complexion seemed blanched, which only intensified the blue eyes. "I've heard quite a bit about you from your sister. My only regret is the circumstance I've finally gotten to meet you under."

Felps, Felps. Patricia struggled. Then she remembered. "Oh, you're the construction magnate."

The man chuckled. "I wouldn't call myself a magnate by any means, but I am a builder, yes."

"The luxury condos that are going on up on the river side of the Point." Her lawyer's instincts instantly engaged. "And you'd like to continue building on this side of the Point. My sister mentioned that you'd already made an offer for her property, so you'll need to know that I'm Judy's acting legal counsel for all personal and business matters." A cordial smile as she handed him her business card. "Please feel free to contact me in the future for any inquiries regarding my sister."

Felps wasn't fazed by her polite show of force; if anything he was impressed. He pocketed the card. "I will, thank you—not that I suspect it will be necessary, not at this point. Judy's made her desires clear to me. She doesn't want to sell the family land, and I respect that. Actually I've made several offers, but anything more than five million wouldn't be practical from my standpoint."

Five million? I thought she said one million. . . .

"I fully understand her loyalty to Everd Stanherd and his people. She doesn't want to put them out; regrettably, if I took over the property, I'd have no choice. I'd build an entire community where they're living now."

"The Squatters have always been sort of a surrogate family—they worked for my mother and father when they started the crabbing business in the fifties." But in the back of Patricia's mind, she kept thinking, *Five million? Wow . . .*

"Of course. I'll have to keep my project on the river side, but I'm sure it will still stimulate the town's growth." He looked around the reception. "Anyway, it's uncouth of me even to be discussing it at such a time—sorry."

"Oh, I'm so glad you two could meet." Judy emerged from the crowd and squeezed between Patricia and Felps, draping an arm around each of their shoulders. "Mr. Felps is the man I was telling you about, the construction man."

"Yes. We were just having a chat," Patricia said.

Judy was obviously in her cups, stooping over a little. But at least the tears had dried. She hugged Patricia harder. "Oh, and it was Gordon who supplied all the liquor for Dwayne's reception. Wasn't that kind of him?"

"Yes, it was." But then Patricia thought, *Probably hoping you'd get drunk and sign a bad purchase agreement.*

"It was nothing, Judy," Felps said. "For the short time I've been here, you and Dwayne have been good friends, and my heart goes out to you now in this sad time. I hope it goes without saying, but if you need anything—anything at all—just ask."

"Thank you, Gordon." Another tear now; then she looked glitter-eyed to Patricia. "He's such a sweet man."

He may be a con *man, but I don't know how sweet he is,* Patricia thought. She was just being protective, of course. Felps was probably a fine person and a legitimate businessman, but since lawyers tended to despise businessmen, and vice versa, she supposed her guarded reaction was normal.

Felps stood his ground in spite of the sudden discomfort. Judy was close to drunk now, and she was a *sloppy* drunk. Was she clutching Felps so hard on purpose? Was she deliberately pressing her left breast against him, or was she just unaware of it in her inebriation? The stooped pose lowered the vee of her black dress, showing a depth of cleavage. *Could my sister possibly have a crush on this guy?* came Patricia's off-key thought. Judy's bosom was almost as formidable as Patricia's. She watched Felps's eyes, hoping to catch them straying to the cleavage . . . but it never happened.

Then Patricia berated herself. *My head has been in the gutter since the minute I came back here. I'd better straighten up.*

"I've got to visit the ladies' room, but you two keep chatting," Judy slurred next. She gave Patricia a kiss on the cheek, then a squeezy hug to Felps, and she was gone.

"I'd better get going myself," Felps said, glancing at his watch. "Early day tomorrow. But it was very nice meeting you."

"You, too."

Interesting, she thought after he'd left. *He could be the greatest guy in the world, but . . . I don't think I like him.*

It was just more attorney cynicism, but what did it matter? When she looked back into the dining room to see if Ernie was still there, all she caught a glimpse of was his back as he disappeared into the kitchen.

Was she suddenly obsessed with him? Had returning here sparked some until-recently-dormant middle-aged biological clock? *We weren't even high school sweethearts,* she reminded herself. *He wanted to be but I didn't.* Was some fossil of regret inching out of her soul?

Ridiculous, she dismissed the thought. Even in her darkest and most personal hours, she knew she'd found total happiness—as well as sexual satisfaction—with Byron. When she'd called him on her cell phone just before the services, simply hearing his voice had sparked a few sexual wires. Her nipples had hardened even as she related her very dull goings-on thus far. *I don't know what this Ernie thing is, but it's stupid and nonsensical, so I'm going to put it out of my mind,* she determined.

"Howdy, Patricia. My condolences, a' course. Sorry it took me so long to welcome ya back to town."

Another startlement as she'd been musing. It was Chief Sutter who'd approached her. She'd always thought of him as a clichéd country-bumpkin-type chief, complete with the suspenders and big belly, but she'd always remembered him as a considerate man who very much cared about the residents he was employed to protect. She remembered how gentle, how caring he'd been in the aftermath of the rape, as well as the delicacy with which he'd handled her during the grueling but necessary questioning.

She smiled warmly, shaking his hand. "Chief Sutter. I'm happy to see you. In fact, I waved yesterday when I was coming into town."

He winked. "The Qwik-Mart. Yeah, Trey 'n' I caught a glimpse of ya in that shiny new car of yours. Judy's always tellin' me how well things are going for you 'n' your husband up in D.C. We're all so happy for ya."

It was just small talk, but Patricia appreciated it, and it truly was good to see him. "Thanks, Chief, and I hope things are going well for you, too." She quickly glanced around. "Where is your deputy, by the way? I know I saw him at the service."

"He had to go back out on patrol, but he sends his condolences as well." Suddenly something like concern touched the chief's face, and she noticed that he was holding a dark plastic bag with some official-looking seal on it. "But if I could trouble ya for just a minute? Could you take this and see that Judy gets it when the time is right?" He held up the bag. "It's from the country police lab, and they're done with it now."

"What is it?"

"Dwayne's personal effects, stuff he had on him when his body was found. They released it me today, but it ain't really appropriate to give it to Judy just yet."

"Oh, of course."

"Just his wedding band, watch, wallet 'n' all."

Patricia opened the bag and looked inside. "Did the crime lab find anything in the way of evidence?"

"Unfortunately, no. And there's some cash in there too, just so ya know. A goodly amount."

Watch, wallet, gold wedding band? Patricia thought, thinking it odd. She opened the wallet, saw some cash, but also noted five hundred-dollar bills in the bottom of the bag. "That's strange, isn't it, Chief?"

"You mean that whoever killed him didn't take his valuables and the cash? Yes, it is. A' course, anyone's first guess is that Dwayne was murdered, ya know, on account . . ."

"On account of him losing his head, sure," she finished.

"Right. But, uh, the cause of the decapitation itself was officially labeled as 'undetermined.' In other words, the coroner wasn't convinced it was a murder. Could've been a fluke accident, who knows?"

Patricia withheld an overt frown. Instead she asked, "Is it true that no one ever found . . ."

"Dwayne's head? Yeah, that is true, I'm afraid."

Patricia doubted it was an accident, but the point wasn't worth belaboring. *Oh, well. An "undetermined" decapitation.* "I'll put this in a safe place, Chief," she assured him, "and show it to Judy when the time is right."

"Thanks much, Patricia. And thanks for comin' all this way. It means an awful lot to Judy." He shook her hand again. "But I'd best get along now. I'm sure I'll be seein' ya again before you leave."

"I hope so, Chief. Good-bye for now."

Chief Sutter wended off through the crowd. *I guess I'll put this in the den,* Patricia concluded of the bag, but in her mind it kept occurring to her that the only thing stranger than the notion of the decapitation's being an *accident* was Chief Sutter's sudden uneasiness when talking about it at all.

Like something bothered him more than the obvious facts. Dwayne's death was indeed a mystery, but . . .

It's almost like the chief knows more than he's telling, she thought.

She looked into the living room and was content to see Judy on the couch, surrounded by friends. *She's getting drunk again, but she's more than entitled to do that today.* Then she slipped off down the hall and switched on the light in the small den that Judy used for an office.

The room seemed sterile with its wall of file cabinets. *Company records, I'm sure.* On the wall over the desk hung Judy's very first incorporation certificate and her business license that had been changed over since their parents' deaths.

A picture on the other wall left her morose—a shot of her father, long ago, hauling bushels of crabs off a small trawler. *I'll bet that was taken before I was born.* Her father, though spry and muscular in the photo, still had the same cold, humorless look in his eyes she'd always known him for.

Then something else on the wall—an old poster—utterly depressed her.

COME JOIN US ALL!
THE FIRST ANNUAL AGAN'S POINT CRAB FESTIVAL!
MONDAY SEPTEMBER 6.
NOON TIL EIGHT AT BOWEN'S FIELD!

Patricia turned away, a lump in her throat and a knot in her stomach. *Bowen's Field, my God . . .*

And suddenly that everlasting look in her father's eyes seemed more accusory and disgusted than cold.

Next thing she knew she was standing in a daze. The images in her mind began to tumble backward, pulling at her. . . .

She'd been thinking about it all day at school. It didn't seem like her. She didn't know why. Skinny-dipping?

It was a big deal back in eleventh grade, and Agan's Point and some other nearby towns hosted a number of suitable ponds and small lakes. Patricia was constantly being invited by her friends, yet the invitations had never threatened her sexually because it was only her circle of *female* friends always asking her to go. Boys went too sometimes, but from what she'd heard nothing much ever went on. Safety in numbers. She supposed it was all harmless and normal. It was something sixteen-year-olds did on Saturday nights.

But Patricia never went.

She wasn't inhibited, nor self-conscious about her body. If anything she felt the opposite. Not only had good grades allowed her to skip a grade, it seemed that her body had all but skipped adolescence and hastened toward womanhood faster than the others'. Many times, in the showers after gym class, she felt certain some of the other girls spied her naked body and full bare bosom with strained envy. It was fine with her. "What are you afraid of?" one girl had asked in objection. "Patti, in Agan's Point we skinny-dip every weekend, so don't be a prude. If I had your body, I'd show it off every chance I could!"

But Patricia would have none of that. Showing off wasn't her nature. She hadn't even come close to having sex yet—it was something she'd save for the right man. Most of the other girls seemed a lot less choosy, and even this young, Patricia saw that as a pitfall. She wanted to go to college, forge a career, while most of the local girls rushed to get married right after high school and start having kids. *Not me,* she resolved. These girls would wind up living here their whole lives and never even know what opportunities might be waiting for them out in the rest of the world. Patricia was determined not to miss out on what was out there simply to have a routine life in the place she was born.

As for sex . . .

She'd never had it, nor had she ever noticed in herself any trace of the sex drive that seemed to propel everyone else. She'd dated a few boys, but only once got past French-kissing. One twelfth grader she'd kind of liked from her geography class had gotten her bra off one night at the old Palmer's drive-in, but the film—something about killer worms—had grossed her out more than scared her. He'd clumsily groped her breasts and sucked her nipples for a few minutes, then evidently spent himself in his pants. He'd also tried to rub between her legs but was only rubbing just below her navel. She hoped he did better in high school geography than he did in female geography. In other words, this excursion left her uninterested. The local boy she'd most been expected to date seriously was Ernie, but when she was asked about the prospect, her response was always akin to: "Ernie's been my friend since first grade! He's like a brother! I could never date him!" Only later, just before she graduated, had she learned how badly he'd pined for a romance. She simply wasn't interested in Ernie—or in any boy, for that matter. Even when friends described their experiences "doing it" (and the fabulous multiple orgasms that *always* resulted), her response was typically a frown. Masturbation seemed ridiculous, at least from the descriptions she'd heard. *What if someone saw me?* And what could possibly be that great about it anyway? When she'd been younger—fourteen or so—she remembered leaving volleyball practice—and being late—so she'd cut home through the woods, where she'd accidentally happened upon a boy from Hodge's Hardware Store coupling naked with one of the Squatter girls. *So that's what sex is,* she presumed, unshocked and unimpressed. The boy's fastidious performance of lovemaking had lasted about three minutes, whereupon he'd re-dressed quickly and left. But the Squatter girl remained, one hand alternately kneading her breasts, the other playing with her sex. Her body had flexed, her back curling backward in a noisy finish that only left Patricia amused and absolutely convinced she had no need to do this to herself. *Why? If I made all that noise, my parents would hear!*

Ultimately, by the end of the eleventh grade she found all the talk of boys and dating and junior proms and sock hops—and sex—to be annoying. *I guess I'm just different from everyone else,* she concluded, and didn't feel at all unusual about it. In not being sexual, she never once thought she might be missing out on anything. But what she *wouldn't* miss out on was life, her career, the future. Sex would have to wait.

It was right before school would let out for

summer—for some reason she remembered that—and she recalled nothing sexual about her motive, the business about skinny-dipping. She and Judy had gone to a late double feature at the town theater. She'd asked several friends to join them, but, alas, they were all going on to another skinny-dipping party. She and Judy had both passed on the invite—electing instead to go see *Star Wars,* which everyone was talking about—but regrettably they were forced to sit through some grueling first feature about an Egyptian cannibal in the catering business. Patricia found the schlocky farce hilarious in its bad production, but Judy had left halfway through, too revolted by the hokey violence and fake blood that looked like house paint. *Star Wars* was fun, though, and exciting. However, while walking home . . .

. . . Patricia got to thinking.

Maybe I'll try it, she dared herself. *In case I ever decide to do it with my friends, I'll know what it's like.* It wasn't sex she was considering; it was merely skinny-dipping.

I'll try it alone first, see if I like it.

But where? Everyone else was out at the lake in Luntville. *I know,* she thought. She saw the sign right there as she walked along Point Road:

BOWEN'S FIELD.

There was a pond there, and the field itself was almost entirely surrounded by woods.

Perfect.

Her parents were at the fire hall tonight—bingo—and would be home late. The heat and humidity were skyrocketing as the summer deepened; Patricia was sticky with sweat just minutes after leaving the cool movie theater. *A late-night dip in the pond is just what I need.*

She cut through more woods, her sandals snapping twigs. Peepers cheeped like parrots, and she had to walk slowly, keeping her eyes on the ground for toads. Then the woods broke, and there she was. . . .

The clearing opened, ringed by tall trees. The moon was just edging over the tallest oaks. Bowen's Field was a little-used municipal lot: mainly county softball games and holiday gatherings. Picnic grounds with tables and grills dotted the area, and off to one side was the pond.

Patricia looked around guardedly. *No one around.* She felt satisfied. She walked off to the trees, then thought nothing of skimming out of her shorts and top. A moment of hesitation; then the rest came off, panties and bra dropped atop the sandals. And one last look around . . .

Everyone else is skinny-dipping in Luntville, and I'm skinny-dipping here. . . . Simple. There was no need to be self-conscious or embarrassed—she was a logical girl. So she shrugged her bare shoulders, then, and walked nude across the field. *See? No big deal.* She giggled. When she looked down at herself, the only shock was how white she was. She was fair-skinned; she didn't tan well. Her natural hue touched over by the moonlight made her look ghostly.

The warm air caressed her skin as she moved on. Another giggle: *I'm walking naked in public!* The night's heat licked up and down her body.

Cicadas buzzed in their unique drone. The pond lay flat and still before her, a solid black mirror with the moon's reflection floating on top. Mud squished up through her toes when she stepped in, first to her ankles, then to her knees. She lifted her foot and took the next step, which should've brought her hip-deep, but—

Splunk!

—she dropped into a surprise gully deeper than she

was tall. She sprang back to the surface, laughing, then began to dog-paddle around. Where the night's heat had felt heavy on her skin, the cool water felt absolutely luxurious. A sudden liberty swept her as she let the water devour her: *No one knows I'm here; I'm totally alone.* She liked that feeling, a forbidden independence—being naked and by herself, as though the world existed solely for her, and she were its only inhabitant. The moon looked down, a luminous voyeur. Her flesh felt buoyant; cool water rushed between her legs and over her stomach and breasts. She smiled to herself, kicking out farther, totally tranquil in the water.

Patricia was at peace. . . .

It was some sort of a sack, canvas, or maybe several layers of burlap; she'd never figured out what it was exactly. And she never saw it coming.

He must've been in the water the whole time. Waiting? But that was impossible, because no one knew she was out here. She'd told no one she'd be skinny-dipping tonight; in fact, she hadn't even made the decision until after leaving the theater. Nevertheless, as she'd turned to come back closer to the pond's edge, a heavy, wet sack was pulled over her head from behind and tightened immediately by a drawstring. It couldn't have been more effective. . . .

It smothered her scream.

A strong arm girded her neck. Her attacker was breaststroking back to shore, Patricia in tow, but as he did so his hand plowed into her most private area as though it were a squeeze ball. Fingers tried to wriggle in. Each time she attempted to suck in a breath and bolt out a scream, the wet sack sucked against her lips, and all she could do was wheeze. And when they reached the edge and her ankles began to kick through mud—

Thwack!

—a fist hard as a stone knocked her unconscious.

Deathlike blackness filled her mind. Was she dead? No, but as her consciousness began to trickle back, her previous terror had been supplanted by an all-encompassing nausea. She opened her eyes but couldn't see. It wasn't the sack; instead, the only thing she could figure was that a wide strip of tape had been pasted over her eyes. When she tried to move, her wrists and ankles rose . . . but only an inch.

She'd been tied down.

More of her senses began to fall back into place. Her eyes had been taped but her mouth hadn't, and just as she sucked in a deep, deep breath to try another scream, a palm slapped across her lips.

Then something very sharp and very pointed pricked the side of her neck.

"Feel this?"

A coarse whisper.

"It's a knife. If you make any noise at all, I'll cut your throat. Understand?"

She felt burning hot yet immobile, as if frozen solid. At first the terrified paralysis wouldn't even allow her neck muscles to work.

The knife point pricked a little harder.

Patricia nodded.

Next: "If ya bite, I'll cut'cher tongue out 'n' slice yer big tits off and leave 'em on yer mama's doorstep. Understand?"

Patricia nodded.

The clammy palm left her mouth, only to be replaced by a slavering mouth. At least her rapist was passionate—he wanted to kiss first. The dirty mouth sucked her lips, a tongue pushing through. Reflex caused Patricia to squeeze her eyes shut in spite of the blindfold, and from there . . .

Her mind went blank.

More reflex, more defensive instinct. Earlier it was the moon, but now, blinded and lashed to the ground, she became her *own* voyeur, sight replaced by sense. It was as though she were watching herself with her mind. Her mouth fell open and she simply let him do it—*Don't fight your rapist*, she'd read in a women's column once—so she admitted his tongue, tasting liquor and bad breath. The tongue continued to slaver, his drool falling into her mouth. Then the strange mouth sucked her own tongue out, sucked it hard, and that was when she noticed the gap.

His two front teeth were missing.

Eventually the abominable kiss ended; the mouth lifted, then fell right back to her breasts. Wet, ugly suction drew each nipple between the gap in his teeth, and the tongue began to whirl furiously. She could feel that he was naked himself—that hot, hard weight pressing down. All the sensations and mental images collided with revulsion, but Patricia now was disengaged, her own self not part of what was happening.

He never said another word.

She simply lay there and let him molest her, her belly sucked in, her arms and legs pinned out straight as steel rods. Her nipples buzzed now from the furious tendings of his tongue and the way the gap in his teeth isolated the dark areolae. A moment later he sat upright as though her stomach were a seat. His scrotum lay like a hot bag of pudding on her belly, his manhood no doubt inflamed by his own demented desires. His hands opened and closed over her breasts, intent, as if he expected to wring out milk. The sensations hurt; she imagined handprints bruised into her flesh. Next, his fingertips closed on her nipples, tweaking at first, then grinding. Patricia's hips squirmed beneath his weight as he twisted her nipples as if turning screws into a wall.

The weight began to shift. He kneed himself backward, off of her. Was he done? A foolish question. Of course he wasn't done—he was just beginning. Only now did she realize how widely her legs had been parted. Hands gripped her upper thighs, and then the mouth lowered.

Oh, God . . .

Her revulsion collapsed on her like a brick wall against the fiercest wind. The most secret and personal part of her body was brazenly invaded by the detestable tongue. First the tip traced around the opening of her vagina, stimulating the outer ridges, then delving up and down the groove. It was a long tongue, too, evidenced by how deeply it delved inside after each revolution. These ministrations lasted for a long time, until she thought the body she was perceiving so distantly would go nuts and simultaneously choke on vomit.

Could she actually feel the moonlight on her skin even with taped-shut eyes? Patricia could almost see herself writhing, half in arousal and half in utter repugnance.

The mouth rose and its new target was no surprise. . . .

Now the wicked suction drew over the assailant's true target in a variety of movements: back and forth, up and down, then hard circles. And all the while it continued to suck, drawing the nugget of her sex through the gap in the front teeth—a macabre inversion of fellatio.

The sensations rose and rose. Loops of rope abraded her ankles and wrists, and every muscle in her body began to clench up; a feeling she'd never experienced seemed to sear into her, something scalding hot but delicious. Then that detached kernel of her consciousness—that seemed to be spectating the crime from afar—snapped back into her brain like something yanked inward off a cord, and at last the thing that all those sensations had been building up to . . .

. . . broke.

Patricia went out of her mind, and that was all she remembered.

Some early risers found her at sunup. When the duct tape was peeled off her eyes—taking quite a bit off her brows—she dizzily saw that she'd been staked to the ground. She felt humiliated and insensible, naked and laid out for all to see. A man who'd been walking his dog gave her a light jacket to wear until the police came.

Of course her assailant had raped her after his oral invasion, yet she remembered none of it. She could feel her virginity ruptured between her legs, but at least there was little blood, and she recalled no pain. But she could feel the sperm deep in her like some devilish slime. Her mind spun in rings of disgust; she couldn't have felt dirtier than if she'd been defecated on. Worse were the pitying looks in the eyes of the people who'd found her, as though she were crippled, an elderly invalid who could no longer control her bowels. "Poor girl," a woman said. "Like to kill the sick animal that did this," said a man. But Patricia could barely even cogitate. Eventually a much younger Chief Sutter arrived to take her home. Her mother and Judy were aghast, Judy breaking into tears when she'd heard what happened. Chief Sutter couldn't have been more considerate in dealing with the sensitive aftermath of physical examinations and questioning. There'd been no DNA profiling back in those days, no way to type her assailant with technology, just a vaginal smear for rudimentary disease screening. And Patricia supposed—even now, after the passage of over two decades—that if anything could be worse for her than the rape itself, it was her father's reaction when he'd learned of the details.

"Skinny-dipping!" he bellowed, red in the face when he'd gotten home from the crabbing docks. "Runnin' around with no clothes on like a common tramp! Life's hard enough, and now I got a daughter shitting on our good family's name, makin' us look like trash!" He slapped her in the face with a sound like wet leather snapping. "How could you let something like that happen?"

The words were worse even than the blow; Patricia felt as though she'd been shot with a gun. Tears flooded her eyes, and when she looked to her mother for support . . . her mother just looked back with a face set in stone.

So long ago, she thought now, looking at the poster on the wall. *I'd forgotten all about it, until I came back here.*

Enough of this . . .

She shook off the flash of despair, focusing instead on the bag that Chief Sutter had given her. *I guess the desk is as good as anyplace,* she thought, and tucked it back in the bottom drawer. The recollection of her father—and Bowen's Field—seemed to hasten her out of the cramped room, but before she would leave, she made an abrupt decision.

She tore the poster down and crunched it up in her hands. The gesture provided little satisfaction, but that was better than nothing. She was about to drop it in the small wastebasket by the desk when something caught her eye.

Something inside.

An envelope and a crumpled letter.

Perhaps the only reason she'd noticed them at all was because the items were the only things in the basket.

She picked them out, focusing. . . .

The envelope was addressed to Dwayne, handwritten, not typed. There was no return address; the local postmark was dated one day before Dwayne's death. Junk mail wouldn't be handwritten, but it was obviously something Dwayne had opened, looked at, and immediately discarded.

Her curiosity pecked at her, though she couldn't imagine why; Patricia wasn't ordinarily nosy. *The bastard's dead, so it's not like I'm invading his privacy,* she reasoned.

Paper crinkled as she uncrumpled what she could only guess was a letter, but she saw in a moment that it was not really a letter at all.

Just a sheet of paper with one word inscribed neatly at the top.

Wenden.

(III)

It's heavenly, he thought. He stared up in wonder, drinking up the sight of the stars. *My whole life is heavenly. . . .*

The night couldn't have been more beautiful, nor could his love. The God that he believed in was much more nebulous than the God of most people, but just as real. Wilfrud knew, in fact, that they were all essentially the same, and it was to that great ethereal and omnipresent being that he now offered his unbounded thanks.

Ethel, his wife, puttered in the woods, focused on their task. It was Wilfrud who was the dreamer of the pair, the introspective one, which she often, in her loving way, dismissed as laziness. *But it's only my love that makes me a dreamer,* he thought, and she knew that, of course.

Besides, she was the better diviner.

Divination could be very effective in obtaining knowledge of that which one desired, so long as the practitioners were faithful people. Faith was in the heart, in the soul. Wilfrud and Ethel had been the clan's diviners for decades, since their late teens. They solicited the spirits of nature tonight for nothing more complex than finding honey morels for the weekend's clan banquet. Ethel made a delectable mushroom roux that specifically depended on this rare edible fungus, but they were very difficult to find.

Diviners, however, could find them a little easier than others.

Earlier they'd both prayed over the boiled pig knuckle, and now Ethel meandered about the woods, holding the clean bone in a cupped hand. It was not with anything like tactility by which she read the telltale signal—it would be more like a vibration in her head. She was naked, of course, to further appease the spirits, and Wilfrud's eyes couldn't resist that raw beauty of hers as she stepped through the brambles, sensing the air. Her bare skin shone so white in the moonlight; it looked so perfect. No, neither of them was young anymore, but looking at her now, in the quiet night's glow, Wilfrud got short of breath. He couldn't be more grateful to God for giving him so beautiful a wife.

The decades had blessed her body; she didn't look at all like a woman in her mid-fifties, and the gray had barely touched her long, raven-black hair. Even her bosom barely sagged; her breasts glowed like lambent orbs in the moon's light, centered with large, dark nipples. About her neck hung the pendant he'd made for her when they'd gotten married, a deep blue-and-scarlet pontica stone that diviners and mediums often wore, to maximize their visions. The stone hung between her breasts and seemed to change color when her own passions inflamed. Wilfrud himself wore the cross she'd given him just as long ago: two meticulously carved shavings from an eddo root.

For a moment Wilfrud felt bolted to the ground; he couldn't move; he could only swallow up this nighttime image of her. *Oh, heaven,* he thought. *I am such a lucky man. . . .*

She pivoted on her bare feet, not looking down but staring out into the night, listening for the secrets it would tell her, and then in a second she quickly got down on her knees and bent over. Wilfrud almost collapsed now, his desires reeling. This alternate glimpse of her—kneeling, naked, buttocks jutting—was the last thing Wilfrud needed to see just then. He was supposed to be helping her. . . .

"Oooh, Wilfrud, look!" she nearly squealed in excitement. Her free hand tilled the soft earth between the vee of a tree's roots. "We're finding so many tonight!"

Only a woman after my own heart could be so enthused over finding morels, he realized absurdly. He walked over with his collection bag, tried to focus, but only remained dizzy in the fugue of his passion. Her breasts bobbed when she jerked upright, grinning. She extended her earth-smudged hand, which was full of morels.

"Five more!"

He smiled back, so distracted, and put the morels in the bag, then . . .

He dropped the bag.

"What are you doing?" she exclaimed.

"You know," he whispered, embracing her. He urged her back against the tree, his groin pushing into hers. His voice was parched in his need. "Let me make love to you—right here. In the forest, with the moon and stars watching." His hands ran up her bare sides; sweat misted her skin from the warm night. She felt so soft. . . .

He was tasting her neck, breathing hard already. The jasmine essence in her hair stiffened him at once.

Ethel giggled. Her fingers slipped around his back. She pressed her breasts more urgently against his chest, then raised one leg and half wrapped it around him. "Hmm," she breathed into his ear. "So you want to take me right here, on the ground?"

"Yes, yes!"

"Hmm, let me think about that. . . ."

Her thigh slid up and down his leg. Her hand squeezed his buttocks; then it came back around, dawdled over his chest, then began to pop open his shirt buttons.

"Let me think," she repeated.

Wilfrud was going nuts in his passion now. He kept trying to kiss her, but each time their lips met she jerked away, smiling. Eventually her fingers spidered down his unbuttoned chest, lingered a moment, then proceeded to his crotch, which she slowly—and excruciatingly—began to caress.

"My love, my love, my love," he kept murmuring into her neck. "Please! Now!"

"Hmm, yes, let me think . . ." As her fingers were toying with the top button of his trousers, were just about to open them—

"On second thought," she said abruptly, "no."

Her hand pulled away, and she gently began to push him back.

"Don't torment me!" he pleaded.

"Wilfrud, you're so much fun to tease!" She was grinning at him in the moonlight, her bare breasts standing right out. Then she picked up the collection bag and gave it back to him. "We've got to get back to our gathering." The grin sharpened. "We'll make love later. When we get back home."

Wilfrud groaned, his eyes rolling in agony.

"Thinking about me more will make you want me more," she cooed at him.

"No, it won't! I want you now!"

"Oh, Wilfrud. You're a wonderful husband, but honestly, sometimes you're just like a goat. You can wait a bit longer." And then she disappeared around a stout tree to continue her search.

Wilfrud stood like a horny fool. *Women,* he thought uselessly. *Oh, how they love to make idiots of men.*

He shuffled after her into thicker woods. Denser networks of boughs overhead drained off the moonlight—he could barely see. After a time he wanted to call out but thought better of it: he mustn't distract her while she was divining. Instead, then, he filled his mind back up with images of her nakedness, her breasts and the pebble-hard nipples, all that smooth, warm, white skin that he could indulge in, the nest of down between her legs soft as kitten fur. . . .

Minutes more, and he still hadn't found her. He stood and listened . . . and heard no traces of her footfalls.

"Sweetheart?" he finally called out.

Ethel didn't answer.

"Ethel?"

Another step, then—

"Oof!"

He stumbled and fell.

What a clumsy clod. . . . He must've tripped on a downed limb. But when he put his hand out to push himself up it landed on a bare foot. Alarmed, he patted upward, up a bare leg. . . .

In slivers of moonlight coming though the trees, he saw Ethel lying prone on the forest floor.

"Ethel! Are you all right?" He slid up to her, got an arm around her back to lean her up.

But her head just lolled on her shoulders.

And he noticed blood on her forehead.

No!

Wilfrud felt crazed in the sudden fear. "Ethel! Ethel!" He shook her. "Please be all right!"

A voice snapped behind him. "Don't worry, Squatter. She ain't dead. All's I done is conk her lights out."

In the dimmest darkness, he spotted the figure standing over him. Enraged, Wilfrud attempted to jump up, to fight.

"Yes, sir. Conked the bitch's lights right out with this here beer bottle."

Conk!

The unseen swipe knocked Wilfrud out cold.

It was a harsh gagging sound that Wilfrud regained consciousness to. Grainy, sooty vision began to fire in his eyes; each time his heart beat, a heavy *thud* of pain throbbed in his head. In a few more moments, he could see. . . .

Ethel lay naked on her back in some deep, moonlit clearing. A beefy man humped vigorously between her sprawled legs, his overalls pulled down to show pasty buttocks.

The atrocity raged but for a split second before Wilfrud's mind managed to separate the horror from logic. *What happened to me?* The pain in his head felt like a nail had been driven into his brain. He and Ethel had been gathering morels, hadn't they? Yes, the clan cookout was coming up. And she'd dashed off into darker woods with her divining bone. *That's when I found her,* he remembered. *I tripped over her and—*

That figure . . . All Wilfrud recalled was the stocky shadow before he'd been hit in the head with something, and now he was waking up . . . to this.

Wilfrud realized now that he'd been tied to a tree, his wrists bound behind the trunk with rope, and a shorter length of rope had been tied around his head—between his teeth—to gag him. In horrid glimpses, he noticed that Ethel had been gagged similarly. All either of them could do was croak out some feeble noises, nothing even close to a scream that could be heard by others.

The man raping his wife looked over his shoulder while his fornication didn't miss a beat. "Oh, looky there, sweetie. Your husband's finally woked his old ass up." A chunky face grinned back. "Hey, Wilfrud? You don't mind me raping the holy ever-livin' *shit* outta this old bag you got fer a wife, do ya?"

Wilfrud's eyes bugged in rage; he recognized the portly face at once: Junior, one of the Caudill boys. Wilfrud struggled uselessly against his bonds, the rope digging into his wrists, and when he tried to shout, the only vocal objection he could muster was more of the same croaking.

Worse were Ethel's croaks. Junior was choking her with the leather cord of the pontica stone around her neck. He'd twist the cord down tight till her face darkened and her tongue began to protrude, but just before she'd either pass out or die, he'd release it—to rape her harder. He wanted her alive for the entire ordeal.

But why was he doing this?

And what would happen when he was done?

Junior began to grunt, twisting the pontica cord harder, and then his pelvic thrusts slowed and stopped.

He straggled to his feet, hitched up the overalls, and dusted himself off. "Ain't exactly the best piece a' ass I've had, but not bad fer an old box. What is this bitch, Wilfrud? About sixty? Me, I prefer 'em a tad younger, like about ten, but in a pinch? Any piece a' ass is better than none, huh?"

Junior belted out a piglike noise that sufficed for a laugh, but then his eyes darted back down to Ethel, who now lay utterly still. "Aw, shit! Don't tell me she's *fuckin'* dead! I need her still kickin' for the rest a' the party !" He dropped to his knees, slapped her face several times, then put an ear to her bare chest to listen for a heartbeat. "Whew!" he said next. "Ya lucked out, Wilfrud. Her ticker's still tickin'." He stood back up. "Let's give her a splash or two a' water in the face, to spark her up. . . ."

Wilfrud roared in his throat through the gag, surging against the bonds. Junior had opened his fly and was now urinating liberally into Ethel's face. The revolting process did indeed revive her, soaking her.

"Well, there goes another six-pack!"

By now Wilfrud was oblivious to the pain of the flesh around his wrists grinding away. He brokenly barked out through his gag, "Cut me loose! Cut me loose!"

Junior zipped back up. "What's that, Wilfrud? Cain't rightly understand ya, what with the gag. Oh! You want me to cut ya loose?" Another piglike guffaw. "Come on! Why in tarnation would I wanna do that?"

Now Junior leaned against a tree, arms casually crossed. "You don't even know this, Wilfrud, but in yer own little way you n' this creepy old tramp are playin' a part in a *big* plan that'll make things around here a damn sight better fer everybody." He scratched his belly. "Well, I should say *almost* everybody, 'cos things just got a damn sight worse fer you and the little missus." Junior looked up at the moon in the sky. "And I'm afraid it's gettin' late. Time for this party to end, don't ya think?"

Ethel shuddered in the dirt, hacking up urine through the gag. Without a moment's hesitation, Junior reached behind the tree and pulled out an inordinately large fire ax, then stepped up, parted his legs, hoisted it up over his head in a great arc—

"Nooo!" Wilfrud gagged.

—and—

Thhhhwunk!

—dropped the massive blade into Ethel's belly. Then—

Thhhwunk! Thhhwunk!

—two more downward plunges of the blade cut her naked body in half in a straight line just above her hips.

Her bare heels thunked in the soil, white legs quivering. The upper half convulsed, back trying to arch reflexively.

Wilfrud was choking on his tongue, straining ever harder against his bonds, but all for nothing. He choked out some final, faulty bellows as the whites of his eyes hemorrhaged red in outrage.

Junior grinned, his own eyes beaming down. He set the ax aside. "How's that for a piece a' work?"

Ethel's legs finally fell still, while the upper half of her body remained miraculously alive. She actually managed to flip herself over and began to crawl toward Junior.

"Bitch's got some spunk; I'll give her that," Junior remarked. He grabbed the pendant cord, hoisted her up, then looped the cord over the crook of a broken branch. He stood back to watch as Ethel slowly strangled against the tree, innards uncoiling.

"God, that was fun. . . ."

By now Wilfrud's horror and exertion left him limp. Junior unsheathed a buck knife and approached. "Her ticket's punched, so I guess it's time to punch yours too, Wilfrud."

"Uuugh!" went Wilfrud.

Junior pigstuck him low with the knife, one deep jab just below the navel.

"But I got tell ya," Junior went on, "all this choppin' and chokin' and stabbin's got my dog barkin' again, if you know what I mean." He chuckled, showing brown teeth. "And there ain't exactly anyone around who's gonna call me a pervert, huh?"

Wilfrud groaned in the lowest agony, blood and bile eddying from his wound.

Junior shrugged and approached the sprawled legs on the ground. "So I just say . . . what the hell!"

He lowered his overalls again, then crawled between the legs, and this was what Wilfrud Hild got to watch for the remaining ten minutes it took him to die.

Six

(I)

Looks like she's sleeping in, Patricia realized. It seemed understandable. Patricia had risen early to the sound of cicadas and chirping finches. She'd left her window open last night, a luxury she was beginning to enjoy—the fresh night air flowing over her as she slept, and no police sirens and ambulances, like at home. And unlike yesterday morning, she didn't waken feeling guilty and embarrassed. She recalled snippets of intense sexual dreams, but this time her frolics didn't involve making love to Ernie in front of her husband. Simply strangers this time, and dreaming of strangers didn't constitute infidelity. *Just a bunch of silly, dirty dreams,* she dismissed them. *Everybody has them. Byron has them. I'm not going to feel guilty.* It was a solid resolve to begin the day with.

But at one point during the night, had she awakened and imagined herself being watched by a peeper through the window? She even recalled masturbating again, to a delicious climax, but that had to have been a dream too.

And dreams are harmless, so I'm not going to stress over it.

After she'd dressed for the day, she noticed Ernie's door open, and when she peeked inside she found it empty. That was when she went upstairs to check on Judy—to find her still heavily asleep. Last night she'd eventually passed out, but maybe now that Dwayne's ashes were officially scattered, Judy could put her despair behind her and focus on pursuing the positive things in her life. *I can only hope,* Patricia thought, and gently closed the door.

Back downstairs, she rejected the idea of making herself breakfast, and instead headed out to the backyard. Something she couldn't identify seemed to be pushing her out of the house, and she could only suppose she was ignoring what "home" had always reminded her of, and, in place of that, she was enjoying the beautiful natural environment here. This was opposite of the city; this was refreshingly different from what she'd grown so used to looking at every day in D.C. She stepped out onto the fieldstone path and stood stunned for a moment. A cloudless sky hung overhead, the clearest blue, which only made the sun seem more vibrant. The patches of grass between the flower beds almost glowed, they were so green, and the flowers themselves were explosions of razor-sharp reds, yellows, and violets. *Yeah, I guess coming back home this time isn't going to be as bad as I thought. . . .* Perhaps she was evolving past her trauma, and was proving Dr. Sallee wrong in his insistence that she should avoid Agan's Point at all costs. Racy dreams, an inexplicable burst of sexual awareness, masturbating far more than usual?

This was so unlike her, but today she was feeling better and better about it.

She kicked her sandals off to stride barefoot across the more expansive tracts of grass farther off in the backyard. *I don't know where I'm going and . . . I don't need to know,* she realized. Finally a day without an agenda.

Then she thought: *The Point.*

Why not? She'd spend the morning walking around the Point.

More stretches of deliriously green grass took her away from the house. Stands of high trees seemed to funnel her down. If anything the Point appeared more beautiful than she could ever remember it, and it seemed much larger. Agan's Point could be described as a wedge of verdant land that shoved itself out into Virginia's widest estuary off the Chesapeake Bay, while the other edge of the wedge was determined by a sprawling river. She hopped over several meager creeks, noticing salamanders and toads, then found herself wandering the path that marked the river side of the Point. Across the water, next, she could see several office trailers and what appeared to be foundation molds for the construction project that would hopefully instill the local economy with more money from a new, well-heeled community of residents. Nothing seemed to be going on at the project today, though: cement mixers sat static, tractors and backhoes unmanned. When a door on one of the office trailers opened, a man walked out toward a parked pickup truck, and Patricia could tell by the short, bright-blond hair and purposeful gait that it was the man she'd met last night at the reception, Gordon Felps, the executive of the entire construction endeavor. *Not quite sure what to make of him,* she thought. Her sister clearly found him enlivening, but Patricia's own first impression was one of suspicion. *He's a businessman trying to throw money at Judy, to get her land,* she reminded herself. *I don't care how much money he's got . . . I don't trust him.* She half frowned and half smiled at herself. *But then again, I'm a lawyer. I'm not supposed to trust anybody, because nobody trusts me.* Across the river the distant form of Gordon Felps paused at the open truck door, spotted her, and waved. Patricia put on her best fake smile and waved back.

A flock of crows squawked overhead, and at the crest of the riverbed she noticed butterflies sitting idly atop tall blades of grass. Down here near the water the always-heard but seldom-seen cicadas flew to and fro in dramatic numbers. Patricia felt staggered by this outburst of raw nature that she'd banished from her mind long ago. But then she frowned at the dichotomy. *Nature untouched right here . . . and another condo project over there.* It was the way of the world, she supposed, and as a real estate attorney she was as much a culprit as Felps.

She dawdled on, the sun in her face. A half mile of ambling through the woods eventually brought her to the widest spur of the Point—Squatterville was the area's nickname. There, surrounded by trees, was their little plantation, so to speak, a crude but close-knit community of shacks, tin sheds, and age-old trailers. Set in the background stood the Stanherd house; it was the oldest dwelling on the Point, and it looked it, dating back to the original plantation days when Virginia broke from the Union. A rickety wraparound porch defined the home's shape of sloping angles and high, peaked rooftops. A century of periodic whitewash left its wood plank walls more gray than white, shingles blown off in storms had been replaced with cedar slats and tar, and most of the functional shutters had long since been nailed shut. Judy had no use for the house, so she let Everd Stanherd and his wife live there for nothing, along with several other elder couples of the clan. Judy, in fact, charged no rent of any kind to any of the Squatters; nor did she charge for electricity—which was wired to every dwelling—nor water or sewage, which was provided by the communal washhouse where Squatters could shower, get water for their homes, and go to the bathroom. It wasn't much, but it was better than welfare, and the Squatters themselves couldn't have seemed more content with their lives here, however unsophisticated those lives were.

Looks like happy simplicity to me, she mused, looking down at the ramshackle community. Women were taking laundry out to hang on myriad clotheslines, chatting, laughing amongst themselves as they worked. Patricia thought a moment then. Was it really happy simplicity, or ignorance and oblivion that milled before her? It was easy for an elitist attitude to dismiss the Squatters as subcitizens with no education and unable to achieve anything more in life. *Maybe this happy simplicity is just holding them back, blocking them from any real achievement.*

It was an idealistic concern, to say the least. *You're a metropolitan lawyer, Patricia,* she told herself. *Don't pretend to be a sociologist. . . .*

She saw no men down among the quiet network of trailers and shacks, but of course she wouldn't. Most of the male Squatters would be out on the water right now, hauling in today's take on the crabbing boats Judy provided. *Maybe it's just like anything else,* she considered. *Give and take. Judy gives them a free place to live, and they work to keep her company profitable.* Judy owned the boats, the land, the processing plant and warehouse and delivery trucks—everything. And the Squatters worked it all for her.

A closer look showed children prancing around their mothers and/or grandmothers, squealing with innocent exuberance as they played tag amid the sheet-flapping labyrinth of clotheslines. Older children emerged from the woods with armfuls of wild berries, edible greens, duck eggs, and even rabbits and squirrels they'd caught in traps handmade by their fathers. Other children returned with stray firewood they'd culled from the forest; though the shacks and trailers all had electricity, the Squatters often preferred to cook their family meals outside in cauldrons braced over communal fires and long barbecue pits. What Patricia was looking at now seemed like a hidden crosshatch commune that gladly let the modern world slide over them without notice. Primitive yet undeniably efficient, tribal yet organized. It was a system that worked.

She traipsed down the hillock toward an outer footpath, and when she turned the corner around the washhouse, several Squatter boys—ten to twelve years old, they appeared—broke off in the opposite direction the instant they noticed her. *What was that all about?* she wondered without much interest. It was as though she'd surprised them; they ran off the way children did when caught doing something bad. *But what?* She made her way along the white-painted brick wall that formed the rear of the washhouse. The long, clean wall stood unblemished, except . . .

Hmm . . .

A squint showed her there *was* a blemish of sorts. She walked up closer. *What is that?* The wall seemed to bear a single pock; the closer she got, the more she thought she heard something. A steady hiss.

And voices?

Patricia wasn't sure.

She looked right at the "blemish." It was a hole, not even a half inch wide, drilled into the mortar between two of the wall's cinder blocks.

And she realized the hiss was a running shower.

A peephole, she knew. She put her eye to the hole and looked in. Three hardy Squatter girls in their late teens stood in the long shower room, sudsing themselves with soap, and chatting and giggling obliviously. This would explain the fleeing youngsters; Patricia had caught them spying on the older girls inside, and though she didn't know the boys at all, she was certain they knew who *she* was: the sister of the woman who gave them a place to live and provided jobs for their parents.

No doubt this peephole had been used for some time for such shenanigans; she couldn't help but notice what could only be tracks of dried semen streaking the wall beneath the hole. She smiled to herself then, amused. *Boys will be boys,* she realized.

She walked on, but for some reason felt distracted now. By what? The thrumming cicada trills seemed to wash in and out of her head, and in some strange way urged her to recall the hiss of the shower.

Peepholes. Peeping. Voyeurs.

It was harmless enough, sure—just a few boys about to enter puberty, following their hormonal curiosities. So what was bothering her?

My dream, she remembered then.

Last night she'd dreamed of being spied on herself,

hadn't she? Only slivers of the dream seemed vivid, while most of it had turned to fog by now. *I dreamed that someone was watching me from the window,* she remembered, *while I was touching myself.* The more she thought about it, the more clearly it came to mind. She remembered being even more turned on when she'd realized someone was watching; her voyeur remained unidentified, yet the longer she knew he was watching, the more aroused she became, and it hadn't taken long for her climax to overwhelm her.

The only thing that remained unclear was the sequence of events. *Was I masturbating in the dream,* she asked herself, *or was I masturbating for real, after I woke up from the dream?*

Probably the latter, she suspected now. The spate of dirty dreams? Sex with Ernie while her husband watched (more exhibitionism)? Sex with strangers? The sudden flux of heightened sexual moods since she'd arrived? To the most secret part of herself, she admitted it all now. She couldn't recall a time when she'd felt so sexually stoked than over the last two days, and it only reminded her of the senselessness of it all. Agan's Point symbolized her rape—the ugliest and most *un*arousing thing to ever happen to her. *So why don't I feel unaroused now that I'm back?*

Her musings stretched. She couldn't help it; she couldn't get it out of her head. Now she imagined *herself* in the Squatters' shower room, alone, and somehow knowing she was being watched from the peephole. That knowledge made her desire burn harder. The fantasy cocooned her; she could not only see herself standing naked in the stark-white, brick-walled room, she could feel her hand gliding the bar of soap between and around her breasts, then down her belly and up between her legs. Soon she was dressed in a suit of lather, her pink nipples and the tuft of soft red pubic hair the only things breaking the surface of the soap's white froth. She stared fast at the hole in the wall; some ethereal force seemed to emanate from it like a wizard's totem. Now her hands were sliding all over herself—she was no longer washing; she was making love to herself, her nerves winding up, her nipples engorging. Then she stepped back into the cool spray, the lather sloughing off her skin down into the drain between her feet.

In the hole she could see the unblinking eye. . . .

Come in here, she panted to the hole. She parted her legs. Her hands splayed her sex. *Whoever you are, come in here. . . .*

She closed her eyes, waiting, her fingers teasing herself. She was almost there already. Her breasts felt hot, twice their normal size. The bladelike sensations between her legs nearly toppled her over, and then from behind the large calloused hands of her unseen voyeur slipped around under her arms to her breasts, and when they squeezed she began to—

"Howdy, Patricia. You're sure up early."

The fantasy snapped like a broomstick across someone's knee. Patricia spun in place, bristling in stifled shock. Ernie was striding across the grass, jeaned and workbooted, a toolbox in tow.

"Ernie. I didn't see you coming," she faltered.

He hoisted the box. "I was just cuttin' across. Judy wanted me to go to Squatterville to turn the electricity off on a few of the shacks."

Patricia had barely recovered from her startlement.

That was the most vivid daydream of my life! She brought a stray hand to the bottom of her throat. *I hope I'm not blushing. . . .* The fantasy hadn't lasted long enough for her to see the face of her imaginary peeping Tom.

Had she hoped it was Ernie?

He chuckled, looking cockeyed at her. "You okay?"

"Daydreaming," she muttered back. "What were you saying? You had to turn *off* the electricity?"

"Just to three of the Squatter shacks. No point in electricity going into an empty place."

"What do you mean?"

He set the toolbox down and crossed his arms. "Well, things ain't changed much since you moved outta the Point. Back then, a' course, there weren't quite as many Squatters. But unlike back then, it seems that a lot of 'em are leavin'."

"Leaving—as in leaving the Point?" she asked.

Ernie nodded. Somehow the streak of sweat going down the center of his tight T-shirt struck her as sexy, and the way his long hair was slightly disheveled, like he'd just gotten out of bed. "Three of 'em have left just in the past week, and eight or ten more since the beginning of the month. Kinda strange . . . or maybe not, really. Just 'cos I love livin' on the Point don't mean everyone does. Look at you."

"But where did these Squatters go?" she asked the logical question.

Ernie shrugged his strong shoulders. "They didn't leave forwardin' addresses, if that's what you mean. Most a' the folks who left was younger Squats, late teens, early twenties. Growin' pains and all that, I guess. It ain't unusual for kids to wanna leave home to check other pastures."

No, it's not, she realized.

"But me?" Ernie continued. His long hair gusted in a sudden breeze. "I love it here. Cain't see myself ever leavin'. The city ain't for me. I went to Roanoke once, couldn't believe it. The air stank, the traffic was awful, everything was expensive. I don't know how you stand it in D.C."

"It has its ups and downs," she said. "But I'm actually liking it a lot here this time. I didn't last time I was back."

"Oh, yeah. When Judy 'n' Dwayne got married. Well, that's all over 'n' done with. I'm hopin' Judy gets out of her funk soon."

"Me, too."

"She got drunk as a skunk last night, but you could tell—even as heartbroke as she was—there was a lot of worries and hassles gone from her life."

That was good to hear.

"You just out for a mornin' walk?" he asked her.

"Yes. It's been so long since I've had a good look at the Point. It's much more beautiful than I remember."

"I gotta head down to the pier to check 'n' see if the new crab traps got delivered. Why don't'cha come with me?"

"Sure," she said, and followed him down the trail. They went in and out of several stands of pine trees. Around them the fields behind Squatterville blazed green in the sun. The scenery lulled Patricia, but not enough to take away all of that irritating sexual edge left over from the daydream. As she walked behind Ernie, she had to consciously force herself not to look at him: the toned, tan arms, the tapered back, the strong legs. *This damn place is becoming an aphrodisiac,* she thought, *and there's no reason why.* She tried to clear her head, following on.

"I love that smell off the bay," he observed. "Salty, clean."

"Mmm," she replied, taking a breath herself.

"No pollution, like everywhere else on the bay. Christ, most other places think the bay's just a place to dump their garbage."

Yeah, like D.C., Patricia had to agree in her thoughts. Now, through breaks in the trees, she could see the mirrorlike shine off the water, and, high in the sky, the finches and crows were replaced by seagulls and pipers. Another few minutes of walking took them down to the town dock, where a dozen piers jutted out into the water. Some wooden buildings stood up front, where several Squatter men looked up, nodded briefly, then resumed their tasks of sorting rigging ropes and stacking bushel baskets. Ernie briefly walked to one of the dock buildings, grabbed a clipboard, and began counting what looked to be several dozen brand-new crab traps that had been stacked there: simple chicken-wire boxes dipped in black latex to prevent rust. A cylindrical compartment inside each trap held the bait, and then each trap was dropped out in the bay, marked by a floating buoy. The boats would all go out as early as four in the morning, drop their traps, then dredge oysters and clams for a few hours, after which they'd haul up their traps, empty them, and size the crabs. Almost all of the boats were gone now, but Patricia did notice a few moored to the piers—long, wide, shallow dingies with little motors at the back.

She walked over to Ernie, who was still busy counting traps. "I'm always reading in the papers about how bad the crab harvest is in the bay. What's so special about Agan's Point?"

Ernie pointed outward, where the bay stretched several miles across. "Out there? The current's too strong, not many crabs." Then he pointed to a series of sand berms that could be seen just breaking the surface a mile or so out. "But those berms cut the current way down in the Point, which is ideal for blue crabs. Then there's the freshwater runoff, keeps the water cooler and lowers the salinity. That's why Agan's Point crabs are bigger 'n' heavier than crabs anywhere else. The perfect environment."

"So why don't the big commercial crabbers come out here?"

"It's not worth their time or money. They have to come too far, and their boats are too big. Agan's Point waters are too rocky 'n' shallow for their big rigs. So they all go south 'n' leave us alone. The Squatters use flatboats to get around these shallow waters, and they always bring in the same number of bushels a day, and not one more than that, ever. The rest of the bay's been fished out, but not Agan's Point. The Squatters stick to their daily haul limit and never break it; that way there'll always be plenty a' crabs. We only sell our meat to the better restaurants and markets in the county, and that's it, and because Agan's Point crabs taste so much better than the other stuff, our buyers pay more per pound."

"What makes them better?" Patricia asked. Now she was sitting at the edge of the pier, waggling her feet in the cool water.

"The meat's sweeter 'cos the salinity's perfect and the water's cooler 'n' cleaner. It's that simple." Ernie hung up his clipboard, apparently satisfied with the trap delivery. "And another reason the company's got a higher profit margin per pound is 'cos of the lower overhead." He pointed to another pier, where several men sat down at tables next to some large picnic-type coolers. "Most crabbers use chicken necks fer bait, but what ya need to know about the Squatters is that they don't waste *anything*."

Patricia didn't get his meaning; she leaned up higher from where she sat, squinting at the men. Now she heard a continuous series of *thwacking* sounds. . . . "What are they doing?"

"Like what I was sayin'," Ernie went on, leaning against a stack of traps. "The Squatters live off the land like nobody's business; they don't spend a dime on food unless they need to."

Patricia's bosom jutted as she leaned more urgently to see what the men at the tables were doing. "I still don't—"

"It ain't just crabs the Squatters trap; it's everything. Rabbit, possum, muskrat, squirrel. When they're done guttin' and trimmin' what they catch to eat, they chop up what's left. Scraps, guts, feet, 'n' tails. And that's what they use fer crab bait."

Patricia shuddered a moment when she finally realized what the men were doing: chopping up animal scraps and innards with butcher knives and then depositing the portions into plastic jars punctured by holes. Each jar was then put into a cooler.

"Them jars there?" Ernie explained. "When the boats go out tomorrow, they put one a' them jars in each trap. Best crab bait ya can get. And it's free."

It sounded very practical—but grisly. "I can understand rabbits and squirrels—I ate plenty of that when I was growing up," Patricia noted. "But you said the Squatters even eat *muskrat* and *possum?"*

"Oh, sure. I do, too. Muskrat's tough to dress, but it tastes like ham, and on a possum the only thing ya eat is the back strap. Tastes like the best pork tenderloin ya ever had if ya marinate it right, and the Squatters know how to do it." He tapped her on the shoulder, looking down. "You'll be able to try some. This weekend is the Squatters' celebration feast. You'll think you walked into the county fair, and they'll be cookin' up everything. These people know how to cook."

Her feet in the water relaxed her. She looked up at him, frowning. "Ernie, I don't mind eating a little squirrel and rabbit, and crabs are fine too, but now possum and muskrat? That's roadkill, if you ask me."

"You'll try some," he assured her. "One thing I remember about you from way back is that you were always adventurous."

"Not *that* adventurous," she declared. It occurred to her in the briefest moment that her position—sitting down at the pier's edge as he stood over her—afforded Ernie a considerable view of her cleavage and possibly even her nipples, given the leeway of her loose ivory blouse. Again, she hadn't put a bra on, and she'd been oblivious to that fact until just this second. But when she glanced back up at him to say something, he was looking out at the water, not at her. *What the hell is my brain up to now?* she asked herself. *It's almost like I want him to be looking at me . . . but if he's not, I'm disappointed. I'm so screwed-up!* Then her original question resurfaced. "You said they're having a *celebration* feast?"

"Yeah. Every month—every half-moon, whatever that means. They got some weird ways."

The Squatters were notoriously superstitious but . . . *Half-moons?* she wondered. "So what are they celebrating?"

"Life, I guess—in their own way. Nature, the crab harvest, the food they get from the woods. But when ya think about it, it's the same thing as our Thanksgiving."

Patricia supposed so. All societies, even today, seemed to have some ritual of giving thanks for the abundance of the land. "What religion are they, though?" she asked next. "I never quite got it."

"I asked Everd once, and he said they're worshipers of nature and love, or some such, and left it at that. But then ya see a lot of 'em wearin' crosses along with all those knickknacks and stones around their necks. Their own kind of Christianity, I think it is, mixed with other stuff."

How interesting. Like Cuban Santeria and the obia of the Caribbean, these religions amalgamated old African folk magic with traces of Roman Catholicism and Protestantism. Even Haitian voodoo borrowed patron saintdom and idolatry from Christianity. And now that Ernie had mentioned it, she looked back at the men chopping up the crab bait and noticed that one of them wore around his neck what appeared to be a cross made from small animal bones.

"See, right out there," Ernie said, and pointed out to the bay.

Patricia focused out on the water. At the end of the berm, near the inlet's mouth, she spotted a wide plank sticking up out of the water; on its face someone had painted a cross.

"Everd supposedly blesses the Point every morning," Ernie said.

But Patricia was still looking out. There were actually two planks, she noticed now, the second sunk directly into the sand berm. But it wasn't a cross painted on it; it was some sort of a squiggly design. "What's that second one there?"

"Some kind of clan good-luck sign," Ernie said. "Don't rightly know exactly."

More superstition, Patricia realized.

One of the Squatters approached them, a knobby-kneed man in his fifties, with a sun-weathered face and the trademark coarse, jet-black hair of the Squatters. He seemed to be bearing the lid of a bushel basket as a waitress would with serving tray.

"Howdy, Regert," Ernie greeted him.

Regert, Patricia thought. *What a strange name.*

The man kept his eyes downcast, the way servants wouldn't look directly at their masters, another thing that had always struck Patricia as strange. "Miss Patricia, Mr. Ernie." He returned the greeting with a curt nod. He set the basket lid down on a dock table. "We made ya both a clan breakfast. Hope you like it. It's a blessing from the land."

"That's mighty nice of ya, Regert," Ernie said, then to Patricia: "This is great; come 'n' have some."

Patricia got back up to look. Two tin tumblers of liquid sat on the tray, along with a plate of shucked oysters and a bowl of . . .

What are those? she wondered. *Prunes? Figs?*

"Try our home-brewed *ald,* miss," Regert said, passing her one of the tumblers.

"Thank you, Regert," she said, mystified. Ice cubes floated in the tumbler full of a thin pink liquid.

Ernie took a glass for himself. "You could almost call it a Squatter highball."

Patricia rolled her eyes. "I'm not going to have a cocktail at nine in the morning!"

But Regert sternly responded, "The clan do not imbibe, miss. Our bodies are gifts from on high, temples of the spirit. Everd the *sawon* says so, and we follow his word. The clan will not disgrace our bodies with alcohol, the elixir of the devil."

Patricia was amused. *This guy sounds more like a Southern Baptist.*

"There ain't no booze in it," Ernie assured her. "It's stuff they make from roots 'n' bark, stuff like that."

It didn't look terribly appetizing. "Well, you're the one who said I was adventurous," she dismissed, and took a sip.

Her lips pursed at once. *It doesn't look good, and guess what? It tastes like it looks.*

Ernie laughed and downed his in one swig. Patricia elected not to offend Regert's hospitality, so she just said, "It's . . . very interesting."

"Tastes like chalk at first, but give it a minute."

Patricia would give it more than that. Then she noticed that Regert, like some of the others, also wore a cross pendant, which appeared to be made from tiny vine twistings, and a dark stone hung from a second pendant. By now she had to ask, "That's an interesting cross, Regert. So you're a Christian?"

Regert nodded, still not making eye contact. "Yes, miss, the clan believe in God's only Son, and in the earth that He has bestowed and in the deliverance that He has promised, and in the earth and in the water and in the holy universe."

Now that's *a mouthful,* Patricia thought, nearly bidden to laugh. *The holy universe?*

"And earlier you referred to Everd as—what did you say? A *sawon?* That means he's, like, the governor of the clan, right?"

"No, miss. Only God is our governor. Everd is our seer."

The comment piqued her. "You mean like a psychic person, a visionary? He sees the future?"

Regert seemed on guard for some reason, less enthused to answer. "No, miss. The *sawon* sees the paths that God wants us to travel in life, and he shows us those paths."

Patricia was about to ask him to elaborate, but he quickly nodded again with the same downcast eyes, and excused himself. "Good graces be with you both, but I must return to my work, which is a gift from on high."

And then he was walking away.

"Thanks, Regert," Ernie said after him.

Patricia watched the man amble back to one of the dock sheds.

"Yeah, they definitely got their own ways," Ernie commented.

Patricia agreed. "They're very gracious people, but . . ." She slid her tumbler away. "I can *not* drink any more of this."

"You'll have some oysters, though," Ernie said, eyes alighting on the plate. "Remember how you 'n' me used to see who could eat the most when we was kids?"

Patricia felt touched by the memory. "Of course."

"And you always won them contests, if I remember right."

"Yeah, I guess I did." But oysters, like crabs, she'd always loved; she'd practically been raised on them. "These are huge," she remarked, looking at the sprawl of six-inch shells on the plate.

"The Squatters dredge a couple a' bushels every morning." Ernie slurped three in a row raw off the shell. "Then we sell 'em to a few of the local markets for two bucks a dozen; then the markets resell 'em for about four."

Patricia sucked one down, curling her toes, it was so fresh and briny. "In D.C. they'll charge close to twenty dollars for a dozen oysters in a restaurant. And these are ten times better." When she turned up the next shell to swallow the oyster meat, a gout of juice ran down her chin and neck. *Great. Now I'll smell like oysters all day.*

Ernie ate a few more. "I never did figure out if it was true what they say, though."

Patricia stalled over the comment. Earlier she'd been abstracting that Agan's Point seemed to be working some obscure aphrodisiac effect on her, and now here was Ernie—whom she'd already had a sexual dream about—mentioning the same supposed effect of oysters. But did he mean anything more? *He had a crush on me for years,* she thought. *And we never did anything. We never even kissed.* "I think that's just an old wives' tale," she finally said. Her next oyster spilled more juice on her. "Jeez!"

"Gettin' more on yourself than in your mouth." Ernie laughed.

This time the juice ran down her chin and continued right down into her cleavage. She felt spaced out for a moment, and suddenly she was fantasizing again: Ernie pulling her blouse off without a word, and licking the delectable juice out from between her breasts. Next she imagined herself fully naked, right here on the dock, more and more juice running salty rivulets down her stomach, filling her navel, trickling down. . . .

And Ernie licking it all away.

God, she thought, feeling flushed.

The oysters were gone now, and Ernie addressed the last object on the bushel lid. "Naw, I don't know about oysters, and I don't know about these, neither. But just ask any Squatter. They'll tell ya these are the best aphrodisiacs in the world."

Patricia was glad for the distraction; she looked at the bowl. "Figs?"

"Naw. They're pepper-fried cicadas, and the ones we got here are the biggest of 'em all. They dust 'em in wild pepper, then fry 'em in oil."

Patricia simply shook her head. "Ernie? There's no way on earth I would *ever* eat one of those things. They're *bugs*. And I don't eat *bugs*."

Ernie grabbed a handful from the bowl, munching on them. They crunched like fried wontons. "Aw, don't chicken out. Believe it or not, they taste kinda like asparagus, but crunchy."

"Bugs don't taste like asparagus; asparagus tastes like asparagus," Patricia said. "I'm not eating bugs."

Ernie ignored her. "You grab one by the wings, like this. . . ." His finger plucked one up. "Then pull it off with your teeth. But don't eat the wings. They're like wire." He demonstrated, eating another, then plucked one up for her. He held it right before her mouth.

Patricia shook her head with vigor, insisting, "No!" Then she closed her lips tight.

"Come on. Like the Squatters say, it's part a' God's bounty. Don't be a chicken. Won't kill ya to try somethin' new."

Patricia smirked. *Shit. I can't believe what I'm about to do,* she thought, then ate the turd-looking thing off his finger. It crunched between her molars, but actually tasted interesting, not repulsive. "Not bad," she admitted.

"Good. Have another."

"No! One bug's my limit. Now let's go!"

Ernie chuckled as they walked off the pier, the sun beaming on the water behind them. "What's that building there?" she asked of a long white-brick structure just up from the dock. "Another washhouse?"

"Naw, that's the line."

"The what?"

"The new pickers' building. We call it the line."

Patricia noticed small windows and a number of window-unit air conditioners. "It looks new."

"Three, four years old. In fact, I think Judy told me once that it was you who lent her the money to fix things up. So she had that built. You remember the old pickers' shack that your daddy built, don't ya?"

"Yeah, and now that you mention it, it was . . . a shack," she said, thinking back on the old rickety open-aired building. Squatter women would sit together at long wooden tables inside, monotonously picking the meat out of hundreds of crabs each per day. "Can we look inside?"

"Sure. In a way, it's yours." He opened a metal door, after which cool air gusted out.

A peek inside showed Patricia why they called it "the line." *Like a production line,* she thought.

Over a dozen Squatter women—from eighteen to sixty—sat at long wooden tables. Cooked crabs would be dumped in the middle of the tables, and from there the women would dismantle the spiny, bright-orange creatures and begin to pick the meat out of them. Each woman wielded a small, unsharpened knife with which she'd tease chunks of the white meat from intricate inner shell channels. The meat would be flicked into plastic one-pound containers, which, when filled, would be scurried back to a walk-in refrigerator by a younger Squatter girl. Another girl would hurry back and forth, removing the shell debris.

"They do it so fast," Patricia remarked.

The women's hands pried apart and demeated each crab completely, in only minutes.

"They get a lot of practice," Ernie said. "I can pick a pound pretty quick myself, but nothing like them. Couple of our girls can fill a pound tub in ten minutes. We wanted to enter 'em into the annual pickin' contest up in Maryland, but they wouldn't go, and that's a damn shame, 'cos they woulda won."

"Why didn't they want to go?"

"They said it was ungodly, or some such. To them, crabs, like all food, are some kind of gift from the heavens, and shouldn't be turned into a sport."

More weird philosophy, Patricia thought.

She couldn't imagine more tedious work. *Picking crabs all day, every day?* But as she looked inside, the women couldn't have appeared more content, chatting quietly amongst themselves as their hands and fingers blurred through the process. In the background—barely audible—an evangelical radio station murmured oral missives from God.

"Just wait'll the Squatter cookout," Ernie promised. "They got their own recipes for crab cakes, Newburg, and cream a' crab soup that're better than anything you've ever had, even in them upscale D.C. restaurants."

Patricia believed it, and she could even remember a bit of it from her childhood.

Ernie closed the door and showed her back to the path. "Guess we better be headin' back to the house—

er, I should, at least. Gotta cut the grass. What'choo got planned today?"

"Nothing, really. I'll go back with you, check on Judy. Then I might go into town, or maybe go for a walk in the woods." This was another refreshing aspect of being back: not having to follow any agenda. But she knew she should at least check her e-mail and give the firm a quick call. Then she thought: *And Byron! I haven't called him in a day and a half!* In fact, she'd actually spoken to him only once or twice since she'd arrived. *He'll be worried....* But when she patted the back pocket of her shorts, it occurred to her that she'd left her cell phone back in her room.

The tree-lined path wended further upward; spangles of heat draped across her face and chest from the sun pouring in through leafy branches above them.

"There's another one," Ernie said without stopping. He pointed to a tree as he walked on.

But Patricia paused.

A small plank, painted white, had been nailed to the tree in what appeared to be a crude decoration. But out here? In the woods? It seemed so peculiar. A simple but ornate drawing adorned the plank, some squiggles and slashes; they seemed symmetrical, in some disordered way.

"Another one of their good-luck signs?" she asked.

Ernie had stopped just ahead of her, looking back. "Yeah. Ya see 'em every now and then out in the woods. The woods are blessed land to the Squatters."

Patricia peered closer at the design. "It just looks so . . . unusual, doesn't it?"

"I guess," Ernie said without much interest. "It's more creepy than anything, if ya ask me."

Creepy . . . Yes, she supposed it was. The color of the

paint used to form the design was odd, too: a tannish slate. *Is it even paint?* she wondered, touching it. Her finger came away smudged almost black. *Doesn't feel like paint. More like crayon.*

Then she realized what it reminded her of. *Last night . . .* The note she'd found in the garbage, addressed to Dwayne. Since then she'd paid no mind to the weird sheet of paper she'd found, the sheet with one word written on it. . . .

Wenden.

Was it a name? She could look in the phone book but . . . *Why?* There was no reason for her to care, so why did it seem to bother her now? The word looked as though it had been written in some kind of thin-lined chalk, similar to this good-luck sign on the tree.

"What'choo doing?" Ernie asked with a smile. "Hopin' some a' that Squatter good luck'll rub off on ya?"

"Maybe," she said, and broke away.

But Ernie was right. The design was . . . creepy.

A narrow creek broke the path, its crystal water burbling. Ernie stepped over it in one easy stride; then Patricia hopped across herself. She sighed as her mind cleared—a rarefied luxury for a city attorney—and concentrated only on the cicada throbs, the babbling creeks around them, and the steady crunch of Ernie's boots as he strode onward. This odd sequence of sounds and sensations seemed to tranquilize her as effectively as a low dose of Valium.

Ernie stopped and turned around. "Well, here's a problem."

"What?"

Another creek crossed the trail, several yards in girth and full of jagged, algae-covered stones.

Then it occurred to Patricia that she was barefoot.

"You don't wanna cut'cher feet all up on them rocks," Ernie said.

Patricia laughed. "Ernie, I don't think I'm quite the city priss you take me for. It won't kill me to walk barefoot through a creek." She grinned, about to take her first careful step onto the stones. "Of course, you could always carry me."

She'd said it as a joke, and was completely taken by surprise when he grabbed her and picked her up. "I was only kidding!" she exclaimed.

"Ain't no trouble." He chuckled, hefting her. "Us country boys're strong. Feels to me like you don't weigh much more than a bag a' peanut shells anyway."

"You say the sweetest things, Ernie," she joked back. "Now, if you'd said I weigh more than a grand piano, I'd know it was time to join Weight Watchers."

He carried her easily with one arm bracing her back, the other under her thighs. Her feet jounced in the air with each step, while her own arm clung fast to him around his shoulders.

"I hope there's another creek," she kept joking. "Then we can try piggyback."

"Don't'cha be teasin' me now."

But the rocking motion that came with each step lulled her more. She let her head rest against his shoulder. He seemed to grip her tighter under her rump, which increased the friction between her legs—a pleasurable but aggravating sensation—and the position caused her right breast to rub against his chest.

Did the cicada sounds begin to drone louder? She felt deceptively relaxed in his grasp, rocking, rocking, as he stepped over more rocks; she could've fallen asleep. Some strands of his long hair brushed her face. The vee of her blouse looped up; then she drowsily realized that one nipple was showing.

She pretended not to notice.

Oh, God. The thought moaned through her mind.

She felt so strange, burning up with pent-up desires but lazy, slothlike. The cicada drone continued to fill her head, and the rocking motion continued to stimulate her sex, her breasts. But he remained the perfect gentleman; he couldn't have *not* noticed her nipple. It tingled, felt like it was swelling. . . .

"Here we are. Ten cents for the ride . . ."

On the other side of the creek he set her back down on her feet, and she wasn't even aware of what she was doing when she pressed right up against him, reached around and squeezed his buttocks, and kissed him, and it was no friendship kiss. It was a famished one, a kiss incited, even crazed by desires she couldn't identify, just some sexual arcana that had swept her sense of reason away and left nothing but cringing nerves and raw, animal impulse.

Ernie seized up in the sudden shock and leaned back against a tree, his opened hands out—the roots of some moral reaction, perhaps: that though this was a woman he'd been in love with so long ago, she was married now, off-limits. But Patricia only pressed closer, slipping her tongue into his mouth and squeezing his buttocks with even more deliberation. Finally, threads of his resistence began to slacken. She moaned into his mouth, put her arm around his waist, and squeezed her groin to his.

Patricia's mind raced in a desperate delirium. The suction of her kiss drew his tongue into her mouth. She was never even aware when she unbuttoned her blouse and bared her breasts. It was almost violent then, when she grabbed some of his long hair and urged his head lower.

His lips attached to an already swollen nipple and sucked. "Harder," was the only word she uttered. She was cringing, like someone in a prickly heat desperate for relief . . . but the prickly heat here wasn't rash; it was an agonized desire, the crudest horniness that blocked out all thoughts from her mind and simply demanded to be tended. Her groan was barely even feminine when her earlier whimsy came true: after sucking each nipple to a beating soreness, he licked up and down her throat, sucked lines in between her breasts, tonguing off the oyster juice she'd dribbled.

She moaned more, deeper in her throat. Then she grabbed his strong hand and coaxed it down the front of her shorts, beneath the panties, pushed some more and made him feel her there. Without hesitation, her own hand roved his crotch, her fingers testing the already throbbing rigidity. . . .

Then she prepared to haul his pants down and drag him to the ground, make him take her right there in the blazing sun.

She didn't know what she was doing.

She was out of her mind. . . .

If this sudden departure from her traditional monogamous values could be thought of as a *thing*, that thing fell apart a second later, just as she was getting his pants open.

Her hand froze; then her eyes vaulted wide and her mouth shot open in a silent scream of self-outrage.

Oh, my God, oh, my God! What am I doing?

She quickly backed away from him, almost tripping over a tree root.

Ernie glared at her. "What the hell?"

"I'm sorry, I'm sorry!" she blurted. "I-I-I . . . *can't!*"

He stood there appalled, his pants open. "You're shittin' me! What the hell's wrong with you, pullin' such shit!"

Patricia's shoulders slumped. Her face was beet red in shame. She fumbled to button her blouse. "I'm sorry," she peeped.

"*Damn* it!" He refastened his jeans, clearly outraged. "Patricia, you cain't be comin' on to guys like that 'n' then changin' yer mind!"

"I know. I'm sorry," she said yet again.

His glare sharpened. "What, thought you'd git your kicks by gettin' the big dumb country boy all worked up 'n' then pullin' the plug?"

She shook her head desperately, fighting tears. "No, no, I'd never do something like that, not to you or anyone."

"What then? What the hell's your problem?"

"I'm . . . I'm married—"

"Married? Yeah, I know you're married! And you were married a minute ago when you grabbed my hand 'n' put it down your pants! You were grabbin' me by the hair to shove my face in yer boobs! Don't sound to me like you were all that worried 'bout cheatin' on your husband!"

More embarrassment flushed over her. She struggled for something logical to say, but what could be logical about this? She was mystified at herself. *I was about to have sex with him right here in broad daylight. I had every intention of doing that. . . .* "Ernie, I don't know what to say. Something just . . . came over me." She rubbed her eyes. "I've just been . . . weird lately, for some reason.

Since the day I got back. I haven't been myself, and I can't understand it for the life of me. For those last couple of minutes, I wasn't even thinking. It's like I was out of my mind."

"Well, you are out of your mind for playin' around with a fella like that," he grumbled. But at least his frustration appeared to be abating. He sat down at the base of the tree and just shook his head.

Patricia stood in frustration of her own. Her breasts, nipples, and sex seemed to throb in objection, as though her mind had betrayed her body. All that desire building up, building up, about to be relieved, and now this guillotine of last-second morality. "I'm really sorry, Ernie," she kept apologizing.

His own frustration urged a laugh as the moment cooled down. "Well, at least we know now."

"Know what?"

"That it *is* true what they say about oysters and fried cicadas."

She shook her head, smiling. "Come on; let's go back. I promise not to accost you."

But Ernie had already stood back up; he didn't seem to hear her. "I wonder what *that's* all about. . . ." He was staring across the hill.

"Huh?"

"Look."

Her eyes followed his finger.

The town police car was parked at the Stanherd house, its red and blue lights flashing.

"Never seen nothin' like it," Sergeant Trey was telling them in the foyer of the old Stanherd house. It had been so long since Patricia had been inside the dilapidated plantation house that seeing it now refreshed no memories. Nothing had been replaced, just repaired, however expertly, such that she could've just walked through a time warp, back to the 1850s.

"And I guarantee there ain't never been nothin' like it, ever, in Squatterville before, and not in Agan's Point either," Trey finished. "Except for Dwayne last week, we ain't *never* had a murder in these parts. And like that?"

It was too much information too fast. She and Ernie had jogged up to the house upon seeing the cruiser's flashing lights, when Sergeant Trey had told them that two of the clan's elders, Wilfrud and Ethel Hild, had been murdered. Patricia thought she remembered the name, but simply couldn't place faces that far back.

"Craziest thing I ever heard," Ernie murmured.

The old house smelled of incense, potpourri, and handmade candles. It stood in dead silence, like something watching them in disapproval. Wide, bare-wood stairs led up into darkness at one end of the foyer, but Trey showed them through a sitting room full of throw rugs, faded, intricately patterned wallpaper, and sunlight filtering through dusty bay windows.

"Is the house empty?" Patricia asked.

"Only one here's Marthe," Trey said.

Everd's wife, Patricia remembered. "So the Hilds lived in the house too?"

"Yeah, along with some of the older couples. All the men are out on the crabbing boats. That's why Everd ain't here. And the women are all out gatherin' for the picnic comin' up. Ain't gonna be much of a picnic now. Shit."

He took them deeper into the house's first floor, and more sun-edged darkness. No pictures hung on the walls, which seemed strange, but instead all kinds of inexplicable handmade decorations: corn-husk flowers, oyster-shell mosaics, and crosses, of course, some that appeared to be made of small-animal bones. In frames, she also noticed more of those squiggly designs, their mystical good-luck sign.

In the room farthest in back, Chief Sutter was grimly taking pictures with a Polaroid, and making notes. From his face he looked like a man experiencing stomach pains.

"You tell 'em?" he asked Trey.

His deputy nodded.

"Damnedest thing. Murders. In Squatterville, of all places."

Patricia frowned her confusion. "Chief, I don't understand. The Hilds were murdered? Where are the bodies?"

"No, no, they weren't murdered here. Couple miles away, on the Point's where their bodies were found. Old Man Halm came across 'em doin' his morning walk. So me 'n' Trey checked it out." He put his notebook down next to the camera, then sat down on a big poster bed that must have been fifty years old. A purplish stone hung above the bed from a piece of red yarn, and on the nightstand sat a jar of what appeared to be pickled eggs.

"What's that in the jar?" she asked. "Eggs?"

"They call 'em creek eggs," Ernie said. "Just regular hen's eggs that they bury in a creek bed for a coupla months, turns 'em black. Supposed to ward off sickness, more clan superstition."

"Rotten eggs," Sutter muttered. "What a bunch of loonies."

"Stinks something fierce if ya open that jar."

Gross, Patricia thought.

The rest of the room stood as sparse as the house: a

cane chair and small walnut table for a desk. A closet full of clothes. A claw-foot dresser and some candles in metal holders. Above the bed hung a cross made of acorns glued together, and below it, yet another of the good-luck designs.

Guess it didn't bring them much in the way of luck.

"Shit, poor Marthe's sittin' in the other room practically in shock." Sutter rubbed his big face. "Couldn't get nothin' out of her when I was questionin' her. Trey, go in and see if she's all right."

Trey nodded again and left the room.

"You were taking pictures," Patricia pointed out.

"Yeah, evidence. We're just a small-town department, Patricia, so whenever something happens here that qualifies as a major crime, we write up the report and collect whatever evidence there is, then turn it over to the county sheriff's. They'll be doin' the investigation. Right now, the county coroner's office is out on the Point, pickin' up the bodies."

"But if the Hilds were murdered several miles away . . . why are you treating this bedroom like the crime scene?"

"'Cos it is, now that I looked around." His hand tiredly gestured the closet and some open dresser drawers. "The Hilds were murdered like a city drug execution. Are ya squeamish?"

"Try me," Patricia said.

"Ethel was stripped naked and chopped in half at the waist with an ax. Wilfrud was tied to a tree and knifed. And he had a couple bags a' crystal meth in his pocket." He pointed again to the closet and dresser. "Then look what I find in there."

Under some linens in the dresser drawer, she noticed dozens of little plastic bags containing either yellowish granules or yellowish chunks of something that looked like pieces of rock salt.

"Crystal meth," Sutter said. "Redneck crack. In the city where you live, crack is the big drug, but out here in the boondocks? That stuff's the ticket. They snort it, smoke it, shoot it up—one of them little bags costs a couple bucks to produce; then they sell it for twenty. It's superspeed, keeps ya high for eight hours. And it's just as addictive as crack."

Patricia looked at the bags, astonished. "The Hilds were using this stuff?"

"Not using, selling, it looks like. See all that other stuff in the closet?"

A large plastic bag sat on the closet floor. When Patricia opened it, she couldn't have been more bewildered.

"Matches?" Ernie said when he looked in too.

There must've been a hundred of them in the bag: matchbooks. Just plain old everyday books of matches. "What does this have to do with—"

"It's part of the process. Meth-heads soak the matches in some kind of solvent to get some chemical out of it—not the matches themselves, but the strike pads on each book. Then, up there on top, that's the main ingredient."

On the closet shelf sat about a dozen bottles of store-brand allergy and sinus medication that could be purchased over the counter in any drugstore.

"They soak the cold medicine in alcohol, then boil it and filter it," Sutter informed her. "That becomes the base for the crystal meth. Then they mix it with the stuff from the strike pad and add some kind of iodine compound, and cook it all down and distill it. I don't know the whole process—it's pretty complicated. But any cop in the world'll tell you that's what Wilfrud and Ethel Hild were into."

"Cain't believe it," Ernie said. "I known Wilfrud 'n' Ethel all my life. They were weird, sure. But drug dealers?"

"More than dealers," Sutter reminded him. "Producers. It takes all kinds, Ernie, and sometimes—a lot of the time, actually—people ain't what they seem."

Patricia supposed he was right about that. Sometimes people changed, became corrupted, and not much else could corrupt a person's values more effectively than poverty. But this was utterly shocking. With all her education, and all her experience living in a large modern city, Patricia was inclined to think that she knew a lot about human nature and the world in general. But now she felt oblivious, even ignorant.

This was a *different* world from hers.

Chief Sutter rose, walked his girth to the open window, and what he said next provided an eerie accompaniment to what Patricia had just been thinking. "There's a secret world out there that folks like us either don't see or just forget about 'cos it don't affect us." He was looking out at the fringes of Squatterville, the ragtag tract of Judy's land covered with tin shacks and old trailers. "And the world of crystal meth is right out there somewhere, right under our noses. The shit's been poppin' up more and more in our country over the past few years. Shit, just the other day me 'n' Trey caught a couple of punks from out of town tryin' to sell this selfsame shit down here. Crystal fuckin' meth." Then he pointed out the window. "And all that out there is why they call it redneck crack. Any one of them little shacks or trailers could be a meth lab."

Patricia knew she couldn't *not* believe it; that would be naive. *And what's Judy's reaction going to be when she learns that some of her Squatters are selling hard drugs?*

"So you say Wilfrud and Ethel were murdered by other drug dealers?" Ernie asked.

"Had to have been," Sutter answered. "That's how these people do it—real psycho. The Hilds' operation must've been cutting in on someone else's territory."

"The same thing happens in the city with the crack gangs." Patricia at least knew that much. Just a month ago in the *Post* she'd read about how drug dealers would kidnap and dismember the girlfriends of rival dealers. "In the corporate world you buy out the competition, but in the drug world you *kill* the competition."

"Sure." Sutter knew as well. "Old as history. The Hilds were probably movin' in on someone else's turf, and now they got themselves killed for it."

Car doors could be heard thunking from outside.

"Now the fun starts," Sutter muttered. "You two better git on back to Judy's. County sheriff's just pulled up, and when they see all that shit in the closet, they'll be callin' the state narcotics squad."

"Do you think they'll get warrants to search all the Squatters' homes?" Patricia asked.

"Oh, I'm sure. Let's just hope this is isolated. If there was a whole lot of other Squatters workin' with the Hilds, we're all in for a big headache."

Patricia and Ernie walked back out to the foyer with Sutter. The door stood open in another room; inside, Sergeant Trey could be seen quietly questioning a very shaken Marthe Stanherd. The thin, elderly woman looked like a bowed scarecrow as she murmured answers to Trey's queries.

Trouble in paradise, Patricia thought. *Serious trouble . . .*

She and Ernie slipped out, leaving Chief Sutter to brief the incoming county officers. As they walked back across the rising hill—the sun beating down, and the cicadas out en masse—Patricia took another glance back at the humble sheds and shacks of Squatterville, and wondered if last night's brutal murders were a fluke, or a new beginning for Agan's Point.

The fringes of Squatterville were marked with small, uneven vegetable patches that the clan's children would tend, mostly spring onions, soy beans, radishes. Patricia thought of Marthe Stanherd once more when she spied a genuine scarecrow mounted at the field's edge: old straw-stuffed clothes and a grimacing potato-sack face beneath a corroded hat. The crucified thing seemed to reach out to them with skeletal hands fashioned from twigs.

Around its neck hung, not a cross, but a small wooden board acrawl with elaborate squiggles. . . .

"Patricia! Goodness!" Judy called to her the instant she stepped into the kitchen. Despite last night's overindulgence with liquor, and the mental aftermath of her husband's funeral, Judy looked peppy, vibrant, her grayish-red hair flowing in a mane around her face. "Byron called and he's worried *sick* about you! Shame on you for not calling him!"

The exclamation caught Patricia totally off guard. "Byron called the house?"

"Yes," Judy sternly replied. "A little while ago. He said he's been leaving messages on your cell phone since yesterday."

Oh, God . . .

Judy wagged a scolding finger. "Don't you *dare* neglect that wonderful husband of yours—"

Ernie stepped up, interrupting. "Uh, Judy, lemme talk to ya a minute. The police are at the Stanherd house right now. There was some bad trouble last night. . . ."

Patricia edged away, leaving Ernie to make the grim report of the Hilds' murders to her sister. She was back in her room in a few seconds, then retrieved her cell phone and called Byron.

"Oh, God, I was so worried, honey," he expressed. "Are you all right?"

"Yes, Byron, I'm fine—"

"I left messages and you never called back, so I thought—"

"Everything's fine, honey," she said, feeling like a complete lout. What could she say? "Things were just so busy here with the funeral service and the reception, and all the people. There're so many people here who remember me—I didn't really expect that."

"But that was all yesterday, right?"

"Well, yes—"

"So why didn't you call me this morning?"

Patricia stalled. She looked, horrified, to the clock: it was almost noon. "I'm so sorry. I slept late—I was so exhausted. Then I went for a walk to get the gears turning. But I was going to call you when I got back, and I just got back a minute ago." She frowned at herself. Now she was simply lying. How could she tell her own husband that she'd completely forgotten about him? That she'd been out "for a walk," all right, with a man she'd been having sexual fantasies about and . . . and . . . *And whom I practically just screwed in the woods?* she finished for herself.

"I'm sorry," he said. "I guess I'm overreacting. I know how that place distresses you. Plus, I just . . ." There was a pause on the phone. "I guess I'm just a big, whiny, insecure pud, but I had a horrible dream last night that you were having sex with another man."

Someone should've given Patricia an Oscar for the skill and immediacy with which she next tossed her head back and laughed and said, "Oh, Byron, you're so ridiculous sometimes. There's not one solitary man in Agan's Point who isn't a redneck hayseed with a busted-up pickup truck. At least have enough respect for me to dream that I'm getting it on with Tom Cruise or Johnny Depp, someone like that." But even through her recital, she was thinking, *Holy, holy, holy shit!*

Now—to Patricia's relief—Byron laughed. "Yeah, I guess it was a pretty dumb dream. I'm just glad everything's okay."

Finally she had the opportunity to change the subject but to something not so okay. "Actually, there was a big shocker just this morning. The police have been here—"

"Police?"

"—and evidently two of the Squatters who live on my sister's land were murdered last night."

"What!" he exclaimed.

"Yeah, it's the craziest thing. There have never been murders here ever; then all of a sudden Dwayne gets killed, and now this."

"I want you out of there right now," Byron insisted. "Sounds like that backward boondocks place is boiling over. Get in the car right now and come home!"

"Byron, now you *are* overreacting. It was drug-related, the police said, and it happened miles away out in the woods. Judy's just finding out about it now, but even though it's tragic and all that, it's nothing for us to get all worked up over. A Squatter couple were secretly dealing drugs, and they got murdered by a rival drug gang—that sort of thing. It's not like there's a serial killer prowling Agan's Point."

"Well, I don't like it," Byron affirmed. "The funeral's over and done with, so there's no reason for you to stay. You hate the place anyway."

"Byron, the whole reason I came in the first place was to give my unstable and fairly heavily drinking sister some support in her time of need. I'll be back next week, just as we planned."

"Well, all right. But I still don't like it. And you need to call me—"

"I will, honey," she promised. "Most of the commotion's over now, so there won't be any more distractions. And once I got Judy back on her feet, I'll be home in a flash."

"Good." He paused. "I really miss you and I really love you. You've only been gone for a few days and I'm already realizing how important you are to me. I guess I don't show it much. . . ."

"Byron, of course you do, so stop it." She truly did love him—more than anything—and she did want to get back to be with him. Her little mishap in the woods with Ernie was just a fluke brought on by the stress of being back; it was simply a loss of control in a moment run amok. *I do love Byron,* she attested to herself. Ernie was no more than a man in a magazine ad whom she'd happened to notice.

On the other hand—and as loving and genuine as he was—Byron *did* have his moments of insecurity. He was an overweight middle-aged man, and Patricia was still a well-endowed, beautiful woman. She knew it must be hard for him to deal with sometimes.

"You never have to 'do' things to prove your love to me," she continued. "Just being you is the proof. Please remember that. And I love you too, very much. Remember that too."

"I will," he replied, a bit choked up.

"I'll call tonight, and every night I'm here. And I haven't forgotten. I even have a cooler."

"What?"

"Your Agan's Point crab cakes, silly!"

"Good. And the minute you get back here, I'm going to eat them off your beautiful, naked body. That's a promise."

"Byron, nothing turns me on more than culinary sex," she said, laughing, and then they bade their final "good-byes" and "I love yous" and rang off.

Patricia lay back on the bed and let out a great sigh. The conversation left her relieved and ashamed at the same time, not a good combination. She had lied to him—little white lies, but lies just the same—and she had offered invented excuses, and maybe that *was* good, because it helped her confront something important about herself.

It's all me. It's not Byron. There's nothing wrong with my marriage, and there's nothing wrong with him. So . . .

And the coincidence jolted her. *He's been having dreams about me cheating on him, and I've been having dreams about me cheating on him. And today, with Ernie, I almost* did *cheat on him.*

It was with a total spontaneity that she roved through her cell phone's address book and found herself looking at Dr. Sallee's number, and before she knew what she was doing, the line was ringing.

He probably doesn't even remember me, she thought. She'd seen him only once, when she and Byron had returned from Agan's Point after Judy's wedding. When the receptionist answered, she said, "Hi, my name's Patricia White. I had a session with Dr. Sallee several years ago. I was wondering if I could arrange a phone consultation. I could give you my credit card number over the phone."

"Is your home address still the same?"

"Yes."

Keys were heard tapping. "Yes, we still have it on file."

"Great. Then if possible could you give me a time to call back for a consultation?"

"One moment, please."

As Patricia waited, she didn't even know what she would say once she got the consultation. *I don't really even know why I called. . . .*

"Dr. Sallee is available now," the receptionist told her. "I'll put him on."

"Thank you—"

"Patricia White?" the next voice asked.

"Yes, Doctor. You probably don't remember me but—"

"The real estate lawyer with blazing red hair—of course I remember. How are you?"

She was flattered he remembered her. "All in all, I'm fine, but . . . I've been having some problems for the last several days."

"When you came to me last time, we'd nailed your problem in general as a reactive symptom of monopolar depression. You'd left town to attend your sister's wedding, at a place called . . ."

"Agan's Point," she helped him.

"Yes, the crabbing town. Your depression was activated by memories of a sexual trauma—a rape—that you suffered at age sixteen. We agreed that this depression was entirely location triggered, and decided that as long as you kept your distance from Agan's Point, the depression would not recur. I presumed this theory worked, because I never heard from you again. Am I wrong?"

"It did work," she said. "I felt fine after that and have for the last five years. But for the last few—"

"Where are you right now, exactly?" he interrupted.

"Agan's Point," she slowly admitted. "This time for a funeral—my sister's husband."

Dr. Sallee's voice came after a long pause. "That's regrettable. So your depression *has* recurred. . . ."

"No, that's the surprising part. It's almost the opposite. For the days I've been back in Agan's Point, I haven't felt depressed at all. I've felt great; I've felt enthused."

"Strange," the doctor said, "but considerable."

Now Patricia mulled over words in her mind, trying to choose the right ones. "I don't really know how to say it, but—"

"Just say it," Dr. Sallee suggested.

The words leaked out slowly: "Something about coming back has made me feel more sexual than I've felt in years. It's actually scaring me, and I'm beginning to feel out of control." In spite of the miles between them, her face reddened. "I'm . . . masturbating much more than normal, and every night I have very intense sexual dreams, which is unusual for me—"

"Sexual dreams? Masturbation? There's nothing abnormal about that," the doctor told her. "This is all an aspect of passive sexuality. There's nothing out of control about it."

Passive sexuality, she thought. She was even more embarrassed to tell him the rest. Her throat choked up. "I'm almost ashamed to continue. . . ."

"Patricia"—he chuckled—"I'm your counselor. We're essentially strangers, not to mention the fact that everything you say to me is in professional confidence. My rates are high, so you might as well get your money's worth. Make me work for it. I can't help you unless you tell me everything that leads you to think you're out of control."

It made perfect sense. So she said it: "I almost cheated on my husband about an hour ago. That's *never* happened before. And I was going to do it. . . ."

Dr. Sallee didn't seemed the least bit fazed. "Is there trouble in the marriage?"

"None," she said. "It's the best marriage any woman could ever ask for. I've never *not* been sexually fulfilled with my husband. We're perfectly compatible in every way, even sexually—*especially* sexually."

"Was the person you almost cheated with a stranger?"

"No. A boy—er, I should say a man my age—whom I grew up with. We were best friends since childhood."

"Any sexual experiences with him in the past, before your marriage? A high school romance, perhaps, experimentation when you were younger—playing doctor, and the like?"

"No. I know he wanted that, but I was never interested back in those days. I was always very goal-oriented as an adolescent, and even through college." *Ernie, Ernie, Ernie,* she thought. *I never really noticed you over all those years. So why now?* "I've seen him maybe three times since I left Agan's Point over twenty years ago. But this time, when I came back for the funeral . . . something happened. I just all of a sudden find him very attractive."

"Hmm," came the counselor's response. "From a clinical standpoint—so far, at least—this all sounds very good."

The remark astonished her. "Good? I'm in total turmoil!"

"I said from a *clinical* standpoint. In the past, whenever you returned to Agan's Point, you'd become clinically depressed. Today you've returned to Agan's Point, but you're not depressed at all. You feel great—to use your own words of a moment ago. You feel *enthused*. Your depression is gone, so that's a good thing."

Now she saw his point, but he still wasn't seeing hers. "Yes, I feel enthused, but I also feel very, very sexual—"

"To the point that you nearly committed an infidelity," he added, "and *this* is what's bothering you now."

"Exactly. It doesn't make sense. It makes me feel like I must be sick or something, because—"

"Because," he kept finishing for her, "it doesn't seem right for you to feel sexual in the very place that has always reminded you of the worst trauma of your life, which just so happened to be a *sexual* trauma."

"That's exactly what I mean," she said, sighing in relief that he'd made it easier for her.

His voice almost sounded bored as he continued. "In my job, I've had many patients who were victims of sexual abuse, multiple rape, sexual torture, and worse. You'd be surprised how many women, for instance, will go years or even decades without ever telling anyone—even their counselors—that they experienced orgasms during their trauma, because in their minds it seems wrong, it seems shameful, it seems *sick* to experience pleasure during a revolting ordeal. In truth, quite a considerable percentage of rape victims experience a sexual release, and it doesn't mean they're sick at all. It's just their body reacting to a primordial function. It's not sick, it's not shameful, and its not abnormal."

Patricia calculated this with a reserved interest. She, too, had experienced orgasm during her rape—the first orgasm of her life—and she'd never told anyone for the same reasons the doctor had just cited. *I never even told Dr. Sallee,* she realized, *and now I guess I know why he never asked.*

Suddenly there was a tear in her eye, but it was a quietly joyous one. "You have no idea how good that makes me feel."

"I'm glad," the doctor said. "And you should be glad, too, of a lot of things—at least based on what you're telling me today. Most rape aftercare revolves not so much around psychotherapy, medication, and group counseling, but around the evolvement of the individual, coming to terms and dealing with it. It's clear to me that you've done this."

This was good to know, but it still didn't solve her problem. "It's like the old problem is gone, but now there's a new one."

"But is it a grievous one?" he asked, already knowing the answer. "Is it a debilitating one? No. In fact, it's got nothing whatever to do with your trauma of so many years ago. Let me allegorize. Are you computer literate?"

She frowned at the question. "I think so. We have a network at the office, and I do all right."

"Good, then I'll use my favorite comparison on you." He chuckled. "Lawyers tend to be objective thinkers; they deal in black-and-white terms. But this is not a black-and-white issue, is it? The human brain is the most sophisticated 'thing' in the world. Ten trillion brain cells, one hundred trillion synaptic connections. Think of it as a computer. That computer is programed by the experiences of life, good and bad. Well, sometimes the files glitch; sometimes they get viruses and have to be cleansed. A rape, for instance, can be thought of as an infected file, a file gone bad, a file that's no longer functioning in synchronicity with the other files it's been programmed to operate with. When we can't delete a bad file, we try to quarantine it, and sometimes we can't even do that because the file is so out of sorts. Your rape experience is a bad file, Patricia. You've been quarantining it for years, which has worked, but now the computer is appending that file, to make it more serviceable to the system—rewriting the file. This is a sophomoric analogy, but it might help you understand. As far as your rape is concerned, the file has been rewritten; it no longer has a negative effect on the system."

Dr. Sallee's simile did let her see the problem in a clearer light. "But what about—"

"An unexplained heightened sexuality in a nonsexual setting?" he finished for her yet again. "Same thing, different program. Only in this case there was never a bad file. Think of it, instead, as a scheduled maintenance activation. The way a calendar program will flash reminders on your screen at a preset time?" Another chuckle. "You're approaching your mid-forties, Patricia, which is the actual sexual peak for most women. Consciously, you've been groomed by your social and professional environment—a very *specific* environment. You've never wanted children, for instance, because it doesn't suit the course you've chosen for your life, and part of the reason you chose your mate is because he doesn't want children, either. Some people simply don't, but *all* people—all mammals, in fact—have an inborn instinct to reproduce. It's in our genes whether we like it or not. It's in our brains, our computers, so to speak—it's one of the operations programs. As we get older—women, especially—that program begins to run faster, to try to become the priority over other programs. It's trying to beat the inevitability of still one more program—one called menopause—an *infertility* program. In ten years—less, perhaps—your body knows that you will no longer be able to reproduce, so it's lighting up your sexual awareness, going for that last chance of reproductive success. It's all genetic, subconscious. It exists independent of your values and domestic and personal desires. What I'm trying to tell you, Patricia, is that an inexplicable sexual spike at your age is *perfectly commonplace.* It has nothing to do with your rape, and it doesn't mean there's anything wrong with you. It doesn't mean that you're a tramp or a cheat or a deceptive person. All it means is that you're a perfectly healthy middle-aged woman. For your entire adulthood, you've excelled in everything, and you've been in total control of yourself. You still are. The reason it's happening now is simply because you're in a different place, away from your spouse, and your subconscious mind is selecting 'targets' of sexual opportunity. Almost every single female patient I have in your age group is experiencing the same thing. It's normal, Patricia. And you won't cheat on your husband even when it seems that your body and your mind want to. What'll happen instead is you'll return to your home soon and probably have a lot of great sex with your husband."

Now Patricia was the one chuckling.

The doctor began to finish up. "But until you do return home, you'll still experience this, so just be ready for it. It's *okay* to masturbate; it's *okay* to have sexually vivid dreams. It's all part of your sexuality. The important thing is not to worry about it, and don't get yourself worked up. Nobody knows you better than yourself, Patricia. You know you're not going to cheat on your husband, don't you?"

It was with every confidence now that she answered, "Yes."

"In that case, I can say that I'm happy to have gotten to talk to you today, and unless there's anything else bothering you, then we should hang up now so I won't have to erroneously bill you for therapeutic services that I haven't earned."

The man was a hoot. "Thank you very much, Doctor."

"And thank you. The disappearance of your depression proves that . . . I must be a fairly good doctor."

"That you are. Have a great day."

Patricia hung up, feeling exuberant. *I'm not a cheating, conniving sex maniac after all. And he's right. I'm cured of my Agan's Point depression.* This knowledge was an optimal way to commence with the rest of the day.

With that off her mind, though, she was reminded of more serious matters. *Judy,* she thought. *Just when she gets over one tragedy, she gets hit on the head with another one: the murder of the Hilds.* By now, she was sure Ernie had explained what he knew of it, and Patricia supposed she should check on her soon to see how she was taking the news. But first . . .

She started up her laptop and went online. Her mailbox remained free of anything from the firm, so next she took to Googling around a little.

Crystal meth, she thought. She'd heard of it, of course, just errant pieces sometimes in the news, but she really didn't know anything specific about it. In a moment, the Drug Enforcement Administration's official Web site opened before her. *A highly addictive Class II narcotic as defined by the Controlled Substances Act*, she read. *A superstimulant that produces long-lasting euphoric effects.* When she added the word *ingredients* to her search, other, more obscure pages came up. *Active ingredients: pseudoephedrine.*

Never heard of it, she thought, until she read on and discovered that the chemical was derived from a complicated distillation and filtering process that began by dissolving over-the-counter allergy medications in certain types of solvent. She'd seen the cache of allergy remedies in the Hilds' bedroom.

The next primary ingredient listed was a phosphorous compound called RD, something else she'd never heard of, but more recognition bloomed when she read the first few lines: that the easiest way for "guerrilla meth-heads" to obtain this compound was through another complicated distillation process using striker pads on paper matchbooks. *Chief Sutter mentioned the same thing*, she recalled, and she also recalled the veritable garbage bag full of matchbooks in the Hilds' closet.

It's hard to believe, she thought. The Hilds? But it didn't matter how hard it was to *believe*; it still must be true. Judy wouldn't believe it either, but she had a tendency to be naive. *The Squatters are like her children, even the older ones. Nobody wants to believe their "children" manufacture hard drugs in secret.*

And now they'd been brutally murdered by outside drug dealers.

Patricia read on. Crystal meth was a man-made stimulant; it didn't occur in nature. Even small doses could last up to twelve hours, and the street price was relatively cheap: twenty dollars per dose. Clinical addiction rate? Around ninety percent, close to that of crack, and like cocaine it could be administered effectively several ways: snorting, injecting, smoking. The smoking form was called "ice," (small crystalline chunks were placed in a pipe); the inhaled form was called "tweak" on the street.

Patricia was nearly amused when she came across the next street term: "redneck crack," something Chief Sutter had mentioned. It was all logistical, she read. Cocaine was typically transported to large urban centers for the already existing market. It was harder to get, and riskier, because the base form for any type of cocaine was derived from the tropical coca shrub, which grew only in Africa and northern South America. But since crystal meth was synthetic, it could be produced anywhere, and didn't require constituents that needed to be procured from other countries. Many a trailer park contained secret meth labs—hence the nickname of redneck crack. A thousand dollars' worth of equipment and ingredients—all available at drugstores and hardware stores—could generate five to ten thousand in profit, if the person knew what he was doing. Crystal meth, in other words, was the perfect illicit drug for remote areas. . . .

Like Agan's Point, Patricia deduced.

And, according to the government Web sites, crystal meth use was growing, reaching into society's less accessible nooks and crannies. It was considered an epidemic in the drug culture, and like all narcotics it piggybacked HIV, hepatitis, and crime right along with it.

Jesus. And now this stuff is here. . . .

Patricia went back to the living room, dreading her sister's reaction. Judy looked drawn-faced now, partly confused and partly infuriated. Ernie was pouring her some coffee as she mused: "I guess that's the modern world. In the old days, people used to have stills in the woods and make their corn liquor. Now they're making this stuff . . . this crystal stuff. And not just *any* people. *My* people. My Squatters."

"It's probably just isolated, Judy," Patricia said when she came in and sat down. She wanted to sound optimistic, but didn't really know if that was honest or not. "It was probably just the Hilds doing it."

"You think you know people," Judy said, oblivious. "You like them, you help them, and they seem perfectly normal, perfectly decent, hardworking folks. Then one day you find out the truth. I give 'em a free place to live; I give 'em work when they ain't really suited for work nowheres else. And they do this to me. They been takin' the money I pay 'em to make this drug stuff. And we got a lotta Squatters on the Point. I'd be plumb stupid to think it was *just* the Hilds."

"Aw, Judy, you don't know that," Ernie said. "I think it *was* just the Hilds. They was always a bit strange anyways, more'n most of the Squatters. And may God forgive 'em, but it looks to me like they got what was coming. Ain't no way I believe there's a whole lotta this goin' on at the Point. These people are crabbers, for Christ's sake. Everd's got 'em cowed like he's Jesus Himself. The Squatters don't even drink. I ain't never even seen one smokin' a cigarette or chewin' chaw. They all think it's a sin to drink 'n' smoke, so makin' hard drugs is ten times worse. The Hilds was bad apples, is all. Every basket has a few."

Judy leaned backed in her chair, brushing hair from her eyes as if exhausted. "But that's all I been hearin' lately. Squatters gettin' in fights, Squatter's turnin' lazy at the line, Squatters leavin' the Point 'cos it ain't good enough for 'em no more, like the work I give 'em ain't good enough. I'm hearing all the time these days that somea' the prettier clan girls're sellin' theirselves—whorin'—but all Chief Sutter 'n' everyone else says is the same blamed thing. 'Oh, don't worry, Judy. They're just a few bad apples.' Well—Christmas!—it's startin' to look like we got the whole orchard goin' bad."

Wow, she's really riled up, Patricia realized. This was rare. "Judy, I think you're overreacting. It's inevitable. Anywhere you go, bad elements can work their way in and have a negative effect on otherwise good people."

"She right," Ernie agreed. "You don't need to be worryin' about this, 'specially after what'cha just been through."

Judy's large bosom fell as she sighed. "I guess things do change, no matter how bad we don't want 'em to." Her eyes sought out Patricia's. "Mom and Dad never had problems with the Squatters, but the world ain't the same place as it was back then."

"No, it's not," Patricia said. "As society progresses, good things come with the progress, but so do some bad things."

Now Judy's eyes seemed to be looking more at herself than anywhere else. "I don't know, Patricia. Maybe I really should just up 'n' sell the company, the Point, everything. Maybe it's time."

Oh, Lord. Here we go . . . The image of Gordon Felps flashed in her mind—and it was a shifty image. "You don't need to be thinking about anything of the sort just yet. Things will probably be back to normal in no time."

Another long sigh. "Gracious, I hope so. Ernie, will you get me a glass of wine, please? I need something to relax."

"Sure."

Great, Patricia thought. *She's going to get drunk again.* "I'll go fix lunch," she offered, if only to keep things active. The day had turned sour fast: first notice of two murders as well as drug activity on her sister's property, and now Judy all wound up again. *At least one good thing happened,* she thought with a slight smile. Her talk with Dr. Sallee left her feeling much better about her recent dreams and behavior. *There's nothing wrong with me, thank God. . . .*

But when she headed for the kitchen, Ernie cast a quick glance at her when she passed. Was it a neutral look? Or did his eyes brush over her breasts? *Just my imagination,* she insisted. He'd been quite a gentleman in the aftermath. But she couldn't shed the reminder. Dr. Sallee or not, she was attracted to him, and—

I almost had sex with him today—in the woods. . . .

She busied herself over cold cuts in the kitchen, preparing sandwiches. A simple cross hung by the bright window—a normal cross—but for whatever reason she was reminded of the much stranger crosses used by the Squatters, and their bizarre good-luck charms. She truly did believe that the Hild tragedy was isolated, but somewhere deeper in her spirit she feared that something else just as bad was about to happen.

Seven

(I)

Think I'll have me a jerk, Junior thought. His brother Ricky was out right now, took the truck over to Crick City to pick up some things at Wordon's Hardware: muriatic acid (whatever that was, some kind of cleaner, he guessed), acetone, and some special kind of alcohol called "denatured." Junior didn't know shit about crystal meth, but the way Trey explained it, these were the things that rednecks used to make the stuff in their trailers. He already had a bag of matchbooks and several bottles of allergy medicine ready to go—all for appearance' sake.

Junior had done the rough stuff last night, so tonight was Ricky's turn, which was fair enough. This Felps fella was paying righteous bucks for the work, and it was fun—it got their dander up—and it sure as hell beat real work.

Yeah, he thought again. *I need a jerk, all right. Still all hot 'n' bothered from last night. Get one off quick, before Ricky comes home.* He rooted through their box of video porn, hunting for his favorite: *Barnyard Babes #4,* but then thought, *Aw, shit, that's right.* The tape had broken a few weeks ago, so he'd ordered a new one. *Fuckin' post office is slower 'n' molasses. Shoulda got it by now.* Such were the disappointments in Junior's existence. He started to hunt through the box of tapes again but then realized, *Hell, I can do without it, I guess,* because he was indeed still a bit tingly with the image of Ethel Hild in his head. The old bitch was actually pretty good-lookin'—for an old bitch, at least—and Junior had had a good time putting the blocks to her, and then, when he thought about chopping her in half with the ax . . .

He felt his crotch, nodding in satisfaction. *Who needs porn? I'm ready to go without it.* Yes, Ethel Hild . . . She'd been something. For some reason, making that weirdo husband of hers watch as he'd dropped the ax made it that much more of a turn-on. Junior had especially liked the way her titties jiggled as he'd chopped, and then when she'd started crawling away . . . ?

The recollection enticed him further. But soon other images entered his head. *Judy,* he thought next. *Not a bad-lookin' dish either, and those big tits?* Junior wouldn't mind doing a similar job on her, just tear the clothes right off her and get her really screaming. And then another image . . .

Patricia.

She was about the cream of the Agan's Point crop: one hundred percent pure-grade fox. That silky, bright red hair? And the tits on her? *Jeez . . .* Junior was breaking out in a sweat just thinking about that one.

Maybe get her 'n' Judy at the same time, have me a double stack.

Then chop them both in half when he was finished.

All these delicious images challenged Junior's power of decision. Who to think about? It got downright maddening sometimes. . . .

He sat down on the couch, was about to pull his pants down and get to it, when—

There was a knock on the door.

Junior sputtered. *Jesus, a man can't even jerk off in peace around here!* Grunting, he got back up, shifted his pants a little, then opened the door.

"Howdy, Junior. You got a package."

The mailman, Charlie Meitz. He was a big guy with a shaved head, and a mustache that made him look sort of like Hitler.

Junior frowned. "Why didn't ya just leave it in the mailbox?"

"Too big. Plus, I wanted to say hi."

Shit. Charlie shook the box, offering a sly smile. "What's this? A videotape?"

"Don't you be shakin' my mail around," Junior complained. God, he hated interruptions.

Now the postman looked at the return address. "Hmm, T and T Video, California. Sounds like one a' them porn companies—"

"Gimme that!" Junior barked. He snatched the box away and closed the door. *Fuckin' nosy pain in the ass . . .* He peered out the side window, looked down the driveway of the crappy little house he and his brother shared, then muttered, "Aw, shit! Cain't even beat off in my own house!" Just after the mail truck pulled away, Ricky pulled the pickup up into the driveway.

Fuck. Business would have to wait; Ricky'd be going out late tonight to do more of the job they'd both been hired for. He opened the box that the mailman had brought him and, sure enough, out slid a brand-new copy of *Barnyard Babes #4.*

Cain't wait to watch this one again. It was a real hoot what some of those dirty chicks did.

He bellied over to the kitchen table and put the tape down. That nutty postman had also given him the rest of the regular mail, which Junior flipped through now. *Buncha' shit,* he thought. Here was one letter from the county supervisor of elections, urging him to register to vote. Fat chance. Phone bill, power bill, water and sewage bill. *Least we got the money to pay,* he thought. Felps paid well, and he and Ricky both were hoping the man would want more work.

There was one more letter in the pile, but . . . *Don't look like no bill, at least.* It was addressed specifically to Junior, in scratchy handwritten scrawl.

There was no return address.

(II)

It was dirty work, but that was what Ricky Caudill was cut out for. He didn't like to be bored. His brother had done a good job last night, real down and dirty, and the effect was exactly what they'd been hired for. Junior had killed the Hilds in grand style, and Trey had flaked their room at the Stanherd house. So . . .

Tonight's my turn.

It should be a fast, easy job. Those first dozen or so disappearances hadn't done the trick. *No dice,* Ricky thought. As it turned out, only a handful of Squatters had left. So Felps had this new idea, something on a bigger scale. If the state cops thought the Squatters were running an extensive meth operation, they'd roust them big-time, and Judy would just say to hell with it, and sell the land out from under them anyway. Then . . .

Problem solved.

The moon hung low beneath reefs of clouds. Ricky slipped through the woods along a barely visible trail. He didn't hear many cicadas tonight; their season would be ending soon. Ricky felt totally alone and totally at peace. Another hundred yards or so and he'd be at the tree line around the Point.

In one hand he carried his bag of "supplies": two bottles of denatured alcohol, some Breathe-Free sinus medication, a smaller bottle of acetone, matchbooks, and a couple of grams of crystal meth. Most of it would be destroyed in the fire, but there'd still be enough traces left over to convince the police and fire department what had happened. The plan sounded perfectly plausible; all the time you'd hear how meth-heads would accidentally spill a little solvent on their stove elements, and next thing they knew, their trailer was burning down. That was what was going to happen tonight.

In his other hand, he carried a hubcap mallet.

Almost there, Ricky thought. At the wood line, he slowed. The only trick was getting in and out without being seen. He'd already had the place picked out; some Squatter named David Something-or-other had himself a small wooden shack at the western edge of the woods, fairly far away from most of the others.

He crept up, careful not to let the bag crinkle. Moonlight painted one side of the shack luminous white. *Shit* . . . He slipped by quickly, then plunged into the darkness of the shack's front side. No lights could be detected from the makeshift windows, but he did hear snoring—a good thing.

And another good thing: out here in the quiet, peaceful boondocks, nobody ever locked their doors. Hell, most of these Squatter shacks didn't even *have* doors, just curtains or hinged planks, or sheet plastic, like this guy had.

Ricky ever so quietly set the bag of incriminating supplies down on the front stoop; then he stepped through the sheet plastic.

He'd seen David Something-or-other on the docks and around town in the past. Didn't know the guy, but then Ricky didn't associate with Squatters, except maybe some of the trashier girls for twenty-dollar tricks, but there weren't many who did that. This guy was in his thirties, it looked like, short like all the Squatters, but built up pretty well from working his ass off all his life hauling crab bushels. Ricky, on the other hand, was more fat than muscle, and without some backup or a knife—or, in this case, a big hard-rubber hubcap mallet—he probably wouldn't stand a chance against this David cracker.

Except when he's asleep, Ricky thought, smiling in the dark.

He supposed about the only thing more despicable than shooting a man in the back was cracking him in the head with a hubcap mallet while he slept like a baby in his own home. This was Ricky's speed.

When he'd slipped through the facsimile of a front door, he plunged into more darkness. Bars of moonlight fell in wedges across the floor. Upon entering, he'd rustled the plastic a little—not much of a sound under regular circumstances, but loud as holy hell when you were trying to kill a man. Ricky gritted his brown teeth at the rustle, then stepped quickly aside so that no moonlight might give him away. He stood dark as a shadow himself.

He let his eyes adjust, roving. A cheap, shitty little place like most of them, but it looked clean, much cleaner, in fact, than the cheap, shitty little house he shared with his even more demented brother.

He spotted some bookshelves and some cabinets, and a cubby of a kitchen with what looked like a thirty-year-old refrigerator. There was also one of those mini stove/oven combos that folks had in efficiency apartments. *Perfect,* he thought. His instructions were explicit: drop some of the allergy pills in the bottom of the saucepan and leave it on the stove. It would look to the fire marshal and cops like good ol' David Something-or-other had been cooking the shit down with denatured alcohol, the stuff had ignited, and then the whole joint burned down. He'd leave the other stuff lying around, too, and drag David's dead or unconscious body out of his bed and let him burn up with everything else. If Ricky did it right, the hubcap mallet wouldn't crack the skull, so it wouldn't look like murder.

But . . . where is the guy? Ricky wondered.

He could hear him snoring. He strained his vision, then let more things become visible in the room.

There's the cracker.

It was just an old spring cot the guy slept on. Ricky could make out the form of his body, and the short ink-black hair that almost looked darker than the darkness.

Time to rock, he thought, hefting the mallet's weight in his hand. He moved forward in short, silent steps. When he got closer he noticed a roughly cut stone of some kind hanging over the guy's bed; Ricky wouldn't know in a million years that it was specifically a chrysolite stone, said to bid good dreams and protect one's home from evil. The stone wasn't exactly doing a great job tonight.

Another few steps and he was at the head of the cot, looking right down at the stupid rube. The mallet froze high over his head, and in that moment Ricky could see his own shadow thrown against one wall: a shadow of death, a haunter of the dark.

At that single image he smiled, his heart beating faster, because he looked bigger now than he ever had.

"Who the—"

The Squatter's eyes glimmered in the moonlight, wide open. A hand shot upward, but—

Thud!

—too late.

One whack with the mallet was all it took. Ricky patted the top of the guy's head, felt no fractures. *Good job.* Didn't matter if he was dead or not, because he'd surely die in the fire that Ricky would start in a few minutes. David Something-or-other's lights were out for good.

A macabre realization occurred to him then. *The last thing this weirdo hillbilly saw in his life . . . was me.*

Ricky liked that.

He went back out and grabbed the bag. It didn't take long to put the matchbooks up in a cupboard, along with the acetone and the first bottle of denatured alcohol. Next he pulled a small boiling pot off the wall, set it on the stove, and dropped in a handful of allergy pills.

Now all I gotta do is drag the cracker out of his bed, empty the other bottle of alcohol around the joint . . . and light 'er up.

Ricky liked fires. He'd liked to look at them since he

was a kid—when he'd burned his mother and stepfather's house down with them in it. *Bitch had it comin' fer lettin' her old man make me 'n' Junior . . .* He didn't finish the thought, but it would suffice to say that fires made him feel like a success. They made him feel transcendental . . . not that he had any clue what *that* meant.

With some huffing, he dragged the Squatter out of the cot and left him to lie across the floor. Ricky didn't notice his chest moving up and down, so he guessed he was dead. Burning the fucker up alive had more kick to it, but that was the way the cards fell sometimes.

He noticed a jar on the kitchen counter. Pickled eggs, it looked like. *Shit, yeah! I love pickled eggs.* He and Junior had loved them as kids; their mom had made them all the time, before she'd started boozing hard and passing out every night, leaving their stepfather free to come into their rooms, and—

Well, that was another story.

He opened the jar, was about to grab an egg, but—

Holy shit!

The stink from the jar hit him in the face like someone dropping a flowerpot on his head.

Smells worse than a fuckin' pile a' dead dogs.

He put the jar back, revolted; then—

"Daddy?"

—his eyes bolted open, and he spun.

Shit!

There was someone else in the shack.

A slant of moonlight fell right on her, like a spotlight. A girl—mid-teens, he guessed, but it was hard to really tell with these Squatter girls because so many of them blossomed a few years before other girls.

It must've been something in the water.

But whether it was or not scarcely mattered to Ricky.

He was all fucked-up in the head to begin with, and now—razzed and bristly over busting the cracker's coconut in his own bed and about to turn the joint into a late-night bonfire—he was even *more* fucked-up.

His blood felt hot, excitement tingling on his skin with his sweat. His crotch felt tight.

"You're not my daddy!" she objected in that weird slur of clan dialect. She cast a worried glance down at the empty cot.

The guy was lying in darkness behind Ricky. *She can't see him,* he realized. He saw her own cot now, wedged in the corner of the room out of the moonlight. "Aw, now don't'choo worry 'bout your daddy, sweetheart. He's outside runnin' a errand, but he'll be right back. Me 'n' him are good buddies."

The girl's lower lip trembled, not that Ricky was looking at her lower lip. He was looking at the rest, though, his lust holding his eyes open.

"But I ain't never seen you before," she questioned.

"Oh, well, that's 'cos me'n yer daddy, see, we work together on them crab boats."

Yeah. Ricky was all fucked-up in the head, all right, and as for the girl?

Well, never mind what he did to the girl before he set the place ablaze and slipped out into the night.

(III)

Patricia dreamed of smoke and fire. She was running through the woods somewhere near the moonlit water, and though fires raged around her, she felt nothing even remotely like fear. Instead she felt invulnerable, safe. Heat wafted about her, but caused no injury. If anything, it only stoked the heat of her own desires.

"That's what the heat is," a voice calmly pointed out. It was Dr. Sallee sitting in a chair by a stand of trees. "The symbology of the dream mechanism. Our will is guided by conscious and subconscious impulses. It defines us as individuals, in subjective terms that are too complex for the concrete world around us: dreams."

The voice drifted like the smoke. Patricia tried to focus on the doctor's words and discern what they might mean with regard to her specifically, but too many other things nagged at her, such as her calm in the midst of this raging forest fire, and the hot tingling of her skin. She felt flushed; she felt . . .

Oh, God . . .

"Just a dream," she muttered to herself. At least she knew that. "It's just a dream, so I don't have to worry about it."

"That's right," Dr. Sallee agreed. But why did he look dead all of a sudden? Face drawn and pallid as old wax? The dark suit he wore was dust-tinged, its fabric frayed.

As though he'd just climbed out of a coffin after being buried for a long, long time.

"The death of Freudian dynamics, I suppose," he said, disheartened. "Psychological thesis is dead in this day and age, I'm afraid. I'm dead."

For whatever reason, then, Patricia laughed.

"But you're right," he repeated. Why had his voice reduced to a dark gurgle? "This is a dream, so you don't have to worry about it."

Patricia peered at him through smoke.

"And you don't have to worry about what you do."

The smoke engulfed him. The fire blazed behind her, so she ran, though she still felt no fear. Her feet crunched twigs and leaves, the earth warm beneath them. Her sexual urgency—her feminine *heat*—rose with the flames. At one point she broke through the trees, the smoke hanging behind her, and realized she was wandering along the edge of a lake—no . . .

A pond.

The realization seized her then.

This is the pond at Bowen's Field. . . .

Moonlight blared in her face. Even this late at night she could clearly make out her reflection on the pond's glass-flat surface.

The vision gave her a mild shock.

She stood pantiless in a sheer nightshirt made even more sheer by profuse perspiration. She seemed a caricature of female sexuality, her *parts* exaggerated by some aspect of the craft of the dream. Her breasts were ample in life; in the dream, though, they were even larger, higher, so swollen she could've been pregnant. The damp nightshirt clung to them, making no secret of nipples just as magnified, with fleshy ends prominent as olives. The dream had deepened her curves and widened her hips, and when (with no volition whatsoever) she raised the hem of the nightshirt, she saw that she was not only missing her panties, but missing pubic hair as well.

Her desires squirmed with her nerves. The night's heat drew more sweat from her skin, leaving her in a veneer of indeterminable lust.

It was Ernie who rose from the water: naked, his smile sweet and eyes reaching. Patricia's eyes yearned back, but her own smile was clearly one of wantonness, the greed to slake her own needs moistening her. She simply stood there, lifting her hem again up past her navel.

Why should she feel guilty now? It was a dream, and even Dr. Sallee—evidently a doctor whose professional philosophies were dead—had affirmed that she could do what she wanted. And when she'd talked to the real Dr. Sallee on the phone, he essentially told her that she had defeated the trauma of her past.

This dream proved that, didn't it? Here she was at the very site of her rape, but she stood now as a normal and very untraumatized sexual being.

Her sensibilities corroded. She felt lewd, trampish. Was this her real self coming out? Was this the *real* Patricia? Or was the dream just giving her the luxury of cutting loose in a way she couldn't in real life?

"It's only your sexual socialization evolving," Dr. Sallee's unseen voice guaranteed. "Superego versus id. The societal verisimilitudes of modern man reinforce the self-maintenance of our regrettable sexual repression."

She tried to make sense of it, but couldn't.

"We're all animals, Patricia. We just act like we're not. Hence the repression and its debilitating effect. Ultimately, it's *what?* Unnatural."

What am I doing? This is a dream. Am I waiting for my doctor's permission to have sex? She nearly laughed at the absurdity—in a dream no less. The idea behind his comment hawked down on her. *We're animals but we pretend that we're not.*

"Cavemen didn't repress themselves," the doctor's voice assured her next. "Neither did cave*women*."

Well . . .

Her eyes hooked on Ernie. He was naked in the water, on his knees. The dream, too, had augmented him into a puppet of male sexual features all optimized. A broadened back, shoulders, and neck. Chest and biceps like pumped bands of meat. The surreally large genitals rising at the vision of her.

"Come here," she said, a slut now. "And bring your mouth. You're going to need it."

Ernie obeyed without pause, a slave to her summons. He crawled to her on hands and knees: every woman's perfect man. Patricia remained standing, the dream enforcing her need to be higher than him, to reduce him to subservience. She gave her plumpened breasts a shameless caress through the top and felt their gorge of nervous desire gust to her loins. She parted her legs some more, closing her eyes with a commanding smile, waiting for his mouth to give her succor. . . .

But nothing happened.

She looked down again and saw that he was gone without a trace.

Unless the gentle ripple in the water could be called a trace.

What crawled out next wasn't Ernie. It was something thin, gray, and very dead.

A woman. She couldn't have weighed ninety pounds. Gray skin seemed stretched over a struggling framework of bones, and Patricia could see those bones moving as the woman crawled hence. Hollow eyes looked up from the skull-like face showing through the open vee of straggly, waterlogged hair. Patricia wasn't sure—not that details mattered in a dream—but it seemed that the corpse woman possessed crude stitches about her waist, as though she'd been cut in half and later reconnected by slipshod surgeons. A pendant with a stone of some kind swung about the starved neck as she continued to crawl.

"Flee this evil place, child," rumbled some semblance of a voice. Was that a Squatter accent leaking through the corrosion that death had brought to her larynx? "Run outta here now, and beg God's grace to go with ya. Run. Run."

"Run from what?" Patricia asked.

The cadaver collapsed as though all of her joints at once had lost their connective tissue.

Patricia's query wasn't answered, and when she heard stomping behind her—something coming out of the woods—she didn't need an answer to run just the same.

Her feet kicked up splotches of mud when she dashed along the edge of the pond. Before she could turn off in another direction . . . were there things in the pond, close to the surface, looking at her or addressing her in some way?

She didn't want to know. She plunged back into the woods and their moonlit darkness, the fire still blazing deeper within. Smoke stung her eyes, and when she felt small, fragile things crunching under her bare soles, she realized what they were: cicadas, having been cooked to crisps while trying to fly away.

The stomping still pounded behind her.

She thrashed farther into the woods, hoping she was heading away from the fires. *Who's following me?* But was it even a *who?* This was a dream, and that fact, now, she had to keep reminding herself of.

"It's something you're never meant to see." Dr. Sallee's voice somehow suffused her head. He was nowhere to be seen, of course. "Sometimes we chase ourselves. We're our own worst predators. Could it be that the person or thing that's chasing you is actually an aspect of yourself?"

I don't care! she thought at this point. Now she truly

felt fear, and she expected more Freudian backlash when it became apparent that her previous sexual arousal had increased tenfold. *I don't believe that I subconsciously want to be raped again!* She felt absolutely sure. *Freud can kiss my ass!* Her dream-enhanced breasts swayed vigorously beneath the tight fabric of the nightshirt. Her nipples buzzed. Then—

Shit!

Patricia fell to the ground belly-first. She'd tripped over something. A vine? A branch?

No, because when she looked back, she saw in a network of moonlight what it had been: a severed head.

Dwayne's head, she knew.

And the wild footfalls of her pursuer drew closer. But . . .

What's . . . that?

Did she hear a pounding in the back of the dream? *Like someone knocking on a door,* she thought. But there were no doors here in the burning woods. The woods signified her desires, she knew, and the dangers that accompanied them, and her pursuer: the unknown.

But what of the pounding?

It scarcely mattered. She heaved herself up, was about to sprint off again, but then she saw another slant of moonlight painting the tree right before her.

There was a design carved in the tree's bark . . . but was the bark bleeding? No, of course not, it must be sap. And it was the design that riveted her: a crude yet elaborate cross framed by the intricate etchings and squiggles of the Stanherd clan's symbol for good luck.

She squirmed, flat on her back now. The dream was gone, and all she could feel were the throes of orgasm, her nerves pulsing, her hand fervid between her legs, and then—

"Patricia! Patricia!"

Her sister's voice.

Patricia snapped away. She was confused at first, for the moonlit darkness of the bedroom matched that of the woods in her dream. Of course, she'd wakened, and it was Judy who'd wakened her.

"Patricia, I'm so sorry ta wake ya at this hour, but—"

Oh, Jesus . . . The first thing she noticed was that her nightshirt—the same one from the dream—was pulled up over her breasts. Her nipples throbbed in delicious pain, and she knew how they'd gotten that way: from self-plucking. The sheet lay aside, her legs splayed. She knew she'd been masturbating in her sleep again, to the point of climax.

She second thing she noticed was the smell of smoke.

"Is the house on fire?" she blurted. Why else would Judy be waking her up so late and so abruptly?

"No, no, dear me, no. But—"

"And . . . I heard this loud pounding," she said, quickly dragging the nightshirt back down.

"That was Sergeant Trey, knocking on the front door."

The police? "What did he want?"

"To tell me what happened. There's been a burnin' on the Point, in Squatterville. Now hurry up 'n' put somethin' on so's we can go see."

A fire on the Point. Real smoke, evidently, had pursued her in the dream. "I'll be right there," she said.

Judy turned before she left, the slyest smile in the dark. "You were havin' yourself one racy dream, sister."

Thank God she couldn't see Patricia blushing.

"Ain't nothin' wrong with a gal takin' care a' herself," Judy added. "Now hurry! We'll meet'cha out front."

My God, Patricia thought when she left. *My own sister just caught me masturbating. . . .* She pulled on a blouse, shorts, and sneakers. Before she left she glanced out her open window and saw flames from afar.

It wasn't the kind of sight anyone would ever expect to see in a place like Agan's Point. Ever. Blossoms of flashing red, blue, and white lights throbbed out into the night. Several fire trucks parked askew, tentacle-like hoses reaching out. A half dozen police cars bracketed the end of the perimeter—several state cars, Patricia noted—with poker-faced officers prowling the scene. Patricia, Judy, and Ernie looked on in macabre awe.

"Oh, Lord, no." Judy gasped.

"It's David Eald's shack," Ernie said, "so I guess that's—"

Ernie didn't finish as the three of them watched firemen bring out a black body bag atop a stretcher.

A smell in the air nauseated Patricia; it wasn't a stench she might expect; it was an aroma—something akin to pork roast. *Oh, Jesus,* she thought, her stomach flipping.

"That ain't the worst of it, I'm afraid," Sergeant Trey told them. His face shifted in various luminous shades from the flashing lights.

"David Eald has a daughter, doesn't he?" Judy choked out the question.

Both Trey and Ernie nodded at the same time, and a moment later a second stretcher was carried out.

Had a daughter, Patricia thought.

The trucks had put the fire out, a fire that had incinerated the dilapidated wooden shed that had comprised David Eald's home. Several trees had caught fire too, leaving blackened posts in their place, smoke still wafting.

"I know all the electrical connections 'n' junction

boxes were good," Ernie said. Did he seem worried that someone might think he'd made a mistake? "They're all to spec. I installed 'em myself, every hookup in Squatterville."

"Just one a' those things," Trey offered. "Happens all the time, bad as it is. He 'n' his daughter probably went to bed and forgot to turn off the stove. The smoke conks 'em out in their sleep; then the place burns down."

A common tragedy. *You read about accidents like this all the time in the paper,* Patricia acknowledged, *and you never really think much about it. . . .* "There're an awful lot of police, though. And why all the state troopers?"

"That does seem strange," Judy added. "The nearest state police station is a half hour away."

"On account a' what happened earlier," Trey said. "With the Hilds. They're still investigating *that* . . . and now *this* happens."

"But the Hilds' murders and this fire can't possibly be related," Patricia supposed.

"I don't know about that, not now." Another voice sneaked up from behind. Chief Sutter's disheartened bulk stepped out of the darkness.

Judy looked puzzled. "Whatever do ya mean, Chief?"

"The Hilds were closet druggers—crystal meth." The chief's eyes roved the cinders that were once the Eald shack. "Ain't much left a' the place now, but the state cops found some charred chemical bottles inside, and a burned pot on the stove with somethin' at the bottom of it that they say ain't food."

Patricia immediately remembered what she'd read on the Internet earlier. "A methamphetamine lab," she said. "Is that what the police think?"

"They're sendin' the bottles and other stuff to their

lab for tests, but it sure looks like it." Sutter shook his head. "Kinda makes sense when you think about it."

It was pretty sad sense.

Judy stood in something like a state of shock as she watched the police and firemen stalk about.

Patricia asked the grimmest question yet. "How old was this man's daughter?"

"Thirteen, fourteen, thereabouts," Ernie replied.

Judy stifled a sob.

"It's all the damn drugs," Sutter regarded. "God-damn evil shit . . ."

Patricia could feel streams of heat eddying off the cinders. The night felt more and more like something she was disconnected from—she was a watcher looking down. *This quaint little town really is going to hell fast. Four deaths just in the few days I've been here. Plus Dwayne . . .*

The night swallowed the heavy thunks of the ambulance doors. Radio squawk etched the air. Patricia put her arm around her sister, who was already blinking tears out of her eyes. Judy's lower lip quivered when she finally said, "I might have to sell this land after all."

No one said anything after that.

And no one noticed the split second in which Sergeant Trey smiled.

Eight

(I)

Ricky felt high on drugs when he got back home, the tantalizing garbage thoughts filling his brain as effectively as any opiate. The girl had really gotten him tuned up. *I love it when the bitches twitch like that,* he thought, replaying the atrocity in his mind. *And right there on the floor next to her dead daddy!* Yeah, it was a great night, all right. He'd torched the place perfectly, too, afterward, and was all the way back in the woods before the fire started to really catch.

Ricky was a consummate sociopath.

Can't wait to tell Junior, he thought. He was cutting through the woods all the way back home, so as not to be seen. This was something they needed to have a few beers over. And he couldn't wait to tell him about the girl. . . .

Yeah, my little brother'll be a mite jealous 'bout that!

He could hear the sirens in the distance, which simply brought more satisfaction to his heart. It filled him up very happily, like a big, rich meal.

Night sounds pulsed around him. Eventually, the trees broke and he was suddenly standing in his backyard. He didn't see any lights on in the house, though. *Guess Junior went beddy-bye,* he thought. Usually they both stayed up late, drinking and watching porn. It seemed a brotherly thing to do.

But Ricky was too keyed-up to go to bed himself. Couple beers and another chew, first, and maybe he'd also pop in his favorite porno, *Natal Attraction.* He crossed the backyard, stepping over moonlit junk, and went in through the back screen door.

At once, the inside of the house felt . . .

Weird, he thought.

Darkness hemmed him in, and when he closed the door behind him the silence felt cloying, like the faintest unpleasant smell in the air. He snapped on the kitchen light, yet felt no better. He couldn't shake the feeling, and he didn't even know what the feeling *was.* When he opened the refrigerator for a beer, he stalled, hand poised.

Ain't that the fuckin' shits.

The full case of brew he'd put in there this afternoon was untouched. *Junior must be sick as a dog to not've knocked out ten or twelve bottles by now.*

He grabbed one and closed the door, then walked slowly, brow furrowed, into the front room, switched on the light—

The bottle of beer shattered on the floor.

Ricky stared, gut churning.

Junior Caudill lay in the middle of the floor, eyes and mouth wide open, not breathing. His face could've been a pallid mask, gravity pushing the blood to the lowest surfaces of the body, leaving the flesh white as a turnip.

Ricky's mourning escaped in a shrill gasp from his throat. He couldn't say or even think anything about what he was looking at. Junior had obviously been dead for several hours, but that wasn't why Ricky stared.

Junior's pants looked several sizes too large; in fact, they hung so loosely they surely would've fallen down were he standing up.

When the shock snapped, Ricky yelled, "Junior!" and rushed to him, dropping to his knees. His hands floated in the air; he didn't know what to do.

"Junior! What happened?"

In his mind he knew his brother was dead; it was obvious from the pallor. He felt the neck for a pulse, found nothing but cool fat. Then he straddled his brother to administer some inept CPR, like on TV, but he may as well have been straddling a bag of fertilizer.

"Junior . . ."

He climbed off then, numb, remaining on his knees.

Musta had a heart attack or somethin' . . .

What else could it be?

He just looks so fuckin' weird, he thought.

Indeed, the arms and legs still held their usual girth—Junior, like his brother, was a *big* man. Fat, in other words. The big, fat arms and legs looked normal, and so did the fat-covered chest and chubby face. So . . .

Why did Junior look so strange?

Ricky pushed his brother's spotty T-shirt up over the blubbery, hairy chest and belly.

He shook his head in the utmost dismay.

There was no intricate way to put it. Junior's once-proud and very prominent beer gut . . . was gone.

Had he been dieting? *Fuck, no,* Ricky knew. His

brother had never been on a diet in his life. Diets were for sissies!

He remained there awhile, sorting his thoughts. He supposed he should call an ambulance, but that might not be the smartest thing to do right now. The local ambulances were at the Point, no doubt recovering the burned bodies of David Something-or-other and his little fox of a daughter. It would seem an odd coincidence. And an ambulance call might bring some police questioning with it. *Guess I'll have to wait,* he reasoned, but there was still no reasoning *this* situation.

In time, Ricky straggled up. *Damn it, Junior. Why'd ya have to die? Never even got the chance to tell you 'bout the hot job I did on them two crackers . . .*

He went to the kitchen, grabbed another beer, then wandered open-eyed around the house. He didn't turn the lights on; he needed it calm and dark, to help him think on what to do.

Musta been a heart attack. Couldn't be nothin' else. Hash 'n' eggs every morning of his life? Shit, I guess the one who needs ta go on a diet is me. . . .

He wandered around some more in the dark, then found himself in the living room. He didn't know where he was going, what he was even doing. This was redneck mourning: shuffling around in your dark house with a beer in your hand and a thousand-yard stare. . . .

With his next step, something crinkled under his foot.

A glance down showed him a sheet of paper. *The hell's this?* he wondered, and picked it up. He was about to turn the light on to look at it when—

Movement snagged the corner of his eye. He spun around, and—

His second beer of the night shattered, full, on the floor.

A thin figure stood staring at him from the hall that led to the bedrooms. It was so dark Ricky couldn't see. Just a figure there, something barely more substantial than a shadow . . .

A burglar? It must be. But, boy, did he pick the wrong house to burgle! There was nothing to steal in *this* dump. *This dumb-ass burglar's about to get his ass* killed, Ricky thought with some confidence.

Unless . . .

"Who the fuck're you, scumbag?" Ricky challenged.

The figure looked grainy standing there in the dark. It said nothing.

"I'm gonna . . ." But Ricky stalled through a thought. It finally occurred to his not-so-spectacular brain that maybe this figure was the guy who killed Junior somehow.

The figure said this, in a low, grating voice like some slow, black liquid oozing up his throat:

"Your brother is in hell. . . ."

And the figure, in a split second, withdrew into the hall.

"I am gonna kill you so motherfuckin' dead, you motherfucker!" Ricky bellowed out in his loudest sociopathic rage. His bulk tore down the hall, boots thudding. In the dim darkness he spotted an edge of the figure disappearing into Junior's bedroom. A second later Ricky was there, eyes sweeping back and forth in the dark.

There was no one else in the room.

But the window stood open, framing moonlit darkness.

Then that utterly bizarre voice seemed to gush around his head in a mad circle:

"Your useless brother is now a fat whore for the devil's minions, as you too will be, very soon. . . ."

Ricky stared in the dark. This time the voice had seemed to have no source. It came from everywhere, or nowhere.

He thrust his head out the window and saw the figure standing between some trees at the very end of the yard.

That is one fast motherfucker! How'd he get all the way out there so fast?

A cloud moved off; then a bar of moonlight fell ever so briefly across the figure's face, and Ricky's teeth ground, because he knew who it was. . . .

And then the figure's voice returned one last time, not from the figure itself but again a mushlike gurgle churning around Ricky's head as it bade its final promise before the figure disappeared.

The voice said this: "Curse thee."

Running after him would be pointless. Ricky pulled back into the room, confused, sick, and enraged. But something tempered that rage—even sociopaths felt fear.

He took deep breaths in the dark bedroom. Now instead of the evil voice it was the sound of cicadas that flowed into the room, and it was then that Ricky realized he was still holding the piece of paper he'd found in the living room.

He turned on the light and looked at it.

A single word was scrawled on a sheet of white paper, in something like brown chalk: *wenden.*

(II)

"I want you out of there right now! More murders? That place is dangerous."

Patricia sat comfortably on the bed. Sunlight

streamed into the room, warming her face. It was Byron she was talking to on her cell, and the previous, very loud exclamation had been his response when she'd told him about the burning last night, and the gruesome deaths of David Eald and his daughter. "Honey, you're overreacting again. It's just some people way out on the Point who got involved with drugs—"

"And those two people who got murdered the other night—what was their name? The Hilds? The Halds? Whatever! They were involved in drugs, too! Which is why I want your butt in your car right *now,* heading north!"

Patricia rolled her eyes. "There's plenty of drug-related crime in D.C., but we don't move because of it."

"That's four murders in a week," Byron countered. "No, five. Don't forget about Dwayne, the whole reason you went back to that nutty place."

"The Ealds weren't murdered. Their place burned down, probably an accident. It's actually kind of common in makeshift meth labs. Making the stuff involves several flammable solvents."

"That's supposed to put me at ease? It's okay because it's *common* for drug labs to burn down?"

"No, but I'm just saying—"

"And it could just as easily be that someone else torched the place, couldn't it? Another turf murder. Didn't you say the Hilds were murdered by a rival drug gang for operating on their turf?"

"Well, it's possible. That's what the police think. But . . ." She paused over the phone. *How can I argue with him? He's actually right. The place very easily could have been burned down by a rival drug gang.* "Honey, still, you're overreacting. Everything's fine here, and we're perfectly safe. Judy's still shaken up over the funeral and all, so that's why I'm here. I told you, I won't be gone longer than a week."

"Promise."

She laughed. "I promise!"

"So what are you going to do today? Chew tobacco? Sit on the porch in a rocking chair?"

"Agan's Point isn't quite *that* backward. I'm just going to go for a drive into town this morning—"

"You shouldn't be driving into town; you should be driving *out* of town."

She just shook her head and continued. "And then I'll probably just hang around the house and help Judy with some things." She began to tell him about the big clan cookout tomorrow—if the Squatters still had it now—but as she talked, her focus dissolved. Was that a splattering she heard? Yes, and a hiss. She noticed then that her bedroom door was open a crack, and as she peered down the hall, she saw that the bathroom door, too, stood open a few inches.

Ernie's in there taking a shower, she realized. *He's so used to having this wing of the house to himself that he forgot to close the door. . . .* This wouldn't have meant anything to her, but . . .

She could see flesh.

A convenient angle allowed the shower to reflect in the bathroom mirror, which she could see a significant slice of through the crack in the door.

She kept talking to her husband without even thinking, and suddenly had gotten up and walked to her own door for a better view. She could see him in there, all right—he hadn't closed the shower curtain.

My God, what am I doing? What if he saw me? He'd think I was a total perv . . . which I guess I am. A female voyeur?

Looking at other people in secret had never been a desire of hers, but then a lot of things about herself had changed since she'd gotten back. *What would Dr. Sallee say about this?* she wondered. It was just the midlife sexual peak of all women, so . . .

Was it that bad?

Her sense of guilt struggled to cut into her thoughts—as she continued to talk to her loving husband, no less—but she easily blocked them out.

And watched.

And then imagined.

Suddenly she saw *herself* in the shower with Ernie, and the more deeply she thought about it, the more clearly the vision focused. . . .

He wasn't even surprised as she stepped in; it was as though he were expecting her, as though his flesh were a summons to her desire, and he knew it. When the cool spray hit Patricia's breasts, her nipples shot right up. Something else shot right up, too, when she put her hand to his sudsy groin. She could feel it beating in her hand.

Then, in gestures that nearly seemed rough, his calloused hands spun her around by the hips, and then he was feeling her up into a suit of suds. He stood behind her, his manhood hot against her buttocks. He was manipulating her flesh the way a sculptor manipulated clay. Patricia grew short of breath at once, rising on her tiptoes, her mouth and eyes wide open. The rough fingers skipped back and forth between corkscrewing her nipples and massaging her sex. She just stood there and let herself be *felt*. . . .

She talked on to Byron, locked in some split stream of consciousness, communicating to him and regarding his replies with no real awareness . . . while the rest of her mind delved deeper into the sexual musing. Ernie still stood behind her, the shower hissing over them. One strong forearm locked around her waist, and then he was lifting her up. Her feet came off the shower floor. She could feel her buttocks sliding over his penis as she continued to rise, as if he would penetrate her from behind with her feet off the ground. Her sex burned; she was squirming—

Oh, God, no . . .

"Patricia?"

It was about to nudge into her all at once.

"Patricia? Damn, I think your cell phone cut out. Can you hear me?"

Her legs were tensing, her back arching as her inflamed breasts and nipples thrust outward, and she was already beginning to cli—

"Patricia!"

Reality slapped her in the face. No, she wasn't in the shower with Ernie; she was talking to her *husband!* "I'm here," she assured him, waiting for her heart to slow down.

"You sounded way off in space."

Not in space, she thought, visibly blushing. *Just in the shower.* "The reception down here isn't always that great. When I call tomorrow, I'll use Judy's phone."

"So how is Judy doing, considering?"

Patricia tore herself away from the gap in the door, then went back and sat on the bed. Her last real image of Ernie had been of him stepping out of the shower, in the reflection. She struggled to reengage her mind against a backwash of guilt. "Actually, okay, I think. She's seemed to be handling Dwayne's death pretty well since I got here, but now she's kind of rocked by what happened last night. She even said something to the effect that it might be a good idea for her to sell the Point."

"I think she should. Sounds like the whole place is turning into Drugtown. Sell it before all the property value goes down the tubes."

"Really, Byron, it's not that bad. There're luxury condos going up on the other side of the river. That'll drive any bad elements out faster than anything."

"I hope you're right."

"You get back to work now," she said, "and I'll call tomorrow. And there's something you need to know."

"What?"

"I love you," she said.

"Well, I love you, too, so come back *soon,* will you?"

"I will," she promised, and then they hung up.

Patricia sighed. *My fantasies are out of control!* It aggravated her so much now. But at least there was *some* solace: *Dr. Sallee said this is common for women my age. There's no reason to feel guilty, because they're just fantasies. I'd never really cheat on Byron. . . .*

Before she could consider anything further, she spotted Ernie coming down the hall in a robe.

"Hey, Ernie?" she called out.

He stuck his head in, his long hair combed out in wet lines. "Oh, hey. I didn't even know you were here."

Yeah, I'm here, all right, spying on you in the shower. "I meant to get up early, but it took me a while to fall back to sleep once we got back from the fire. How's Judy?"

"It's funny," he said. "She's more pissed off than depressed about the Ealds. She don't like the idea that Squatters are makin' dope on her land."

"Well, it's just a few of them."

"Yeah, I know. She'll be all right. It's just too much goin' on at once. She ain't handlin' it well."

Patricia deliberately avoided eye contact. Just his being in the same room relit some of the shower fantasy's fire. "I wanted to ask you something. Do you know who officially declared Dwayne dead? I know he was cremated at the funeral home, but where was he autopsied? Is there a family doctor or something?"

"It was the EMTs who picked his body up just off the Point," Ernie informed her. "And they took Dwayne's body to the county hospital there, to the county morgue. So I guess that's where they did the autopsy, but that's about all I know. You might wanna ask Chief Sutter."

"I already did," she said, looking off. *And he seemed vague.*

"What'cha wanna know that for?"

She shrugged. "I just want to see the autopsy report. Nobody seemed to know any details about the murder, not even Judy."

"That's 'cos Judy doesn't want to know 'em. You know how she is. She coulda got a copy of the autopsy report, legal-like."

Legal-like, Patricia thought. Even the backwater way he talked seemed attractive. "I do know how she is, and I can't really blame her. Learning the *details* of how her husband got his head cut off would just rub her face deeper in the tragedy. But I keep hearing funny things about the incident, and no one seems to know exactly what happened."

Ernie nodded. "Just like any small hick town. Everything's rumors."

"What other rumors are there?" she couldn't help but ask.

"Well, over the past coupla months a lotta Squatters have disappeared—that's the biggest rumor goin'."

"I've heard something along those lines. But they didn't really *disappear,* they just pulled up roots and moved somewhere else. Even Squatters can get sick of living in the same place."

"Sure, and that's probably true. But that's what I'm talkin' about. The way people are in a town like this. There's always gotta be a mystery goin' on, even if it ain't true. Rumor is some of these Squatters was actually murdered. By Dwayne."

The comment jolted her. "Dwayne?"

"Um-hmm. And you wanna know the rest?"

Now Patricia was almost laughing. "Of course!"

"Rumor is that Everd Stanherd used his boondocks magic to kill Dwayne—for revenge."

"And people actually believe this?" she asked, astonished.

"Oh, yeah."

"I don't believe in 'boondocks' magic, and I'm sure you don't either." She paused, looking at him hard. "Do you?"

He paused himself, which seemed strange, then cracked a smile and said, "A' course not. All I meant is to show ya how things work here. There's rumors for everything. And that'd be great if you really *could* see Dwayne's autopsy report, and put an end to *that* rumor."

"Oh, don't worry, I will."

"I got work to do in the yard, so I'll see ya later," he said, and disappeared from the open door.

What a strange conversation. *But at least it got my mind off . . . him. Middle age is turning me into a closet slut!* And he was right about the rumors. People made them up to make their lives feel more interesting. Patricia had to admit she was intrigued herself, and that was why she picked up her cell phone again and called her office.

Her associate put her through to the boss, the chief managing partner, Tim McGinnis.

"So how are things down there in . . . *where?*" he asked.

"Agan's Point, southern, southern Virginia."

"Never heard of it. Sounds like a hillbilly town."

"It sort of is," she said through a laugh. "D.C. and this place are two different worlds. Everything all right at the firm?"

"Well, other than the roof threatening to collapse since the day you left, things are great. I hope you get back here soon, because the Walton account wants to go to settlement."

"Give it to the associates; I don't have to be there."

"They want you, nobody else. I guess you're the only lawyer in D.C. they trust. Please come back soon."

"God, you sound like my husband. Don't worry; I won't be more than a week."

"Thank God."

"But I also wanted to ask you something." She got to the point of her call. "Didn't you tell me once that some buddy of yours works for the governor of Virginia?"

Tim laughed snidely. "Yeah, but he's not my buddy; he's my brother. He's the number four man in the state government, director of public safety. Oversees every police department in the state, every fire department, county sheriff's—everything."

Perfect, she thought. "Are you in any position to ask him a favor?"

Now Tim laughed harder. "Since I practically put his boss in office with private fund-raising contributions, I think I can safely say my brother would shit turkeys and whistle 'Dixie' if I told him to. Why?"

Patricia was amused by the talk. "I need access to an

autopsy report, and I don't have the time to do a FOIA request. My sister's husband—Dwayne Parker. Nobody knows the exact cause of death, and I want to find out."

Tim's incredulity could be sensed over the line. "I thought you said he got his head cut off! That's the cause of death: head cut off."

Patricia felt guilty getting a laugh out of the tragedy. . . . *But it is kind of funny when you put it that way.* "There's this rumor down here that there was some oddity relating to the decapitation, and I haven't gotten anywhere with the local police chief. I really need this, Tim. The autopsy report is in the morgue at the county hospital in Luntville."

"I'll make a call. Just go to the place tomorrow, and it shouldn't be a problem."

"Thanks, Tim. It's just that there's some weird stuff going on here, and I'm curious about it."

"Hmm. Well, remember what curiosity did to the cat. I don't really like the idea of my star attorney running around down in Hooterville inquiring about decapitations."

"The weirdest part is that there have been several more murders just since I've been back—"

"What!"

"Drug-related stuff. It's very uncharacteristic in a place like this."

Now her boss lost his levity. "Why don't you just come home? Don't tell me some *other* people got their heads cut off too."

"No, but it was pretty brutal stuff. I just want to check some things out, get my sister squared away; then I'll be back."

"You'd damn well better, 'cos let me tell you something. If you wind up getting *your* head cut off . . . I'm going to be pissed."

A final laugh. "Thanks for your help, Tim. And I will be back soon, with my head securely attached to my neck."

Nine

(I)

Chief Sutter was looking at Pam's legs as he pretended to write up his daily operating report. He needed diversion—from the very loud fact that people in *his* town were suddenly dying right and left—and Pam's legs provided this necessary diversion and then some. Pam was a local cutie whom he'd hired as the department's radio dispatcher and office manager. She was great at both jobs, so the fact that she had a body that could start a riot in a monastery maximized her purpose in the office. She made for a positive working environment, and that was important to hardworking, overstressed police officers, wasn't it?

Trey sat at the opposite desk, pretending to go over the county blotter, and he, too, seemed to be musing over Pam's legs as she sat at her own desk, typing. The legs, by the way, could be described as coltish. Long and lean, well toned without being "muscular"—ultimate legs as far as men were concerned. The rest of her was equally flawless: trim and curvy; alert, prominent-nippled breasts; and a tight, to-die-for little butt. Short auburn hair framed a cute little angel face with bright hazel eyes. Any male sexist slob's archetypical meat for a spectacular daydream: the total office package.

Sutter seethed to himself when she suddenly crossed her legs. The delectable—and tiny—triangle of fabric shouted at him. *Fuck, she's wearin' a T-back. Just what I need . . .*

Then she got up to take something to the file room. The chief's eyes riveted to the shifting little butt in the tight blue-jean miniskirt, then slid down to the legs. All that tight, fresh, tan skin seemed to glimmer beneath fishnet stockings. Her high heels ticked across the floor until they disappeared.

Trey was shaking his head. "Jesus, Chief. Those are some damn fine walkin' sticks on her, ain't they? Wouldn't mind havin' 'em wrapped around my head for an hour or three."

Sutter shot a reproving scowl. "Is there anytime when your mind *ain't* in the trash can, Trey? That happens to be our employee you're lustin' after."

Trey grinned, slapping his knees. "Chief, you practically been droolin,' lookin' at those gams for the last twenty minutes."

"I have not," he insisted. "And shut up. We need to be thinkin' on what we gotta do about this drug business in Squatterville."

"Not much we can do. State narcs are investigatin'."

"Yeah, but this is *our* town, Trey. So maybe some a' this is our fault."

"How do ya figure?"

"All these years we took it for granted that Squatterville's crime-free. Maybe if we'd had a better presence out there, none a' this would have happened."

"Horseshit. People turn to scum because it's their time. We cain't be lookin' over every damn shack on the Point."

"That ain't what I'm sayin'. What I mean is—"

Pam came back to her desk, the image of her legs chopping off the rest of the chief's remark like a carrot end. *Oh, God, those legs are killing me. . . .* Just as she was sitting down, the hazel eyes flashed at him once. Then she smiled and returned to her work.

Jesus, save me.

He and Trey both looked up from their desks when the bell on the station door chimed.

It was Ricky Caudill who strode in. He looked like he always did: slovenly, fat, not particularly clean. But his usual cast of arrogance made no appearance on his face today.

Instead he looked scared.

Just as peculiar—Sutter noticed—was the expression on Sergeant Trey's face upon noticing their abrupt visitor. For a split second, something like dread washed over his face, but he quickly buried it beneath his authoritative police veneer.

What's with that? Sutter wondered. Was it just his imagination?

"Well, look what the cat drug in," Trey said, and stood up at his desk.

Sutter was too tired, so he didn't bother. "What'choo want, Ricky, 'cos the only thing you're gonna get here is somethin' you *don't* want: an ass kicking."

"I wanna be locked up," Ricky declared from where he stood.

"You have to break the law to be locked up," Pam told him, surprised. "You broken the law lately?"

"My brother's dead," he said with no hesitation.

Now Sutter stood up. "You confessin' to murder, Ricky?"

"Hell, no. I didn't kill Junior."

"Then why you wanna be locked up?"

"'Cos I want protection from the person who did. They'll be after me next."

Sutter frowned and sat back down. "You're drunk, Ricky. You're talkin' shit. Now get out of here unless you want a big pile a' trouble to leave with."

"I ain't drunk—"

"You smell like a brewery," Trey said. "I can smell it across the room."

Ricky's hands curled up into frustrated fists. "I'm tellin' ya, my brother's been murdered. Go to the house 'n' look. It was Squatters who done it."

Sutter stood back up. "Go check it out," he told Trey.

"Why don't you check it out, Chief? This guy can be a handful. Let me take care of him."

Sutter stared Trey down. He didn't like the innuendo here. "Go check it out. Now. I wanna talk to this one."

Addled, Trey grabbed the cruiser keys and left.

"You want me to call an ambulance?" Pam asked the chief.

"Ain't no reason to," Ricky spoke up first. "My brother's dead. Call the undertaker. But lock me up."

"You're talkin' crazy, boy. Now you're gonna turn around and walk out of here right now. I'm too busy to be foolin' around with you."

"Lock me up," Ricky repeated. "Otherwise I'll be killed."

Sutter smirked. "Yeah, sure, by the *Squatters.* So you're sayin' it was Squatters who killed Junior, huh?"

"Yeah."

"You saw 'em?"

"Yeah."

Sutter pinched the bridge of his nose, a headache coming on. "Ricky, you're tellin' me you *saw* Squatters kill your brother?"

"I didn't see 'em *do* it, but one of 'em was in my house. Everd Stanherd. He was *in my house,* and it was that weirdo clan magic a' his he used to kill Junior. And he put a curse on me. He'll be comin' for me next, so's you gotta lock me up, Chief, for my protection. I'm beggin' ya, man."

Sutter came around the desk, shaking his head. "Ricky, you're a scumbag and a no-account loser, but I can't *lock you up* just for that. You gotta commit a crime, boy, and unfortunately talkin' shit ain't a crime."

Ricky stalled, thinking. "Okay," he said, then spun around, cleared Pam's desk with his stout forearm, and yanked her top down. Even in the midst of the outrage, Chief's Sutter's eyes bulged at the beauteous sight. Razor-sharp tan lines bordered each firm orb of flesh, and the well-delineated nipples stuck out as if iced, plucked, and sucked out in advance. At least Chief Sutter's day would have one high point.

But the rest was certainly a low point. Pam shrieked at the assault, pushing herself back in her chair, while Ricky stalked off and began hauling bookshelves over. Training manuals scattered. The *Virginia State Annotated Code* flew across the room, and a moment later so did the office coffeepot, which was full of java. It shattered against the wall. Sutter's reaction was delayed a moment by sheer disbelief. He broke from his stance just as Ricky now manhandled the five-gallon bottle of Polar Water out of its stand.

"Don't you dare, you crazy redneck!" Chief Sutter bellowed.

Ricky shoved the bottle across the room. It exploded spectacularly against the wall, gushing springwater everywhere.

Sutter hauled on a sand mitt and lunged. He was a fat man, but he was still a strong one. Three hard belly shots with the mitt doubled Ricky over; then a loud belt across the face sent him reeling conveniently in the direction of the station's three-unit jail. Ricky hit the floor like a 250-pound pallet of sod.

"Crazy shithead!" Sutter yelled. He doubled over himself now and grabbed Ricky's bulk by the belt, then began to drag him into the first cell. "You just fucked up my office! Take me all damn day to clean this mess up! I ain't got time for this grab-ass bullshit!"

Ricky lay wheezing on the cell floor. He groaned a few times, then dizzily sat up against the wall.

"You wanted to be locked up, you dickhead! Well, you got it!" Sutter continued to yell. He slammed the door shut with a clang.

Cross-eyed, Ricky grinned back at him. "Thanks, Chief," he said.

What a fuckin' kook! Sutter lumbered back toward the office, frowning as he heard the phone ringing. All he wanted to do was sit his ass down and have a nice, slow day, especially after being up half the night at the Eald fire.

Pam's hazel eyes looked foreboding when he sat back down at his desk. She'd just hung up the phone.

"Please tell me it was a wrong number," he pleaded.

"Sorry, Chief. It was Trey. He needs you down at the Caudill house—says Junior's lying in the middle of the floor, stone-cold dead."

(II)

The hand reached out in tranquil dark. He *liked* to sit in the dark. The colors of dusk were filtering into the room.

He picked up the phone.

"Yes?"

"It's all fucked-up like you wouldn't believe."

"What are you talking about? I saw a dozen Squatters pulling up stakes today, packing. They're beginning to leave town. It's working beautifully, and faster than I thought."

"No, no, you don't know the rest. It just happened a few hours ago. Junior's dead."

A pause drew out along the line. "How?"

"Don't know. There's no wounds, there's no—"

"He probably had a heart attack. He was a fat slob."

"No, no, see, Ricky's in lockup."

"What? What for? He didn't—"

"No, he didn't squeal. But he says it was Everd Stanherd who killed Junior, says he saw the guy in his house last night. He wanted to be locked up for his own protection, but Sutter wouldn't do it. So then he trashed the place. But he's talking crazy shit. And . . . and . . . and . . ."

"And what?"

"I'm scared, and Sutter was looking at me funny earlier today when I left the office. I'm about to shit my pants worrying what Ricky might say."

"Ricky's in as deep as us."

"He don't care! He thinks the Squatters killed Junior with some sorta hocus-pocus!"

"In other words, you think Ricky might be a liability now?"

"Damn right. He starts running his mouth to save his ass, you and I're both gonna be neck-deep in shit."

Another pause. The solution was obvious, though he would've preferred not to clarify it over a phone line. "Rectify the problem, for both our sakes. Use your position to your advantage. It'll be easy once you think about it. . . . Am I clear?"

"It'll cost."

"I'll pay. Rectify the problem. Do it quickly."

He hung up.

His hand retreated back into the dark.

(III)

I don't believe it, Patricia thought. She looked up the hill, lit by morning sun, and saw what appeared to be a Squatter family leaving the Point. A ragtag man and woman, plus a child, trudged up the hill toward the main road out of town, carrying sacks of clothes and beaten suitcases.

They're leaving town. . . .

At the end of the trail she spotted a figure coming her way, a toolbox at the end of one strong arm. She scarcely had a minute to contemplate the idea that Squatters were actually moving away out of fear, and now more of this distraction.

Oh, no, not again.

It was Ernie who headed toward her. He smiled and waved.

Patricia had hoped for a nice, leisurely walk by herself, to clear her head. But the instant she saw him . . .

All that sexual tension returned.

Damn it.

He wended up the rest of the trail, the Stanherd house looming in the background.

"Mornin'," he greeted her.

"Where have you been?"

"I just come from the Stanherd house. Last week Everd asked to borrow my tools to replace some missing shingles, so I thought I'd drop 'em off with Marthe for when he comes back from the boats." He set the toolbox down, suddenly looking confused. "But he ain't there."

"He works the crabbing boats every morning, I thought. He's probably on the water."

"His boat's still tied up at the dock, and so are half a' the others. What I mean is Everd and his wife are *gone.* They left town's, what the men at the pier told me."

"They . . ." Then Patricia looked farther up the trail and saw yet another Squatter family trudging away. "It looks like quite a few clan people are leaving."

"Things change. I guess it was bound to happen." Ernie's face looked deflated.

"I guess if I had a family, and drugs started popping up in the neighborhood, I'd move too," Patricia reasoned.

"The others are sayin' that ain't the real reason," Ernie said. "I just talked to some a' the men at the docks, said a lot of clan are leavin' 'cos they're just plain scared."

"Scared of what?"

"Well, it's like we were talkin' the other day. Rumors everywhere—ya never really find out what the true story is. But some a' the clan are sayin' that this whole drug business is a setup, and that somebody murdered the Hilds and the Ealds to scare the bejesus out of the rest a' the Squatters, to get 'em to clear out."

"That's ridiculous," Patricia replied. "Nobody wants the Squatters to leave. . . ." But then the rest of her sentence trailed off as she considered her words.

"Uh-hmm," Ernie edged in. "That Felps fella would *love* for the Squats to leave. With nobody to run the crabbing business, Judy'd be much more tempted to just say to hell with it and sell the land."

"To Felps, you're right." A breeze ran through her red hair. "He's already made offers. But that's still crazy. I don't believe for a minute that Gordon Felps is *murdering* Squatters for the sake of his condo development."

"Neither do I, but ya gotta admit the coincidence." Ernie pointed to one of the shanties, where a man hauled a suitcase out the front door. "Looks like a lot of 'em are figurin' they'd be safer somewhere else. They don't wanna wind up like the Hilds 'n' the Ealds."

Like a chain reaction, Patricia thought. *The murder of the Hilds, plus the fire, has started a mass exodus.* Ernie's suspicion of Gordon Felps was an overreaction; nevertheless, she wondered how long it would be before he came back to Judy with another offer to purchase the property.

"Let's just go ask someone," she said off the top of her head.

"Huh?"

"Come on. . . ."

He followed her back down the trail. High grass on either side shimmered in sunlight, while lone cicadas buzzed clumsily through the air. Patricia wasn't sure what lured her down the hill; perhaps she just wanted to see more directly for herself. They approached one larger shack made of roofing metal. Outside was a chicken-wire pen that caged, of all things, several seagulls.

"Seagulls as pets?" she questioned.

"Not quite," Ernie said. "The Squatters use gull fat to make candles, and they eat the meat. Roasted gull tastes just like—"

"Let me guess. Chicken."

"Naw, tastes like mallard duck."

Patricia shook her head. "I've never heard of anyone eating *seagull.* They're like pigeons, I thought. Don't taste good."

"They pen 'em for two weeks, and feed 'em nothin' but corn. Just wait till the clan banquet tomorrow. You'll have to try some."

Patricia doubted she would. "I'd be surprised if they even *had* this banquet. With four of their own killed in a couple of days . . . that's not exactly a festive occasion."

"That ain't how the Squatters see it. Every day they're alive they consider a gift from God."

Patricia appreciated the positive philosophy. *Eat, drink, and be merry,* she thought, *for tomorrow you may die?* But she honestly wondered how many of them believed the others had been murdered as a scare tactic.

A little Squatter girl—about ten—moseyed about the pen. She wore a frayed and obviously handmade sundress, and had a mop of black hair.

"Hi, there," Patricia greeted her. "Are these your birds?"

The little girl looked up despondently and nodded. She looked on the verge of tears. Then she opened the makeshift door of the pen and began shooing the gulls out with a branch.

"Why are you letting them go?"

In a rush, all of the hefty birds scampered out of the pen and flew off at once. "Cain't take 'em with us, my daddy said," the little girl told them.

"Where are you goin'?" Ernie asked.

The girl's accent warbled from her small mouth. "Someplace called Norfolk, 'cos my daddy says he might git a job on the big crab boats. But we cain't stay here, 'cos someone might kill us." And then the little girl ran back into the shed.

"That's so sad," Patricia said.

"Yeah, but like I said . . ."

Patricia tried to unclutter her mind as they meandered back toward her sister's house. She frowned to herself when Ernie turned his back to her.

It was that same distraction again—raging, fraying her sexual nerves. Whenever she tried to focus on something else, his aura kept dragging her eyes back to his unknowing body: the long flow of his hair, the strong legs in tight workman's jeans, the strong back. *What if I weren't married; what if I weren't . . . ?* Her thoughts kept betraying her.

Just remember what Dr. Sallee said. Women my age experience their actual sexual peak. It's normal for me to feel this way . . . as long as I don't act on those feelings.

His boots crunched up the trail before her, and that alternate voice kept asking her: *What if I weren't married?*

It didn't matter.

"Well, how do ya like that?"

Patricia reclaimed her attention; Ernie had stopped on the incline of the trail, looking up toward the main road.

"What are you . . ." But then she spotted the vehicle herself, a new large pickup truck parked at the shoulder. Even at this considerable distance she could see the man sitting in the driver's seat peering down into the center of Squatterville, as though he were actually watching the clan families trudging away from their homes in order to leave town.

The man in the pickup truck was Gordon Felps.

Ten

(I)

Less than a twenty-minute drive took Patricia to Luntville and the rather drab county hospital. She knew it was her imagination, yet it bothered her the way two clerks at the information kiosk gave her the eye when she asked directions to the morgue. The basement, of course. They were always in the basement.

The downstairs unnerved her; it was dark and dead silent. Her footsteps clattered about her head as she made her way to the yellowish glass-windowed door that read, OFFICE OF THE COUNTY CORONER.

Let's see how much pull my boss really has, she thought. Getting a morgue to release recent records was usually akin to pulling the teeth out of a ferret. When she entered, she expected more odd looks from the personnel here and was nearly shocked to find herself standing before a human dichotomy: an utterly striking blonde in tight jeans and an open lab coat that revealed a haltered bosom and a perfect bare abdomen. She had the kind of body that spurred jealousy even from the most extraordinarily attractive women.

Her body's ten times better than mine! Patricia thought. *I'm pissed!* "Hi," she began, and got out her driver's license. "I'm—"

"Patricia White, right?" A sexy Southern accent preceded the blond woman when she hurried around the registration desk. She spoke very quickly. "The governor's office called this morning, and I'd just like you to know that we'll do whatever we can to accommodate you." Then she pulled out a folder. "You wanted to see the post records for a decedent named Dwayne Parker?"

That's what I call the red-carpet treatment, Patricia thought, amused. *Tim's brother lit a fire under somebody's butt.* "Yes, and I'm sorry it was such short notice. I'm the attorney for the decedent's wife, and I won't be in town long, so I didn't really have time to file a FOIA request."

"Oh, well, there's no reason to do that"—the beautiful woman kept speaking very quickly—"because, after all, we're a branch of the government that exists to serve the taxpayers' needs."

Now she's absolutely kissing my ass, Patricia realized. The coroner's office for a rural county like this probably didn't keep the best records anyway. *The last thing they'd want is a government inspection.* But it was working, and that all Patricia cared about. "Are you the receptionist? I was hoping to talk to the county coroner himself."

"Herself, and you are, ma'am," the blonde corrected, and gestured to the nametag on her lab coat. It read C. BAKER, RUSSELL COUNTY CORONER. "And I'd be happy to answer any questions you have, since the postmortem report might be . . . confusing to you."

Patricia opened the folder and scanned the top sheet: *Anomalous death—COD*, it read. *Decapitation via smooth Transection of levator scapulae muscular process and #5 & 6 cervical vertebrae. Mode of transection as yet undetermined and curious.* She blinked, looked back up at Baker, and admitted, "I'm only good with legalese, not medical tech talk. I guess this means that the manner in which Dwayne Parker lost his head . . . *that's* what they're calling 'undetermined and curious'?"

The coroner nodded curtly, but she was obviously curtailing something. "It's just kind of odd, and its difficult to explain in any way that makes sense. But every now and then any medical examiner's office will get a cause of death that simply can never be determined."

Patricia frowned at the sheet. This was much less than she'd hoped for. "How was his head cut off, is what I want to be able to tell the family. Was it cut off, shot off? Was it knocked off in some sort of freak accident?"

Another curt look from the pretty coroner. "It was . . . none of those things, and that's about the only thing we *do* know. No blade striations, no evidence of severe impact to the body, no evidence of firearm discharge."

"But the head was never recovered—that's what I heard from the locals, anyway. Is that true?"

"Quite true, ma'am."

This was frustrating. "I'm sorry, but I just don't get it."

"Look on the next page, Ms. White."

Patricia followed the instruction and immediately fell silent.

What she looked at now was the most macabre photograph she'd ever seen in her life. . . .

The clarity of the bright digital picture—Dwayne's autopsy photo—seemed to shout at her. "This . . . can't be real, can it?"

"Oh, it's real, ma'am. I took the picture myself. It hasn't been altered, and there weren't any defects in the film or processing. I took several with several different cameras."

The photograph framed Dwayne's chest and shoulders, as well as the area of space that his head would occupy, if he'd *had* a head. Patricia expected a clot-caked stump or some other kind of ragged wound to indicate the decapitation. But there was nothing.

There was just skin.

"There's not even a—"

"Not even a neck," Baker finished. "And the osteo X-rays actually show a round—not a severed—cervical vertebra. There's actually no clinical evidence of a decapitation—which I know is silly, because he's got no head. But the picture looks like he'd never had one. Look at the next picture."

Patricia, with some trepidation, turned to the next sheet: a close-up of where the "stump" should be.

"This," she started, shaking her head, "this . . ." She tried to frame words. "This looks like there's just skin grown over the place where his neck should be."

"Um-hmm."

Patricia looked up again, grateful to take her eyes off the creepy photograph. "You're the coroner. How do you account for this?"

"I really can't. It happens in this business, and I realize that's not an acceptable answer, but it's all I can give you. It's just one of those rare deaths that's a big question mark."

"And you're sure this is Dwayne Parker? You're sure it's not some elaborate stage dummy or something, some kind of joke?"

"It's no dummy, Ms. White. I personally performed

the Y-section and a clinical evisceration. I weighed every organ in that man's body. There are pictures of that too, if you'd like to—"

"No, no, that won't be necessary," Patricia hastened to say.

"The Bureau of Prisons verified the fingerprints, along with two five-probe DNA profiles. And the body that I autopsied had tattoos that matched the county corrections inductee log of distinguishing marks. The body in the photograph is Dwayne Parker, and I'm very sorry I can't give you any useful information regarding his decapitation. One of the dermatologists at the hospital suggested that maybe some kind of mold or fungus grew over the transection area—"

"Is that possible?"

"In my opinion, no." The coroner shrugged, just as frustrated now as Patricia. "That's why we call this kind of death undetermined and curious."

You can say that again. . . . Patricia passed back the folder. She was glad not to have it in her hands anymore. *What am I going to tell Judy?* She struggled with the thought.

Nothing, I guess. I just won't tell her anything.

"What's stranger," Baker said, "is the fact that Dwayne Parker was a resident of Agan's Point, the crabbing town out on the water."

"Why is that strange?" Patricia asked.

"Because it really is a quiet little place. I don't think I've ever seen a decedent from Agan's Point who didn't die from old age. Then all of a sudden, in little more than a week we get Dwayne Parker, plus two brutal mutilations and two people burned to death."

The Hilds and the Ealds, Patricia knew. "All from

Agan's Point. Did you find any evidence of drugs in any of the bodies?"

Baker shook her head. "The narcotics unit *and* the Agan's Point police chief both asked me for full tox screens—something about crystal methamphetamine. There was nothing in any of them, no CDS of any kind, no marijuana, not even any trace alcohol. But that's not even what I was going to mention. *That's* not the strange part."

"What is?"

"The body that came in this morning."

Patricia's brow furrowed. "Not another Agan's Point resident . . ."

"I'm afraid so. The sixth one now."

"Who?"

"Forty-five-year-old male Caucasian named Robert Caudill, aka Junior."

The name rang a bell. "I remember when I was a kid, he and his twin brother were the neighborhood bullies." Patricia pinched her chin. "And he was murdered?"

"Don't know," Baker replied. "I don't see how it *could* be a homicide, but . . ." She sighed, blowing a tress of blond hair. "Since the governor's office told me to open all doors to you . . . I guess I can show you. You want to see?"

She's asking me if I want to see a fat redneck's corpse. Patricia told herself. She gritted her teeth and said, "Yes, please."

Whatever it is, it can't be any weirder than the picture of Dwayne.

Patricia was quite wrong about that, which she would discern in a moment. She followed the attractive coroner through the front office and into a door that read, SUITE 1—DO NOT ENTER. At once a strong scent accosted her nostrils. "It's formalin; you'll get used to it," Baker said. "All-purpose preservative." Overhead fluorescent tubes threw the ghastliest tint about the room; Patricia supposed it was just her imagination—she was in a morgue—but somehow that tint made her feel unnaturally close to death. Ranks of storage shelves behind them sat heavy with big smoke-colored glass bottles: JORE'S, ZENKER'S SOLUTION, PHENOL 20 PERCENT. A tin tray marked AMYLOID/FAT NECROSIS PREP held several bottles of iodine and copper sulphate. A large sink and heat-sealing iron hung on the same wall. Basically the room could've passed for any high school biology lab, save for one fact: high school biology labs didn't have a covered dead body sitting in the middle of them.

Patricia's stomach flipped when she glimpsed the covered bulk. White light glinted like abstract art in the crinkles of the black plastic sheet.

Baker seemed nonchalant when she whipped the sheet off the table.

What am I doing here? Patricia yelled at herself.

The body lay there so candidly it seemed surreal, like the graphics in a CD-ROM game—a spooky veil like tulle that somehow enhanced details instead of detracting from them. The body lay on a stainless-steel morgue platform that came equipped with a removable drain trap, gutters for "organic outflow," and a motorized height adjustment. The corpse's image was blatant, like a surprise shout in the dark.

"Here he is," Baker announced in her snippy Southern drawl. "Robert—Junior—Caudill."

Patricia didn't allow herself to look at the body directly, opting for peripheral side glances. The pallor of the flesh reminded her of the water chestnuts that Byron used to make rumaki at home; the unused chestnuts would always sit in the fridge too long, and start to turn brown. Junior Caudill was a big man—and a plump one—much of his body fat settling like raw lard on the stainless-steel table. One morbid glimpse at his groin showed her the purple nose of a penis shriveled so severely that it could've been a mushroom in a bird's nest. *Oh, my God, I'm looking at a cadaver. . . .* When she closed her eyes she found the formalin fumes seemed to sting. The afterimage of the white face lingered behind her eyes. She only vaguely remembered the man from her youth, a problem child and troublemaker who'd dropped out of school early. Had she seen him and his brother at Dwayne's funeral? Probably, but she didn't even care. Come to think of it, she didn't even care that he was dead. At least the body hadn't been cut open yet. Had Baker been able to establish cause of death without a full autopsy?

Finally she choked out the question: "Okay, it's a dead body, so what's so strange about it?"

Baker snapped on a light board on the wall. "Here's a transabdominal X-ray of Dwayne Parker," she said, clipping a large sheet of film to the board. Murky shades and shapes seemed to throb. "It's normal." Her lithe finger pointed. "Normal GI tract, cardiopulmonary process, liver, bladder, spleen. Everything that's supposed to be there *is* there."

"Except his head," Patricia noted when she looked higher and saw that the boundary of the X-ray ended at the shoulders.

"Yes, but this isn't about Dwayne Parker's head. This is about Robert Caudill." And then just as quickly as she spoke, she pinned up another sheet of X-ray film.

Patricia caught the dissimilarity in an instant.

Dwayne's X-ray clearly showed the presence of his internal organs.

Junior Caudill's X-ray clearly showed an *absence* of internal organs.

"Where are his organs?" Patricia asked baldly. "You haven't autopsied the body yet—I don't even see any cuts on it."

"There aren't any cuts, and, no, I haven't done the post yet. I've only done some preliminaries so far." Baker sat down as if fatigued or repressing an agitation. "The only thing I can think of is maybe the decedent was exposed to a strain of flesh-eating bacteria, like an internalized version of the one in England, or maybe he died from a corrosive digestive virus."

Patricia asked the strangest question, then, ever to pass her lips: "So his organs dissolved?"

Baker's sleek shoulders shrugged. "I don't know. Maybe. There are no other contraindications if that's the case. E. coli, for instance, has been known to liquefy parts of the digestive system, and then the effluent drains from the rectal canal—"

Patricia was suddenly delighted she hadn't eaten yet today, for surely she would've deposited her last meal right here on the floor or perhaps even *on* the corpse of Robert "Junior" Caudill.

"But there's virtually no clinical evidence of an effluent void from the rectum, because I inspected his rectum *thoroughly*," Baker insisted, as though her competency were in question.

Patricia closed her eyes. *This woman has a* lousy *job. . . .* She let her eyes stray around the room, to any place away from the corpse. Her mind was ticking with questions. But then something snagged an eye: something on the counter, at the other side of the room.

Two clear plastic bags, one large, one smaller.

"What's that? In those bags?"

Baker looked over, uninterested. "Oh, that's some stuff the EMTs brought over; some of it was in his pockets or near the corpse on the floor. I bagged it as evidence."

Patricia walked over; she was pretty sure she noticed what was in the larger bag. "But what is it exactly?"

"Looks like a couple of pieces of crystal meth in the little bag, and—"

"An envelope in the other bag?"

"Yes."

Patricia leaned over and saw the outside of the envelope. Junior Caudill's name and address, in craggy handwriting.

"Don't open the bags," Baker reminded her. "You don't want *your* fingerprints on police evidence."

No, of course not . . . Patricia came back toward the table. "What was in the envelope?"

"Just a piece of paper with a weird word written on it," Baker replied. "Wend-something. I'm not sure."

Just like the letter to Dwayne. Patricia already knew.

"So," the coroner continued. She stood up with an exasperated sigh. "I might as well show you what I already know." And next she skimmed off her lab coat, flapped on a rubberized apron, and snapped on rubber gloves.

She's as confused about this as I am, Patricia realized, *and she's getting mad.*

Now Baker donned a clear-visored face shield and flipped the shield down, blond hair shimmering around the straps. She snatched up a silver device that looked like a metal can lid fixed to the top of an electric toothbrush. A brand name could clearly be made out on the tool's body—STRYKER—and a moment later Patricia realized with a jolt of adrenaline that this tool was an autopsy saw.

Patricia's hands shot up. "Oh, no, really, it's not necessary for you to show me. . . ." But her plea was too late.

Her skin crawled as if aswarm with cockroaches, and her shoulders contracted when the extraordinarily genteel and preposterously attractive coroner revved the saw like the most monstrous dentist's drill and began to cut a straight line from Junior Caudill's pubic bone to the bottom of his sternum. With the saw's grisly whine, flecks of clotted blood flew out of the groove and specked her apron and face shield. As the blade continued to cut upward, Junior's dead, pallid body fat jiggled on the slab.

I've got to get out of here, I've got to . . . Patricia began to feel faint. This was not a place for her. She liked to think of herself as a realist—and this was indeed reality—but by now she'd simply had enough. Just as she would have turned around and run out of the morgue suite, though, the saw's awful whine stopped.

It was obvious now that the coroner's perplexion and sheer rage at the anomaly had been building up within the constraints of her temper, and now those constraints were snapping.

She threw the saw down on the counter, flipped up her visor, then slapped her gloved hands down onto the corpse. She pulled open the great rift sawed into Junior's belly, then thrust a hand in and felt around like someone searching for a lost object under the bed. "See? See? I'm showing you what we already know. Look!"

Patricia ground her teeth, her eyelids appalled slits, and she leaned over and glimpse into the absolutely vacant area of space that was Junior Caudill's abdominal vault.

"There are no fuckin' organs inside this fat fuckin' redneck!" the coroner nearly wailed.

Patricia turned away, stumbled to a lab table, and sat down, exhausted.

Moments of silence passed. Baker was now finished with the outburst that had obviously been mounting all morning; she daintily hung up her apron and face shield, and dropped her rubber gloves into a pedal-operated garbage can that read, HAZARDOUS WASTE ONLY. At once she was demure-voiced again, totally out of place here with her tight jeans, magnificent body, and lilting Southern accent.

"So much for that," she said.

Patricia struggled to banish the imagery from her mind. She looked up wearily at the other woman. "So what will you put on the death certificate as a cause of death?"

"Undetermined and curious," Baker said.

(II)

"Magic, huh?" Pam asked, looking over her shoulder from the coffee machine.

"That's right," Ricky Caudill sputtered back at her. Through the jail bars he looked like exactly what he was: a busted, washed-up, no-account rube. "It's that Squatter voodoo they got goin' on," he assured her. All morning long, in fact, he'd elaborated on the details of last night, leaving out the part about killing David Eald and his daughter and then burning their shack down. "Everybody knows that Everd 'n' that nutty wife a' his are into it. Fucker cursed me right in my own house, and it was that magic a' his that he used to kill my brother."

"Ricky, it was *alcoholism* that killed your brother," Pam replied. "Same thing that'll kill you someday."

"Shee-it."

Pam traipsed back to her desk, perky as ever. *These redneck losers are just so funny!* They'd blame anybody and everything for their dysfunctional lives. She'd heard it all from similar folk sitting in that cell. *At least this dolt is original. He's not blaming the police or his wife or his boss for his problems. He's blaming the Squatters! He's telling me that Everd Stanherd is a warlock and he's cursed him!*

"And if y'all ain't careful, Everd'll curse the whole town; then you'll all really be in the shit."

"Ricky, you already *are* in the shit. You're in *jail.*"

"Only safe place for me. You'll see."

"Sounds to me like you're just scared," Pam challenged him. She loved to toy with these local white-trash hooligans, play on their phony macho self-concepts. "Big, tough, strong man like you, scared of a bunch of hillbilly mumbo-jumbo. Scared like a little baby. Any minute now you'll be curled up in there sucking your thumb and crying for your mama." Pam fully expected the big moron to talk down her challenge, to assert his masculine bravado.

Instead, Ricky replied, "You're right," very quietly. "I am scared."

Pam shook her head. *How do you like that? He really is spooked.* He was the last guy on earth she'd expect that from, especially admitting it so plainly. *Must be serious DTs,* she supposed, and got back to filing the week's DORs and expenditure invoices. *And he hasn't looked at my boobs once today.* The low-cut sleeveless summer dress she wore always had the male heads turning. But not this one.

Ricky Caudill was genuinely preoccupied with his fear.

Charlie the postman *wasn't* preoccupied, though, and when the bell clanged and he walked in with his mailbag, his eyes darted immediately to her cleavage. "Howdy, Pam," he greeted her. His baldhead and small mustache always reminded her of some of the Nazi honchos she remembered from history classes. Ernst Rohm. Heinrich Himmler. "How's the purdiest woman in all of Agan's Point?"

"I don't know, Charlie. How's the biggest bullshit artist in Agan's Point?"

"God!" he said. "I love it when you talk dirty!"

He was such a card. "You should've been an airline pilot, so you could bullshit all those bimbo stewardesses."

"You'd always fly first-class with me, baby."

"You want some coffee before you *leave?*"

"Naw, you know what I want. A date with you."

"That'll be happening, Charlie. Hold your breath. Did you come in here to actually deliver mail, or just stand there with your Hitler mustache and act like you're *not* looking down my top?"

"Both," he admitted. He began rifling through his mailbag. "I know you'd love for me to stay and chat all day, but I'm a little behind."

"Actually, Charlie, you're a *big* behind, but that's what I like about you," Pam said. She decided to let him keep on looking down her top. *Why not? Gives him something to think about when he's walking his route.*

"I'm not just a big *behind,*" he said. "But I'll leave the rest to your imagination." Suddenly, though, the levity on his face faded. "That's weird."

"What?"

"I got a letter for Ricky Caudill, but it's addressed to him care of the Agan's Point police station."

"Well, that's good, because the redneck bum is right down the hall—in the drunk tank."

"You don't say. Saves me a trip out to his house." He put the police mail down on Pam's desk, along with the letter, which she picked up immediately. "No return address," she noted. And it was handwritten, without a great degree of penmanship. She felt through it, feeling for any objects that might serve as weapons, but it was flat. *Just a letter.* "Thanks, Charlie. I'll give it to him myself."

Charlie just stood there as if he didn't hear her, his eyes still playing over her outstanding bosom.

"I said thanks, Charlie! Have a good day!"

"Oh, right," he said, and walked out.

Men were such sexist pigs, but... *But they're* so *amusing!* At the very least, Pam got her share of laughs in this town.

She also had her share of boredom. *Jeez*... She could drink only so much coffee. She'd finished her filing, so all she could do now was sit and listen for anything on the police radio. Trey and the chief were out in Squatterville for that big clan cookout, though Pam was surprised they'd even be having it after all the recent commotion. Now she felt more at home with her boredom. *I guess I should be grateful nothing's going on,* she reminded herself with the deaths, the burning, and all the talk lately, Agan's Point had been anything *but* boring.

Then her mind strayed.

The letter.

She picked it up, looking at the crude scrawl. It was

strange that it was addressed to Ricky Caudill, care of the police station. *Word travels fast in a gossip town. . . . Oh, well.* There was nothing else to do.

Pam got up with the letter and walked back to the jail cell. "Hey, Ricky, you got some mail," she announced, but when she looked through the bars she saw that he was asleep on the jail cot. He lay belly-up on the mattress, snoring. *The fat slob . . . Sounds like a cave full of bears.*

Pam slipped the letter through the bars on the floor and walked back to her desk. He could read it when he woke up.

Eleven

(I)

More white lies, Patricia thought when she set her cell phone down. She'd just hung up with Byron, having kept the conversation innocuous. She was still so befuddled over her trip to the county morgue. *What could I tell him, for God's sake?* So she'd told him nothing of significance. Dwayne's head seemingly disappearing off his body as though it had never been there? Junior Caudill with no internal organs? Patricia *was* confident there was a scientific explanation, but she simply couldn't imagine what it was just yet. Of course, they'd do more tests. . . .

Nevertheless, there was no need to tell Byron. *It'd just give him one more thing to worry about.*

She stepped out onto the little patio off her bedroom to stand amid part of the garden. The cicadas thrummed—she was finally getting used to it. It just kept taking her back to her childhood. The scents off the myriad flowers smelled luscious. asters, pyxies, and goldenrod. Being here continued to supplant her. She was no longer the high-roller attorney from the city; she was the country girl at home in the midst of nature. But now so many ugly facts kept dicing that image of the peaceful—and very sane—backwoods town.

Murder. Drugs. Turf wars by some unseen dope gang.

Every place has something, she thought. *Doesn't matter if it's the city or the sticks.*

At the end of the yard, near the kiosk, she spotted Judy wandering about the flowers; the troubled look on her face was no surprise. *Talk about being thrown for a loop,* Patricia thought. Judy was not a sophisticated woman. Since Dwayne's death, too many things that were wrong about her environment threatened her ability to view her life and the world.

She doesn't know which end is up. . . .

"Hi," Patricia greeted her, meandering up the path.

"Oh, hi, Patricia. I'm just out moseying around. Beautiful day, isn't it?"

Small talk is all she can deal with, Patricia realized. "Yeah, it sure is. And your gardens really top it all off. Everything looks the same as it did when we were kids."

Judy sat down on a stone bench, her hands clasped in her lap. "Yeah, but just because they look the same don't mean they *are* the same. It's like everything's gone mad overnight. Chief Sutter just called me, said Junior Caudill's dead."

Here we go. Patricia knew the day would be a tailspin now. "I heard about that myself—"

"Drug dealin', murder, arson—all on my land. And God knows what killed Junior. Never thought much of him—he was always into trouble—and now *he's* dead too."

"Judy, there's no reason to believe that his death is related to anything that's been happening in Squatterville." Patricia knew at once that this was going to be a long day. "He probably had a heart attack," she urged, not adding the little part about Junior not even *having* a heart. "They're still doing tests is what I heard, and there were no signs of foul play. Anyway, all these things that are happening lately don't have anything to do with you. There are a lot of Squatters living out here. It stands to reason that a few of them will get up to no good. It's human nature."

Judy looked up dolefully. "I hate to think of what Mom and Dad would say about this. They never had problems with the Squatters, but now that I'm in charge around here, everything's goin' to hell. And now I just feel worse about it. You come all the way out here to help me, and look what happens. Folks killin' each other. I wouldn't blame ya if you *never* came back to this godforsaken place."

Patricia knew that she had to work around her sister's mood swings, not confront them head-on. "Of course I will; you're my sister. And you should come out to visit Byron and me sometimes, too. But let's just take things one day at a time. Look at the good things. Your company's doing better than ever, and the Squatters who *haven't* turned bad have never been happier or more productive. You have this beautiful house in a beautiful place. You're a successful businesswoman with lots to look forward to."

Judy shrugged, noncommital. Some people just had it in their heads that everything was terrible. *That's my sister,* Patricia thought. "So what's on the agenda today?" she asked.

Before her sister could answer, a horn honked. Past

the shrubs Patricia saw an old pickup truck idling on the dirt road that descended the hill toward the Point.

Judy looked at her watch. "My, where has the day gone? It's time to go."

"Go where?"

"The Squatter cookout. Oh, that's right, you ain't been to one since you were a kid, but they are a lot of fun. Come on."

Patricia honestly didn't remember these cookouts. When she looked at her own watch she saw that she, too, had lost track of time. *Where's the day gone?* She followed Judy down the path that exited the backyard. "Who's in the pickup truck?" she asked.

"Ernie. He'll be driving us down there."

This is just what I need. Patricia thought. The truck jostled down the dirt road, springs creaking. She and Judy had squeezed up front on the bench seat, the pickup's back bed loaded up with baskets of food and chests full of ice. Of course, Patricia ended up being in the middle, pressed right up against Ernie behind the wheel. Ernie wore his typical work jeans and boots but also a nice white dress shirt. *Redneck high fashion,* Patricia mused. *Why does he have to look so* good *all the time?* By now the situation amused her as much as aggravated her: how fate kept putting them together. Every time he shifted gears, his hand slid against her bare knee. *Yeah, that's* just *what I need. . . .*

"Really whacked out about Junior Caudill, huh?" Ernie made conversation.

Don't bring it up! Patricia wished she could tell him. *Don't bring up anything that's been going on. Judy's enough of a basket case as it is.* "He probably just had a heart attack; it happens." She desperately shifted subjects. "So what kind of food did you prepare for this banquet?"

"Oh, just side dishes," Judy answered glumly. "All the main courses they make. The Squatters really do have a talent for usin' what the land gives 'em and turning it into a cuisine a' their own."

Ernie laughed, nudging Patricia. "Aw, yer sister's a big fan of Squatter food, Judy. Just the other day she drank a whole cup of *ald* that Regert made for her down at the pier. Said it was the best thing she ever tasted."

Patricia frowned, remembering the drink's tang. "Actually, Ernie, it *wasn't* the best thing I've ever tasted."

He raised a finger to denote an additional point. "Oh, yeah, and she also ate a whole bowl of pepper-fried cicadas."

"I ate *one!* And never will again."

Ernie winked at her with a cocked grin. "She never did tell me if they worked, though."

Patricia almost blushed at the inside joke, recalling the wives'-tale insistence that cicadas had an aphrodisiac effect.

She also remembered the dense sexual fugue state she'd experienced after eating it.

I was going to have sex with him. . . . She choked before she could respond. *And I can't blame the damn fried cicadas. I can only blame my own weakness and immorality.*

But she'd stopped short, hadn't she? *I said no at the last minute, so I never really cheated on Byron. . . .*

Judy was scowling at her. "Patricia, one thing you *don't* need to be eatin' are cicadas, not unless your *husband* is with ya."

Ernie chuckled softly to himself, their inside joke still

alive. Patricia wanted to wilt right there on the front seat. *My God . . .*

Ordinarily the acre or so of land before Squatterville was barren, but now it looked more like a fairground. Savory smoke drifted off of open-pit fires over which abundant meats were being cooked. Squatter women busied themselves at fold-down tables, serving up plates heaped with steaming meals. Lines of people, Squatters and townsfolk alike, trailed around the table, chatting amiably. As the sun faded, the scene appeared almost surreal: faces seemed diced into wedges of firelight. Chatter warbled in and out, and laughter rose up.

"There's pitchers of *ald* over there." Ernie pointed to another table. "Too bad there's no booze."

"Hush," Judy whispered. "Just 'cos Squatters don't drink don't mean we can't." And then Patricia and Ernie saw her lower a silver flask into a pocket.

"This is some feast," Patricia said, marveling over the various dishes set out. Ernie appeared behind her with a loaded plate. "Try some duck. The Squatters do it up great. It's slow-roasted."

Patricia took the plate. It smelled delicious, the skin dark and crisp.

"And you *must* have some of this, big sister," Judy insisted, thrusting a pewter mug toward her. "Squatter *ald*."

"I *had* that the other day. It tastes like swamp water!"

"Shh! The Squatters'll be offended, dear. You can't decline their hospitality," Judy whispered lower. "And don't worry; I tuned it up with a drop of vodka."

"Oh, terrific . . ."

"Come on," Ernie coaxed her further. "When in Squatterville, do as the Squatters do."

When Patricia took a sip, her brow shot up. *Oh, yeah, just a* drop *of vodka . . .* "You're just trying to get me drunk," she joked to him.

"Why?" he said, deadpan. Then he cracked a smile and laughed.

Oh, that's right. She'd never forget what almost happened in the woods. *I'm just a tease.* The roasted duck came apart fork-tender beneath crunchy skin. "My God, this is probably the best duck I've ever had."

"Glad ya like it," Ernie said. "It's not really duck. It's seagull."

"You're so funny. . . ."

Her eyes roved the other offerings on the table: stout sausages, steaming kettles of stew, homemade biscuits and seasoned flatbreads. The aromas were almost erotic. *Byron would go to town here,* she thought. Another table sat heavy with various crab dishes. Something like a Newburg cooked in empty shells, crab-stuffed wild peppers, crabmeat po'boys. She helped herself to several fried crab fritters and found them delectably crunchy inside. "These are fantastic!" she exclaimed, cheeks stuffed.

On her third one, Judy tugged her arm. "Not too many a' the fritters, hon. It's the Squatter crabcake recipe wrapped around a fried cicada."

Not those things again!

Ernie laughed.

Next Patricia scanned around in general. The quiet revelry buzzed around her; it all seemed so hearty and honest. But again she thought it strange to have such a feastlike cookout so soon after four Squatters had been killed. *The positivity of their religion,* she remembered. *Almost like evangelists. Even death is a joyous occasion, be-*

cause death is just another step toward eternal life in heaven.

Patricia hoped that was true.

She sampled more food, finding the cuisine complex and fascinating. Judy wandered off, tipsy already, while Patricia and Ernie stood aside to eat and people-watch. *I must be getting tipsy, too,* she suspected, or maybe it was just fatigue compounded by the perplexities of the day . . . especially her experience at the morgue. She pushed the morbid images from her mind and instead just tried to relax, melting into the lazy, darkening atmosphere. Squatters greeted her happily, offering her more of their wares. Music—a quavering violin, it sounded like—echoed around the grounds, yet she couldn't pinpoint the source. As the sun died completely, faces seemed brighter and more focused somehow, in spite of the seeping darkness.

"There's the money man," Ernie commented. At the last table she spotted Gordon Felps sampling a cobbler-like dessert. He seemed to sense her notice, looked up and nodded to her, then returned his attention to the person talking to him: Judy. *She doesn't really have a crush on him, does she?* Patricia asked herself. She could tell by Ernie's sedate expression that he found it amusing. But at least her sister was getting over Dwayne; perhaps it took his death to make her realize what an awful person he truly had been, not even worth mourning. Chief Sutter and Trey cruised another table full of plank-roasted bluefish and large soft-shell clams whose necks stood out straight from steaming. Sutter actually manipulated two plates of food, which wasn't surprising. Eventually he wended his way over to Patricia and Ernie.

"Some spread, huh, Patricia?"

"It's incredible," she said. "I didn't think I'd like much of this type of cuisine, but so far every single thing I've had is delicious."

"Even the crab-and-cicada fritters?" Ernie joked.

"Even the crab-and-cicada fritters, Ernie," she admitted.

"Oh"—Sutter changed the subject—"the county coroner told me you'd been in today."

Damn. She hoped this wouldn't open a can of worms. "I just wanted some details on Dwayne's death."

"Pretty off-the-wall. So you also know about Junior Caudill, then."

It wasn't a question; Patricia sensed he was fishing for something. "Yes, she did mention it."

"Even stranger than Dwayne." Sutter shook his head.

"Damn near everyone in town's heard that news," Ernie piped up. "Some contagious disease that dissolved all his insides."

Sutter smirked. "There ain't no contagious disease, Ernie, and don't'cha be tellin' folks anything of the sort. The rumors're bad enough around here."

Ernie shrugged. "Just tellin' ya what I heard, Chief."

"I don't think it was anything contagious, Ernie," Patricia added. "But I don't guess we'll know anything until more tests are done on the body."

"The kick in the tail is there ain't no evidence a' foul play, yet everyone thinks that's exactly what it was," Ernie said.

Patricia kept her mouth shut and her ears open.

"And it don't help for Junior's brother to be accusin' Everd Stanherd of being involved and then for Everd to disappear," Sutter stepped up the gossip. "I don't believe nothin' that comes outta Ricky Caudill's yap, but that don't change the fact that I got no choice but to drag Everd 'n' his wife in for questioning."

Interesting, Patricia thought. "I hadn't even noticed. Neither Everd nor Marthe is here."

"Probably never see 'em again," Ernie said.

"Maybe they ain't disappeared at all," Sutter offered, stuffing his face. "Maybe they're dead."

"How would they come to be dead?" Patricia had to challenge.

"Well, it was something Trey was kickin' about, and now that I think of it, it makes sense. Already had a couple a' turf killings over dope. Maybe Everd 'n' his wife were part a' the same dope ring that David Eald and the Hilds were in."

Both Patricia and Ernie frowned at that one.

Sutter looked like he regretted the suggestion a moment later. "Well, I guess that is stretchin' things a bit." Suddenly he was looking around. "Speakin' of Trey . . ."

"He was just here a minute ago," Ernie said.

Patricia looked around herself, straining her vision in the fire-diced dark. Sergeant Trey was nowhere to be seen.

(II)

Got no time to fuck around anymore. It was a steadfast thought, and a calmly determined one. It was dark now, and the main drag stretched on in vacant silence. *Good . . .* Pam got off duty at five P.M.; then the Agan's

Point police channel was taken over by the county dispatcher.

In other words, there was no one else in the station house right now. No one else except . . .

Good ol' Ricky, Trey thought. He came in through the back with his key. Killing people wasn't really that big a deal. Trey couldn't say he *enjoyed* it—he just didn't mind, not if it served his own best interest.

Killing Ricky Caudill was definitely in his best interest.

Big dumb redneck's gonna spill the beans, Trey thought. *Can't have that. I've put too much work into this gig to lose it all because a' that fat fool's big mouth. He's just scared. Well, in a few minutes he won't have anything to be scared about . . .*

Unless, a 'course, there really is a hell, 'cos he sure as shit ain't goin' to heaven.

Such were the limits of Sergeant Trey's theological perceptions. He was like most folks: just wanted his share plus a little more, and if Felps's plan worked, Trey stood to walk away with a *lot* more.

The Squatters were already hightailing it off the Point. In another month or so they'd *all* be gone, and that was when things would really pick up. But with Dwayne gone—and Ricky and Junior, too—that would leave all the dirty work up to Trey.

I'll just have to get the job done.

He didn't turn the lights on in the station when he slipped in. A radio was playing; Pam must've left it on for Ricky before she clocked out. *Shouldn't be too hard,* Trey thought. Ricky was a big guy—but soft. *It's simple. I jack the fucker out and hang him.* Earlier that day Trey had pinched one of the fresh sheets that they used for the jail cots; then he'd cut it into fat strips and made a noose. He'd hang Ricky in his cell and throw out the sheet already on his cot.

Yes. Very simple.

"Take this job and shove it," the radio crooned very softly. The only light on was down the hall, in the cell corridor. Trey had his blackjack in his pocket already, which he could slip out in an instant. But he'd have to distract Ricky first, and open the cell.

"Hey, Ricky, ya big dolt. You awake?"

Ricky didn't answer.

"Wake up, moron. Sutter told me to stop by 'n' check up on ya. Ya need to take a piss before beddy-bye time?"

Still no answer. Trey walked up to the cell, looked in.

"Hey! Redneck! Wake up!"

Ricky lay on his back on the cot, one arm dangling. *Good. The fucker's sound asleep. Easier to take him out.* Trey, as quietly as possible, unlocked the cell and eased open the door.

The cell light itself was turned off; only the light from the hall bled inside. But even in the weak light Trey could tell something wasn't right when he was several steps inside, blackjack poised in his hand. The arm hanging off the side of the cot looked oddly pale, blue veins almost black against white skin.

"You sick?" Trey leaned over. He shined his flashlight into Ricky's face—or, it should be said, Ricky's very *dead* face.

Fuck!

It was a corpse that lay on the cot now.

The fat face seemed thinner now, and the flesh appeared a translucent white, like a fresh cod fillet.

There was no pulse. The body felt cool.

Trey couldn't have known it at that precise moment, but Ricky Caudill had lost all of his blood.

Not even one irreducible fraction of a drop remained in his body.

Twelve

(I)

The feeling made Patricia think of the few times in college she'd smoked pot. A warm buzz, a mental *lightness*, as though an aspect of her persona were floating. She'd been at the cookout for only an hour before it plainly occurred to her that she was not herself, and this—to a high-strung D.C. attorney—was not necessarily a bad thing.

It must've been that stuff I was drinking, she decided rather giddily. Ald *or whatever they call it, kicked up with Judy's booze.*

But . . .

So what?

It was a party, and there was no reason why she shouldn't have a good time. She picked at more food off and on, and drank more *ald*. Judy was already drunk, but that was to be expected. Everybody seemed to be fading off into the darkness tinged by firelight. Patricia found herself chatting happily with townsfolk and

Squatters she didn't even know, and several times, when she noticed Ernie talking to some Squatter girls, she felt some pangs of trifling jealously, after which she just laughed at herself.

Eventually she lost track of Judy entirely, and when she couldn't make out Gordon Felps anywhere in the crowd, she had to wonder, but that just caused her to laugh too. *I'm getting hammered!* she realized next, but with Judy not around to top off her *ald* with vodka, where was the inebriation coming from? Had somebody else spiked the Squatter concoction and not told anyone? That had to be the answer.

"How come we never dated in high school?" Ernie appeared out of the dark to ask right up front. He looked a little crocked, too. But what would compel such an overt question?

Maybe the fact that I practically pulled his pants down in the woods the other day? she chided herself. Suddenly, though, she seemed remorseful. "I don't know, Ernie. I guess it was all me. I didn't care about anything except getting an education and getting out, after . . . well, you know. What happened at Bowen's Field."

Ernie nodded, probably not expecting his question to cause such a dark note. He just nodded, then thrust a plate at her. "Try a mushroom stuffed with crab roe. They're great."

Patricia laughed. She ate one, then said very quickly, "I wish we had, though, Ernie," and wandered off.

"Wish we had *what?*" he practically shouted after her.

She giggled and wended through more people, sensing him behind her. "Where's Chief Sutter?" she asked to change the subject. "I haven't seen him in a while."

"I think I saw him leave earlier."

Patricia stopped, peering between some shoulders toward the woods. She grabbed Ernie's arm. "Is that Everd Stanherd out there?"

"Can't be," he said, squinting himself. "He's wanted by the police."

Even now she could see the figure standing between some trees, firelight from one of the cooking pits shifting across the thin, old face. For a moment it appeared as though his intensely bright eyes looked right at Patricia. "Don't you see him? He's right . . ." But before she could point, a pretty Squatter girl stepped right in front of them. Her ripe young body filled the skimpy shorts and makeshift top. A trinketlike cross dangled about her swollen cleavage, and the smile on her face seemed wanton, mischievous. Squiggles of some kind of dark face paint adorned her cheeks—like a child at a carnival. More bizarre lines curved down her bare belly and around her navel, while still more traveled down voluptuous legs.

Patricia was taken aback when the girl kissed both her and Ernie on the cheek, then placed pendants around their necks, after which she scurried away into the crowd.

"What is this?" Patricia touched the object about her neck, a furry preserved animal foot of some kind. "A rabbit's foot?"

"Not quite. It's a badger's foot."

Patricia winced. "Gross! Why would she . . . Like the Hawaiians and their leis, some kind of welcoming gift?"

Ernie snorted a laugh. "It's sort of a fertility thing with them, a romance thing."

"Huh?"

"Lemme put it this way. The Squatters must think

you 'n' me would make a great couple. Guess they didn't see your *wedding* ring."

Patricia's fingers were unconsciously diddling with the dried foot. "How strange."

Ernie was obviously frustrated and maybe even embarrassed. He peered back through the crowd. "What were you sayin'? You saw *Everd?* If ya did, we should probably call Chief Sutter."

"I don't think for a minute that Everd Stanherd had anything to do with Junior Caudill's death, and neither do you."

"No, I guess I don't," Ernie verified, "but why'd he 'n' his wife head for the hills the minute folks started sayin' he did?"

Patricia couldn't answer. She stood on her tiptoes to look over the crowd. The fire pit raged, but there was no one standing between the trees where she thought she'd seen the Squatter elder. "Maybe it wasn't even him," she dismissed. "Just someone who looked like him. What was it they called him? Remember the guy who gave us the oysters the other day?"

"Oh, Regert, yeah. That name the clan has for Everd is *sawon*. It means 'seer,' or somethin' like that."

Patricia kept looking out. "Damn, I'm sure it was him, though." Without even thinking, she grabbed Ernie's hand and pulled. "Come on; let's go check."

She was tugging him gently through the crowd. More firelit faces grinned at them as they passed, many of them adorned as the girl had been, with the carnival-like face paint. Again, and even more strongly, Patricia didn't feel like herself, but whoever that other self was . . . she enjoyed the sensation. Another part, though—some remnant of her rational self—probably knew what her subconscious was up to. Lewd thoughts shouted at her in the baldest truth: *I'm drunk, I'm horny, and, gee, look what I'm doing now. I'm hauling this man into the woods on a stupid pretext—the same man I almost had sex with the other day. I keep telling myself that I'd never cheat on Byron, but . . . what am I really doing?*

She couldn't even fool herself.

Their footfalls crunched into the woods. *I should let go of his hand now,* she thought. But she didn't. She led him in deeper, until the moonlight showed them a foot-path. "Let's go this way," she said. "He probably came this way."

Ernie said nothing, but he was frowning.

Moonlight painted one tree whose bark had been scraped away, and into the bare wood beneath more odd Squatter etchings had been cut around a makeshift cross. Would this be her good luck? And what of the bizarre badger foot the painted girl had christened them both with?

The night shimmered. As the cicadas thrummed, Patricia felt herself merging into that other self. Her heartbeat had already picked up; she could feel her nipples aching against the fabric of the sheer blouse. The evening heat was caressing her, sensitizing her skin through pores seeping sweat.

"Everd ain't out here, Patricia," Ernie finally spoke his mind. He likely had already deciphered her motives, even before she had herself. "This is dumb. Let's go back."

"No," she whispered. She was secretly desperate. "I'm serious. I really did see him." Now her fingers seemed manic, diddling with the dried foot as though it were some talisman that would embolden her.

"I'm goin' back," he insisted, agitation in his voice. "We both know what's goin' on here."

"What?" she questioned ineptly. "What do you—"

"If we stay out here, we're both gonna get in trouble, and it ain't gonna lead to nothin' no ways. I ain't comin' out here just to be jerked around."

Patricia let go of his hand and stopped. "Ernie, that's ridiculous," she insisted, but her head was reeling—not so much from inebriation as from lust. Lust felt *stuffed* in her head. Her knees were almost shaking. "I really do want to talk to Everd Stanherd—"

"Fine. Then go *talk* to him. I ain't gettin' myself set up again to wind up lookin' like a fool. I'm goin' back."

When he turned, her heart twisted in her chest. All reason was lost now, along with her values and self-respect. "Ernie, wait. . . ."

He gruffed a sigh, stopped midstep, and jerked back around.

Patricia had already unbuttoned her blouse. Her breasts felt hot and very heavy on her chest now, as though all that drunken desire had pushed more blood into them. She skimmed off the blouse and let it fall to the twigs. She was leaning against the skinned tree, her head just under the crudely adorned Squatter cross. Her eyes riveted into him.

"Christ, I feel sorry for your husband, Patricia, 'cos you are one right pain in the ass when you drink."

She barely heard him. She arched her back against the tree, elucidating her breasts, and next she actually caressed them in her hands. When she pliered the nipples between her fingers, she moaned out loud.

"You're drunk," he declared.

"I know, but so what?"

She slipped her shorts down to midthigh, then openly played a hand through her scarlet pubic hair.

Ernie gnawed his lip, then decided. "You're all bark and no bite, Patricia. You got some midlife fucked-up city-chick thing goin' on, like teasin' it up with some redneck sucker who had a crush on you since junior high's gonna show ya somethin' about yourself you didn't know. It's just bullshit, and I ain't buyin' it, and even if you *were* game, all that'd do is make ya feel guilty in the morning 'cos you're fuckin' *married* and you and I both know you ain't gonna cheat on your husband. You might *act* like you'd cheat on him, but you ain't gonna do it, so's I'm wastin' my damn time standin' here like a fuckin' idiot."

Ernie turned around and walked back to the cookout.

The reality collided with her. She was almost in tears when she pulled her shorts up and got back into her blouse. She stumbled to the fringes of the gathering, finally letting some common sense reach through her drunkenness. *I am really one screwed-up woman. It doesn't have anything to do with my childhood, or the rape or my parents. It's got nothing to do with Dr. Sallee or Byron or Ernie or* anyone. *It's me, and I've got to get my act together, and I've got to start* right now. . . .

The party was still in full swing as some of the older Squatters lit the great bonfire in the middle of the field. Patricia edged around the crowd, cloaking herself in shadows. She didn't look to see where Ernie was and she felt too embarrassed to allow herself to be seen. After several deep breaths, she felt a little less drunk, and she walked back up the hill.

The only person who even noticed her leaving was Everd Stanherd himself, who was looking out from the trees he'd been hiding in. He watched her walk home.

"Maybe she can help us, like you said," Marthe Stanherd remarked. She held her husband's hand in the dark.

"Maybe, my love," he replied in his strange, buoyant accent. "Or maybe I'm wrong about everything, and the great Lord God has deemed me unfit to be a seer even for myself. . . ."

(II)

Chief Sutter had felt not quite right all day. This morning, for instance, he'd wakened with a grand erection—rare for a man his age—but when he took a look at his wife snoring next to him, he realized he'd sooner attempt to copulate with a grounded manatee. The box of jelly-filled doughnuts he'd picked up for breakfast at the Qwik-Mart was stale. He'd had a headache and a half since morning, which turned into a headache and seven-eights by noon from the pollen and the heat. All kinds of shit was going down in his town, none of which Sutter could reckon, and the only thing he had to look forward to all day was the Squatter cookout, which had kicked off just fine, and then he got a call from Trey on the radio. Something happened at the station. *Jesus.*

"What are all the damn lights doin' off?" were the first words to exit Sutter's mouth when he came in.

Trey looked up from his desk with an expression like bewilderment. The younger man rubbed his face. "Things are startin' to get really fucked-up 'round here, Chief. I don't know where to start."

Sutter looked at his watch, his patience ticking away with it. "Why'd you call me down here at midnight,

Trey? And why'd you turn off the lights? Start talkin'. Now."

"Ricky Caudill's dead, Chief," Trey blurted.

"Bullshit." Sutter bulled past Trey's desk to the cells. The only light that remained on was the hall light, which bled into Caudill's unit. The cell door stood unlocked.

"Fuck!" Sutter shouted.

Eventually Trey came down the hall. He was edgy, fidgeting. "That's how I found him, Chief. Looks like . . ."

Sutter was leaning over the cot. "It looks like all his blood's gone is what'choo were about to say." The wizened face looked pale as old candle wax. There was no blood on the floor, none on Caudill's clothes, no evidence of a wound. "It's fuckin' crazy," Sutter murmured, staring.

Trey turned on the cell light. Sutter unbuttoned Cauldill's shirt to reveal a sheet-white chest underscored with blue veins. The lack of color in the flesh made Ricky's chest hairs look like jet-black wires. The nipples were purple. Sutter lifted up the arm that dangled off the cot, then pushed Caudill's body on its side. "No lividity," he said.

"What's that, Chief?"

"We've seen corpses before, Trey. After they're dead an hour or two, the blood settles to the low points a' the body and turns blue. But not here. It's impossible."

"I know, Chief," Trey agreed wearily. "Lotta impossible shit been goin' on lately, and you know what folks're sayin'."

Sutter turned and bellowed, "I ain't believin' no shit about Everd Stanherd hexin' people! Ain't no reason for Everd to hex Ricky or Junior anyway!"

Trey shrugged where he stood. "There is if it was Ricky 'n' Junior who killed the Hilds and the Ealds."

Sutter's face was reddening. "Why would they do that? You're sayin' the Caudills were into selling crystal meth, too?"

"I don't know, Chief. Gimme another explanation, then. Somebody killed Ricky in his cell, drained all his blood without spillin' a drop? You tell me."

"There ain't no fuckin' such thing as hexes 'n' curses 'n' magic! We're *cops,* for God's sake!" Sutter yelled. "You hear me?"

Trey waited through a moment of silence. "Roger that, Chief. I don't believe the shit either, but then again . . . I don't know what to make of any a' this."

"Did you call the coroner's office?"

"No."

"Why?"

Trey let out a breath at the same time he took an inadvertent glance at Ricky Caudill's grub-white corpse. "This place is givin' me the creeps, Chief. Let's go back out front and talk."

Sutter's temper was ranging up and down. He didn't like not knowing things, and right now the only thing he *did* know was that something was seriously off-kilter. "Turn some fuckin' lights on," he griped in the station lobby. "It's dark as a fuckin' tomb in here."

There was a click. Suddenly a cone of light blossomed at Chief Sutter's very own desk. But Trey was standing beside him.

Then who the hell was sitting at Sutter's desk?

"Good evening, Chief Sutter," Gordon Felps greeted him. Only the bottom half of his face could be seen in the light. "We were going to talk to you eventually, but certain events have expedited that need."

"Mr. Felps? What are you—"

"It's best if we just begin as openly as possible," the blond man said. "You are the law, after all. But sometimes the law is malleable, for the greater good. The Squatters, for instance."

Confusion immediately swept Sutter. He looked to Trey, who remained standing beside him. "What's going on, Trey?"

Trey sighed. "Chief, it's like last week, when we shook down those shitheads in the Hummer. Common drug dealers. We fucked 'em up and took their cash, and booted 'em out of town, right?"

The reference threw Sutter for a big loop. That had been *private* police business, the details of which he didn't particularly want to admit in front of Felps or any citizen. "Trey, you better level with me about what's goin' on here."

Trey nodded, crossing his arms. "That's what I'm doin', boss. And you *are* the boss; don't get me wrong. We want you in with us."

"I'm not likin' the sound of this."

Trey held up a finger to make a point. "Lemme put it this way. Those scumbags in the Hummer, okay? What if we'd gone a step further, Chief? I mean, what we did was illegal. You weren't exactly keepin' the Constitution in mind when you knocked that black dealer's teeth out and busted his leg—"

Sutter was enraged. "You were part a' that, too, so don't ya go sayin' that—"

"Chief, Chief, that's not what I mean, so *listen* to me. We *both* fucked those guys up, and we took their watches and their cash—you *and* me. And we've done stuff like that before because—let's face it—the common man don't give a shit if the police steal from criminals and bust their faces in. Forget about the letter a' the law—this is commonsense stuff we're talkin' 'bout, stuff that *all* cops do, 'cos if we don't take the law into our own hands when we can get away with it, criminals'll drag this great country of ours right down the shitter. You agree with that, Chief. We've talked about it. What it all boils down to is this: so what? We fucked up a coupla criminals. We stole from a coupla thieves. And in doin' so, we did help make the world a teeny bit better, didn't we? 'Cos those two assholes are probably *still* in the hospital. They ain't never gonna sell drugs here again, right?"

Sutter's blood pressure was starting to creep. "Right, Trey, so stop dickin' with me and tell me what this is *really* all about."

Trey nodded again, sticking to analogies. "Let's go one further, okay? Let's just say we'd *killed* those two losers in the Hummer. They kill innocent people with the drugs they sell. We know they're guilty. Sure, the Constitution 'n' all says they're innocent until proven guilty in court, but—shit, Chief—we saw it with our own eyes. We don't need no judge to tell us. Those guys sell hard drugs, and folks eventually die from those same drugs. So say we killed 'em to boot. That's against the letter a' the law, too. But what about the common man's law? It ain't that big a deal, right? We killed a couple of killers and the world's a better place for it. Right?"

Sutter's eyes shone hard on Trey. "What the fuck are you tryin' to tell me?"

"What Trey's trying to relate to you, Chief," Gordon Felps stood up and said, "is that we're all trying to make Agan's Point a better place, while we're serving our own better interests at the same time."

"The Squatters," Sutter croaked.

"Yes, Chief. They're a negative element, and they need to go. I won't lie to you. I want them gone so that I can make a lot of money by turning Agan's Point into the clean, upscale community it deserves to be. Trey wants them gone so that he can benefit financially as well. The Squatters are slowly sliding away from acceptable levels of morality. They're getting into the drug trade themselves, which can only be bad for Agan's Point. If the Squatters leave, then Judy Parker will sell the land to me and we can get on with the business of progress."

"What Mr. Felps is sayin', Chief," Trey spoke up, "is that we want the Squatters gone . . . so we're helpin' 'em along."

The silence seemed to tick along with the darkness, and with Sutter's contemplations. "Helping 'em . . . along."

"That's right," Felps continued in a monotone. "We knew that the Hilds were selling hard drugs, so I paid Junior Caudill to kill them, and to make it appear to be part of a turf-war scenario."

"He jazzed up the facts," Trey added. "To make it look more convincing to the state cops."

"And then I paid Ricky Caudill to burn down the Ealds' shack, because we also had it on good authority that they were running a meth lab out of it. Dwayne, too, by the way. He was the first contractor on my payroll. He killed about a half dozen Squatters who we also knew were working drugs."

Sutter stood stock-still. Now it was all unfolding before his face and his very life. "Ah, and you say you *knew* that these Squatters were into drugs, so you were takin' the law into your own hands by killin' 'em. To make Agan's Point a better place."

"Yes," Felps said. "And to serve our own gain."

"So how did you *know* the Hilds 'n' the Ealds were into meth?"

"Street intelligence, Chief Sutter. The best kind, which, as a police officer yourself, you already know."

"I'd been hearin' about it for a while, Chief," Trey said.

"Hearin' about it from who?"

"State cops here 'n' there, and county. Plus just bits 'n' pieces I'd been hearin' on the job. It's all legit, boss. We wouldn't have done it if we hadn't known it was rock-solid."

"So what do you think, Chief?" Felps asked outright. "Are you going to join us? It will change your life if you do. Your financial problems will be over, and you will get to be chief of police in a much, much better place—the kind of job you deserve."

Sutter stared.

"So what do you think, Chief?" Felps repeated.

The cards all fell down. Sutter turned straight to Felps and stared at him. "I think that you murdered them Squatters in cold blood. I don't believe for a minute that the Hilds 'n' the Ealds or any other Squatters had anything to do with crystal meth. I think ya killed 'em and flaked 'em with dope to make it look like they did. Just to get rich off the land."

Felps's lips could barely be seen in the darkness hovering over the desk. "That's regrettable, Chief."

Sutter reached for his gun, but—

Click.

—Trey already had his own revolver cocked against Sutter's head. "Damn it, Chief. Ya done buggered everything up." He reached around and hit his boss's thumb snap, then took his gun.

"I can't believe this," Sutter said, remarkably stable. "You growed up white trash, Trey. I pulled ya out, gave ya work, trusted ya, and now after all that, you got a gun to my head? Are you really gonna kill me after all I done for ya?"

Bam!

Muzzle flash lit the station up for a split second when Trey's piece bucked in his hand. A chunk of skull blew out of Chief Sutter's head in a way that reminded Trey of the old JFK assassination footage he caught every now and then on the History Channel—the old melon shot. Sutter's last act in life was to collapse before his own desk with a considerable thud.

At least he got to die with a bellyful of food.

"Good job," Felps said. "An unfortunate happenstance, but there was no other option available. I need his body buried deep. Will that be a problem?"

"Naw. Won't be the first time I been up all night."

"Bury him and Ricky in the foundation trenches at my construction site. I'll see to it that they're cemented over. It'll look like Ricky and Sutter were part of the meth network, too. Sutter let Ricky out of jail and then they fled. Be sure to plant some crystal in Sutter's personal vehicle and Ricky Caudill's house. In addition, that other job we discussed—the pier. I'd planned to have Ricky and Junior do that too."

"But now they're dead, so you need me to do it," Trey finished what he already knew.

"Correct." Felps looked blankly yet confidently to Trey. "Do you foresee any of this presenting a problem?"

"Nope."

"Here's something to tide you over for the time being." Felps handed Trey a very fat envelope. "I'll talk to you soon. And congratulations . . . *Chief* Trey."

Yeah, Chief *Trey*. Trey rolled the title over in his head. *I really like the sound of that.*

Felps left the station through the rear exit. Trey pocketed the sheaf of cash, then began to mop up Sutter's blood.

It would be a long night, but a productive one.

Thirteen

(I)

It was the last thing Patricia needed: another steaming, piping-hot dream. . . .

Faceless, well-muscled men spent themselves in her one after another. When one rolled off, another took his place, hot skin veneered in sweat sliding across her tingling flesh. Something felt soft beneath her bare buttocks and back—her bed?—but through the woozy slits of her eyes she was certain she saw trees, moonlight, the woods. *Oh, God, oh, God, oh, God,* she thought as another orgasm broke. The gustlike sensation racked her, forcing her to lock her ankles and wrists around the broad back of her current suitor, but he shrugged away, dragging his manhood out of her just to make way for still more unidentified men. Teeth clamped her nipple ends and pulled; calloused hands wrung her inflamed breasts. Patricia was going crazy in the anonymous sexual frenzy. She was allowing herself to be used, to be squashed, humped, and emptied into, yet through that debasement—she knew—she received pleasures far more intense than those she was giving. Who were these men, these roughened, lust-charged strangers? It didn't matter. They were but sexual animals, just as she. They were symbols of her repression and the designs that society nowadays demanded of successful, married "businesswomen." *It doesn't matter,* she panted to herself in the dream. *None of it matters. The only thing that matters is me. . . .*

She quaked at the ensuing orgasms. Mouths licked greedily over her body; tongues roved her sex. Stout fingers manipulated her clitoris with a jeweler's finesse, then roughly burrowed into her folds as well as other places.

Moonlight blurred in her eyes. The orgy seemed to be abating, but she could still see shadows of people around her. The aftermath of her ecstasy left her gleefully exhausted, but . . .

She felt herself becoming aware of something. The trees around her, the woods—they seemed pushed off at a distance. Did she hear water lapping somewhere? She thought of a pond or a lake, and as more water gently splashed, she thought it could mean that someone was coming out of this body of water. Details shifted, and her vision began to clear.

Then her heart froze in her chest.

I know where I am now, she realized, and she might as well have come to this conclusion inside of a coffin.

She'd been having sex with all those men . . . at Bowen's Field.

She lurched upright, screaming. She ran for the woods, thrashing into their midst. Her scream followed her like a contrail, but when it occurred to her that she was being followed—by some bizarre, giggling horde—the fringes of the nightmare began to dissolve, and the next thing she knew she was standing before the dresser mirror in the bedroom, naked, hair disarrayed, terrified. Her bosom heaved. The badger's foot on the cord about her neck seemed to be vaguely alive, moving about the valley of her breasts. In the dark mirror she saw that she'd been finger painted with Squatter graffiti: gleaming, slate-colored lines and squiggles inscribed about her nipples, bracketing her navel, traveling about her thighs like crestwork on an old house. Her face had been painted likewise—an ancient fertility mask, a rictus of either wantonness or horror.

The giggling tittered behind her. Had something followed her from the nightmare into reality? Her eyes bloomed at her horrid likeness in the mirror, and in the reflection she could see the window, and a faceless figure standing there.

She sat upright in bed as if awakened by a shriek. She remained naked, the sheets kicked off the bed. Her first instinct, though, was to look very closely at herself.

She slid off the mattress and walked gingerly to the dresser. *Please, please, please,* she thought. The badger's foot still dangled between her breasts, but her face and skin were clean—no evidence of the Squatter clan's body paint. Finally she let out a long breath. The cicadas trilled sedately from outside. Moonlight tinted the quiet room.

Just a nightmare, she assured herself.

She was tired of her dreams, and tired of never feeling like herself since she'd arrived. *I need to go home soon. This place is weirding me out.*

In the dream she'd been drenched in impassioned sweat, but now she felt equally drenched in shame and unmitigated sin. She'd enjoyed the raving sexual fest of the dream, which only made her feel guiltier about Byron. *I'll bet he's not dreaming of orgies with a bunch of women,* she thought. *He's home worrying about me, and missing me.*

Patricia didn't do well with guilt. . . .

The clock on the nightstand read 3:20 A.M. *Jesus . . .* Now that the terror of the dream had subsided, her head throbbed. *I'm half-drunk and half-hungover at the same time.* The dark room hovered around her. Eventually the comforting moonlight and cicada sounds turned annoying. Then—

Creeeeeak.

Patricia snapped her gaze toward the open window. "Who's there?" she abruptly called out.

A creak.

As if someone had been standing on the wooden porch below the window. *It's probably nothing,* she dismissed, yet quickly pulled on her robe.

Someone had been standing by the window in the dream. . . .

Yes, it was probably nothing, but she got up nonetheless and leaned out the window. "Is anyone there?" she asked too quietly. What if someone answered? Who would be out here at this hour, and for what purpose?

She wouldn't let herself contemplate answers.

She squinted, set her hand down on the sill to lean out further, but . . .

What is . . .

Her hand came away wet. Something viscid.

Gross. Whatever it was, it felt warm. Slug trails. Annoyed, she wiped her hand with a tissue, then grabbed the flashlight and went outside.

At first she couldn't reckon what she was seeing in

the flashlight beam: a splotch like melted wax pooled on the sill, the overflow running down the outside wall in a trail. It was still wet, but now she noticed other similar trails that had long since dried.

The window, she thought.

Then, revolted, she knew.

Like the peephole at the Squatter's shower. *Oh, my God.* The realization bloomed in totality.

Some man was out here, masturbating. Looking at me naked in bed . . .

Then a rustling came from the hedges out in the yard, and she saw a figure slinking away. It was Ernie.

He stumbled drunkenly down the path, then through the trees, and disappeared.

Fourteen

(I)

Bam, bam, bam, bam, bam.

The knock on the door sounded like someone hitting the frame with a hammer.

Oh, my God, I'm so *hungover,* Patricia thought, a hand to her head. She'd passed back out on the bed last night, and when she looked to the clock now, it shocked her to see that it was noon. And—

Bam, bam, bam, bam, bam.

The knock was maddening, painful against her headache. She dragged herself out of bed, making sure her robe was sashed. Who would be knocking that loud? *It's so fucking* rude!

When she opened her door, it puzzled her to find a poker-faced Virginia state trooper looking back at her, with sergeant stripes on his sleeve. "Sorry to bother you, ma'am. Are you Patricia White?"

"Why, yes, but—"

"I'm Sergeant Shannon, with the state police narcotics unit. I need to ask you a few questions," he said. The trooper had gunmetal hair and no trace of the local accent, more like a Wisconsin accent than anything Southern. His eyes seemed critical of the fact that Patricia was in her nightgown past noon. "It won't take very long at all."

Patricia immediately put her guard up. She was a lawyer; such a question from a police officer had to make her wonder. "What are the questions in reference to?" she asked back.

"Ernie Gooder . . . and your sister, Judy Parker."

Patricia's head throbbed; she couldn't concentrate. "What on earth . . . Is everything all right?"

"No, ma'am. There was more trouble last night," the officer said. "Do you have any idea where Judy Parker or Ernie Gooder is?"

"Well . . ." She rubbed her eyes. "Aren't they here at the house?"

"Nope. We checked the house."

Another flag shot up. "You need a search warrant for that, Sergeant."

He put a piece of paper in her face. "I have more than that, ma'am. I have an arrest warrant for Ernie Gooder. The magistrate just signed it."

This is crazy! "Why do you want to arrest Ernie?"

"Did you know that most of the Agan's Point boat docks burned down last night? The boathouse, and about half of your sister's crabbing boats?"

Patricia couldn't think past the shock. "No, I had no idea."

"The fire marshal's down there now, says it was arson. Some coincidence, isn't it? One night after someone burns down the Ealds' shack—a crystal meth lab—then someone burns down the docks. Looks like more turf war; at least that's what we think."

"But what does this have to do with Ernie?"

"Several witnesses saw him in proximity to the docks shortly before the fire."

Patricia pushed through some mental cobwebs. *Wait a minute. I saw Ernie last night at 3:15. . . .* "What time?" she asked.

"About three-thirty in the morning."

The pause in her mind yawned. That didn't sound good at all, especially when she remembered what else Ernie had been doing last night. *He was peeping in my window, and . . .* It didn't add up, though. "I don't understand why you're here instead of Chief Sutter."

Shannon's rugged face remained blank. "Chief Sutter appears to be missing, too, along with your sister and Ernie Gooder. Sergeant Trey is down at the scene right now."

The confusion was piling up on her headache. "My sister? You're saying that my sister is *missing?*"

"Not officially, but no one can find her. Her vehicle's in the driveway, and she's not in the house. She's the property owner, but she's not anywhere on the property. We think Ernie Gooder might be working in collaboration with some kind of rival drug gang—"

"That's ridiculous," Patricia had to admit, even after what she'd caught Ernie doing last night.

"There's been quite a bit of evidence lately involving sales and manufacture of amphetamine-based narcotics. These vagrants who live on your sister's land at the south end of the Point. We already know that some of these vagrants or squatters or whatever they are have been producing and selling drugs in an operation run by a man named Everd Stanherd."

Patricia sighed. *More craziness.* "Look, I don't know about the Squatters—I guess some of them are involved in that—but there's no way that Ernie Gooder is, and . . . what? You think my sister is too?"

"No, we just think it's odd for her to have disappeared when all of this is going on. Two burnings in two days, a rash of missing persons, and drug-related murders between what are obviously rival drug gangs."

Patricia couldn't argue with the trooper. "And what did you say? Chief *Sutter* is missing too?"

"That's correct, ma'am. Do you know where he is?"

The tone of Sergeant Shannon's voice unsettled her. "Why would I know where the town police chief is, Officer?"

"I'm just asking, ma'am."

"You seem to be implying something that rubs me the wrong way."

"No implications, ma'am. We'd just be very interested in knowing why he's not around when the town docks get burned down. It appears that sometime last night Chief Sutter released a prisoner at the town jail, a man named Ricky Caudill. He's missing, too. And wouldn't you know it? When we checked Caudill's house, we found packets of crystal meth. Sutter's personal vehicle is still at his house, and his wife doesn't know where he is. And . . ." The snide trooper paused for effect. "Wouldn't you know it? The wife's car is gone, stolen. In a town that hasn't had a single stolen car reported in ten years. I got men at the Sutter house right now, searching the premises and his personal vehicle. And on top of all that, your sister is missing too.

We'd be very interested in knowing where she is. A lot of people have been disappearing around here lately. More than anything else, we're very concerned about the well-being of Judy Parker and the whereabouts of Chief Sutter and Ricky Caudill. And we're going to arrest Ernie Gooder at the earliest opportunity." Shannon held up the warrant again—a stolid reminder. Then he gave her his card. "I'm sorry to have to wake you up so earl—" He paused, looked at his watch, and raised a brow. Then he discreetly sniffed the air, as if to say, *Would that be alcohol I smell on your breath?* "Sorry to intrude on your day. But please give us a call if you think you might be able to help us out."

"I will," she said, trying to not grind her teeth.

"Hey, Sarge!" a younger trooper called out behind him. "Check it out."

Shannon walked away without further word, retracing steps back to Ernie's bedroom, where several other officers milled about.

Jesus, that rude bastard! She had a mind to file a harassment complaint. She closed the door, repressing her lawyer's rage, and dressed quickly. Then brushed her teeth and gargled, hoping to quell any more remnants of last night's drinking. *Now let's see what the fuss is in Ernie's room. . . .*

When she walked in herself, she didn't need to be told. *I don't believe it,* she thought.

A state trooper with acetate gloves was plucking tiny bags of crystal methamphetamine out of Ernie's dresser drawer.

There were many such bags.

(II)

I'm not doing too bad here, no, sir, Trey thought. Even with those couple of surprises at the last minute, Trey was sure he'd done the right thing. Burying Sutter and Ricky Caudill had been a cinch; Felps had left some holes already dug at the condo site, as promised. And taking care of the docks, too, had been easy and kind of fun. *But I sure as shit didn't count on that fuckhead Ernie catching me at the pier last night. Son of a whore followed me all the way from Judy's house!* Trey had been caught by total surprise when he'd been pumping twenty or thirty gallons of marine gas from the boat pump all over the pier and the closest crabbing boats.

Ernie was a bigger, stronger man, for sure, but Trey was harder. He'd jacked the redneck out after not much of a tussle, busted some teeth, cracked a rib or two, then knocked him out cold with a bop to the head. *Never did like that fucker. Shit, I shoulda just let him burn up in the boathouse. . . .* Why hadn't he thought of that? *Can't think a everything every time.* Instead, he'd hogtied Ernie and driven him out to the abandoned shanty way off from Squatterville on the Point. *Nobody even knows about this place,* he thought, unlocking the front door now. He'd tried to look as official as possible for the state cops and firemen once the burning docks had been discovered. They'd all been out there for hours. Close to nightfall, the state began wrapping things up, so Trey took off in his patrol car to "start canvassing the neighborhood. Try to get me a line on Ernie Gooder," he'd claimed.

Instead, he'd come straight to the shanty.

"Howdy, folks," he proclaimed inside.

No one responded, but how could they, with gags in their mouths? Trey lit the lantern; light flowed around him when he proceeded to the center of the room. "There she is, the little cutie," he mocked Judy. Snatching her last night couldn't have been easier. She'd been stumbling toward the edge of the woods beyond the cookout, drunk out of her gourd. "Why, sure, Judy," he'd answered her blabbering request. "I'd be more'n happy to drive you back to the house." He'd driven her back to the shanty instead, handcuffed and with her D-cup bra stuffed in her mouth. Drunken bitch didn't even know what he was doing, she was so stewed. Now she lay on the floor, on her side, tied up like a trussed goose. One ample breast had fallen out of the torn blouse, the nipple large as a beer coaster. Trey, of course, did the gentlemanly thing, saying, "Ah, now, that ain't right. A gal can't be havin' a tit hangin' out." And then he ripped back the blouse some more. "She needs *both* hangin' out. There, that's better." He gave them both a good feel. Trey had plans for these breasts, and for everything else connected to them . . . but not just yet. He'd be setting her up for another psycho job; this one would look like some of the clan did it, the ones who were running meth. Only Trey knew that there were actually *no* Squatters selling anything except fucking crabs—but that was beside the point.

"You first, buddy-bro." Trey grabbed Ernie by the back of the belt and dragged him to the car. He mewled beneath his gag, eyes blooming with rage. Trey hocked on him once he got the cracker loaded into the truck. "Time for a road trip," the dutiful officer promised, then slammed the trunk closed.

Trey cleared his head as he drove, smiling to himself. The moon was just up over the trees, gibbous, yellow as a grapefruit. Even closet sociopaths like Trey found their moments of existential harmony. *I'm gonna kill a couple more people tonight, and you know what? I dig it.* All part of the plan. He particularly liked the notion that on the same day he'd unofficially become Agan's Point's new police chief, he'd disposed of two bodies and was about to dispose of two more.

I'm really gettin' the hang of this, he thought.

The spur he was looking for sat about five miles north of the Point, inaccessible to boats—due to rocks and a low-tide margin—and well hidden by a wall of trees. When Trey was a boy, in fact, he'd come down here on his own to drop chicken necks. The crabs were humongous and so plentiful he could pull a half bushel in an hour. More of that same existential harmony seized him now when he parked and opened the trunk. Cicadas trilled, the moonlight bathed his face, and the lapping water along the shore made him truly feel one with the universe, the master of his own destiny.

"Out'cha go," he said, hefting Ernie out of the trunk and carrying him like a heavy suitcase by the back of his belt. In the other hand, Trey carried his crowbar.

"Ain't no one to hear ya way out here," Trey said, and cut off his gag.

"You fuckin' piece a' shit, Trey," Ernie wheezed, crooking his neck to look up. "I always knowed you were a twisted motherfucker."

"I *did* fuck my mother, Ernie. Lotsa times. And I'm damn proud of it. Now let's get you fixed up. Hot night like this, you need a cool dip." Trey shoved Ernie on his side, raised the crowbar high, and—

Crack! Crack! Crack!

—hammered the crowbar's elbow hard between Ernie's shoulder blades. Ernie grunted a salvo of less-than-eloquent objections, then began to shudder. Several more cracks between the shoulder blades sufficed to achieve Trey's purpose. He leaned over and cut the hogtie, watched Ernie's limbs slump.

"Are ya dead?" Trey asked, slamming his shoe down on Ernie's hand. There was no recoil, no movement whatsoever. But Ernie's eyes were still blinking, his chest rising, and his throat gulping.

"I-I cain't move," Ernie choked. "Cain't move my arms or legs, ya motherfuckin' sick piece a' shit . . ."

"That's 'cos I just paralyzed ya, dickhead." Trey nodded a secret approval, like an acknowledgment shared exclusively between himself and the night. He'd fractured the spine high enough to cause total paralysis but not quite high enough to kill. "You always were a no-balls, do-good hayseed, Ernie. Well, now you're a *quadriplegic* no-balls, do-good hayseed."

Ernie drooled, only his head moving. "You'll burn in hell, so I guess that's good enough."

"Sure, but you'll get there first. And when you're down there suckin' the devil's dick, I'll still be here, havin' a ball." Trey chuckled as he took to his next task. He tore open Ernie's shirt, pulled off his boots, then yanked his jeans down to his knees.

"What are you, queer?" Ernie challenged. "I figured ya for a lotta things, but not that."

Trey guffawed. "Don't worry, Ernie-boy. I ain't gonna pack your fudge. I done told ya—you're goin' fer a nice cool dip in the good ol' Chesapeake Bay." And then Trey dragged Ernie into the shallow water until the water came over his chest.

"All you're gonna do is drown me?" Ernie managed. It could be discerned by the straining expression on his face that he was trying to move his limbs, but those nerves were no longer firing at all. "Figured a sick fuck like you'd cut me up or hang me or somethin'."

"Naw, Ernie, this is much better, and no, I ain't gonna drown ya neither." Now Trey leaned Ernie's head up against a rotten log in the water. He couldn't move, and was braced enough so that there was no way he might sidle over into the water and indeed drown.

A moment passed; then Ernie figured it out, to his extreme misfortune. "Aw, no, God . . ."

Trey grinned down at his work: Ernie's head and shoulders were propped out of the water, but the rest of his body was submerged.

"Agan's Point crabs'll eat good tonight," Trey said, then walked back to the car and drove off.

Fifteen

(I)

"It's all beyond belief," Byron said in a very low voice over the phone.

Patricia was looking blankly out the window as she talked, her cell phone to her ear. "I know," she said. "I feel useless. I don't know what to do. I came out here to *help* my sister, but now I don't even know where she is."

"Well, enough is enough. You have to come home now."

She chewed her lower lip. She *did* want to go home now, but how could she? "Byron, Judy is *missing*. I can't leave until I know she's safe."

Byron's dissatisfaction could be sensed over the line. "At this point, I don't even care. All I care about is you being *back here* with *me*. I want you here *now*, in *our* house—safe. I don't care about Judy, I don't care about those nutty Squatter people, I don't care about docks and lean-tos burning down. People are getting murdered there, Patricia. So you get in your car—right now—and drive home. Now. This minute."

It was rare for Byron to be this bent out of shape; he was even mad, something rarer. "I want to come home, too, Byron. But I can't leave until I know Judy's all right—"

"She probably passed out drunk in the woods!" Byron exploded. "Whoever's doing these burnings—these drug people—they could burn Judy's house down next, with *you* in it!"

"Honey, calm down," she tried to pacify him. The sun from the window glared in her eyes. He was right, and by now . . .

By now, I'm sick to death of Agan's Point and hope I never see the place again. "I'll be home soon. . . ."

"Damn it! You're so fucking stubborn!"

I know I am. But I can't leave yet. "I'll be home in three days, no more. I promise."

"What if you can't find her by then? What if she's dead? I'm sorry if that sounds insensitive, but I don't give a shit about your sister compared to you!"

Patricia sighed. "I'm sure she'll turn up by then."

"But what if she doesn't?" Byron blared.

"Then I'll come home anyway. I'll come home Sunday no matter what."

Now Byron sighed, too. "I just miss you so much, and I love you. I want you home, away from that crazy place."

"I'll *be* home, honey. On Sunday."

He calmed down in a moment, and they said their good-byes for the moment, Patricia promising to call him several times a day until she left. *Indulging me is wearing him out,* she realized. *I'm not being much of a wife, am I?* She remembered her failed antics with Ernie, her drunkenness, and her complete disregard toward Byron since she'd been here. *Yeah, I've been a really lousy wife lately.* About the only thing she could look forward to was making it up to him.

Did she hear sirens in the distance? She wasn't sure. *Don't tell me something else was set on fire. . . .* She called the town police station, inquiring, "Has Judy Parker been located yet?"

"No, ma'am," a woman replied quickly.

"What about Ernie Gooder?"

The receptionist seemed hurried. "He hasn't been found yet either, and neither has Chief Sutter."

"Is Sergeant Trey available now?"

An exasperated sigh. "No, ma'am. He's out helping the state police look."

"Well, if anybody turns up, could you please call—"

"I'm sorry, ma'am, I have a radio call. I have to go. Call back at five or six. Sergeant Trey should be back by then. Have a good day."

Click.

The little bit of radio squawk Patricia had heard in the background sounded urgent. *Maybe those really were sirens I heard. . . .*

She showered and dressed, feeling awkward, even uneasy. *I'm the only one here,* she reminded herself. Last night she'd slept fitfully, the only one in the house then, as well. But she'd been sure to wear her nightgown this time, and close and lock the window and her bedroom door. She'd refused to admit to herself that she was afraid.

The beautiful morning outside should've heartened her, but it didn't. *What's happening here?* she thought, driving through some of the town's side roads. Modest homes from sparse yards looked back at her. Yes, the town *appeared* normal, quaint, and very sane. But this past week assured her of the falsehood of appearances. *Who knows what's going on behind some of those doors?* she thought.

She took the Cadillac off the Point, vaguely heading in the direction from which she thought she'd heard sirens. An ambiguous nausea flirted with her stomach, and it took her a few moments to realize why: this was roughly the same direction as Bowen's Field. . . .

Forget about it. You're long over all that.

And she *did* feel long over the incident, just as Dr. Sallee had explained. And miles before the road would lead to Bowen's Field, she saw a state police car turning down a trail into the woods.

Something is *going on out here,* she realized.

The road wound down to a rutted dirt lane. Around the bend, she stopped short, startled. *My God! What happened here?* An ambulance and three police cars sat parked with their lights flashing. Sergeant Shannon, the rugged state trooper she'd talked to yesterday, stood with the other officers, arms crossed and looking down toward a fingerlike estuary cutting into the woods from the bay. Shannon turned at the sound of her tires, then broke from the others and approached.

"Ms. White," he said, holding up a cautious hand, "you don't want to come down here."

"What happened!" she blurted, heart racing. She spotted two EMTs dragging a gurney from the ambulance. One of them also unfolded a black body bag. "It's not my sister, is it?"

The trooper blocked her way. He looked a little pale.

"No, it's not. It's one of the other missing persons—Ernie Gooder. I'm afraid he's d—"

Patricia pushed past him, wild-eyed. *No! It can't be!* But even as the plea left her lips, she knew the worst.

Her eyes shot down at the water. She blinked. Then she jerked her gaze away.

"I told you you didn't want to come down here, Ms. White," Shannon said. "There is some rough stuff going on in this town."

Rough stuff. What Patricia had seen in the several seconds she'd actually been able to look was this: Ernie's dead body being dragged out of the shallow water . . . or, it could be said, something significantly *less* than his dead body.

From the chest down the body looked corroded, or even eaten. All the skin and quite a bit of muscle mass was absent, leaving raw white bones showing. The waist down was the worst—there was essentially nothing left but tendons and scraps of muscle fiber along the leg bones and hips: a wet skeleton. Skeletal feet pointed up at the ends of the lower leg bones. Ernie's sodden shirt had been torn open and hung off the shoulders, while his pants looked congealed at what was left of his ankles. Some arcane process had whittled away the flesh, leaving this human scrap, and in the final second of her glimpse, Patricia realized what that process was.

At least a dozen very large blue crabs let go of those skeletal legs when the body had been pulled out, whereupon they skittered back into the water. Ernie had been used for crab bait.

Patricia wanted to throw up. She felt dizzy at once, and braced herself against a tree. "My God," she wheezed.

"Sorry you had to see that," Shannon said. "These drug wars can get down and dirty."

"I knew him very well," Patricia mumbled over the nausea. "He simply wasn't the type to sell or use drugs."

Shannon seemed convinced otherwise. "We found crystal meth in his room, so how do you explain—"

"Sergeant Shannon?" one of the EMTs called out. He knelt at Ernie's horrific corpse, as gloved cops prepared to slide it into the body bag. "Found some CDS in his pants pocket. Looks like crystal meth. You'll want to bag it as evidence."

"You were saying?" Shannon said back to Patricia.

When she heard the bag being zipped up, some morbid force caused her to steal one last glance. Ernie was now mostly in the bag, but his head hung out, neck craned back. That was when she saw . . .

His teeth . . . My God, his teeth . . .

"You all right, Ms. White?"

"His two front teeth are missing," she croaked. "It's impossible for me to not have noticed that in the past."

"Ever hear of false teeth? They probably fell out when his attackers were putting him in the water."

Patricia didn't hear whatever else he said before he departed and went to secure the drug evidence.

His two front teeth are missing. The words droned in her head. It was the one thing she'd never forget: the man who'd raped her over twenty-five years ago had been missing his two front teeth. . . .

Patricia could barely maintain her composure. She stood up at the end of the road with Shannon. They both watched in silence as the ambulance and other police cars drove away, leaving a veil of road dust hanging in the air. When the last vehicle had left, Patricia stood in numb shock, the cicada sounds beating in her ears.

"I can tell you," Shannon began, "nothing will ruin a town and its people faster than dope. It's happening everywhere. And half the time it's the people you least expect."

"It's just . . . Ernie," she said. "He wasn't the type at all."

"All it takes is one hit off a meth pipe and you're done. Every addict I ever busted says the same thing. It changes you overnight. And once the stuff tips you over, you're making it or selling it just to maintain your own supply. It turns decent people into thieves, killers, criminals—human animals. And good luck making it through rehab. This stuff and crack? The success rate is so low it's not even worth bothering with. You can put a meth-head in prison for ten years, and he's back with the pipe the first day he gets out. That's how addictive this stuff is."

Patricia shook her head, looking out into the woods.

"So you knew this guy pretty well, I take it," the trooper observed.

"I thought I did. I grew up with him as a kid. I live in D.C. now, but I came back to Agan's Point for a visit—the first time in years."

"Well, now you can see what happened to him over those years."

"I guess I knew something was wrong—I couldn't imagine he'd gotten involved with drug people. He wasn't the type."

"There isn't a *type*. It can happen to anyone. You experiment with something like this, think, 'Oh, I'll just do it once to see what it's like.' Then you're never the same. We're pretty sure Ernie Gooder was the person who burned down the docks two nights ago."

"What time did you say the fire occurred?"

"Three thirty."

Patricia smirked. "He was peeping in my window around quarter after."

"Really?" Shannon said. "You're lucky that all he did was peep. Anyway, it's obvious what's going on out here—a meth war between two gangs. Ernie and some of these other locals are in one gang, and a bunch of these Squatters are in the other. And now they're duking it out. It might seem impossible for a place like this, but like I said, the same thing's happening all over the state." Shannon shrugged. "Chief Sutter being missing doesn't look good either."

"So you think he's involved with drugs?"

"A cop, especially a police chief, is the kind of power person any dope gang will pay to work for them and protect their runs. You wouldn't believe the kind of money a crooked cop can make."

"Is that what you really think? That Chief Sutter is working with a drug gang?"

"It's either that or he got killed trying to make a bust. A police chief doesn't just *disappear*."

Even in her civilian naïveté, Patricia was coming to grips with Sergeant Shannon's suspicions.

The heat was steepening, the humidity drawing beads of sweat on her brow.

"And I'm sorry I'm the one to tell you this, but I'm sure you've already considered it anyway," Shannon told her. "There's a pretty big chance that your sister was involved in some of this too. She's also missing. There's a good chance—"

"I know, Sergeant." Patricia faced the facts. "My sister's probably dead. Her body's probably lying in the woods somewhere."

Shannon didn't say anything after that.

When he went back on his rounds, Patricia headed back toward town. She drove aimlessly, cranking the air-conditioning up. *What am I thinking?* she asked herself. *That I'm just going to see Judy walking down the road? She's going to wave to me, with a big smile?* She knew that wasn't going to happen.

She drove through more of the town proper, and then the outskirts. *I've never seen anything like this,* she thought; Agan's Point looked abandoned, evacuated. *Not even one person out walking their dog . . .* When she pulled into the Qwik-Mart, she found the little parking lot empty, noticed no one in the store, then spotted the SORRY, WE'RE CLOSED sign.

Hours passed without her notice. Patricia tried to keep her mind off what was becoming the greatest likelihood. Eventually, she forced herself to admit why she was driving so pointlessly.

I don't want to go back to the house.

The comfortable old house she'd been raised in now seemed utterly haunted, not just by her dour parents but by murdered people she didn't know, and by Judy, by Ernie, by every dim, sad memory, and as she pulled up the long cul-de-sac out front, those memories massed and urged her away. She drove to the southern end of the Point. . . .

Where the town looked evacuated; the tract of land that comprised Squatterville looked evacuating. *It's a mass exodus now,* she saw. She wondered how many Squatters actually had been involved in drugs. Just those few? Or had the Squatters become a secret drug culture of their own?

We'll never know. They're all leaving now.

In small salvos they trudged up the hill and away, beaten suitcases and sacks of possessions in tow; Patricia thought of refugees leaving a bombed city. *Where they go next is anybody's guess, and it's not like anyone cares anyway. . . .*

The sun was sinking. Patricia drove the loop around the crab-picking house and then winced at the burned pier. The boathouse had been reduced to cinders, while the boats that had been burned had been moored ashore, the hulls like blackened husks. She could still smell the char in the air, thick as the cicada trills.

Out in the bay she saw the pale wood plank sticking up: the Squatter graffiti, their good-luck sign. The plank appeared to overlook the ruined docks, a symbol now of the clan's *bad* fortune, not good fortune.

The inevitable approached quickly, like a beast running down a fawn. The sun had now been replaced by a fat yellow moon that stalked her back to the dark house.

She parked the Cadillac out front, then sat for several minutes staring, the engine ticking beneath the hood. *I don't want to go in. There's nobody there anymore.*

She trudged up the steps, frowning at the odd door knocker that was a half-formed face. The fantasy beckoned her: that she would walk in, smell homemade biscuits baking, and Judy would look up from the oven and explain where she'd been the last two days, and it would all be so innocent, and they'd laugh and hug and everything would be okay again.

Patricia's hands were shaking when she entered and crossed the foyer. Darkness saturated the house. She walked around downstairs, wide-eyed, snapping on lights, but the illumination she sought only made the house feel bigger . . . and emptier. Her feet took her listlessly to the kitchen and no, the air didn't smell of biscuits; it smelled sterile, lifeless. Instinct urged her to call out for Judy, but she didn't bother.

Her sister wasn't here, and probably never would be again.

She checked the answering machine. Had anyone called? Had the police left a message to relate that Judy had been found, had been rushed to the hospital for an appendectomy or something, and was recovering now and waiting for her?

"You have . . . zero . . . messages," the machine's generic voice told her.

She turned and went to the refrigerator for some juice, but her hand froze in midair. A strawberry magnet held a note to the door—*Things to get: flour, milk, eggs, coffee*—a shopping list in Judy's unruly scrawl. Patricia stared at the list and began to cry.

She wore her clothes to bed, too unsettled to undress. The bedroom window stared at her. It was locked now, its curtains drawn, but just knowing what Ernie had been doing on the other side of it several nights ago gave her a grim fright. *A dead man's sperm is on my windowsill,* she thought absurdly. *Just a few feet away . . .* The notion knotted her stomach. She could go sleep in another room, but that idea distressed her as well. Which room would she take? Ernie's? Her sister's? Or what about her parents' old room upstairs? No, they were all chock-full of ghosts now.

She stared up at the ceiling, at the room's grainy

darkness. Were faces forming in the grains? *The window, the window,* part of her mind kept whispering to her.

There's nothing there, so forget about it and go to sleep! she shouted back at herself, but she couldn't take solace even in her own sense of reason. Eventually she threw back the sheets, sighed to herself, and pulled back the curtain.

See. No one there. No peeping Toms, no monsters. Beyond the glass the yard looked normal, sedate. Night flowers in the expansive garden opened their petals to the night. The moon had risen higher now and turned white, flooding the backyard with a tranquil glow. There was nothing out of the ordinary for her to see.

Back under the covers, she curled into a ball. Did she hear the hall clock ticking? The house frame creaked a few times, causing her to flinch. *Please, Judy. Please come home. Please be okay,* she prayed, drifting off.

The maw of a nightmare opened wide. She was in the same room, in the same grainy darkness and on the same bed, only naked now, splayed. Moonlight flooded the room and, in turn, her bare flesh. It painted her in a translucent lambency: bright, sharp-white skin, the rim of her navel a shadow dark as black ink. Her legs were spread to the window, her furred sex shamefully bared.

She couldn't close her legs for the life of her.

She couldn't cover herself.

How can there be moonlight in the room? she thought. *The curtains are closed. I know they are. I just closed them.* But of course she thought that, for it didn't occur to her yet that this was a dream. . . .

She thought on through a tingling fear, concluding her question: *Someone must have opened the curtains.*

Then:

The window . . .

She was determined not to look, but just as she'd given the order to herself, some force—the ghost of her father's hand, perhaps—pushed her head up and *made* her look.

She looked straight ahead between the mounds of her breasts, down her stomach, through her spread legs. The tiny tuft of pubic hair drew a bead like a gunsight to the window.

The curtains weren't merely open; they were gone. The moonlight shimmered in an unwelcome guest now. She felt humiliated, ashamed. If someone was outside, they could look in and see her totally bared, the most private part of her body displayed as if on purpose. What would they think of her, lying on the bed like that, utterly naked?

But . . .

Thank God. There's no one there.

The hall clock began to tick louder than normal, and more rapidly. She kept looking down her body at the window, saw her breasts rising and falling faster now, her flat abdomen trembling, and then, beyond the ticking, she heard something else.

Crunching.

Footsteps, she knew.

Patricia's paralysis intensified; she felt made of cement, a prone statue. When the shadow edged into the window frame, her scream froze in her chest.

It was Ernie.

Cadaverous now, he leered in with a rotten grin, his eyes like raw oysters, his skin fish-belly white. He was masturbating, his dead hand shucking a rotten penis with vigor. Worse than the act—and the dead, wet gleam in his eyes—was the gap that shone through the grin: the two front teeth missing. At one point he pushed a black tongue through the gap and wriggled it.

Soon another figure joined him: David Eald and his dead young daughter, both blackened corpses, the Hilds now naked, gut-sucked stick figures. Chief Sutter, as bloated in death as he was in life, his dead face the color and consistency of cheesecake, with two thumbholes for eyes. And finally Judy herself, naked and sagging, the skin of her face stretched across her skull like a stocking mask, the steam of rot wafting off her flesh.

Yes, they'd all congregated now—this cadaverous clique—to paint Patricia's nakedness with their spoiled grins. Ernie painted the windowsill with something else, his bony hips quivering and cheeks bloated—putrid semen spurting. In his enthusiasm, Patricia noted that he'd actually wrung the skin off his penis at the climactic moment. She also saw that maggots frenzied in the sperm as it shot out.

Thank God the window's locked, Patricia thought.

Then Ernie's and Sutter's cheesy-dead fingers began to open the window. First they'd reveled just to see her, but now they were coming to touch. . . .

When the stench poured into the room, Patricia wakened and screamed loud as a truck horn.

Oh, God, oh, God, oh, God . . .

Was she going insane? Her hand shot to her chest; her heartbeat felt like something exploding in her. But at least her clothes were on—at least now she knew it had been a dream.

The grainy dark hung before her, a veil. The hall

clock ticked but was back to its normal, quiet pace. When the house frame creaked again, she actually found it comforting—because she knew it was real.

The window seemed to beckon her, though. Of course its curtains remained closed, just as she'd left them. But . . .

Her paranoia raced back to snare her. *Damn it,* she thought. *Damn it,* damn *it!* She needed to know, just to be sure. . . .

She swung her feet out and rose, giving herself a moment to fully come awake. When the time came to move, she faltered. *Come on, Patricia. What are you thinking?*

What *was* she thinking? That she'd pull the curtains back to find a cluster of dead faces leering in?

Ridiculous.

But still, she had to prove it to herself; otherwise she'd get no sleep at all.

There! See? She was almost ecstatic when she looked behind the curtains to find nothing there. The backyard faced her exactly as it had earlier. No movement, the night flowers standing open, moonlight shimmering.

Then her heart slammed once.

Wait a minute. . . .

There was one thing outside that hadn't been there when she'd looked before. At first she hadn't seen it.

Ernie's pickup truck.

The first foot of its front end protruded into her view. *That's impossible!* She closed her eyes and took several deep breaths. *Ernie's dead. I saw his* dead *body. And his truck wasn't there before!*

She was certain, absolutely *certain* it hadn't been there before.

And next the thought exploded:

Oh, my God, maybe it's Judy! She must've borrowed his truck earlier and gone off somewhere! And she came back but didn't wake me up when she came in!

Now it was joy that propelled her out of the bedroom. "Judy! Are you back?" She raced down the hall, out to the foyer, and up the stairs. She swung into her sister's bedroom and snapped on the light.

"Judy?"

The bed lay empty, neatly made.

Then she's downstairs somewhere! Patricia felt convinced. *She has to be! That's the only thing that could explain Ernie's truck being in the backyard. She's downstairs right now in the kitchen, getting something to eat!*

Patricia collapsed when she burst in and flicked on the light. Her knees thudded to the floor. She shrieked.

Judy was in the kitchen, all right. But she wasn't getting anything to eat. A cane chair lay tipped over on the floor, along with two sandals. Judy was hanging by the neck from a kitchen rafter.

The rope creaked, a sound not unlike the house frame. Judy's face ballooned, bright scarlet tinged with blue, tongue sticking out. She wore the flowered sundress Patricia remembered her wearing at the clan cookout. To make it worse, the process had snapped the neck entirely, and now beneath the noose, the neck stretched a foot. Lividity had turned her sister's bare feet something close to black, and the lower legs too, veins bulging fat as earthworms.

Oh, Judy . . . Oh, my God, my poor sister . . .

She'd never been that stable to begin with, and she'd never liked change. That was why she'd stayed with

Dwayne so long, even in the midst of all that abuse, and that was why she'd never left this house. *She was happy only when things were the same.*

But suicide? Patricia dragged herself up, the horror replaced by the reality of the despair. *Squatters betraying her, selling drugs while they took a paycheck from her? Police on the property every other night for murders and burnings? Yeah, things have definitely changed around here.*

It was inexplicable, but it happened every day: people killing themselves. It was the only cure to a horrid symptom they had to live with for God knew how long, and with nobody else even knowing there was a problem.

I have to call the police right now, Patricia realized. Knowing that her sister's body hung dead behind her couldn't have been more distressing, but Patricia simply didn't have the strength to take her down herself. She turned for the phone—

—and almost collapsed again.

Sergeant Trey stood in the doorway to the laundry room, as if he'd just come in through the back. He seemed as startled as she.

"Damn, Ms. White. Ya scared the bejesus outa me."

Patricia looked at him, confused.

"I just come in from outside. About an hour ago I was looking out the station window and thought I saw Ernie's truck drive by, with Judy drivin' it," he explained. "So I run out and jump in the cruiser, but the damn gas tank was on E, so I had to fill up at the station pump. By the time I was done with all that, Judy'd already got back to the house and—"

He looked up the the body.

"You . . . saw her driving?" Patricia's question faltered.

"Yeah, and I'm really sorry. If my damn tank hadn't been empty, I probably coulda gotten up here in time to stop her."

"But . . ." The information bewildered Patricia. "But what were you doing walking in just now? You didn't seem surprised to see that she'd committed suicide."

"I already knew. I found her about five minutes ago." He explained more details. "So I went back out to the cruiser to call the state cops on my radio. Then I walked back in and found you standing here."

"Oh." Patricia continued to look at him. Something wasn't right. "But . . . your radio's right there on your belt."

Trey's eyes darted down to his gun belt, the Motorola heavy in its leather holder. "Well, yeah, sure, but that's just my, uh, my field radio." Trey's eyes shifted. He bit his lip a moment, but by then his cool delivery was falling apart. "S-see, this radio ain't got the, uh, the state police frequency on it. Just the station frequency and the county."

"Why the county and not the state?"

Trey blinked. "That's . . . just the way the . . . bands work."

Patricia didn't consciously decide to say what she said next. She simply said it. "I don't believe you. You're acting like you're lying. You're acting like a prosecuting attorney who knows his case is bullshit."

Trey blinked again, blank faced. Then he sat down in the chair by the kitchen table, but by the time he did so, his gun was drawn and pointing right at her. "Holy ever-livin' shit, Patricia. Why couldn't ya just leave it?"

Patricia's heart hammered so loud she could hear it. "You killed my sister, didn't you?"

"Fuck," Trey muttered. The expletive was directed

toward himself, not Patricia. "Yeah. Wanna know what I did? I snatched her after the Squatter cookout, kept her tied up for a day at one a' old shacks way out at the Point. Fucked the daylights out of her a couple of times, then hung the bitch in the woods." He shrugged noncommitally. "Then I throwed her in the back a' Ernie's truck and brought her here and just threw the same rope over the kitchen rafter. Easy. And who ain't gonna believe it? Alcoholic and a head case to begin with, been depressed since Dwayne got offed. Looks like a typical widow who just couldn't stand to live no more without her man. Happens every day."

"She wasn't the only person you murdered, was she?"

Trey snorted. "These hayseeds out here? Squatters? No-accounts like Ernie? They don't mean shit. But you're different. You can't just disappear. You can't wind up dead with a pocketful a' dope. No one would believe it. You ain't no redneck; you're a big-city lawyer. Someone would come snoopin' around." He shook his head in the chair, suddenly exhausted. "You fucked everything up."

Trey's attentions seemed diverted inwardly; he wasn't really looking at her. Patricia had backed up against the wall, the entranceway to the foyer only a foot away. But when she edged aside an inch . . .

Trey cocked his pistol. "Don't think I won't do it. Shit, I been killin' folks for a month."

"You and who else? Sutter? He must have been helping you."

"Naw, the fat ol' boy just wouldn't turn crooked, even as bad as he needed the money. It was me 'n' Dwayne at first. The idea was to make a few Squatters disappear—to scare off the rest of 'em. But it wasn't enough, so we had to start gettin' rougher. We did the job on the Hilds and flaked 'em with the crystal, started makin' it look like two dope gangs in a turf war. Then we burned up the Ealds with enough shit in their shack to look like a meth lab."

"So the state police would think the Squatters were one of the gangs?" Patricia asked.

"Sure. And it was workin'. It was Ricky 'n' Junior Caudill we paid for the rough stuff. They come on after Dwayne got killed."

Patricia somehow kept her fear in check. "And let me guess. Gordon Felps is the ringleader."

Trey looked up, duly impressed. "Yeah, the money man. Don't you get it? Agan's Point is a shit town full a' shit people goin' nowhere, and I'm one of 'em. But Gordon Felps was gonna turn this place all around, turn the Point into somethin' special, with some big payoffs for whoever helped him. Shit, all your sister had to do was sell the land to Felps and everything woulda been fine. But no, the dumb bitch couldn't turn her back on the fuckin' Squatters—like they were her fuckin' little sideline family, her orphans. Like one a' these crackpot old ladies ya read about, takin' in all the stray cats." He pointed up to Judy's hanging body. "Well, this is what she gets for her loyalty to the fuckin' Squatters. We couldn't let her stand in our way. When little folks stand in the way of big things, they get run over. I'm tired of small-time. I'm tired of bein' town clown on a no-dick two-man department in a shit-for-nothing town. But once Agan's Point booms, gets all full-up with rich folks buyin' Felps's fancy waterfront condos? I'll finally be a big-time police chief. It's still gonna happen. Don't think it won't. We just have to adjust the game plan a little."

"Because of me," Patricia realized.

"Uh-huh. I think tomorrow you'll be drivin' back to Washington."

"What?"

"You'll be drivin' back to Washington, and you'll have an unfortunate accident in that nice Caddy of yours. Far enough away from here that your people in D.C. will believe it."

"They'll *never* believe it, Trey. And I've already told my boss and my husband that I suspected you and Felps of having something to do with all these murders."

Trey smiled. "I know shit when I hear it, and what just came outta your mouth is a crock of it." He took a breath and stood up. "Come on. Fun time first." He stepped right up to her.

Patricia's heart began to slug in her chest. "I have a lot of money, Trey."

"Not enough."

"Don't be stupid. If you kill me, someone will find out."

"No, they won't." And that was when his hand blurred upward and smacked the side of his pistol across her temple.

Was it the dream again, the nightmare? Patricia lay on the bed, naked, splayed before the window. The curtains were open now, the moonlight pouring in.

It's the dream again, she felt sure, *the dream I had before I found Judy's body. . . .*

But in the dream there'd been no curtain at all, and the clock had been ticking madly, whereas now it ticked normally. In the dream she'd been lying paralyzed on the bed, but now . . .

She craned her neck in four directions and saw that her wrists and ankles had been lashed to the bedposts.

She felt as if she were drowning in dread, remembering the scene from the kitchen. Trey had murdered Judy, then staged the appearance of suicide. He and his cohorts had been doing all the killing, not a drug gang, to frame the Squatters, to get them off the land, thinking Judy would finally sell out to Felps.

But Judy didn't, so they killed her too. . . .

Patricia gulped, nauseous.

And now it's my turn.

Trey would probably strangle her here, then stage some kind of car wreck. But not before he had some fun with her first.

He'd been standing there all along, hidden in the shadows of the corner of the room. He took several steps until the darkness expelled him into the blaring moonlight. He was shirtless, and unbuckling his gun belt now. Then he took his pants off. Patricia was grateful there was only moonlight and not the lamp; it reduced the details. Trey's body was lean, like a jackal's. The thrill of murder—and of what was to come—had already erected his genitals.

"Good, you're awake," he said. "Ain't no fun pluggin' a gal who's unconscious. Let's see if you're a screamer like your sister. Yeah, baby, that turns me on. And ya can scream all ya want, 'cos there ain't no one to hear ya."

Now the dread was piling up on her like a physical weight. Tears drew lines from the corners of her eyes. *I should've gone home to my husband days ago. Why did I have to stay?*

The moonlight painted one side of his body icy white, and left the other half black. He pointed to the window. "Bet'cha don't know that a buncha' nights since you been back, I come up here and watched ya through the window. You are some sight, I'll tell ya, all naked and tossin' and turnin', playin' with yourself in your sleep. Dirty girl."

Her nausea trebled. "Jesus, and I thought it was Ernie."

Trey sputtered. "Ernie? That shuck-'n'-jive piece a' shit? I busted his back before I lowered him in the water . . . so he could *see* the crabs eatin' him alive. The fuck."

"But he was helping you too, wasn't he? He burned the docks last night—the state police told me."

Trey frowned. "That redneck couldn't burn shit. *I* burned the fuckin' docks. He tried to stop me, so I whipped his ass, flaked him with dope, and let the crabs have him."

Even in her horror, Patricia felt astonished, even relieved. "I-I didn't know that."

"Bet'cha don't know somethin' else too." Trey's voice darkened. He reached up toward his face, and then . . .

Patricia squinted in the dark.

He took his denture piece out, a bridge of some sort. Patricia came close to swallowing her own vomit at the recognition.

Now Trey's two front teeth were missing.

"You remember me now, don't'cha?" Trey guttered.

"My God," she choked, "I thought it was Ernie. His two front teeth were missing when the EMTs were taking him out of the bay."

"Aw, shit, that ain't nothin'. When me 'n' him got ta fightin' on the docks, I knocked a couple of his teeth out, busted a rib too, 'fore I jacked him out the rest a' the way. I don't like Ernie gettin' credit for *my* balls—so make sure you know that. It was me who split your cherry on Bowen's Field that night."

Patricia wished she could just die now.

"I done saw ya skinny-dippin' in the water," Trey admitted. "Couldn't help it—hell, I was a young buck myself back then. Chick skinny-dippin' in the woods at night, all by herself? She's asking for it."

"You make me sick," Patricia managed, her muscles tensing against the bonds.

"You were quite a prize back then, and still are," Trey said, feeling her body up with his eyes. " 'N fact, you're a damn sight better-lookin' now. And ya know what else I remember, baby? I remember how much you liked it. . . ."

Trey stuck the tip of his tongue through the gap in his teeth, and then the rest of the disgusting memory swamped her: her clitoris sucked through that same gap over twenty-five years ago when she lay lashed to the ground in the middle of Bowen's Field, much the same way she lay lashed to this bed now.

"Yeah, you liked it then, and you're gonna like it again tonight," he promised. "You ain't gonna be alive much longer, so you might as well just lay back and get into it."

He began to walk toward the bed. . . .

"Wait a minute," she said. "Answer me one thing."

He chuckled. "Guess it's the least I can do."

"Set me straight on something. You've been killing the Squatters and making it look like drug dealers were killing them. Right?"

"Yeah. And it worked."

"So you've been killing them," Patricia repeated. "But who's been killing you?"

Trey fell silent in the moonlight.

"Come on, Trey. Tell me the rest of the story. Dwayne was murdering Squatters; then someone murders

Dwayne. Junior Caudill murdered the Hilds; then someone murdered him. Right?"

Trey hesitated but said, "Yeah."

"And what about Junior's brother? He was working for you and Felps, too—you said so in the kitchen. He killed the Ealds, didn't he?"

"That's right. Burned 'em up in their shack."

"Why do I have this funny felling that Ricky Caudill is dead now, too? Is he?"

Trey nodded. "He died in the town jail cell, some disease."

"Some *disease?* What happened to him?"

Trey was growing flustered. "I don't know—I ain't a doctor. It had to have been some disease or somethin'. Nobody killed him—he was in his jail cell when it happened."

"When *what* happened?" Patricia insisted.

"He lost all his blood, it looked like."

"Really? And Dwayne lost his head, but there was no evidence of a wound, and Junior lost all of his internal organs. I saw Junior's autopsy, Trey, and the inside of his body was *empty.* But there was no sign of an incision. How do you take a man's organs out of his body without cutting him open first?"

"I don't know," Trey said.

"Ricky Caudill lost all his blood. Were there any cuts on him? Did somebody cut his veins?"

"I didn't inspect his fuckin' body; all I did was bury it."

"You said he died in his jail cell. So I guess his blood was all over the cell floor, right? Right?"

"No!" Trey yelled. "The floor was clean, and there weren't no cuts on him!"

Silence.

The clock was still ticking, and outside Patricia could hear the cicadas' drone. "Answer me one more thing, Trey."

"No. Fuck it." He grabbed a pillow off the bed. "I got me a piece a' your ass when you were sixteen—that'll have to do. I'm just gonna smother your ass right now and be done with it."

He raised the pillow and was about to position it over her face, then began to lower it.

"Did Ricky Caudill get a letter on the day he died?" Patricia blurted.

The pillow froze, then fell away.

"How did you know that?" Trey's voice ground out.

"He did, didn't he? A sheet of paper with one word on it, one handwritten word. *Wenden*, something like that, right? It looked like it was written in some kind of dust or chalk. That was the letter he got, wasn't it?"

Agan's Point's new chief of police just stood there in the moonlight. He didn't reply.

"Dwayne got a letter like that, too."

"Bullshit!"

"He did. I found it in the garbage can in the den. The postmark was the day he died. Go look if you don't believe me. It's probably still there. And Junior Caudill got a letter just like it, too."

"No, he didn't!"

"Yes, he did, Trey! I saw it in an evidence bag at the county coroner's."

Now Trey stood with his jaw dropping and his eyes wide, contemplating something in utter dread.

"Trey?" Patricia asked.

Trey just stared.

"Trey?"

He looked down at her almost beseechingly.

"Trey, did you get a letter like that too? Did you get one *today?*"

Trey's Adam's apple bobbed when he gulped. "It's in my pants pocket. The postman delivered it today. No return address. But I know who it's from, and I ain't afraid."

"Who's it from, Trey? Is it from—"

"It's from Everd Stanherd, that little shit. Just some a' his backwoods superstitious bullshit, tryin' to scare us. But I ain't afraid." He gulped again. "I don't believe in black magic or whatever fucked-up mumbo-jumbo he thinks he's pullin'."

Now it was Patricia's jaw that began to drop. "Everybody who got one of those letters died. They died because something was taken from them. Blood, organs, Dwayne's head."

"Ain't nothin' been taken from me." But even then his words began to slur. . . .

"Trey," Patricia implored. "I think you should turn on the light and look at yourself in the mirror. Something's happening to you."

"Ain't nothin' haplen-in'!"

But what was it? Patricia's eyes were riveted.

"Ain't blow-one play-ken bluthin' flum me!" Trey shouted. He turned shakily, tried to stride out of the room, but as he did so, he wobbled in his gait. When he reached out for the doorknob, his fingers turned limp as cooked pasta; then his arm slowly bowed, then fell, tentacle-like.

Before he fell over altogether, Patricia saw his head . . . collapse, as though his skull had dissolved within the sack of his face.

A few seconds later the door creaked open, figures entering. Some held candles made from rendered fat, and in the flickering light Patricia recognized the face of Everd Stanherd.

"Wenden," came the bizarre word from the even more bizarre Squatter accent. "It's from our holy language, from a time even before that of the druids. . . ."

Patricia had been untied, dressed in a robe, and carried out. Then they'd driven her to someplace in the woods, for the woods truly were their home.

Everd Stanherd, his wife, and a few of the elders sat with Patricia in a circle, their candles guttering.

"We owe you no explanations, for they are all secrets. But remember this: long before Christ, God said 'An eye for an eye.'"

Patricia was still regaining her senses. *I'm alive. And it wasn't a dream. . . .*

"You're a wizard or something," she managed.

"No. I am the *sawon*—it means seer," Everd intoned. His face was barely visible—all of them were.

The moonlight shimmered through the branches.

The cicadas thrummed.

"Sawon." Patricia remembered the word. The Squatter on the pier had told them. "You're, like, the clan wise man, some kind of ancestral leader?"

"It means . . . *seer,"* he repeated.

"What does *wenden* mean?" Patricia asked next.

One of the other elders' voices fluttered like a death rattle. "It means *gone."*

Gone. Patricia thought. *Dwayne's head. Junior's innards. Ricky Caudill's blood. And Trey's bones . . . all . . . gone.*

"You cursed them," Patricia observed. "Any of them who harmed the Squatters. It *was* magic."

"We can say no more," Marthe Stanherd whispered.

Patricia couldn't resist. "But . . . how?"

"We can say no—" Marthe began, but Everd leaned forward, overriding her. He held something in his crabbed hand. *A jar?* Patricia wondered. A clay pot of some sort, the size of a masonry jar. A cross adorned with the familiar squiggles and slashes of Squatter artwork had been etched into the pot.

"The burned blood," Everd told her. "It's our sacrament, from the *sawon* before me. And when I am dead, my blood will suffice for the next sacrament, for the *sawon* who is to follow. One of these men here tonight."

Several of the faces in the circle looked startled when Everd removed the strange jar's lid and passed it to Patricia.

She looked in and saw . . .

Dust?

Brownish dust. The dull chalklike substance with which the death letters had been written? There was very little left, just enough to form a rim around the bottom.

Burned blood, Patricia repeated in her mind.

"It's consecrated," someone said.

And someone else: "Through faith older than any religion . . ."

Patricia was confused, but she also knew that there were some things she was not meant to understand. No one was.

"I'm dying," Everd said next, through a smile that seemed to float around them in the dark. "I will soon become the next sacrament. I will soon be *wenden.* I will soon be gone."

They were all getting up now, blowing out their gull-fat candles.

"You're a good woman." Everd was the first to walk away. "Continue to be good."

"But where will you go?" Patricia blurted from where she sat.

"From whence we came: nowhere. Everywhere. Anywhere."

Like shifting ink spots, one by one they disappeared amongst the trees, blending into darkness.

But a final question assailed her. "Wait a minute! What about Gordon Felps?"

A hand patted her shoulder. The creviced face of the final elder whispered, "Don't worry about Gordon Felps. We took care of him."

When Patricia looked again, they were . . .

Gone.

It was an hour before daybreak when Patricia pulled through the gates of the compound. A sign on the fence read: FELPS CONSTRUCTION, INC. BUILDER OF FINE HOMES FOR LUXURY LIVING.

This seemed the most likely place to check first; she had no idea where Felps was staying in town. From the road she could see his truck parked in front of the office trailer.

Gravel crunched under her feet when she walked across the lot. She climbed the short wooden steps before the trailer, then paused. It occurred to her to knock but . . .

She tried the knob. The door clicked open.

He must not be here, she deduced. Darkness seemed clotted in the trailer. For some reason she wasn't afraid of what she might find.

"Felps? Are you here?"

A voice rattled back. "Who is it?"

"Patricia White."

A pause. "Thank God."

"Trey's dead. I know what happened, your plan, the people you paid to frame and murder Squatters, all of it."

"It doesn't matter."

He must've been at the very back of the trailer; she couldn't see anything. And his voice now was beginning to scare her. Something about it sounded so hopeless.

She felt around the wall for a light switch but couldn't find one. *Damn, I can't see!*

"Please come over here," Felps stoically begged her. "There's a gun in the top drawer of the desk. I want you to take it out and kill me. For God's sake—please. Kill me."

She never found the light switch, but in the little bit of moonlight coming in through a tiny window, she saw a flashlight sitting atop a file cabinet.

"Please," Felps pleaded.

She snapped on the flashlight, pointed it, and . . .

Stared.

Gordon Felps looked normal at first glance, sitting in a comfortable office chair. But then Patricia noticed . . .

Oh . . . shit . . .

His sleeves were empty. She lowered the flashlight. The legs of his pants were empty as well. On the desk before him lay the letter she didn't even need to look at now. *Wenden,* she thought. *Gone.* Gordon Felps's arms and legs were gone.

"Don't leave me! I can't live like this!" he shouted.

But she was already backing out of the trailer.

"Come over here and get this gun and shoot me in the fucking head—I'm *begging* you!"

Patricia turned the flashlight off. She walked out of the trailer, closed the door quietly behind her, and walked back to her car.

Epilogue

What could she tell Byron? What could she tell anyone?
Nothing, she decided.
She should never have gone in the first place. *I just want to go back to my life.*
Patricia knew she would never take it for granted again.
The highway breezed by. It seemed like she was driving away from the night, leaving its secrets well behind, which suited her just fine. This early there was scarcely any rush hour, even when she was all the way back to D.C. The smog and the ugly monolithic buildings and potholed roads couldn't have made her happier to see. She'd figure out something to tell Byron later, something feasible to explain Judy's death, and the rest of it. She didn't want to lie, but with *this?*
The truth wouldn't do.
I'm going to forget about everything right now, she promised herself. The resolution made her feel rejuvenated, and a monumental burden disappeared. When

she parked the Cadillac in front of the condo, she felt giddy.

She walked quietly up the steps, and was careful to keep the keys from jingling when she unlocked the door and came in. The instant she stepped inside, she truly felt that she was home. She was back where she belonged.

She traipsed in, hoping Byron was still asleep. *I'll slide into bed next to him and let him find me there when he wakes up.* It would be the best surprise. She'd be right there in bed next to him, two days earlier than he expected.

She kicked off her sandals. She looked around the living room—dim in morning light—and actually had tears in her eyes, she was so happy. Byron's pretentious art prints on the wall delighted her now. The feel of the carpet beneath her bare feet titillated her. Even the air smelled comforting.

She began to unbutton her blouse when she entered the bedroom.

Her hand fell.

Her heart almost stopped.

Patricia stood there for a long time, looking at the be

Indeed, Byron was still asleep, and he would d nitely be surprised to find that his loving wife ha turned two days earlier than he expected.

You bastard, she thought.

A woman lay in bed next to Byron. She young, early twenties, half of her skinny, nak crooked out from under the sheets. A small, p stuck out too, and she had some silly tatt thigh. And as she lay all cuddled up nice an to Byron, she was snoring.

Patricia's mind essentially switched off.

tirade, no lamp throwing, no profanity-laden shouts. There was nothing like that at all. Instead Patricia walked back out to the car, opened the door, and got in.

She didn't drive anywhere. Had she had more presence of mind, she would've driven either to a friend's or a divorce lawyer's. But she didn't even put the key in the ignition.

She didn't know how much time passed when she finally said aloud to herself, "What am I going to do? My husband is upstairs right now—in my bed—sleeping with another woman. What am I going to do?"

The answer sat next to her on the front seat.

The clay pot.

The sacrament.

The Squatters had left it in the woods with her. But there was still a small amount left inside.

Patricia looked up at her bedroom window.

I'm going to go to the drugstore now, buy some paper, and an envelope. Then I'm going to go to the post office and stamp.

hen mail a letter.

EDWARD LEE

FLESH GOTHIC

Hildreth House isn't like other mansions. One warm night in early spring, fourteen people entered Hildreth House's labyrinthine halls to partake in diabolical debauchery. When the orgy was over, the slaughter began. The next morning, thirteen of the revelers were found naked and butchered. Dismembered. Mutilated. But the fourteenth body was never found.

The screams have faded and the blood has dried, but the house remains…watching. Now five very special people have dared to enter the infamous house of horrors. Who—or what—awaits them? And who will live to tell Hildreth House's ghastly secrets?